The
Porcelain Dove

The Porcelain Dove

OR

Constancy's Reward

DELIA SHERMAN

A DUTTON BOOK

DUTTON
Published by the Penguin Group
Penguin Books USA Inc., 375 Hudson Street,
New York, New York 10014, U.S.A.
Penguin Books Ltd, 27 Wrights Lane, London W8 5TZ, England
Penguin Books Australia Ltd, Ringwood, Victoria, Australia
Penguin Books Canada Ltd, 10 Alcorn Avenue,
Toronto, Ontario, Canada M4V 3B2
Penguin Books (N.Z.) Ltd, 182–190 Wairau Road,
Auckland 10, New Zealand

Penguin Books Ltd, Registered Offices:
Harmondsworth, Middlesex, England

First published by Dutton, an imprint of New American Library,
a division of Penguin Books USA Inc.
Distributed in Canada by McClelland & Stewart Inc.

First Printing, May, 1993
10 9 8 7 6 5 4 3 2 1

REGISTERED TRADEMARK—MARCA REGISTRADA

LIBRARY OF CONGRESS CATALOGING-IN-PUBLICATION DATA
Sherman, Delia.
    The porcelain dove : Constancy's reward / Delia Sherman.
        p.   cm.
    ISBN 0-525-93608-4
    I. Title.
    PS3569.H418P67   1993
    813'.54—dc20   92-39860
                                                      CIP

Printed in the United States of America
Set in Simoncini Garamond
Designed by Eve L. Kirch

In memory of my mother, Opal Woodley Sherman,
who loved history, France, and telling stories

CONTENTS

Prologue
In Which I Speak of Beauxprés and the Wondrous Magic
by Which It Is Sustained
1

Chapter the First
In Which Berthe Duvet Begins Her Tale
9

Chapter the Second
In Which Mademoiselle Comes to Woman's Estate
33

Chapter the Third
In Which We Come to Beauxprés
53

Chapter the Fourth
In Which the Future of the House of Malvoeux Is Secured
73

Chapter the Fifth
In Which the Sorcerer Maid Is Born
94

Chapter the Sixth
In Which an Ancient Beggar Makes a Nuisance of Himself
115

Chapter the Seventh
The Curse
134

Chapter the Eighth
In Which the Quest for the Dove Begins
140

Chapter the Ninth
In Which Madame Adventures Far from Home
162

Chapter the Tenth
In Which Monsieur Fouls His Nest
185

Chapter the Eleventh
In Which the Vicomte Proves Himself a True Son of Malvoeux
206

Chapter the Twelfth
In Which Accounts Are Cast Up
231

Chapter the Thirteenth
In Which Wild Birds Are Caged
245

Chapter the Fourteenth
In Which Brother Justin Goes Questing
264

Chapter the Fifteenth
In Which Artide Comes into His Own
284

Chapter the Sixteenth
In Which Berthe Uncovers the Crow's Nest
and Linotte Takes Flight
298

Chapter the Seventeenth
In Which a Curious Document Is Unveiled
320

Chapter the Eighteenth
In Which Both France and Madame Are Transformed
332

Chapter the Nineteenth
In Which the Crows Feast
347

Chapter the Twentieth
In Which We Hear Word of the Sorcerer Maid
354

Chapter the Twenty-first
In Which the Porcelain Dove Comes to Beauxprés
378

Acknowledgments
401

Historical Note and Bibliography
403

In Which I Speak of Beauxprés and the Wondrous Magic by Which It Is Sustained

Once upon a time in the mountainous east of France, there was a duchy called Malvoeux. To be sure, it was only a small duchy, nothing beside the broad lands of Aquitaine or Burgundy, but very beautiful nonetheless, and richly supplied with fat cows and vines yielding cheeses and wines famous from Switzerland to Brittany. Equally famous was the ancestral seat of the ducs de Malvoeux, the noble château Beauxprés.

The duchy is gone now, its meadows and vineyards long since lost to debt and revolution, and its château alone survives to bear witness to its former glory.

As to how and where that château finds itself? Well. According to M. Voltaire, somewhere across the western ocean lies a fabulous land called El Dorado, where want and injustice are inconceivable and the beggar children play with emeralds and rubies. The château Beauxprés is very like El Dorado, only French, and far beyond the reach of even the most intrepid traveler. Furthermore, what jewels we have are set, and not to be played with; but then we have no beggar-children to play with them.

What we do have is a fine palace in the baroque style filled to its rafters with a most sumptuous profusion of glass cases, mirrors, tables, beds, tapestries, paintings, books, and objets d'art. It sits upon a hill that is as round and flat-crowned as a Circassian bonnet and sufficiently broad to accommodate formal, kitchen, and enchanted gardens, as well as a small orchard, an aviary, an ornamental water, and a cow-house. The far prospect is of fertile meadows and tree-covered mountains; nearer at hand, the hill slopes are thick with fir and wild blackberries. Hares run unafraid in those woods, and no wolf howls.

'Tis a pretty picture, is it not? Like a fairy kingdom in a conte des fées?

Ah, and there's more. No starving peasant rebukes us with hunger-hollowed eyes. No malcontent lackey endangers his skin by theft. No servingmaid courts damnation by conceiving a child in sin. Our every need is served by creatures of magic, most of them hands without bodies, or at least without bodies that one can see. Our few completely visible servants are golden-haired, deep-bosomed, and porcelain-faced as fairy-tale princesses. They speak good French in human, if uncommonly melodic, voices and have cloven hooves growing from their dainty ankles. Their tears are dry as sand. Demons, every one of them, and quite unreal.

Our cows and horses and hens are real enough—at least I've seen them born in the usual way, and they bleed red blood when the invisible butcher cuts their throats. Our weather, on the other hand, is not real. Each day is warm and green and fresh and redolent of new-mown hay and lavender, and although Beauxprés lies—or rather lay—high in the third plateau of the Jura mountains, it never snows here. Indeed, it seldom rains, and that only during the soft, fragrant nights. In the course of my life, I have lived in Paris, visited Nice and Marseilles and Geneva and Lausanne, and in none of these places does weather behave as it does in Beauxprés, year in and year out without varying.

In short, the breeding, bleeding animals are entirely out of character, both for an enchanted kingdom and for Mlle Linotte de Malvoeux, the sorcerer maid whose spells enclosed it. They are too natural to have caught her imagination, too peasant-practical. Mlle Linotte would never have thought to magic up cows and chickens for our paradise, and yet here they are. They give me hope, those animals.

And who am I, to hope or to despair? I am one of the seven human souls inhabiting this earthly paradise: Berthe Duvet, who was once femme de chambre to Mme la duchesse de Malvoeux. My former mistress is here as well; also her sons the vicomte de Montplaisir and M. Justin de Malvoeux, in addition to my good friend Jean Coquelet, who was once the duc's groom, and a peasant girl named Colette

Favre. I suppose M. le duc is also in Beauxprés. As he never ventures out of his aviary, I cannot be entirely sure.

Two hundred years in an aviary! I cannot imagine it, me. But then I have never completely understood my former master's boundless fascination with feathered things, nor am I much given to imagining. It is my nature to make what I may from what I see before me: enchantment or revolution, ease or hardship. Oh, I've known hardship, never think I have not, for in the latter days of my servitude, being maid to the duchesse de Malvoeux was a position of some danger. Each night I went to my bed with an empty belly, and each morning I rose expecting to be slaughtered by the peasants from the village at the foot of the hill or eaten by the gray wolves from the forest. Each day I made what shift I could to feed us. Each evening I prayed that we might be saved.

Well, my prayer was answered and more than answered the day Mlle Linotte returned to Beauxprés bringing with her not only the Porcelain Dove, but also her two long-lost brothers. She rode a great horse the restless hue of a thunder-cloud, I remember, and around her shoulders she wore a rusty black cloak pinned with a round brooch.

The brooch was woven of rushes, and that such a piece of trumpery could pierce and hold all those heavy yards of fustian was enough in itself to make me believe that the brooch, and not the cloak, was enchanted. When Jean relates this scene, the girl Colette is accustomed to argue that she has read a thousand fairy tales or more in which she has found hundreds of enchanted cloaks and never an enchanted brooch of rushes. But I, who with my own eyes watched Mlle Linotte call up our cloud-cuckoo land, I know the cloak was no more magic than my second-best petticoat.

'Twas dawn, I remember; a cold dawn, for Mlle Linotte shivered as she walked into the enchanted garden, stood by the bone-white fountain, and held the brooch high over her head. Though there'd been no breath of air before, a wind blew through the ring and blossomed out above her like the canopy of the aerostatic balloon I once saw ascend in Versailles. The sky rippled and swayed in the wake of that wind; the distant mountains drew yet further off. After a space, when the air had quieted, Mlle Linotte threw the brooch into the bone-white fountain. And she took the cloak with her when she departed Beauxprés. All of which seems to me ample evidence that the brooch of rushes is not only magical, but the sole stay and anchor of our fairyland. Were we to lose it, the ballooning magic would doubtless collapse, and we'd all fall to earth again with a prodigious thump.

Ah, bah! Here am I, putting the cart before the horse, which Jean says is as useless an endeavor as setting out on a quest with no idea where you're going, or acting plays to an invisible audience. Bien sûr, Jean is a peasant and scorns any endeavor that does not lead to a full belly or a game of trou-madame. A true history of Beauxprés—that leads to neither, nor to any useful or practical end that even I can foresee. Yet a true history of Beauxprés is what Colette has asked of me, and what I intend to give her, if only I can decide how best to go about it.

A stubborn little witch, Colette. Ever since she began to grow older—oh, a hundred years ago now—she's been asking and asking the same questions. Why? Who? Wherefore? When? Justin, Adèle, and Jean have answered her at length and at large, Justin with sermons, Adèle with ancient gossip, Jean with tales as fair and finely-shaped as his demon mistresses. Me, I have held my peace. I am a dresser of hair and a maker of gowns. My art is in my fingers, not my tongue. And so I've always answered Colette, until this very morning.

That we were in the library goes without saying: we are in the library every morning. Colette was, as always, writing. She's been scribbling ever since I taught her to make her letters: plays and essays in an historical vein. We act the plays—or at least Adèle, Jean, and Colette act them; I am the audience, in which role I am supported by the demonesses and the invisible hands. I cannot know how much the hands in particular understand of our entertainments. But they always attend with every sign of enjoyment and applaud enthusiastically at the end.

I was speaking of Colette.

There she was, sitting at the great table between the windows, papers and books broadcast around her, scratching busily with her quill while I read *Jacques le fataliste et son maître*. There's a scene with the innkeeper's wife, where she tries and tries to tell the story of the marquis des Arcis and Mme de la Pommeraye while her maid interrupts her with inquiries about the key to the oatbin and other irrelevancies until Jacques, his master, and the reader all three are ready to expire with impatience. I laughed aloud. The scratching paused.

"This is prodigious droll, Colette," I said. "Shall I read it to you?"

"You never speak of the past," she said.

I frowned. "What need," I said impatiently, "when there are so many voices to speak of it for me? As I've told you before, you may go to the chronicles for history, to Adèle for gossip, to Justin for theology, and to Jean for romance. Any one of them remembers more of the past than I, and can tell it better."

"Better, Berthe? How better?"

"Well, more beautifully. They take the plain truth and trim it as I would a plain gown so 'tis fit for the finest company. I was a femme de chambre, remember. My past has taught me the value of ornament."

Colette stroked her quill down her jaw. "On a gown, perhaps," she said. "Not on a tale. Consider, Berthe, that ornament, however pleasing in itself, obscures a form that, pleasing or not, is at least itself and not some other thing."

She swept a tumble of paper from one corner of the table, uncovering a leg encrusted with gilded bronze leaves and a mosaic of precious woods, uneven and chipped with use. "This table is a lovely thing, to be sure, but 'twould serve my purpose as well or better if 'twere plainer made. So the history of Beauxprés, which Jean and maman Adèle have between them so carved, inlaid, garlanded, and gilded that its original shape has all but disappeared."

"Very witty, Mlle Précieuse. And just what is it makes you think that I recall these same events in their original and unornamented state?"

"I have seen how you cast up your eyes when Jean recounts how M. le duc de Malvoeux slaughtered the doves and how you smile to yourself when maman Adèle tells me of her so-dear friend Stéphanie-Germaine. I have seen how you watch and listen to everything we say and do, and I am confident that you remember all."

"A good servant is discreet," I said.

"You are no longer a servant," she said.

And that was true enough to silence me for a space, after which I said, "You would need to be patient. 'Twould take time—years, perhaps—for me to recall and write so much."

"I have waited two hundred years to hear your tale. I can wait two hundred more, if need be. Patience is the first lesson of a sorcerer."

"So I understand." Pompey had always said so, I thought, which reminded me of Linotte, which reminded me of Linotte's wedding and a thousand other horrors. Peronel. The beggar-children. The dungeon.

"This truth you desire," I said. " 'Tis not all school-girl pranks and enchanted gardens, you understand. Much of what I have to tell will cause you pain. You know not what you ask of me."

"I do know," Colette said gravely. "I ask you to cast a spell. Like any magic, 'tis dangerous. Like any spell, 'twill unfold according to its own logic, in its own time, by its own will."

"Stubborn little witch," I said softly.

She smiled, her face as bright as a new-blown poppy, a sturdy peasant girl with black hair and ruddy cheeks who, after so many years in the library of Beauxprés, is more learned than all the philosophes in all the salons in Paris. She smiled and then she went to a tall, gilded cabinet and removed from it a writing desk and laid it in my lap.

"I conjured it up myself," she said. "I hope you like it."

For form's sake, I protested a little more, consulted with Jean—who promised to advise me—and at length sat down alone in the library of Beauxprés with my face to the wall for fear of distractions.

So here I am, wondering where to start. My writing desk is open before me. It is plain varnished rosewood and well-stocked with one perfect goose-feather quill, several quires of creamy paper, and a crystal inkpot in the shape of a nestling. A witty touch, that inkpot, and very like Colette.

And now I have taken up the pen and dipped it into the inkpot's gaping beak, determined to write this tale as honestly and plainly as I may, from the beginning.

Honestly and plainly, then, what is the beginning? Was it the February night in 1777 when the beggar laid his curse on M. le duc de Malvoeux? That makes a good, strong beginning, and Jean says it's best to start with your strongest point, like showing a buyer a horse's good legs (if he has good legs) before you get around to his hard mouth or his sway back or whatever else is wrong with him. There's always something wrong with a horse, Jean says, and there are always tedious parts to a story, but good and bad all go together to make a whole animal or a whole tale, and a horse without sound legs or a tale without a sound beginning can never get far.

But the tale did not begin with the beggar's curse, nor yet with his first appearance in our lives, when Mlle Linotte was still in leading-strings and my waist was slender as a willow. The tale began more than six hundred years ago, when the first duc de Malvoeux . . .

No, a story is not like a horse after all, for the history of the first duc de Malvoeux is not at all like a horse's legs (unless the horse has been treading in dung) and not, therefore, the place to begin. Where, then? Well, 'tis Adèle's tale as well as the duc's; and Adèle's tale, at least since her seventh year, is my tale also. So. I will begin with myself, which is at least familiar territory, and let the rest follow as it may.

In Which Berthe Duvet Begins Her Tale

I was born in Paris on the fifteenth day of September, 1745. My father, M. Émile Duvet, was a corset maker. My mother, Mme Louise Duvet, was a lingère. Together they kept a shop upon the rue Montorgueil.

When maman spoke of my father, she'd praise his eye for sound whalebone and his skill at fitting a difficult torso, then shake her head sadly and say that she'd have wished him as careful a provider as he was a corset maker. And then she'd shrug and sigh that such was life, after all, and what would you? Life is seldom fair. From this, I concluded that money had melted in my father's hands, and was just as happy never to have known him. In any case, he died before I was a year old, and maman sold all his whalebone to buy linen so she could set up in business by herself.

She began making négligées for the girls of a nearby house of accommodation. Her work was so fine that before long she was supplying chemises, peignoirs, pockets, and sleeve-ruffles for the artistes of the Opéra and the Comédie Française. While she was not at all ashamed of her clientèle—neither the actresses nor the whores—she intended a better for me, in preparation for which she gave me the finest education she could devise.

That she taught me fine sewing goes without saying; why, before I could lisp my catechism, I could cut and sew a simple chemise. Yet my mother knew that any unlettered grisette might learn to do as well and still spend her life cutting and sewing to plump some other woman's purse. When I was four or thereabouts, she sent me to a petit école where I might learn to write and cipher as neatly as any Jesuit and to read both print and writing. Nor was that the sum of her efforts. To teach me to carry myself discreetly upon all occasions, she took me with her everywhere: to the rue de la Vieille-Draperie to bargain for linen; to the tenements of Saint-Antoine to hire assistants; to the whorehouses of Saint-Honoré to fit chemises; to the tiring-room of the old Comédie Française to deliver ruffles and fichus and embroidered petticoats.

My earliest memories are of that tiring-room: how the famous LeKain bounced me upon his knee; how the beautiful Mlle Huys gave me a spangled scarf to peacock in; how La Clairon and Mme Gaussin pressed me to their fragrant bosoms. I was a pretty child. 'Tis not vanity that I say so. Had I been plain, they would never have made such a favorite of me, nor would the great tragedienne Mme Dumesnil have arranged for maman and me to watch weekday performances *gratis* from a box on the second tier.

Mme Dumesnil was nearly forty then, an old woman to a child of five or six, and years of white-lead had made her look older still, her face and neck wrinkled as crêpe and stained with cheap rouge. I remember watching her dress herself, the way she'd frown into the mirror over the careful placement of her patches and adjust her breasts to swell just so at the neck of her gown. How like a harlequin she looked, with her chalk-white face and vermilion cheeks, her headdress heavy with plumes and paste jewels, her gown trailing yards of train! Yet not twenty minutes later, when I saw her tread the boards as Medea, as Penelope, as Zedima, as Phèdre, I always thought her exquisite.

This nightly transformation of an ordinary woman from crone to queen I may regard as my first experience of the art of magic. That the metamorphosis was achieved by means of paint and candlelight rather than talisman and spell makes not the least difference in the world. For sorcery and acting both are informed by the will and temperament of their agents, and the end of both is to dazzle and to suspend for a time the ordinary course of nature. Their common essence is desire—for power, for adulation, for command. Their common vehicle is passion.

Ah, the passions of actors! How grand they are, and how vital. Like the queens and generals they portrayed, the artistes of the Comédie Française were tossed by emotions as deep and violent as the sea in storm, emotions that could only find expression in voices that reached for the third tier and gestures that encompassed the heavens. On stage or off, my mother's clients were either devastated by grief or transported by joy. They quarreled like angels and loved like fiends. They were as different from my stout, rosy, shrewd maman as peacocks are from wrens, and I adored them. Twice or thrice each week I would weep over their sorrows, laugh at their jests, tremble at their rages, ache when fate or a playwright heaped unbearable hardship on them. And afterwards I would trot home with maman to our tidy shop in the rue Montorgueil and stitch sleeve-ruffles in perfect contentment.

Ah, she was a good woman, my maman. She taught me the value of common sense and of telling the truth—if circumstances per-mitted—of looking neat, of minding my manners, of speaking proper French. She was the very pattern of a bonne bourgeoise, counting it a greater sin to be a debtor than a whore. She died of a summer flux when I was nine years old, and her business passed into the hands of my father's family.

My father's sister was a pinch-penny, low-minded, jealous sort of slut who turned me out of doors before maman was cold in her grave. Too old to apprentice and too young to work in a shop, I could not earn my keep as maman intended, and was forced to look about me for some other means of making my way in the world. When her old clients discovered how things stood with me, they were kindness itself. The proprietress of Saint-Honoré's most expensive bawdy house of-fered me a bed and a percentage of the sale of my virginity. And Mme Dumesnil offered to sponsor me with a company in Bordeaux whose manager was willing to employ an untried actress, provided she was young and pretty.

Oh, I thought about it, you may be sure of that. I loved the theater. Had I been a boy, I might have begged to be made a changer of scenes, and my tale (had I cause to tell it) a history of great loves that endured a week and small jealousies that endured a lifetime. As it was, Louise Duvet's daughter suspected that Bordeaux meant whor-ing no less than the establishment of Mme Godinette, only less well paid. And to say the truth, I'd no real taste for the sound and fury of acting. Even so young, I preferred to watch and listen while others strutted and declaimed. By the mercy of le bon Dieu, I had a third string to my bow: my mother's second cousin Olympe Darnton, who was femme de chambre to Mme la baronne du Fourchet.

When I left maman's shop on the morning of the fifteenth of

August, 1754, I turned my back upon the Comédie Française and bent my steps south-west, towards the Marais.

More than two centuries have passed since I made that journey from the rue Montorgueil to the rue Quincampoix, and this library in which I sit is further from those teeming streets than from Cathay. Yet when I close my eyes, they are there, bright miniatures, like plates in a volume of Rétif de la Bretonne: the carved swan above the shop door, black crêpe tied about its neck in token of mourning; my tante Duvet frowning beneath it, arms folded bonily over her bony chest. The bright cascading ribbons in the windows of the modiste across the way. The slick, sickly pallor of flayed carcasses hung for sale in the butchers of the Halles des Blés. Why, I can smell the dusty, floury, meaty smells of the market; hear its shouting, cursing frenzy and the sudden quiet of the Marais; feel the chill of the rue Quincampoix, whose tall, gray hôtels block the sun from the street, the better to hoard it in their bright courtyards. I can see the rust-red livery of the lackey who answered my knock and how his stone face cracked into humanity when I told him I was Olympe's cousin. And I can see Olympe herself, all fluttering ribbons and lacy apron, tapping towards me in smart high-heeled shoes, feel how her silk-clad arms clasped my shoulders and her easy tears tickled my face.

A little time later, she bathed her eyes, brushed the Paris mud from my skirts, and led me before her mistress.

Mme la baronne du Fourchet was drawing on her gloves to go out. I remember thinking as I curtsied before her that her sleeve-ruffles were clumsily made. Maman would not have let them out of her shop.

"What a pretty thing, to be sure!" the baronne exclaimed. "And what a charming cap! Pray, what can she do, besides curtsy and smile?"

"If madame pleases," I said shyly, "I can sew and make patterns, and I have been taught to read and write as well."

"Why, 'tis a veritable scholar you have brought me, Olympe. Black hair, a brilliant eye, a charming face, a sempstress, educated, and young enough to be malleable! Of a surety, we cannot set such a paragon to sweeping floors! She shall be a femme de chambre, and you shall have the training of her."

My first lesson in waiting upon a lady was to change my mourning black for a gown of painted cotton. When I protested, Olympe told me that I was a servant now and entitled to no grief of my own. I could wear black if a connection of the du Fourchets were to die, and not otherwise. Ladies of the ton wanted none save young, pretty, cheerful attendants around them. Some of these ladies simply desired to possess beauty—another's if not their own—and used their attendants like slaves, turning them out when they wearied of them, fit only for the lowest of brothels. I must count myself fortunate that Mme du Fourchet had an altogether more spiritual image of her women.

"She says that we must think of her as a priestess," Olympe told me with careful gravity, "and of ourselves as acolytes. The goddess we serve is Beauty, and Beauty, she says, is best served by the beautiful. She also says a woman reflects her surroundings like a deep pool. It therefore enhances her if we, who surround her, are pleasant to look upon. Do you understand, child?" I struggled with laughter; Olympe shrugged ruefully. "Moi non plus. My advice is, when she starts on one of her flights, just smile and curtsy and say, 'To be sure, madame,' or 'Fancy! How clever.' "

For one who had spent her girlhood in the company of actresses, that was an easy enough part to play. I put my heart into the rôle and soon, as a thuribular in the mysteries of Mme du Fourchet's Sacred Rites of Pride, hovered with perfumes and unguents at Olympe's elbow and watched each gesture and ritual as if my soul's welfare hung upon it.

How it all comes back to me! Pearl powder for the cheeks and bosom, a dab of serkis rouge here, here, and here, in the valley between the breasts. Lamp black on the lashes—oh, the veriest soupçon—and brushed delicately along the brows. Was that a stray hair? Pluck it out at once! And the patch. Would it be the badine, the baiseuse, the équivoque, the galante? Or perhaps the majestueuse to draw attention to the height of madame's brow? And then there was the coiffure to be decided on, the corset to be laced, the gown, the jewels, and the headdress to be discussed, chosen, tried, and changed.

Two hours were required for Mme la baronne to gird herself to face the world each day. And two hours more were required for Olympe and me to clear her dressing-room of spilled powder and discarded ribbons, to mend what needed mending and brush what needed brushing. After that was done, my time was my own, to be spent walking in the Palais-Royal if I liked, or in the gallery seat Mme Dumesnil had given me for the sake of my dead mother and a little free mending. All in all, 'twas a comfortable life I led on the rue Quincampoix, though at first there was much about it to puzzle the daughter of Louise Duvet.

I remember my wonder, for example, upon discovering that the greater part of M. le baron's household was like a painted scene in a theater, for show and not for use. Oh, the kitchen-boys worked hard enough, as did the grooms and cooks, and monsieur's valet Saint-Cloud. His forty lackeys, however, spent their days lounging and dicing in the antechambers, gossiping with M. le baron's petitioners, admitting the favored and the generous to the master's presence while barring the despised and the miserly. When I remarked that five men would be sufficient to these tasks, Olympe laughed and said that a superfluity of lackeys was simply a sign of monsieur our master's great wealth and power, just as a succession of lovers was a sign of madame our mistress's beauty and wit.

I cannot say I entirely understood this explanation, not at my tender age. I did, however, understand that M. le baron's consequence needed all the ornament he could afford. Bien sûr, I saw very little of him—maids, if they're lucky, are not well-acquainted with their mistresses' husbands. Yet from time to time I'd encounter him: a great, red pudding of a man who stumped over the polished floors with his head bowed and his heavy cheeks falling in worried folds over his jabot. When he saw me, he'd pinch my bum, wink prodigiously, exclaim, "Hmph! Pretty piece, but you won't hear it from me!" and stump heavily on again. A coarse man. And yet—according to Olympe—clever enough to have risen from the Third Estate to the Second, from plain M. Fourchet the banker to M. le baron du Fourchet, Farmer General, collector of his Most Serene Majesty King Louis' taxes, customs, tithes, and levies, purse-keeper to the Crown of France.

As for madame's lovers, her "dear friends," well, M. le baron was often from home and not at all attentive even when present. And backstairs gossip soon taught me that 'twas as à la mode for highborn ladies to have dear friends as it was for actresses to have noble admirers. In all conscience, they seemed harmless enough, full of poems and sighs and pretty little gifts, no less civil to madame's maids than to madame's husband when they chanced to encounter him upon the stairs. No, Louise Duvet's daughter was not shocked by madame's lovers. Madame's indifference to her children, however. That shocked me to the heart.

There were three scions of the house Fourchet: three daughters.

I remember, not long after I entered service, Olympe telling me of them: the two oldest who were off at a convent learning the skills proper to young ladies of noble blood, the youngest who was still in the nursery. Of course I wanted to see them, to know their ages, their natures, their statures and tastes, whether they missed their mother or thought their father a comical fellow.

Olympe laughed at me. In those days, it seemed she was forever laughing at me. "What a funny little shop-girl you are, Berthe! I declare, I quite love you. See them? Why, Mme la baronne herself hasn't seen them above six times since they were christened. Noble ladies aren't like lingères, Berthe. They have better things to do than dance attendance upon their children. Why, I dare say you think she suckled them at her own breasts!"

Not wishing to appear more foolish than I'd already made myself, I shrugged and forbore to ask Olympe whether 'twas accomplishing her toilette or entertaining her lovers that kept madame from her daughters' company.

I think 'twas the next day, though it may have been later, that Olympe made me known to the youngest du Fourchet's nursemaid. I'd often seen her upon the stairs, carrying possets and gruels and such invalid's fare—a sallow, quill-nosed, creak-voiced piece in a shabby apron. She eyed me unpleasantly while Olympe accosted her in her best Mme du Fourchet drawl. "Ah, Christophine. Permit me to present to you my cousin's child, Berthe Duvet. A pretty thing, is she not? And monstrous clever, too. I'm training her up as a femme de chambre."

Christophine's long nose turned pink; she gave me the briefest of nods. "Fancy," she said. "An infant like her, to wait upon madame."

"An infant femme de chambre, and under my eye. Never fear. She's a lot to learn before she's ready to wait upon Mlle Adèle. I'd say you have perhaps two years before you need think of finding new employment."

How Christophine received this shot I don't know, for I was busy goggling at Olympe on my own account. Olympe, having successfully astonished us both, laughed her throaty, careless laugh and flounced away with me chasing behind, pelting her with questions. Was I really to wait upon Mlle Adèle? What was she like? Was she a monster, that she must spend her days hiding from the sunlight? Why had I never seen her?

Olympe, who liked to tease, answered lightly that I needn't concern myself what the girl was like. She was only seven, after all, and me, I had my work cut out learning my new profession.

"I don't understand why I haven't seen her," I persisted. "We live under the same roof, after all. Is she a monster, or is she not?"

"She's often ill," said Olympe shortly. "Never you fear. She'll be a credit to your skill, if she lives."

Mlle Adèle recovered of her fever, and a few days later I caught my first glimpse of a small figure swaddled in a fur manteau wandering up and down the pebbled paths of the formal garden. Thereafter I saw traces of my future mistress everywhere: a scrap of pink satin skirt whisking around a corner; an echo of childish sobbing in a stairwell; a wooden cat on wheels abandoned in an antechamber. Shamelessly, I crept upstairs to see whether I might catch a closer look at her. Christophine, jealous creature, made sure I did not. All I could learn from listening at doors was that Mlle Adèle was a weepy little thing, prone to agues and fits of languor, biddable as a lamb and quiet as a louse. As for her sisters, when Mlles Pauline and Hortense Fourchet visited the rue Quincampoix for a week at Christmas, I learned that Mlle Pauline, the eldest, was the image of her mother, while Mlle Hortense, poor girl, strongly favored her plain, stout father. Mme du Fourchet paid them little attention. I paid them little more. They were nothing to me, not like Mlle Adèle.

A year passed. Knowing that one day I'd be femme de chambre to a baron's daughter (if she lived), I painted and coiffed, laced up and let out, tucked and draped with a will. Mme du Fourchet gave me a castoff robe battante of Lyons silk. Olympe made me free of the society of femmes de chambre, who drank cheap wine in the Palais-Royal and told tales to make me shudder of masters who fumbled at their breasts and mistresses who threw hairbrushes at their heads. I learned to starch fine lace and sponge brocade. By the end of my second year in the Hôtel Fourchet, maman and the shop on the rue Montorgueil had faded into a comfortable memory. My present was Olympe and Mme du Fourchet, her lovers, and her toilette. My future was Mlle Adèle.

What dreams I spun around that unknown child! By what means I forget, I had collected some five or six second-hand volumes of the bibliothèque bleu, which added Charlemagne and Roland, Gargantua, the Princesse Printanière, Chaperon Rouge, and assorted good and evil fairies and sorcerers to a head already crowded with Medea and

Jason, Le Cid and Donna Anna. From this hodge-podge of phantasms I conjured up a fairy child, frail as a cobweb, black-haired, jewel-eyed, with skin as white as snow and lips as red as blood. Tenderly I yearned over this poppet, imagining how she'd bloom under my care, how she'd love me as a sister and share her secrets with me. My own loneliness spoke in these fantasies, I fear, as well as my youth and naïveté. Yet they were closer to the truth than Mme du Fourchet's complexion, as I learned in the summer of 1756, when I met Mlle Adèle du Fourchet at last.

Madame was at her levée, I remember, attended by a young poet and one abbé Pinchet. For some time the young poet had been courting madame with sonnets and sighs, and today he'd brought her his chef-d'oeuvre, a composition in the classical manner. Madame listened politely enough at first, but when her hair had been powdered, her face painted, her garters tied, her gown laced, and the poet still not done declaiming, she took up a letter from the jumble on her dressing-table, beckoned her page to her, and murmured in his ear.

The poet fell reproachfully silent.

Madame was all pretty contrition. "I cry your pardon, *dear* chevalier," she fluttered. "A matter of family business that cannot be put off. So tiresome. I am confident that I may depend upon your understanding."

The poet was still assuring the baronne that her confidence was not misplaced when a lackey opened the door to admit Christophine and a little girl clinging to her skirts. The child hung back a moment, clearly overcome with shyness, then ran and threw her arms about my mistress' neck.

"Ah, sweet child," said madame. "Yes, mignonne, I know you love me, but have a care for my rouge, 'tis only this moment applied. Come, let us look at you." Unwinding the child's arms, she smoothed her dress as though she had been a doll, then gave her a little shove towards the center of the room and bade her turn around slowly. "Ah, abbé, is she not a pretty creature? Much prettier than Hortense, of course, or even Pauline. What do you think?"

"Exquisite," murmured the abbé, and put up his eyeglass to look at her more closely. "Such a sweet naturalness in her dress. The chemise dragged through the lacing—is that the new mode for children?"

Madame gave him a hard look, then took the child by the hand and drew her against her shoulder. "Mignonne, your appearance is so unworldly that I fear the good sisters will think we intend to pledge you to a life of prayer. Alas, 'tis my fault, for forgetting you are grown to be a young lady who needs a maid of her own to attend her.

"Berthe, come forward and curtsy to your new mistress. You may begin your service by doing something with her hair—it much resembles a bird's nest."

My knees bobbed of themselves into a curtsy; Mlle Adèle nodded shyly in return. Her eyes and hair were luxuriantly black, of course, but she was less delicate than I'd imagined her and less ethereal, her mouth being full and rosy and her chin strong and round. Under my nervous scrutiny, she pouted and turned her eyes to madame.

"Isn't Christo to take care of me anymore, madame mère?" I'd never heard her speak before. She had a sweet, high voice, trembling now on the edge of tears.

"Don't be silly, my pet," said madame, giving her a little shake. "You can't take a nursemaid to school, and the girl's not trained for anything else. So say goodbye to Christophine now, and thank her prettily for taking care of you. Then run away with Berthe and tell her what you'd like her to pack. Tomorrow after dinner you go to Port Royal."

Out of the corner of my eye, I saw the nursemaid wringing her apron in her hands. "Oh, madame mère!" cried Mlle Adèle, and threw herself into the baronne's arms. The tableau held for a moment. Then madame put her daughter from her and commenced to hunt amongst the boxes and vials on her dressing-table.

"Olympe, where *are* my patches? No, not those, dear girl—the stars of black velvet. *You* know, the new ones?"

"Stars to echo those in your eyes, Mme du Fourchet?" said the young poet daringly. Madame smiled at him under her lashes. We were forgotten.

The hapless Christophine stretched a quivering hand towards her former charge, who cast a piteous look at her and ran headlong from the room.

Well. I'd no desire to assist at the scene brewing in madame's boudoir. And my new mistress needed me, just as I'd dreamed she would. Why then was my heart knocking in my throat, my feet dragging as I followed her? I loved her already, me, had loved her for two years. Only now did it occur to me that my mistress did not yet love me; that she might, in fact, hate me for displacing Christophine.

I remember all too clearly how I trembled as I came up with Mlle

Adèle in the antechamber, and how she rounded on me, her face flushed and her little hands fisted. It crossed my mind that she might strike me.

"She's going to cry," she said passionately. "She's going to weep and moan and talk about the mercy of God and la sainte Vierge. That's what she always does when she's unhappy. You won't talk about la sainte Vierge, will you, Berthe?"

"No, mademoiselle," I said, astonished. "I will not."

Well, this was beyond question the right thing to say; for "Good!" said she, and smiled up into my face. "Come and see my doll. Christo said I couldn't have her at school, but *you* won't tell madame mère if I take her, will you?"

"No, mademoiselle," I said. Whereupon she vowed that she loved me, seized my hand in hers, and fairly dragged me up to the mysterious nursery. In a daze of relief, I admired her doll, her coral beads, her brocade shoes, her swansdown muff, gratefully accepted the rather stained ribbon-knot she pressed upon me, and coaxed her into letting me brush the tangles from her black curls. At the first touch of the brush, she winced. How well I recall how astonished she looked when she realized I wasn't hurting her, and how she begged me not to stop even when I'd worked out the last knot and her hair fell down her back in smooth, glossy skeins. Glad to please her so easily, I brushed on, and she began to arch her neck luxuriously against each long stroke and half-closed her eyes, for all the world like the kitchen cat when I scratched behind his ears. She's always liked having her hair brushed, my mistress, as much as I liked brushing it. Sometimes 'twas the only link between us, the pleasure we both took in her beautiful hair.

That night, I slept upon a pallet at the foot of her bed. Next morning, I packed up all her clothes into bandboxes and trunks, and duly after dinner, Mme du Fourchet saw us bestowed in the baron's carriage, patted my cheek, kissed my mistress, raised a lace kerchief to her eyes, and waved us on our way.

A long-faced novice welcomed us at the convent gate. Welcomed, I say, though the word's more charitable than her greeting. Hands firmly corked in the wide sleeves of her habit, she nodded to mademoiselle, said "I hope you're quieter than your sister," turned, and entered the gate.

Memory shows us pursuing her swaying black-and-white back down endless miles of wintry corridors set with a thousand tightly closed doors. In truth, Port Royal was not so large a convent, and it could not have been long before the novice was unlatching one of those doors and informing us that mademoiselle's apartment was not a cell or a dormitory such as less fortunate girls had, and devoutly hoping that three rooms of her own would not encourage mademoiselle du Fourchet to think that pensionnaires de luxe were better than anyone else.

Under her minatory eye, my mistress grew so frightened and so very humble that the novice's face softened a degree. "This being mademoiselle's first night," she said, "she need not sup in the refectory. The morning bell rings at half-past six; someone will fetch mademoiselle at seven. You, girl!"—I curtsied hastily—"See that your mistress is awake and neatly dressed by then." Uncorking her hands, she touched two fingers to Mlle Adèle's brow. "Sleep in the arms of la sainte Vierge, mademoiselle."

No sooner had the door closed behind her than Mlle Adèle cast herself upon my neck. "La sainte Vierge!" she wept. "I cannot *abide* la sainte Vierge! How miserable I am! Oh, Berthe, I love thee above anyone, even madame mère. Say that I may trust thee to stay beside me always!"

I wept in sympathy as I returned her embrace. "Ah, mademoiselle," I cried. "You are an angel, and my only wish is to be worthy of your trust. I swear upon the grave of my mother (upon whose soul be peace) that come what may, I will stand by you. As long as Berthe Duvet draws breath, you shall never want for a loving friend."

I blush now to recall that scene, with its immoderate words and immoderate tears. Yet both tears and words were truly felt, and while I blush for them, I do not repent them.

In her seven years at Port Royal, my mistress learned to dance gracefully and to design and execute embroidery as well or better than her teachers. Her singing was sweet, though thin, and she learned, in time, to perform upon the harp and the clavichord with passable accuracy and great feeling. The geography, the history of France, the rhetoric, the grammar, she might as well have done without, for all the good the lessons did her.

Mlle Adèle was not a dull child, you understand. For example, she learned very quickly that a sitting room, a fire in her bedchamber, two windows upon the rue d'Enfer, and a closet for her maid and her clothes attract envy as surely as honey attracts flies. Its first manifestation was a scattering of crumbs between her sheets, which trick she shyly reported to her oldest sister Mlle Pauline du Fourchet when that young lady paid her a formal visit of welcome.

"Only crumbs?" laughed Mlle du Fourchet. "Why, they must love you already, Adèle. For me, 'twas pebbles."

"Poor Pauline," said my mistress. "Were you very much hurt?"

"Hurt? Why no, silly child, 'twas only in fun. I put them in the porridge-pot, and oh, how I giggled when the whole school began to spit out pebbles!" She shook her head fondly, a grown woman of fifteen looking back upon the lost pleasures of her youth.

"Shall I then put the crumbs in the porridge?" inquired my mistress anxiously.

Mlle Pauline stood up. "Silly goose," she said sharply. "What fun would that be? What a tiresome chit you are, to be sure." And off she flounced, with an air of washing her hands of us.

So much for Mlle Pauline. And mademoiselle's second sister, Mlle Hortense du Fourchet, was little better.

Poor Mlle Hortense. What a maladroit she was, to be sure. 'Twas hard to believe we were of an age—I was eleven—for her size and quick tongue made her seem much older. She'd a reputation for cleverness among the pensionnaires, though 'twas not the sort of cleverness that was of any use to her. She was forever being punished for rude and heretical remarks—indeed, one of her punishments is among my most vivid memories of Port Royal.

'Twas in our first week, and I was helping serve dinner to the pensionnaires. How clearly I recall it! The clatter of spoons on pottery, the whispers, the giggles, and over it all, a girl's voice reading, unsteady and hoarse with anger. A savor of fish hangs over the memory—it must have been a Friday. The reader is a lubberly girl, broad of face, coarse of feature, ruddy of cheek—you'd think her the daughter of a carter, save for her accent and her fine white apron and cap. A nun stands behind her pointing out the verses with a birch rod. I move through the tables, ladling out fish stew and overhearing the whispers.

"She said women should be kings."

"*I* heard she said women shouldn't marry men."

"Well, look at her. Can you wonder? What man would marry that, had he a choice?"

The reading at an end, the nun closes the Bible and Mlle Hortense du Fourchet scowls out over the scornful throng, enraged and unrepentant.

At first I was inclined to applaud her spirit. My mistress, however, found it alarming, and held Mlle Hortense in the same terrified distrust that I reserved for the nuns. Indeed, Mlle Adèle was alarmed by most people—her fellow-pensionnaires no less than the nuns and lay-teachers—and annoyingly inclined to shrink when addressed, stammer when questioned, and weep when teased. The little girls, stony-hearted as even the best of children are, greeted both her halting recitations and her shy advances with muffled, disdainful giggles. Under this treatment, Mlle Adèle suffered from sick headaches and nightly fits of weeping in which she sobbed and sobbed that she couldn't bear it, that someone *must* love her or she'd die. During these storms, I held her and petted her and told her to be tranquil, that I loved her dearly, that the pensionnaires, yes, and the nuns, too, were all beasts and fools, that had I the power, I'd spell them to spew toads from their mouths with every word, like the woodcutter's daughter who insulted the twelve months.

So much I'd imagined—how she'd need me and how I'd comfort her. What I hadn't imagined was how, when I left her sleeping at last, I'd curl up on my pallet in the windowless closet and weep on my own behalf.

Oh, how I missed my freedom! All my life, I'd been accustomed to threading the streets of Paris with a basket on my arm and a few coins tied in a scrap of linen, to dodging horses and carriage wheels, to staring as I willed at the fine ladies in their chairs and the beggar-women on their street corners. Now Paris had shrunk to a view of the rue d'Enfer and the dome of the royal observatory, and all its varied multitude of rag-sellers, actresses, carters, petits-maîtres, beggars, artisans, and shopkeepers was reduced to a hundred or so nuns, lay servants, and femmes de chambre, all of them older than I and eager to remind me of it at every turn.

They thought themselves duchesses, those femmes de chambre, and sent me running after their fans and shawls and thread as though my flat chest and childish stature made me a lower order of being. Duchesses. Bah! Apes. Curled and perfumed apes, decked out in cheap lace bought with tips from their young ladies' admirers, boasting of their lovers, how rich they were and how handsome, how long they'd linger in the alley behind the buttery on the chance, the mere chance of a kiss. I couldn't understand it, me. What was so wonderful, after all, about pressing lips with a foul-breathed lackey, or allowing your mistress' brother to put his sweaty hands under your petticoats?

They simpered when I asked, and told me I'd feel very different about it just so soon as my breasts began to grow. Every woman longs for a man's touch, they said.

"The nuns as well?"

They exchanged wise glances, giggles, shrugs. "The nuns as well, my dear. The nuns above all."

Apes, as I said. Yet when all was said and done, they were not unkind to me. Compared to their mistresses, they were ministering angels.

Oh, what torments those infant marquises and comtesses devised for my poor mistress! When she made no public response to the crumbs in her sheets, they went on to cinders, then bricks in her pillow, then a chamber pot's worth of turds spread under her blanket. When I begged mademoiselle to report this last prank to the Mistress of Pensionnaires, she said with some force that she'd rather die than endure an interview with Mme Ursule, a sentiment I understood well enough not to press her.

Not a week later, some wag stole Mlle Adèle's beloved doll and hid it, swaddled in linen, in a young nun's bed. I suspected Mlle Stéphanie-Germaine de Montpelier.

Mlle de Montpelier was a little older than my mistress, wild as a young wolf and sly with it, a child who might have grown to be a great general had she been a boy. Her genius was the planning of elaborate pranks to be executed by one of her faithful lieutenants. In my mistress she found that tyrant's joy, a victim who can be made the willing instrument of her own downfall. Grateful for notice, eager for friendship, my mistress always did just what Stéphanie-Germaine told her to. In catechism once, my poor, innocent lamb brought the righteous wrath of père Méche down upon her own head by asking, at Mlle de Montpelier's suggestion, whether a fairy might go to Heaven if she performed enough good deeds. That ended in her copy of Mme d'Aulnoy's *Contes* being taken from her and a wholly undeserved reputation for blasphemy.

Thus matters stood when, sometime during the first week in Lent, I saw Stéphanie-Germaine and two of her hangers-on creeping out my mistress' door. Their fingers were to their lips, their faces scarlet with suppressed laughter. I smelled mischief on them strong as cheap scent. And yet when I searched mademoiselle's rooms, I found nothing. No full chamber pot balanced on the door, no lard in her powder, no noxious or painful substance secreted in her bed. Puzzled, I held my peace.

A few days passed—perhaps a week—during which Mlle de Montpelier was suspiciously kind to Mlle Adèle, paying her all manner of friendly attentions. The suspicions, of course, were mine alone; my mistress was beside herself with joy, so full of her dear friend Stéphanie-Germaine that I felt quite vexed with her. The sun shone, the sky was blue. Yet I felt in my bones that a storm approached.

It rolled up, as storms often do, with hardly a rumble of thunder or a cloud to warn us. One minute my mistress was sitting cozily by her fire, frowning over her embroidery. The next minute, the door was flung open to admit that dragon among nuns, Mme Ursule herself, her eyes as hard as dried peas and her mouth drawn up in a disapproving knot. She swept past my mistress without a glance and sailed into her bedchamber, emerging a moment later with an embroidered pocket dangling from her hand.

"Malheureuse," she said with a deadly calm. "Little sinner. Thief."

Mlle Adèle's eyes grew large and her bottom lip began to edge into a pout. "That's mine," she said, reaching for the pocket.

Mme Ursule trapped her wrist in a large, white hand. "You admit, then, to your crime?"

"What crime? The pocket is mine. I didn't steal it."

"Not the pocket, little Jesuit—the silver in the pocket."

My mistress looked blankly at her. "There is nothing in the pocket," she said.

Mme Ursule rolled her dried pea eyes at me. "You, girl. Put your hand in the pocket and show us what you find there."

I obeyed her.

I trust that Colette will not judge me too harshly for my want of spirit. I was a child, a servant. I lived by obeying such orders. And the écu was there, after all. If I hadn't found it, another would have. I remember how it gleamed like a moon in my hand: a silver écu of six livres, nearly half of a year's wages.

Mme Ursule looked triumphant, mademoiselle white and sick. Meeting her eyes, I felt like Judas.

"I've never seen it before," said my mistress at last. "I'm sure I never put it there."

"So young and so wicked," said Mme Ursule, shaking her head. "Mother Abbess will be seriously displeased."

I cannot bear to describe the scenes that ensued, mademoiselle's increasingly hysterical denials, Mother Abbess' stony indifference. Suffice it to say that in the end, she decided to try my mistress in a mock court with a mock jury of nuns and Mother Abbess playing Pilate upon the bench.

Thirty years later, in 1790, I recall hearing whispers of the Revolutionary Tribunals that would convict a man of treason upon some informer's oath that once he'd heard the accused drink the health of widow Capet. 'Twas on similar evidence that my young mistress was convicted of thieving. The young nun testified to the doll, and an excited Mlle de Montpelier testified to Mlle du Fourchet's disruption of the catechism class, as well as her wicked inability to recite accurately either the Seven Deadly Sins or the Ten Commandments. One Nathalie des Anges had heard her bemoaning the loss of her doll and her book and wishing for the means to buy others. Then I was called to the stand.

I answered Mother Abbess' questions as best I could, swearing all the while that Mlle du Fourchet had never, that she wouldn't, that she couldn't possibly have stolen that écu, that she was far too timid to attempt such a thing, that 'twas all a trick, like the evidence against her, like the cinders in her bed and the pins in her hairbrush. So far I got and no further before Mother Abbess held up her hand.

"Enough," she said. "Vicious creature! Do you think to help your mistress with these malicious lies? You should be whipped. Sit down and give thanks we've other, graver, matters before us."

"Mother Abbess." That was Mlle Hortense, scarlet-faced and trembling with fury, surging up before the whole school like an untidy wave. "Would you whip the girl for telling the truth? If you'd whip liars, you must whip Mlle de Montpelier and Mlle des Anges, who are as precious a pair of devils as ever salted the sugar. As for my sister, she hasn't the spirit to steal milk from a kitten, far less rob an alms-box."

Mother Abbess heard this speech in outraged silence, and when Mlle Hortense had done, stared silently down her nose for some little time longer before asking, "What is the Ninth Commandment, Mlle du Fourchet?"

"This is not the time for a catechism," said Mlle Hortense angrily.

"Nevertheless, Mlle du Fourchet, you will answer."

Mlle Hortense flushed brick-red, bit her lip, and confessed that she did not remember.

"I am not astonished to hear it, Mlle du Fourchet. 'Thou shalt not bear false witness against thy neighbor.' See you remember it in future. It follows 'Thou shalt not steal.' " She sighed. "What a trial you du Fourchets are to me! Lucifer himself is not so proud as you, Hortense, nor so worldly as Pauline, nor so blasphemous as Adèle." She turned to the jury of nuns. "You are all agreed that Mlle Adèle du Fourchet is guilty of theft as she has been charged?"

The nuns exchanged solemn looks, then as one, they nodded.

"Bon. You are a thief, Adèle du Fourchet. Thieves are felons, and felons are hung. For the sake of your soul and as a warning to your fellow-students, I sentence you to be hanged. You, Mlle Hortense, may meditate upon the sin of pride in the crypt until I see fit to release you."

And so Mlle Hortense was locked for a day and a night in the crypt (which was whispered to be haunted) without so much as a candle or a crust of bread to comfort her. And my mistress was hanged—not by the neck, I hasten to assure you, and not until she was dead, although le bon Dieu knows the shame and humiliation came near to killing her. She was taken to the refectory at dawn by a guard of novices, who packed her like so much dirty linen into a wicker laundry basket and hoisted her up over a beam where she dangled while the school marched under her, singing *De Profundis*.

I've little memory of the affair, save the drumming of blood in my ears and the gnawing in my chest and belly. I do recall that some of the pensionnaires looked up as they passed under my mistress' creaking gibbet. Stéphanie-Germaine, very pale about the lips, did not. And I recall the smallest girl in the school, barely five years old, calling out curiously, "Are you dead yet?"

There was a pause, and then a tearful voice from the basket. "No," said my mistress hopelessly. "Not dead yet."

Afterwards, my mistress was very ill. She could not eat nor rise from her bed, not though Mme l'infirmaresse bled her daily and dosed her with sulfur and salts. At last the rumor began to run through the school that little Adèle du Fourchet lay on her deathbed in such an odor of sanctity that even Mother Abbess was beginning to believe her innocent.

'Twas a very good rumor, invented by Mlle Hortense to breed fear and shame in the hearts of the guilty. After what had passed at the trial no one would have believed it from her lips, and so she enlisted me to scatter it among the servants, who bore it to their young mistresses as rats bear poisoned corn to their nests. That very night, while all were at compline, Mlle de Montpelier crept into the infirmary. She started when she saw me at my mistress' bedside, then bade me be gone in a tearful voice quite unlike her usual lordly drawl. I refused; she shrugged, then knelt by the bed, and with many tears and sighs, begged to be forgiven.

"I'll give you my coral necklace, I'll light candles to la sainte Vierge, I'll do anything you say. I'll even confess. Only don't die, Adèle. I didn't mean for you to die."

Slowly my mistress turned her face from the whitewashed wall. For a space she scanned Stéphanie-Germaine's streaked and swollen countenance as if all the pitiful tale of Stéphanie-Germaine's wolfish heart were written clear upon it. And then she smiled and said weakly that all she'd ever wanted was to be friends. Whereupon Stéphanie-Germaine cast herself upon my mistress' neck and vowed to be her champion and protector forever. She kept her vow, too, at first out of guilt and gratitude, then out of habit, and at last, as they both grew older, for affection's sake.

And did the success of our plot—Mlle Hortense's plot—please me? I no longer remember. I suppose I was disappointed that Mlle Adèle hadn't taken some proper revenge for her suffering while she could, or at the least made the little tyrant confess. I know I never learned to like Stéphanie-Germaine, whose saucy speech and manner mademoiselle soon learned to ape so well that even Mme Ursule forgot how like a beaten puppy she'd been. But if I did not like to see my mistress flirting and gossiping and giggling with the other girls, I did like to see her growing plumper and happier and prettier. And every night I'd brush her hair and listen while she recounted the small events of her day, and she'd kiss me before she slept and vow that she would always love me best.

Seven years passed, seven years of lessons and prayers. Mlle Adèle's sisters were betrothed to suitable men, left the convent, and married. The baron made a brilliant match for Mlle Pauline with the dashing comte de Poix. For Mlle Hortense, he managed the marquis de Bonsecours, who was plain and distinctly hunchbacked, but a respectable catch nonetheless, with lands in Normandy and a moderately lucrative office in the royal treasury. We attended their weddings, and mademoiselle learned to drink champagne.

Then mademoiselle's friends began to be married, schoolgirls one week, wives the next, with no more notion of what marriage meant than babes unborn. I don't pretend I knew much more, for fairy tales all end with the wedding, after all; and while passion is the chief stock-in-trade of messieurs Racine and Corneille, 'tis all poetry with them, and not a hint of action. As for my own experience . . . Well, my breasts were grown, but they'd never known a man's touch, nor would they, so long as I'd any say in the matter. I'd learned the theory of the commerce between man and wife from my friends the actresses, however, and something more from my sister femmes de chambre. And so I felt quite old and wise when, in the spring of 1762, my mistress received a tear-stained letter from the young présidente de Haute-briande, who had only two months since been Mlle Stéphanie-Germaine de Montpelier.

As was her habit, mademoiselle read her letter aloud while I dressed her hair. First came a mournful page or so on the subjects of dreadful loneliness and unbearable pain, and then: *O my Darling Adèle, of my suffering you can have no conception! Night and Morning, he clasps my knees to beg for a Kiss, and the more I shrink, the more he Importunes until at last I must, in wifely Obedience, let him Have His Way.*

"What is 'His Way,' Berthe? Do you know?" my mistress asked, her velvet eyes all wide with curiosity. "What is this 'knowing' of a man and a woman that so alarms poor Stéphanie-Germaine? Is it not inevitable that a man and wife grow well-acquainted once they are wed?"

I could think of nothing to say, me, save that all would no doubt become clear in time, and that the président de Hautebriande was an old man, quite thirty-five, and perhaps his breath stank and that is why the présidente did not like to kiss him.

"Then I shall have monsieur my father inquire particularly after my husband's breath, for I think I should like kissing a man even more than I like kissing you, providing his breath were sweet."

I thought, but did not say, that there was little likelihood that M. du Fourchet would do anything of the sort: it was not my place to turn a daughter against her father. Yet the hoop-backed timeserver the baron had visited upon poor Mlle Hortense was all too present in my mind. Plain as she was, she deserved better than a man whose gaze was fixed unalterably upon her bosom and whose soul was fixed unalterably upon the collection of taxes. At the moment that the new marquise de Bonsecours had turned to leave the church, her face had reminded me of the refectory at Port Royal, and how she would stand before the school, enraged but unashamed at some unjust punishment.

So, "Is this man halt?" I complained to Olympe. "Is that man blind? Does he stammer and spit? Does he have twelve grand-children? Hmph, says M. du Fourchet, the girl will be sure to dote on him—he has six degrees of nobility, all documented beyond the shadow of a doubt."

" 'Tis a great pity, to be sure," said Olympe soothingly. "But what's a father to do, after all? A young, handsome son-in-law is surely more apt to break his daughter's heart with opera-dancers and gaming. And as to degrees of nobility . . . A century of noble blood on both sides of a family can't be a bad thing, can it?"

Well, in the case of Mlle Pauline's husband M. de Poix, a century of noble blood had produced a petit-maître more likely to beget sons upon his mirror than upon his wife. And besides being hunchbacked, M. de Bonsecours was as dull as well-water, and as pleased with the sound of his voice as a trained parrot. Small faults perhaps, when weighed against their names and their fortunes, but proof enough that M. du Fourchet did not think to suit his daughters when choosing their husbands. He'd not notice breath like a tannery, were my mistress' suitor noble enough.

Mme de Hautebriande's letter came in the third week of Lent. At the beginning of Holy Week, we were summoned from the convent to the rue Quincampoix. I scented a husband in the air, and said as much to mademoiselle, who seemed wonderfully indifferent to the prospect. Her mother had breathed no word of such a thing, the visit was not, after all, an extraordinary one, and besides, she'd just been set an essay on the kings of France. Of course we'd return to Port Royal. How could I think otherwise?

Well, I did think otherwise, and with more certainty when I saw a little liver-and-white spaniel awaiting us in Mlle Adèle's bedchamber. Pet animals are not welcome at Port Royal, particularly pet dogs that squeak like rusty doors and make great puddles on the floor when they are excited. My mistress, ignoring the crudity of its welcome, scooped the puppy into her arms, where it wriggled happily, licked her chin, and whined. Delighted, my mistress named the pretty scrap Doucette and carried it down in her pocket to dinner.

Next morning, well before noon, I opened mademoiselle's chamber door to Mme and M. du Fourchet, who, despite the earliness of the hour, were fully dressed. M. le baron marched up to the bed and frowned at his daughter, who had just taken the first sip of her choc-olate. Doucette, curled in a liver-and-white ball on the pillow, was still snoring gently.

"Well, girl, not up yet? Dull work to lie abed alone, eh? You'll soon have something better than chocolate and a fat puppy to keep you there, hmph, hmph. Yes, indeed you will. Yes."

With an exclamation of impatience, madame pushed past her husband, cast herself on the bed, and took possession of her daughter's free hand.

"What your father wishes to say, darling child, is that we have been looking out a husband for you, and have settled upon M. le duc de Malvoeux, who is a *most* estimable gentleman, a creation of Godfrey de Boulogne's, we are told, with no fewer than sixteen degrees of nobility—a true noble immémorial—and such a droll motto: 'Je veux ce que je veux.' His mother being dead, you are to have *all* the family jewels, my pet, the diamonds of a queen, and such emeralds as can only be imagined, if sadly old-fashioned in their setting. I am persuaded you will make a lovely duchesse and be splendidly happy."

Mademoiselle tried to reclaim her hand from her mother's bosom. M. du Fourchet cleared his throat importantly.

"Hmph, yes, my dear, Mme du Fourchet has the right of it, indeed she does. He's only middling rich, mind you, and he came very dear —don't scowl so, Claire, the girl has a right to know how high a price we put on her happiness." For a moment, M. du Fourchet puffed thoughtfully to himself with his hands laced across his little round belly, looking, for all his brown satin and his fine Holland neckcloth, more like a farmer of corn than a Farmer of taxes.

"Hmph, yes, where was I? Oh, the dowry. Five hundred thousand livres, not a sou less, so he was very dear, as I said, but the dukedom of Malvoeux is a very respectable honor—five or six towns of some size, a dozen villages, some forty tenant farms, as well as the seigneuries of Beauxprés and Montplaisir. His landed revenue alone is ten thou-sand livres, and should he take my advice, well, he could easily grow as rich as de Guise. I hear the château at Beauxprés was rebuilt from the ground in 1690, so you needn't think you'll languish in a draughty donjon when you're from Paris. And as for his hôtel here in the rue des Lions, 'tis very fine, I assure you, very fine indeed."

"Yes," broke in madame impatiently. "And his mother was *very* highly placed, maîtresse en titre to the old king's Master of Wigs until ill-health forced her to retire to Beauxprés, where his father was cultivating his gardens, which are, I believe, among the most extensive in all France. He is a famous naturalist, I hear, a great collector of birds, which is *most* acceptable, for 'tis good for a husband to have an interest, ma chère, you must always remember that. I confess I could wish the young man more political: there's both money and position in office, you know, and he'd surely be preferred, an old family like that. Ah, well, husbands are seldom *entirely* satisfactory, and 'tis a small point, to be sure.

"Now, as to his person, he is very distinguished—Hortense will be eaten alive with jealousy. He's freehanded, doesn't game above the ordinary, and furthermore, mignonne, when we showed him your portrait, he seemed quite bouleversé, declared he'd never seen anything so exquisite in his life, and desires me to tell you that he lives only to make you his own."

Here madame fell silent, and both parents looked upon their youngest daughter, who was biting on her under-lip, her chocolate cup still clutched in one trembling hand. Doucette woke, pricked up her ears and began to whine gently. I stood frozen by the dressing-screen, entirely unable even to relieve my mistress of her cup. To be sure, 'twas no more than I'd expected. But to hear my future master thus coldly presented, point by point like an expensive horse—well, 'twas at once not enough and too much to comprehend.

M. du Fourchet, seeing his daughter's blank dismay, hemmed angrily.

"Well, my girl, have you nothing to say? A brilliant marriage proposed and you as dumb as a stone? You don't intend to be difficult, I hope? That would be a fine return for all our care of you, it would indeed!"

"Now, my dear M. du Fourchet, do calm yourself and let Adèle be silent if she wishes. Recollect that we have descended upon her before she is risen from her bed, and that she has had no thought of such a thing as marriage before this very minute."

"Nonsense, my dear! Girl didn't fall to earth in the last rain, after all. Of course she's thought of marriage. Girls think of nothing else —look at her sisters, chattering on about their husbands and their jewels like a pair of magpies. She'd have to be deaf and dumb not to think of marriage. Hmph, yes, indeed."

Madame's face sharpened. "Never mind monsieur your father, mignonne," she said sweetly. "Men never understand these things. You'll thank us in the end, you know. M. de Malvoeux is a duc. You have my word that he is also handsome, cultivated, and a great favorite at the baron de Holbach's salon. The marriage-contract will be signed tomorrow, and the wedding will take place in four weeks' time. Be a sensible girl now, and give your mother a kiss."

Like a cat stooping on a mouse, Mme du Fourchet bent forward to embrace her daughter, and the chocolate cup coming between them slopped its lukewarm contents over Doucette, the counterpane, and the fine blond lace on madame's bosom. There was much barking and exclaiming and ringing for cold water, after which madame and monsieur took their leave. When the door shut upon them, mademoiselle my mistress began to weep and, despite my best and tenderest efforts, was unable to stop until it was nearly time to dress for dinner.

In Which Mademoiselle Comes to Woman's Estate

Writing of my youth and Port Royal, I all but exhausted the crystal inkpot. This morning when I opened it again, the nestling's belly was full to the throat and my pen as sharp and clean as though 'twere newly plucked. Colette followed me to the library with a glass of wine, which she set at my elbow with a wink that has very nearly stemmed my flow of words altogether, saying that I must not think too much of her as I write—what she may or may not know, what she may or may not want to read. This is not a gown, after all, to be cut and trimmed to a client's taste. This is a history. It contains the truth. And if some of it is painful to write or to read about, well, then: that is the nature of truth and of history both.

I was writing of my mistress' betrothal.

On the morning after the marriage-contract was signed, Mme du Fourchet sent up word that M. de Malvoeux was expected to dine, and would Mlle Adèle be dressed by noon, and not in that hideous rose de Grecque sacque that made her look quite thirty, whatever monsieur her father thought. Immediately the page delivered the message, mademoiselle was out of bed so suddenly that Doucette, who'd been curled asleep upon her pillow, was startled into a volley of shrill barks.

"Oh, *hush*, Doucette, do," cried my mistress, and slapped the little spaniel on her nose. "Noon, and it's gone ten o'clock already.

Oh, Berthe, Berthe, I haven't a rag to my back, excepting only the rose de Grecque sacque. Whatever shall I wear?"

I couldn't blame her for being nervous. I was nervous myself. The day before, it had all been "How can he love me? He's never even *seen* me!" until her mother had struck her at last. She'd spent the better part of the evening in tears, declaring she'd not have him, no, not if he were king of France.

I had set myself to change her mind.

How often over the years I've looked back upon that night and wondered at myself. Not for coaxing my mistress into a more complaisant frame of mind, to be sure—her parents would have married her to this duc by will or by force, and a blind man could have seen she'd a better chance of happiness if 'twere by will. No, what I wonder at is the passion with which I set about the task. How excited I was at the prospect of being femme de chambre to a duchesse! Silk gowns! Amber necklaces! A little maid to run upon my errands!

Bah!

'Twas not so difficult to change my mistress' mind, not for one who knew her heart as well as I. The married state has infinite advantages, I told her. Imagine a ball at Versailles, and you all dressed in black and silver to make your first courtesy to the king. As the wife of a duc, you'd have the right to ride in His Majesty's private coach; he's an eye for beauty, they say—he'll be sure to ask you. And that's the least part of a married woman's privileges. A duchesse may stay up as late as she wishes, wear whatever she wants, even play whist if she's a mind. No one asks a duchesse the date of the battle of Crécy or the number of Eleanor of Aquitaine's husbands. Furthermore, this duc de Malvoeux didn't sound so bad a bargain, as husbands went; neither a twittering petit-maître like the comte de Poix nor a grotesque like the marquis de Bonsecours, but a famous naturalist, a collector of birds. She liked canaries, I reminded her. And it was so romantic of him to fall in love with her portrait, like a prince in a conte de fées. Surely her heart must be touched.

If I do say it, I spoke eloquently. And as I spoke, mademoiselle grew quiet and thoughtful.

" 'Twill please madame my mother, will it not?"

"Bien sûr, mademoiselle. And M. le baron as well, and all of mademoiselle's friends."

"Will it please you, this marriage?"

My heart beat high. With pride? With fear? I know I felt my

power over her; I pray I meant to use it only for her greater happiness. Meeting her eyes in the mirror, I said, "Yes, mademoiselle."

She smiled at me; her breast rose and fell in a quivering sigh. "Bon. Then I'll try to love him."

To make promises at night is as easy as brushing hair; to keep them in the morning is more like creating a coiffure à jamais vue. Mademoiselle demonstrated her good intentions by weighing *ad nauseam* the rival merits of white and blue, gauze and silk, coral beads and pearls. I was reminded of nothing so much as Mme Dumesnil dressing for a new play: "These ribbons are hideous, Berthe. I'll have the pink ones after all," and, "Is that a freckle, Berthe? Will the rice powder cover it?" and, "Do you think the cream gauze makes me sallow, Berthe?" I vow 'twas a miracle I didn't pin her garter in her hair.

Yet the thing was done at last, and Mlle Adèle stood up in a sacque of heavy silk brocaded with peacock feathers of pink and apple green, an apron of white drawn-work, and a fichu of the same. Her hair was curled in tiny ringlets à la dragonne, heavily powdered, and garnished with a fetching pompon of lace and pink feathers. With her white skin and her black eyes, she was perfect—like a porcelain figure animated and smelling delightfully of roses. I was just buckling one dainty brocade shoe when a double knock thudded on the front door. She tore her foot from my hand and flew to the window with me behind. We peeked around the curtain in time to see a gentleman in a sad burgundy coat step out of a smart town carriage—the duc de Malvoeux, beyond doubt.

Briskly he ascended the steps of the hôtel and disappeared within, leaving me with a fleeting impression of fashion, height, and extreme thinness. A pie-faced boy in silver-gray livery followed more slowly, bearing a cane and a chapeau-bras and a large flat leather case.

Mlle Adèle clasped shaking hands to her breast. "Oh, Berthe," she faltered. "Is he not . . . distingué?"

Well, I confess I'd thought him skeletal and rather sharp looking, but after my speeches of the night before, could hardly say so. Therefore, "Yes, mademoiselle," I answered her brightly. "Very distinguished, mademoiselle," and knelt to secure her shoe.

Dinner lasted from two until four, at which time Mme and M. du Fourchet took the betrothed couple to promenade in the Tuileries, then to a performance of *Artis* at the Opéra followed by supper at Switzer's. All in all, my mistress was out of my sight for nine hours or more. Words cannot describe how I suffered through those hours, how I wondered whether she'd turn sullen or flighty, whether madame her mother would scold, whether the entertainment would please, whether the duc should prove unbearable after all. By the time my mistress came under my hands again, I was half-frantic and she—she was flushed and animated and most annoyingly coy.

Oh, the opéra had been well enough, though monstrous long and hard to follow; and the supper had been most modishly ill-served. As for the duc, why, he was not such an ill man. For all that his title was four centuries old, he was himself only twenty-five, a veritable infant among ducs. His eyes were very handsome, very bright. To be sure, he had a monstrous long nose. And yet, she vowed, she loved him. During their walk in the Tuileries, he'd pressed her hand most tenderly while declaring that her brow was white as a dove's wing and her bearing more graceful than a demoiselle crane's.

"He told me all about his birds, Berthe. They're not larks or canaries or common swans or peacocks like the ones at Versailles, but birds from strange lands—from the Dark Continent and the Indies. And he's given me this fine parure"—she opened the leather case on a blinding display of diamonds—"Much finer than Hortense's pearls, don't you think?"

The next morning, M. de Malvoeux sent Mlle du Fourchet two lovebirds in a silver cage. Providentially, they arrived at the same moment as the mantua-maker, and their quaint chirpings helped amuse my mistress while the woman measured her for her bride-clothes. Over the next weeks, we had the lingère in as well (*not* my tante Duvet, I need hardly say) and the stay-maker, the milliner, the shoemaker, and the modiste. We also had a number of mademoiselle's old school friends, bearing silver saltcellars, kisses, good wishes, and an endless commentary on the habits of husbands.

"Six months of bliss, my love, and then, pouf! He's off with his mistress, and you might as well be mademoiselle again, except that you have license to do whatever you please." Thus the comtesse de Fleuru, who had been Mlle des Anges. Very worldly she sounded, and very wise. At the convent, I remembered, she'd been thrashed for failing to brush her teeth. Could it have been her foul breath that drove M. de Fleuru so quickly into a mistress' arms?

The présidente de Hautebriande threw her hands aloft. "Lord love you, Nathalie, you'll give poor Adèle the most curious notion of married life, 'pon my soul you will. I assure you, M. de Hautebriande continues most attentive. Why, he's so exigent that I hardly have time for my darling Clémence—you know Clémence de Lys, a bewitching little creature. She puts me much in mind of you, Adèle, all deerlike and breathless. I quite dote on her."

The young matrons exchanged wise looks and smiles, the comtesse de Fleuru making such an exaggerated moue I feared she'd lose her patch. "A lady friend is a comfort, to be sure," she said, "but I hope, Stéphanie-Germaine, that you don't intend to trust her with your heart. She'll leave you for some handsome youth by and by, or worse, attach your husband's interest. No. Give me a handsome chevalier, or a second son, or even an abbé—someone *safe*, you understand—and I will undertake to survive any amount of marital neglect."

The marquise d'Orcy, very demure and nunnish in a gray Brunswick gown, laid down her netting and cried shame upon them all. " 'Tis not neglect if the demands of duty call a husband from his wife's side," she scolded them. "Would you expect a man upon whose word the lives of a thousand Frenchmen depend to spend his time sitting with his wife while she talks of bonnets?"

"Indeed, I would not," laughed Mme de Berline—who not a year since had been locked in the crypt for having rouged and patched old Mme Saint-Antoine as she slept, so that saintly dame attended Matins bedizened like a strumpet. "Depend on it, Adèle. Husbands are a necessary evil, an inn upon the road between virginity and true love. Be presented at court, sit with him at the theater, give him an heir, and then, as Nathalie says, enjoy yourself. It ought to be easy enough. I hear that M. de Malvoeux is forever off to the ends of the earth looking for birds."

Innumerable variations on this theme were played over the four weeks it took for the banns to be called and the trousseau to be made up, and I assure you I grew heartily sick of it. All those silly children—most of them my juniors by a year or more—flounced and beribboned until there was more silk to them than flesh, laying down the law on marriage à la mode! And while they chattered, mademoiselle sat or stood among them mumchance, pretty as a wax doll and no more conversable, turning docilely this way and that to be kissed or pinned or laced up or trimmed.

"I am very happy," she would answer to all inquiries. "M. de Malvoeux is all any woman would desire in a husband." But often at night I would hear her weeping and creep from my pallet to comfort her.

"Doucement, chérie, ma petite colombe, agneau blanc," I'd murmur, and taking up her silver-backed brush, I'd remove her lace nightcap and unbind her black hair. "Hush thee, now, enfant, and thy Berthe will tell thee a story. Dost wish to hear 'La Belle aux Bois Dormant'?" From girlhood, that had been my mistress' favorite story, though the prince's kiss enticed her more often to sleep than waking.

A watery sniff, a small white hand pulling one black tress from the storm-cloud mass and winding it through trembling fingers. "Tell me about my wedding, Berthe."

"Oh, 'twill be very splendid, enfant! Three hundred are invited to the church and two hundred to the wedding supper. A countess will hold thy train, and no fewer than three marquises will support thee at the altar. Why, princesses have gone to their bridals less nobly attended."

"Go on," my mistress would say. "Will I be very grand?"

"More grand than La Pompadour in the days of her beauty, ma colombe. White brocade—no whiter than thy neck, bien sûr—embroidered with pearls and small silk flowers, Alençon lace at bosom and elbow, a train three ells long, and thy diamond parure blinding all who look upon it. I vow and declare, enfant, there will be green hearts among thy schoolmates then."

"Dost think so, Berthe? Dost truly think so?"

I'd set down the brush and cradle her against my shoulder. "But yes, chérie, I truly think so. Thou shalt move down the aisle of the Church of Sainte-Catherine with lace floating behind thee like cloud, and the tapers—six hundred of them, enfant, only think!—will make of thy diamonds a river of light. Thou shalt be a queen, my love, like La Belle and Princesse Rosette, and thy little dog Doucette shall eat no worse meat than partridge wings all the days of her life."

By this time, my mistress would be asleep in my arm, her face calm upon my bosom, her breathing soft and even, her cheeks and eyelids touched with rose. This is something I have always envied her: that her beauty does not diminish when she weeps (which she does as easily as a stay-lace snaps) but only softens, so that even when she'd most enraged me, her tears could always make me love her again.

On the twentieth of May, in the year of Our Lord 1763, Mlle Adèle Hermione Catherine du Fourchet was wedded to M. François Marie Baptiste Armand Maindur, vicomte de Montplaisir, seigneur de Beauxprés, duc de Malvoeux. She looked much as I'd foretold—paler, perhaps, than the Princesse Rosette, but much more à la mode. She moved down the aisle with due attention to the weight of her three ells of train, and from my place up in the balcony of the east transept, all I could see of her as she mounted the steps to the altar was white brocade and lace and the false black curls hanging to her waist behind.

Waiting for her at the altar was a rosary of clerics with the bride-groom in their midst like a gaunt, bright crucifix. His coat was pearl-colored silk with gold buttons, his waistcoat clear green, and his stockings bright primrose yellow. I distinctly remember thinking of birds when he bowed to his bride—a nervous, pecking dip of the head; and when he took her hand, I vow I half-expected him to fly up with her into the dim, high vault. For all the attention the wedding guests were paying, he might as well have done so.

As the priest began his invocation, the guests murmured, rustled, flirted, and moved about the nave of the church. Directly below me, someone sneezed violently: the comte de Poix, his face heavily painted and his coat of peacock satin so embroidered and beribboned, trimmed in crimson and laced in gold that I wondered how he had contrived to lift the snuff to his nose. Beside him, Mme Pauline fussed and fidgeted with her panniers. They were uncommonly wide and sup-ported a court gown in the new shade that dyers call "merde d'oie." Mme du Fourchet, when she had first seen it, declared the color well-named. In the golden light of the tapers it took on a sheen like old bronze, very flattering to a creamy skin. I thought my mistress might look well in it.

The night was warm; what with the crowd and the tapers, the church grew stifling hot. I saw a woman gape behind her fan and another dab at her upper lip with a lace kerchief already stained with rouge and lamp-black. A choir boy nodding in his stall squeaked aloud when the sacristan poked him awake for the *Kyrie*, and the marquise de Bonsecours, who was near her confinement, fainted heavily into her twisted husband's arms. Under cover of the chanting she was conveyed to the vestry, and, her own maid not being present, I was called upon to attend her.

When I entered, Mme de Bonsecours lay groaning upon a bench. Her face was whiter than her sister's gown, the circles of rouge showed like a fever-flush upon her cheeks, and I feared her time was upon her. She assured me 'twas more likely wind, brought on by haricots and champagne at dinner, and she'd do very well if I'd loosen her stays and bathe her face with eau de cologne.

I'd tucked lavender-water in my pocket against my mistress' need, and 'twas the work of a moment to uncork it, dampen a linen kerchief, and lay it to the marquise's brow. She moved restlessly on the bench and put away my hand. "I think I must sit up, Berthe," said she. " 'Tis impossible for me to breathe when I lie flat. You're undoubtedly thinking me a great fool to show my face abroad so close to my accouchement, and you're undoubtedly right. Poor Adèle! How could I not come to see her wed?"

By this time, she'd struggled upright with my help, panting slightly, her belly like a great rock under her satins and laces. As I loosened her corset, I felt a pang of sympathy for her maid Louison, who'd thrown herself so wholeheartedly into the transformation of the lubberly Mlle Hortense into the elegant marquise de Bonsecours only to lose the greater part of her efforts to the bloating and dishevelment of pregnancy.

"That's the *Credo*, or I'm much mistaken," said the marquise presently. "The deed is done, and I not there to see it. Nor you. Poor Berthe."

As we sat listening to the choir's muted whining, tears welled in my eyes. I recall I was puzzled by them. I was no sentimentalist, me, to weep at weddings.

Mme de Bonsecours took the cologne-soaked kerchief from my lax fingers and applied it to her throat. "I know, Berthe, I know. I myself am of two minds about this marriage, as I would be of any match of monsieur my father's making. 'Tis not so bleak, even so. M. le duc de Malvoeux looks to have all the parts of a man. Why, I've even heard him discourse sensibly on art and science." She sighed and stirred uncomfortably. "All M. de Bonsecours knows is taxes. Why, to him, the divine Voltaire is no more than a godless fool who got himself banished from court."

I did not feel comforted. "I pray this duc will make my mistress happy."

"Happy? What fool has told you that happiness is the object of marriage, hein? To most husbands, a wife is a purse to spend from and a womb to spend in. Wealth, position, power, sons: those are the objects of Christian marriage, Berthe."

This, I thought, was a most unsuitable discussion for a servant to be having with a marquise. "La, madame, such things as you say! I am all out of countenance."

She laughed, not unkindly. "I cry you pardon, Berthe: you're quite right. Will you fetch me that cushion, yes, the kneeler from the prie-dieu, and put it here, in the small of my back? Ah, just so. And a little more cologne on the kerchief, if you'd be so good? Thank you, Berthe." She smiled into my eyes. "You're as deft as Louison, and very much prettier. Cleverer, too, I've always thought."

I felt myself flushing. "La, madame," I said.

"Pray don't flutter—it don't become you. We're of an age, are we not?"

I looked at her in some surprise. A servant's precise age is not generally a matter of interest to the nobly born; she is either young and strong or old and useless. But Hortense du Fourchet de Bonsecours had always been an unaccountable creature. "I'm eighteen, madame."

"I thought so. I, too, am eighteen. Listen, ma chère." She leaned forward with difficulty and took my hand in hers. "My sister Adèle, as we both know, has more hair than wit, although 'tis such pretty hair that her lack of wit hardly matters." I began to protest; she pressed my hand and laughed. "Oh, don't deny it: you cannot. Let us be candid, you and I. Here in this vestry, with no one to hear us, we may surely speak as equals."

Well, I knew of a certainty that we could never speak as equals. Wherever we were and whoever heard us, we were forever and always a marquise and her sister's femme de chambre. And, since Mme de Bonsecours was not a fool, she knew it too. Because she was a marquise, however, I could hardly contradict her, so I shrugged—As you will, madame—and knelt at her feet.

"Candidly, then. I don't like this duc de Malvoeux. He fixes me with his sharp, black eye, and I feel like a beetle or a large grub—too large, thankfully, for him to snap up comfortably. He seems to me like . . . oh, I don't know, like a famine or a plague perhaps, that creeps up silently and consumes utterly."

I shivered. "Madame is enceinte," I said uncomfortably, "and very near her time."

"And these are the sick fancies of pregnancy? No, Berthe, I think not. Truly, I fear for Adèle." She took my chin in her hand and searched my eyes. "Madame my mother chose you for Adèle for no better reason than your youth and your pretty face. Nevertheless, she chose well. You've a fine wit, Berthe, and a good and faithful heart."

At this, I blushed and looked away, murmuring that madame was too kind. She released my chin. "Now I've embarrassed you. But 'tis true. I hardly need ask it, I know. Yet I fear he may try to drive you away and put some creature of his own in charge of her. Whatever he does, swear to me you'll stay with her."

Her words were high tragedy; her face and figure low comedy. And yet I never doubted that the lady was in earnest. You may imagine how I stared at her, alarmed no less by her vehemence than by her dark forebodings. My oath, when at last I collected my wits to swear it, was drowned by a consort of horns blaring the news that M. le duc de Malvoeux and his new-made duchesse were leaving the church. If I didn't hurry, they'd be away. I started to my feet, then looked down into Mme de Bonsecours's sweat-streaked face. How could I leave her alone? Whether her pangs were wind or labor, she was clearly unwell. And yet, who'd see to my mistress' train if I were not by? Who'd help her into her carriage?

Mme de Bonsecours laughed. "I am well answered, Berthe. Such a look of dismay! Bien sûr, you must go to your mistress. But first desire Mme de Luce to step inside—I think I saw her standing near. She's a kindly old biddy-hen, and delights in births and deaths." Stricken, I goggled at her; she sighed impatiently. " 'Tis only wind, silly goose. Fetch Mme de Luce and then be off with you."

Gratefully, I curtsied and went in search of Mme de Luce, who was plump breasted, bright eyed, and given to coquelicot ribbons on her caps. I urged her, clucking, into the vestry, then made off down the side aisle for the church porch.

What a throng was there! 'Tis hard to believe, at this remove of miles and centuries, that there were ever so many people in the world, much less in a single Paris street. How can I hope to describe the wonder and the terror of such a scene? In a world populated by seven, four make a crowd; four hundred is inconceivable. And there were upwards of four hundred guests in the church of Sainte-Catherine, and le bon Dieu only knows how many common folk in the street outside. The noise they made was deafening, like a flock of hungry crows cawing, pecking, treading on one another's feet and backs, battering one another with their wings, all eager to be the first to the fresh carrion, to peck out the tender eyes, the soft tongue.

I stood a-tiptoe at the church door, searching for my mistress in among the chapeaux-bras, bow-knots, plumes, and powdered horse-hair wigs swarming on the church porch and steps. In the street below, liveried guards linked arms against the canaille, whose gaunt and filthy faces grimaced in the lurid flare of the flambeaux like so many fiends of hell. Some several caws could be heard above the high-bred shrieking of the wedding guests:

"Hey, sieur! Let me break her in for you!"

"Make her show you what they taught her in the convent!"

"Don't cry, missus. It'll be over soon."

"Aye. From the looks of him, he'll be finished long before you begin to enjoy it!"

"Think she'll pleasure you better than your manservant, sieur?"

Briefly the flow of guests parted around my mistress, who was cringing against M. le duc's arm in an attitude more suitable to a new-caught thief than a new-made bride. I wormed my way to her, then, suddenly shy, smoothed my apron and coughed for her attention. She clutched his arm—I remember the pearly silk wrinkling under her fingers—and turned a frightened face to me.

"My felicitations, mademoiselle," I murmured, curtsying low.

My mistress smiled—a small, tight, cold smile. "I am not mademoiselle anymore, Berthe, but the duchesse de Malvoeux. You must call me madame now."

I swallowed tears. "Yes, madame. I . . . wish you happy, madame."

"Thank you, Berthe," she said more easily, and I think would have embraced me had not M. de Malvoeux put his arm about her waist to bear her down the steps and into the carriage. Nobles and beggars raised a cheer, and then the bridal couple were off, their horses plunging madly and scattering the rabble like rats before them.

That night, while the duchesse de Malvoeux was toasting her husband before two hundred noble guests, I was rattling my bones in the baron's old traveling coach over the cobbles towards the rue des Lions.

In physical distance, at least, the distance between the hôtel Fourchet and the hôtel Malvoeux wasn't far. It seemed to me that M. du Fourchet's coachman had no sooner turned out of the rue Quincampoix than he was reining up the horses and shouting for someone to come untie the duchesse de Malvoeux's trunks while I peeked nervously from the window. Save for a single guttering flambeau, the courtyard was dark as a pit; alighting from the coach, I could see nothing of the hôtel save three stained marble steps and a scarred black door.

The running footman mounted the steps and gave the door six new dents with the knob of his staff. Time passed; he knocked again.

The door opened a little way, grudgingly, and a thin, seamed face peered around it.

"It'll be the new mistress' servingmaid no doubt," said the face sourly. "Well, come in, girl, and bring one of those bags with you. 'Tis not my place to carry bags and boxes. Madame's servants must see to madame's things; I know nothing of women's fol-de-rols."

Reluctantly, I followed the face into a high, dark hall lit only by a branch of candles on a gilded console. "I am Dentelle," said the face's owner, and when I neither exclaimed nor swooned, pursed his lips together like an alms-box. "I am the valet of M. le duc de Malvoeux. Madame's apartments are left at the top of the stairs. Cul-terroux!" —this to the footman, who was staggering under the weight of a banded trunk—"Have a care with that trunk. Those urns flanking the stairs are from Cathay, brought to France by the great-grandfather of M. le duc, and worth twice your miserable hide."

Jean, my friend and faithful adviser, Jean agrees that I've caught Dentelle to the life: the face of a river pike and the soul of a dung hill cock. Timid and strange as I felt that first night, I'm proud to say I retained sufficient spirit to hate him at once.

"Oh?" I said. "And is his great-grandsire's taste in urns the reason M. le duc is too poor to hire lackeys? Is there no one to wait upon him and his new duchesse but one miserable valet? Bah. This is not what I am accustomed to, me."

Dentelle puffed out his chest, drew himself stiffly upright, and clapped his hands sharply together, calling the pie-faced boy and three other lackeys up from the hôtel's nether regions. "Carry this paraphernalia above," he said, disdainfully flicking his fingers at my mistress' trunks. "And one of you keep a watch at the end of the street for monsieur's carriage. Fetch some tapers, and you, Gaston, sweep the floor. Who knows what harm all this to-ing and fro-ing, all these bundles and boxes, might not do the parquet? Well, louts? Do you wait for Our Lord to come again?"

With a great show of energy and speed, the lackeys hefted madame's luggage upstairs, glaring at me the while as though I were to blame for the valet's ill-temper. They dumped everything outside the door and slouched away, leaving me to muddle along alone. For an hour or more, I dragged trunks into the dressing-room and emptied them, hastily laying gowns in the tall presses and stuffing petticoats, stays, sleeve-ruffles, ribbons, chemises and caps higgledy-piggledy into drawers to get them out of the way.

I've always found it a tedious business unpacking and bestowing my mistress' clothes, but never more than on my first night in the hôtel Malvoeux. The dressing-room was cramped and musty; the bedchamber was hot and ill-aired. There was no antechamber. The furniture was as grand as you please, though outmoded and sadly sparse: a bed, a tambour table, a satin-covered bergère by the fire, and a long-case clock, all of them set far apart as feuding relatives and meagerly lit by a pair of wax candles on the mantelpiece. What with the lateness of the hour and the shadows in the corners, I was as frightened and low-spirited as a whore in a Hôtel Dieu. Mme de Bonsecours feared for her sister's happiness: at the moment, I feared chiefly for my own. Olympe, Mignon, Saint-Cloud, LeBeau—all my friends and my family were left behind in the warm, well-ordered house on the rue Quincampoix and the future stretched before me, cold and bleak and friendless. Would my mistress still love me as she had before? Must I trade Olympe for Dentelle?

I broke a nail on the latch of the dressing-case. The long-case clock struck four. I laid a silk gauze négligée ready upon the bed, noticing that the curtains were burgundy silk embroidered in black, more suited to a catafalque than a bridal bed. I tucked them back, thought about going in search of another candle to brighten the room, decided my mistress might be happier not seeing it clearly. Would they never come?

Suddenly in the hall below I heard a great banging accompanied by muffled shouts and cheering and then a man's voice shouting, "Good night to you, my friends, or rather, good morning! You're all very kind, but I can see her to bed myself!"

If that is the duc, I thought, his voice is a measure less merry than his words. I waited. The front door creaked and closed. I heard an obsequious murmur that could only be Dentelle, my mistress' soft voice responding, steps mounting the stairs. A silence, a rustle, and a hoarse whisper in the hall: "I'll come to you soon, madame. Prepare for me."

Timidly, I opened the door. My mistress, very dark around the eyes, entered and sank into the bergère with a most un-bridal sigh.

However strange and melancholy I might feel, I knew where my duty lay. "Come, madame, and let me unlace you," I said gently. "You'll feel much more comfortable without the false hair and the heavy corset. Be of good cheer, madame. 'Tis your wedding night."

"Yes," said my mistress. " 'Tis my wedding night, and I promise you, Berthe, I've heard enough pleasantries on that head to last me until this time next year. As you love me, no more."

Though she spoke very sharp, her lips trembled. I chattered brightly, as I undressed her, of how Mme Hortense had feared she'd drop her child in the vestry and other such nonsense. Gradually she held up her head again and began to look more cheerful.

" 'Tis the long day and the wine and that monstrous corset, Berthe. I'll soon be myself again." She smoothed the folds of her négligée and surveyed her new bedchamber. The hangings catching her eye, she shook her head and sighed. "Tomorrow I shall ask monsieur my husband to order new bed-curtains. And surely"—glancing nervously towards the long-case clock—"he cannot expect me to sleep with that horrid ticking." She gathered her lace ruffle to her throat and glanced again towards the clock. Following her gaze, I saw she was looking at the gilt outline of a door in the paneling.

There was a silence, and then, "My mother has told me a little of what must happen this night," said my mistress in a small voice. "I cannot think what Stéphanie-Germaine found so distressing in it. If the man is skilled, maman says it can be very pleasant." She looked up at me pleadingly.

What, pray, did the child think I knew about it? I was visited by a sudden wild vision of a shrewdness of lady's maids sitting bare-shanked before a convent fire, comparing the manhood of one lover to an anchovy, of another to a battering ram. To conceal my confusion, I bent my face above her head and busied myself with her hair. "So I've heard, madame," I said, very prim. "And consider: why should so many women take lovers to their beds if what they did there were distasteful?"

"Because 'tis à la mode." She flung her arms around my waist and pressed her cheek to my bosom. "Long ago dids't thou swear to stand by me. Surely, Berthe, thou wilt not leave me here alone?"

I rested my cheek against her fragrant hair. "Not alone," I said a little sadly. "Never alone."

She nodded and released me, only to clutch at my hand when the door in the paneling opened in a blaze of light. My heart began to pound painfully and though I could not bring myself to shake her off, I turned away, thus by unhappy chance bringing myself face-to-face with my new master's reflection in the mantelpiece mirror. Night-capped and gowned in dark brocade, he looked more skeletal than ever, and his dark eyes were hungry as a vengeful ghost's. I do not think he saw me.

"My wife," he said, his harsh voice quivering. "My darling little bird, how your heart beats—why, I can see the lace trembling at your breast. Come to me, ma mie, ma chère, ma colombe blanche."

My mistress released my hand and, breathing fast and shallow, rose and took a faltering step. It might have been towards her husband or it might have been away: I did not see, for I ran like a mouse for the dressing-room and latched its door behind me.

How the habits of youth die hard! I've not laid out a gown nor mended so much as a ruffle for a hundred years or more, except by my own will and desire. My former mistress and I sit down at the same table and address one another as "chérie" and "thou." In fine, I am a free woman, me, who may speak her mind to whom she likes. Yet, recounting the days of my service, I find myself haunted by Olympe's lessons in comme il faut.

A good femme de chambre, she taught me, is the soul of discretion and the heart of good temper. She never addresses her mistress uninvited; she neither weeps nor sighs save in sympathy for her mistress' woes. With her fellow femmes de chambre she may unbend, but not so far as to gossip of her mistress' private affairs. For a tittle-tattle's indiscretions will always be discovered, and the brothels are full of maids who could not learn to hold their tongues. Her favorite maxim was: "Better to die of grief unspoken in a noble hôtel than of disease and starvation in a ditch." A cautious woman, Olympe, despite her bright and fluttering ways. How shocked she'd be at this history of mine!

To be sure, I'm half-shocked myself, a little at the liveliness of my memories, more at the anger that curdles my breast as I inscribe them. For Mme de Bonsecours had not been altogether mistaken in fearing that the duc de Malvoeux might drive me from my mistress' side.

Not that he worked against me, you understand—on the contrary, he scarcely gave himself the trouble of acknowledging my existence. I was of less account than Doucette: a pair of hands to dress his wife and disappear. Oh, how slighted I felt! For seven years, I'd awakened my mistress every morning, borne her company every day, lighted her to her bed every night. Suddenly, I was barred from her room until she called for me, often not until eleven or even twelve of the clock. And even then we were not alone, for monsieur her husband loved to watch her toilette, and would lounge on the bergère with his stockings ungartered and his shirt agape, exclaiming upon the pearliness of her skin and the trimness of her ankles while she simpered and preened until I could hardly keep my countenance. Before, we'd often read and talked together. Now all I did was dress her, twice, sometimes four times in a day, for rides in the Bois and walks in the Tuileries, for expeditions to the cabinet du roi to examine birds and to the salon of the baron d'Holbach to converse with famous wits and philosophes. He was monstrous fond of philosophes, M. le duc de Malvoeux, and less fond of balls and musical evenings. Nevertheless, madame seldom laid down her head before three in the morning, which meant that I was forever short of sleep. On the occasion of her formal presentation to His Most Serene Majesty, King Louis XV of France, neither one of us retired until dawn.

The presentation at Versailles—that was the one scene in my fairy tale of wedlock that adhered to the playbook. My mistress has never, save once, been so beautiful. Her gown I remember as though I had it before me—black and silver as custom dictated, with court sleeves and lappets of Alençon lace. The train was two ells long, and so heavy that the little black page monsieur had bought her was hard put to keep it from the floor. Her coiffure was stuck with silver bees. Alone with me in her dark, cavernous bedchamber, she glittered with diamonds and excitement like a starry night. And she insisted that I accompany her to Versailles, where I waited in a hot and gilded antechamber with the other maids while my mistress traded pleasantries with the king and danced with princes of the blood royal.

Her presentation itself I need not describe—Colette has heard it from her own lips often and often, from her first trembling curtsy to monsieur's declaration, as he handed her into the carriage, that she was a bird of paradise among poultry. Decorated or plain, Adèle's account must be truer than mine, for my own memory of that night is painted over with images of a thousand other nights, a thousand other entertainments. When first I walked under the painted ceilings of Versailles, did I think them splendid and astonishing? Or did I judge them immediately as being gaudy, overgilded, overheated, overcrowded? To say true, I don't recall.

For the rest of my romance, well, 'twas false as a gypsy's fortune. Freedom and honor, bah! Bien sûr, I was free to wander Paris as I

would, but I had no friend to wander with. Monsieur kept no maidservants in town, and all the conversation the lackeys had with me was
my beauty and their desire to plunder it. As for Pompey, madame's
little black page, though he ran willingly upon my errands, he did not
speak, and when he wasn't fanning madame or bringing her bonbons,
kept very much to himself. Often in my loneliness I was reduced to
taking Doucette on my lap and fondling her curly ears and hard, round
head until she lost patience with my caresses and snapped at my fingers.

For me, the only bearable hour of the day fell between dinner
and the evening's entertainment. Dentelle attended to monsieur, and
I pinned fresh ornaments in madame's hair while she, as often as not,
pored over a volume of Brisson's *Ornithologie*. In those quiet moments,
she'd confide in me as of old. Well, not quite as of old; for now her
confidences were all of her husband.

"Look, here is the picture of a jacamar, Berthe, just like the one
monsieur my husband showed me at the bird-market. 'Tis not nearly
so lovely as the bird itself. M. de Malvoeux says I am lovelier than any
bird he has seen, and my bosom much softer than feathers." Blushing
furiously, she'd break off and, stealing a sidelong glance into her mirror,
stroke her haresfoot down her breast with a reminiscent smile. "Ah,
Berthe, 'tis so delightful to be loved! I have only to think of him to
feel myself grow prettier. Stéphanie-Germaine de Hautebriande is a
great fool. There is nothing better than an exigent husband."

And here I'd thought she had always known herself loved—by
me. Husbands are different—I understood that. And I understood
that she did not wound me from malice, would, in fact, be vastly
astonished to discover that I felt each word as an arrow to my heart.
Pride and decorum both decreed that I must bleed in private, so, "Yes,
madame," I'd answer coolly. "No doubt, madame. Will madame wear
the pink paduasoy tomorrow or the blue lustring?"

I was happiest when she was telling me the latest on-dit, for
hearing her relate the misadventures of Nathalie and Stéphanie-
Germaine I might imagine that nothing had changed between us. The
best stories were provided by the comtesse de Fleuru, who combined
the carnal appetite of a she-wolf with a monkey's lack of discretion.

"Just think, Berthe, Nathalie de Fleuru has bestowed her favors
upon the chevalier d'Emplumer!" my mistress might declare, all
wicked innocence. "How she could, knowing what he is! Why, he
wears the key to her summer house on his watch-chain, and now all
the world is calling her the comtesse de la Petite Maison. Imagine how

she must feel when she comes to hear of it! I could not endure to have such things said of me, indeed I could not!"

Sometimes I'd catch her eye in the mirror and essay some teasing sally as, "Ah, but madame has no summer house," or "Madame would be much too discreet, I'm sure." Once such small jests had made her giggle. Now they were more likely to make her frown and scold. "Peste, Berthe," she'd pout, "but you are naughty today! You know very well that's not at all what I meant. I am devoted to monsieur my husband."

"Yes, madame."

At times like these, I was greatly tempted to pull her hair or pin her lace right through her feather-soft bosom. What had Mme de Bonsecours called the duc de Malvoeux? A famine that consumed utterly. Well, he'd certainly consumed my mistress. She thought of nothing save him, talked of nothing save him, was deaf to all voices and blind to all faces save his. In thought, in word, even in gesture and mien, she was his faithful mirror, reflecting both the good and the ill in him with unjudging fidelity.

Perhaps 'twas to try this devotion, or simply to display it, that monsieur allowed—more, encouraged—my mistress to hold levées like her mother. He would invite his own friends to attend his wife's toilette, lead them on to talk about her beauty, and watch them ogle her with a painful glitter in his narrow black eyes. Me, I'd run back and forth with pounce-boxes and aigrettes, trying to prevent this gentleman from stepping on Doucette and that gentleman from fondling my bosom, all the while puzzling over M. le duc's odd behavior. On the one hand, he seemed to be dangling my mistress before the other men like a glittering bauble: See, this is mine and not yours. Is it not splendid? On the other, he was clearly jealous of their eyes on her. And the bauble herself, my mistress, postured, preened, and chattered like the sulfur-crested cockatoo he had given her, that fanned its yellow crest and croaked "pretty lady" when you stroked it.

This uncomfortable farce ended at last one morning at the end of August, in the presence of a silk-seller, a modiste, a mariner with a monkey to sell, the baronne's old friend abbé Pinchet, and one vicomte de Tergive.

The vicomte was no friend of monsieur's, nor of madame's either, being one of those youthful lily-knights who amuse themselves with grown men's wives. Mme de Fleuru's chevalier d'Emplumer was another such, and hardly more notorious than this vicomte de Tergive, who must have oiled the lackeys' palms well to persuade them to allow an uninvited guest into madame's bedchamber. Within a bare minute of entering, he'd sprawled himself over the bergère and embarked upon such a pointed catalogue of my mistress' charms as caused M. le duc to throw up his hands and disappear into his dressing-room with a slam.

Madame dropped her rouge-pot.

"Husbands," purred the vicomte in a tone of great sympathy. "They have no generosity of heart."

"That is not true," said madame with some spirit. "I am sure M. de Malvoeux has the most generous heart in the world, and, as I am among the silliest of women, I am very fortunate that it should be so."

"He, too, is very fortunate, madame," said the vicomte, and gazed at her with a kind of melancholy smirk.

"Oh? How is that?" Madame turned upon her stool and tilted her head like Doucette when she thought you had a bonbon for her. Very coquettish she looked in her loose-bodied robe, and yet 'twas so plain she had no idea of the vicomte's meaning that he was quite embarrassed how to answer and took snuff to cover his confusion.

Lifting his cyeglass, the abbé examined first the sneezing vicomte and then the sailor's monkey. "What the vicomte means, madame, is that your husband is very fortunate in the possession of so loving a wife. Although most men, or most husbands, rather, find such love— dare I say it?—rather wearing on the nerves. After a while, of course."

"A while?" said madame. "Three months? La, sir! A very short while indeed. I confess that I have seen no sign of such wearing. But as I have said, I am very silly, so perhaps I've missed the signs."

The vicomte looked very annoyed; his voice took on a malicious edge. "Your femme de chambre is a monstrous pretty piece," he said.

"Yes, my Berthe is very pretty. You cannot conceive how monsieur my husband admires her."

The vicomte smiled, studied his impeccable nails. "Ah," he said. "I think I can." He glanced up at me; I bared my teeth in return and imagined how he'd look wearing a chamber pot.

"The question with maids," said the abbé, shamelessly ogling my ankles, "is whether to have them safely plain and thereby offend one's eye, or pleasingly pretty and thereby offend one's honor. 'Tis a constant temptation to husbands, having pretty maids about."

At last madame understood, for she grew quite pink. "Oh," she gasped. "How you dare!"

Upon her words, monsieur emerged from his dressing-room and stood by the long-case clock with his shoulders hunched up to his ears and his dark eyes ablaze.

"Out!"

At that, the pie-faced boy and one of his fellows threw open the door and advanced meaningly. The abbé Pinchet lifted an eyebrow at the vicomte de Tergive, who shrugged, rose, bowed deeply, and strutted out between them with his nose in the air.

"Out!" shrieked monsieur again, frightening the monkey into a chattering fit. "Out, out of my wife's bedchamber, every damned last one of you!"

There was a general rush for the door, the modiste trailing ribbons and bonnets and the silk-seller clutching her wares helter-skelter in her arms. The last to leave was the abbé Pinchet, who turned at the threshold and leveled his glass at monsieur, then bowed himself out with an ironic flourish. The lackeys withdrew and gently shut the door. I prudently made for madame's dressing-room.

"Stay, Duvet," said monsieur. "You must hear what I have to say. Adèle, I beg you pay no heed to the insinuations of those . . . toads, those popinjays, those poxed sons of underbred whores. Berthe is nothing beside your beauty—a black-browed wench, a bubo. I praised her only to please you."

Weeping now, madame rose and went to him. He seized her head between his hands, thrusting his fingers through the curls I'd spent so long arranging and kissing her with such violence that my lips stung in sympathy. Then he sank to his knees, and, kissing her hands and arms, pulled her down upon the carpet in a froth of lace and satin. He unlaced her bodice and fondled her bosom and still I stood petrified, unsure whether I'd been dismissed, uncertain whether my mistress' moans were pain or passion. Passion, I suspected. I feared he meant to possess her before my eyes.

"We will leave Paris, my love," he murmured as he teased up her skirts. "Paris is a trap, a sink, a brothel. We will go to the country, to Beauxprés." He began to unbutton himself. "Tomorrow," he said. "Tomorrow we will leave this place."

Tomorrow. "With your leave, madame, I will begin to pack," I said, curtsied, and fled.

In Which We Come to Beauxprés

Once upon a time, there was a young femme de chambre who had never seen Beauxprés. She thought herself a connoisseur, urbane, with a fine taste in actresses and argument, a citizen of Paris and therefore a citizen of the world. I can just remember her, blind as an unweaned puppy whose world is a box and a bitch's teat. How frightened she was when there proved to be a wider world beyond! And how quickly that world drew in around her! Haven, prison, burden, bower—Beauxprés has been all these things to me. And after two centuries or more, 'tis grown like my own body, a place to look out of, not at.

Jean, having been born here, I think has always felt so, and also the Maindurs, who have eyes only for their own obsessions. For Adèle, Beauxprés is the sumptuous mise-en-scène of her private dramas. And Colette—in spite of the life she has known here, growing older and wiser as no ghost has been known to grow before—Colette thinks of Beauxprés as the place where she was killed.

Not that she's said so, to be sure; she's freer with philosophy than sentiment, our Colette. Yet from time to time, I've observed it: when her eye by chance alights on a case of fans or painted miniatures and her poppy face blanches with fury. Oh, I understand—never think I do not. I have even shared her rage. And I remember also my first sight of Beauxprés, how beautiful and terrible it seemed to me, like a Heavenly mansion or an enchanted castle.

The journey from Paris to the high meadows of the Juras generally took five days when the roads were dry. Only five days. To me, who'd never ventured farther afield than M. du Fourchet's château in Montmorency, it might as well have been a two years' journey to Cathay.

Besides madame's cockatoo and the lovebirds, monsieur had bought in Paris a dozen or so rarer specimens: redpolls and popinjays and emerald cuckoos from Brazil. These, with Doucette, Pompey the black page, and the unspeakable Dentelle, were my only traveling companions, madame riding alone with monsieur her husband in a second carriage. We set out before light. By dawn we were out of sight of the southernmost faubourgs of Paris; by dinner we were deep in the country. That night, for the first time in my life, I slept at an inn.

This, I thought, was the world: this, I thought, was adventure.

Each morning we rose at four, lashed the baskets of birds into the berline, and bumped along through the dust until two in the afternoon, when monsieur and madame dined. Dentelle, Pompey, and I would bolt down a glass of wine and a slab of meat while the horses were changed, for we must reach the inn in good time to feed the birds, order supper for the duc and duchesse, air their beds, and unpack their dressing-cases. We made a silent company; for Dentelle wouldn't lower himself to gossip, and Pompey (as far as I then knew) couldn't speak at all.

I don't know what I expected to encounter as we drove south and east—flying pigs, no doubt, and men with two heads. The last thing I'd expected was that the land itself would change. For all I knew, the whole world was like the Île de France: flat as stretched cloth, with the sharp, gray steeples of little villages poking up from it like ill-secured pins. Imagine my surprise when the land began to wrinkle and, as we neared Dijon, to gather itself into deep folds thickly sewn with rows of vines. Eastwards towards Poligny, steep meadows were pleated above the road, and cornfields, and long, shadowy stretches of forest. Even the trees were different: shaggy, red-trunked, taller than the poplars and chestnuts I was accustomed to, hung, in the place of leaves, with black needles through which the wind sighed dismally.

'Tis hard to believe, after two hundred years surrounded by firs, that there was ever a time when I'd never seen one, but there you are. I remember thinking they looked like church steeples ought to look —ought to, I say, for to my mind Jura steeples are barbaric things, shaped like flat-sided bells and gaudily tiled in scarlet and yellow and green. As for the villages themselves, I thought their inhabitants must be half-goat, so steeply were the houses canted up hillsides and tucked down gorges. More than once I had occasion to close my eyes against the sight of a bone-crushing drop from the narrow road, with red roofs and tiny green gardens clinging to it like boletus to a tree. I've journeyed a hundred times since then, to Nice and Bordeaux and Brittany and Lausanne, yet 'tis that first journey to Beauxprés sticks in my mind as the longest, the strangest, the most uncomfortable of them all.

I remember the light was golden and slanted when at last we approached Beauxprés. All day we'd been driving through a fir forest—the Forêt des Enfans, Dentelle called it, ancient and masterless, haunted by ogres and wolf-masters and evil fairies. Parisienne as I was, I laughed at him, the louder for the darkness of the wood and the closeness of the air under the bearded firs. He'd scolded me, of course, which served to pass the time. Yet day and forest both seemed interminable, and I was at the end of my patience by the time we broke free of the trees at the edge of a wide plateau.

Absurdly, it reminded me of a soup dish, flat and round and bordered all around with hills, with a great mound sitting in the midst of it like a green dumpling. The bottom of the dish was all meadows dotted with cows and fields in which the ripe corn shimmered like watered silk in the wind. Or perhaps 'twas my tears made it shimmer, tears of self-pity from racketing along mountain roads in an ill-sprung berline with the outraged chirps of a dozen basketted birds dinning in my ears. My stays were poked into my breasts, my spine was jolted through my cap, and I was beginning to fear I'd not live to see Paris and civilization again.

"One hopes," remarked Dentelle out of a long silence, "that madame's servants will know to keep their place when we come to Beauxprés. 'Tis unbecoming to think oneself the equal of those who have served the ducs de Malvoeux for twenty generations."

"La and mercy," I said. "And here was I, thinking your wrinkles and pustules were just ugliness, or too free a hand with the white-lead in your youth. Now I know you to be upwards of four hundred years old, I'll vow you're tolerably handsome."

Dentelle pleated up his mouth very small. Pompey, unexpectedly, giggled. Much heartened, I wiped the tears from my eyes, settled my stays, and straightened my cap under the hood of my cloak.

Soon we reached the foot of the green mound and the end of a chestnut drive that swept up the steep rise in wide curves. At each turn my heart knocked harder in anticipation, and then we were at the mouth of the drive with a long green terrace rising before us, and a great cream-colored palais at its head.

Once the château Beauxprés was a real, fortified château like Blois or the Château de Joux, but the round, gray tower presiding over the enchanted garden is the sole remnant of that ancient fortress. For the rest, Beauxprés is nothing more than a house set on the crest of a hill—a very broad hill, to be sure, and a very large house. Blond stone, three floors above the rez-de-chaussée, balanced ranks of windows answering one another across three large courtyards: Beauxprés is magnificent beyond astonishment. The drive approaches respectfully along one side of the slope so as not to obstruct the view, then curls at the south wing into the forecourt, where cobbles give way to dressed stone laid in an elaborate, shell-like pattern around a marble fountain.

Ah, that fountain! Among so many novelties, I greeted it as old friend, for 'twas a faithful copy of the great fountain of Latona at Versailles. The Beauxprés Latona is much smaller, to be sure, and the frogs besetting her only the size of cats, even the ones that are not entirely frogs, but half-transformed men with wide mouths and eyes bulging in reptilian horror at the sight of their flippering hands. To be sure, 'tis none the less grotesque for being diminished.

Not that I recognized it just at first, mind you. At first, I only had time to glimpse a kind of outsized epergne in the forecourt before we drove round the north wing to the stable-yard and bumped to a halt.

We were home.

A well-set-up youth ran out from the stables to the horses' heads. "Ho, Carmontelle!" he greeted the driver. "Ho, Dentelle! You've been gone so long, we've been selling off your clothes. And who's this?" He eyed me up and down and grinned widely, revealing a mouth full of strong, square, yellow teeth. "Welcome to Beauxprés, mam'selle. We've seen Parisians before, though 'tis seldom they're so comely as you."

Well, I'd heard the like before, and the unwelcome propositions that generally followed, and so I was prepared for the youth's lewd appraisal of my bosom and his lascivious wink. 'Twas like a miracle when he returned my frown with a shrug and a smile of such frank good cheer that I felt the corners of my mouth lift in reply. Dentelle, observing my rising spirits, lost no time in seeking to squelch them.

"Ah, Jean, Jean," he said sadly. "One weeps for the blindness of the unlearned, who can mistake a modish bonnet for comeliness. This is the serving-woman of Mme la duchesse. She is only a city girl, after all, and beyond doubt our new mistress will soon come to her senses and dismiss her."

Jean—very properly, to my way of thinking—ignored this speech. Or perhaps he just didn't hear it, for by this time the stable-yard was alive with lackeys and servingmaids who swiftly stripped the berline of its baskets, boxes, trunks, and cases. As Jean uncoupled the first pair of horses and led them toward the stables, I looked around for Pompey, but he had disappeared as utterly as a shadow at noonday. So I alit, keeping a tight hold on Doucette, and stood in the dust, as uncertain as I've been in my life.

A young girl, sixteen or so, rosy and plump and fetchingly capped, touched my arm and smiled.

"Don't mind Dentelle, mam'selle. Not one of us can bear the sight of him. I'm Marie Vissot, and if it please you, mam'selle, I will be madame's personal laundress. What a pretty little dog! Ah, mignonne!"—this to Doucette, who goggled at her and growled— "Poor thing: she misses her mistress. Are these madame's trunks? Pierre! LeNain! Take madame's trunks to the China apartments. Does your mistress like porcelain? The hangings are silk damask, such a lovely shade of crimson, to set off the china, you know. They'll last another ten years, with care. Unless, perhaps, madame wishes to buy new?" She fixed me with a bright and questioning eye.

I thought her a cheeky, common girl, and answered her very high. "I am Mlle Berthe Duvet, and I'm sure the hangings will do very well until madame has had time to look about her. As for your being madame's laundress, you may wash her linen, but we'll have to see about the lace-work. We are very particular about madame's lace."

Solemnly Marie curtsied to me, all her merriness dampened. I suddenly remembered that I was not yet nineteen and far from my home and began to drizzle like a baby in leading-strings, upon which Marie embraced me, inspiring me to weep the harder. In a trice, she had me in the kitchen with a hot brick at my feet and a dish of tea in my hand. The chef gave Doucette a cutlet and the maître d'hôtel pinched my chin. And that was my introduction to Beauxprés: flattery and kindness and a flood of tears. Not a bad beginning, all in all.

Now that I am arrived at Beauxprés, I hardly know what to write. I found it very splendid, bien sûr; also draughty, vast, and labyrinthine beyond belief—a veritable puzzle-box of a house, with every chamber giving onto two or three others, and odd little stairs and corridors throughout. Why, it took me a week to find my way from the servants' wing to madame's apartment to the kitchen or the laundry without losing myself, and months before I could begin to number all its chambers, salons, galleries, cabinets, chambers, antechambers, pantries, and outbuildings.

A labyrinth, in short, and like all labyrinths, the abode of any number of fabulous monsters. No, not monsters precisely, except for M. le duc—comic types, rather, like the persons of a farce: finical valet, garrulous soubrette, amorous maître d'hôtel, temperamental chef de cuisine. And the lackeys, like all their liveried tribe, much given to lounging in antechambers and leering at the servingmaids. I could not think them real, the servants of Beauxprés, not as my friends Saint-Cloud and LeBeau and Olympe were real, at least not at first. And then one morning on my way to the laundry, I found myself in a long gallery hung with dark paintings, every one of which depicted the Deposition of Christ from the Cross. 'Twas a gloomy enough place to be, and I had no idea where it led or how I'd reached it.

"Merde!" I exclaimed. "Name of a name! Foutre ce dédale infernal!"

"That would be painful indeed, mam'selle," said a deep voice at my back. "And quite useless. Am I to understand that you have lost your way?"

Heart tripping and cheeks aflame, I turned, expecting a towering major domo ready to turn me off without a character for mocking the dignity of M. le duc's ancestral house. Instead, I faced a short, square man with a heavy, cow-nosed peasant's face and a great many crooked teeth. His wig perched high upon his shaven skull and his silver-gray livery strained across his bull's shoulders. A lackey, then, and a low-comic one at that.

"Devil take you, man," I said furiously. "You've frightened me quite out of my wits. Yes, I'm lost, as who'd not be, in such a rabbit's warren?"

The lackey twisted his dark brows into a knot that, however hideous, utterly failed to alarm me. I stamped my foot. "You've no call to glare at me like that. It *is* a warren, and most prodigiously full of steps and corridors. I've been searching for the laundry this hour and more, and I begin to fear I'll still be searching when these chemises have rotted with age, and me with them."

The lackey unknotted his brows and rubbed his nose. "When

Dentelle does that, servingmaids wither and lackeys quail," he said ruefully. "I suspect I haven't the face for it. Artide Desmoulins, mam'selle, at your service." He bowed with a flourish that, had he been thinner, might have been elegant. "You require the laundry, you say. 'Tis in the old donjon tower. To reach it, you must go back through this gallery, turn left through the Violin salon, descend into the cabinet des Fées, through the Snuffbox antechamber and the Fan room, turn right and down the stairs that open by the Triumph of Pompey, and then—" He broke off, halted by my blank incomprehension. " 'Twill be easier to show you." He snatched the dirty linen from my arms. "Come."

For one so heavy he walked very fast and kept up as we went a kind of running commentary upon the rooms we traversed. Trotting behind him, I wondered where he found the breath.

"The cabinet des Fées," he said, "contains memoria of those good fairies whose numerous exploits have been chronicled by Mme d'Aulnoy, M. Perrault, and Mlle de la Force. Observe, for example, this ermine slipper, by means of which the prince's envoy recognized Cendrillon. These are seven-league boots, and this"—pointing to a tiny, rainbow-furred dog curled in a walnut shell—"is the dog Toutou, given to the youngest prince by the White Cat in fulfillment of his father's quest. We also have the linen cloth that will pass six times through the eye of the smallest needle, but not, of course, the White Cat herself, who was transformed into a princesse when the prince cut off her head and tail."

I remember how I laughed, as if his exposition were an excellent jest. Seven-league boots! Magic dogs! What did he take me for? Surely he didn't believe in magic? Had the Age of Reason missed Beauxprés?

He'd already passed through the antechamber; I hurried to catch him in the room beyond. Here the walls were lined with glass cases filled with fans: fans feathered, painted, woven; stiff fans and folding fans; fans of wood and silk; ivory fans inlaid with jewels, shells, mother-of-pearl.

"These," Artide explained, "were gathered over the course of a long life by the present duc's grandsire. As you may have deduced, the rooms take their names from what is displayed there: the Tapestry hall—that's where the Triumph of Pompey hangs—the Box room, the Lace antechamber, the Miniature salon, the Meteorological closet, the Alchemical attic, and so on. I found you in the gallery of Depositions. Don't worry. You'll soon become familiar with them."

I was more interested in the cabinet des Fées. "All that about the White Cat and the ermine slipper, 'tis only a fairy tale. Surely you can't believe it true?"

Artide's ears turned a dark, painful red. "Bien sûr, 'tis true. I read it in a book," he said gravely, and, in a sudden burst of confidence: "I read a great deal, you see. I want to be a maître d'hôtel someday. In Paris."

Of course he believed in fairies and fairy spells. Only through a fairy spell would he achieve his ambition, for in Paris elegance in a manservant is as indispensable as beauty in a femme de chambre. A groom, perhaps, or a running footman, since he was strong and quick. But no man wants a running footman able to read the messages he carries. Only consider the opportunities for extortion!

Jean (whom Nôtre Seigneur designed for a groom; hands, teeth, and voice all complete) has never understood why I liked Artide, who hadn't the sense to be content with his lot in life. Look where Artide's ambition got him, he says, patting a demoness on her perfect funda-ment, and look where contentment got me. On the face of things, I admit that Jean is right. For as Artide lost his illusions over the years, he grew cynical, bitter, and prodigious foul-tempered. The last I heard of him, he had risen to be mayor of Beauxprés—which is to say that he was king of a midden. Yet in the years before the beggar came, Artide was the most interesting man I knew, with his peasant's face and his philosophe's mind that was equally hospitable to Magic and Science, Art and Nature. Ghosts were as real to him as electricity, witches as plausible as mathematicians. I'd never met anyone like him. And besides, he never flirted with me.

The weeks passed. I spent my days arranging madame's wardrobe and finding my place in Beauxprés, which was an altogether more complicated matter than it had been in the hôtel du Fourchet. In Paris, servants are servants, and where you are born is a matter of little interest except to yourself. Can you speak French like a gentleman? Bien! You are a Frenchman, and if you are a Savoyard too, well, only the meanest of souls will hold it against you.

But in a place like Beauxprés! Better than half of monsieur's servants had been born in the nearby village. I, along with M. Males-herbes the chef, Menée the maître d'hôtel, and Jacques Ministre the duc's steward, were foreigners, beneath notice as we were beneath reproach. Artide was friendly enough, and Marie; the rest of them, from Dentelle to the kitchen boys, hardly deigned to look at me. Indeed, when first I made confession to the parish priest, I was tempted to beg absolution for the sin of having been born in Paris.

In the end, 'twas Marie saved me. Dear Marie. So young she was, and so full of questions, all about being a femme de chambre, and Paris, and whether the streets were really paved with white marble and the beggar-women all wore silk, as she'd heard.

"No, they're not, to your first question. And, sometimes, if they're whores." She turned color at that. Perceiving I'd offended her, I gave her a gauze fichu, only a little soiled, and promised to teach her how to sponge brocade and starch thread-lace.

"Then you may go to Paris yourself, and set up as a blanchisseuse, and wear silk every Sunday if you've a mind. 'Tis not every laundress can make thread-lace look new again."

"I don't know about *that*," said Marie. "But I'd dearly like to visit Paris, and see Versailles and the Opéra and walk in the Palais-Royal."

Sudden tears pricked my eyes. "So would I."

"Why, Berthe, you look sad as an owl. Are you not happy here?" Embarrassed, I shrugged my shoulders. "My family is in Paris."

"And you miss them. And your old companions, too—I hadn't thought of that. Poor Berthe, so far from home! I shall have to make you known in Beauxprés."

Well, I'd thought I *was* known in Beauxprés, known and despised, but when I said as much, Marie assured me 'twas only that I'd not been introduced. Next market day, she promised, she'd take me down to the village and present me properly, and then I'd have as many friends in Beauxprés as I'd ever had in Paris.

Doubtfully, I agreed. I hadn't the heart not to.

Shelved into the northern side of the hill, the village of Beauxprés commanded a splendid prospect of the cornfields and fair meadows that gave the seigneury its name. The village itself was most amazingly poor and ill kept. The low houses shed stones and roof-tiles as dogs shed hair in summer, the paths were mud, and the gardens more full of tares than cabbages. Had monsieur kept a chaplain, I'd have had small occasion to set foot in the place. But he was an atheist, and those of his household who were not must needs descend to the village church to hear Mass. There was even a seigneurial pew to hear it in, though from the musty, mousy state of it, no seigneur had sat there for many a long year. Madame, who was most pious in company, went once and never again, vowing she could not pray when surrounded by glowerers and mutterers. I went, me, as I'd been taught, Sundays and saints' days to eat at Christ's table. But whether I stood or kneeled, sang or approached the altar, I could feel the eyes of the peasants of Beauxprés upon me, measuring, judging, condemning.

Be presented to the owners of those stern eyes and pursed-up mouths? Who greets an ass, I thought, is sure to be kicked. Still, I'd agreed. And so, come market day, I accompanied Marie down to the village well. Never let it be said that Berthe Duvet failed to keep her word.

In the year of Our Lord 1763, the shortest route from château to village was down a steep path behind the stable-yard. The village was not far—when the wind was right, we could hear the dogs barking—yet no part of it was visible from the château, save the brazen weathercock that crowned the church steeple.

Ah, the weathercock of Beauxprés! It saddens my heart to think its weathercock is all Colette can ever know of the village, just as bare chronicles and embroidered tales are all she can know of the wide world beyond. She herself feels no lack—the wide world is a cold place, she says, and she saw enough of its cruelties in her short life to haunt her through eternity. For her, the charm of Beauxprés is its impermeability. Thus, no doubt, her delight in the game we used to play with her, Adèle and I, when Colette was just a little thing, a hundred years ago and more.

Hand in hand in hand we'd take the village path, wind down through the blackberries and the bracken to a grandfather fir, and stop and look down the hill to the great fallen beech that marked the village end. The path leads on under the beech, clear as print. Yet when we pressed on, a mist would gather, hiding beech and path and all from our sight. Giggling, we'd twist and turn and double back on our steps, and at last we'd break free—always before the game palled—and find ourselves in the enchanted garden, with our servant hands waving and patting us in happy greeting. And when we looked beyond the walls again, the sun would be shining, and the mountains, meadows, and forest would stand clear and bright as a fresh-painted scene with the weathercock against it, eternally crowing north-north-west, towards Paris. I haven't thought of that game in years.

I was writing how Marie made me free of the village.

Down the village path we went, me in my thin town slippers sliding and tripping over roots and stones, down among the untidy scatter of stone houses where monsieur's peasants lived cheek-by-jowl with their cows.

A village like Beauxprés doesn't have streets or shops or squares like a real town; it has paths between gardens and an earthy clearing in front of the church for market days, with a well and a stone wash-house to one side and a bakery to the other. Here the women gather to draw water, to clean their linen, to bring their daily bread to be baked and, above all, to gossip. Which was what the crowd of women at the well were doing that day, jabbering in a villainous patois I couldn't make head or tail of. They looked alike as dolls to me—dark, solid women with hard, flat cheeks, red skirts, black shawls, wooden sabots, and round caps on their dark, undressed hair. They called incomprehensibly to Marie in their harsh voices, and Marie laughed and answered as she pushed in among them dragging me after. I vow I thought I'd perish on the spot.

"This is Mme Pyanet," Marie was saying. "Her husband is Estienne Pyanet the baker. M. Boudin is a good-for-naught, mère Vissot here is my aunt who raised me, and this is mère Desmoulins, who is Artide's mother."

I don't know why, I'm sure—perhaps 'twas just the weakness of my knees—but I dropped the beldam a curtsy. "I hope to make your better acquaintance, Mme Desmoulins. Your son has been most kind to me, and I am much obliged to him."

Had it been a pig that curtsied and addressed her, mère Desmoulins couldn't have looked more astonished. She dropped her bucket, *crack* upon the ground, and commenced gabbling and rolling her rheumy eyes.

When she'd done, Marie turned to me. "She asks if you want to marry Artide."

Well, I liked Artide well enough, but I'd as soon wed a toad, so, "No," I said, a little quicker than was polite. Mère Desmoulins looked offended, the other women muttered, and even Marie looked startled, so I added hastily, "He's a good man, Artide, sharp as a needle and ambitious. A poor friend I'd be, to marry him and ruin his prospects for advancement."

Marie translated my answer and the women pondered it for a

while. Then mère Desmoulins, grinning toothlessly, took me to her bosom like a daughter while all her gossips laughed and patted my arms with their rough hands.

After that I went often to the village, both with Marie and alone. I can't say I found much to say to Mme Boudin or mère Desmoulins, but Nicola Pyanet the baker's wife had a sister in service in Dijon and could speak good French if she'd a mind. So my life grew less narrow than it had been. Which is why I failed to take note when my mistress began to droop and fade like a rose left too long without water.

Bien sûr, such a failure would have been impossible before her marriage, had I many companions or had I none. At Port Royal, we lived so close and so lovingly that a half-stifled sigh was enough to bring me hurrying to her side. By necessity, her marriage had made me hard of hearing, for when I heard her cry out aloud in the night, I did not dare go to her. The sounds caused by pain and pleasure are, after all, very much alike.

So. One evening I heard a knock at the door of the cabinet where I sat mending a petticoat. Thinking it might be Marie, or even Artide come to read to me as I sewed, I gathered up the petticoat and opened the door to find my mistress, white as death, the rouge showing like wounds upon her cheeks.

"Oh, Berthe," she moaned, and cast herself upon my bosom.

Well, 'twas many months since we had been on such terms as those. I stood like a post in her embrace until she sank down at my feet, sobbing bitterly.

"Am I grown so hideous that you must hate me too?" she cried. "If my husband and my Berthe both spurn me, where then shall I turn for comfort? Death is my only refuge now."

Her words were only so much wind. Her tears, on the other hand, seemed real enough, and her lovely face so pale and woebegone that I quickly knelt down and put an arm around her heaving shoulders.

With a cry of, "No! No! You hate me!" she flung me away.

I sighed. "Indeed, madame, I do not. Come, sit before the fire and I will ring for a tisane—milk and chamomile and warm sweet wine, just as madame likes it. 'Tis the country makes madame so melancholy. I myself find so much peace and quiet trying to the nerves."

She laughed at that, a small, watery chuckle, and I coaxed her to a chair, where she sat holding tight to my hand like a child and confessed to me that monsieur had forsaken her bed.

"I have thought and thought, and can only conclude that Nathalie de Fleuru and Laure de Berline and even that odious abbé Pinchet were right, and my husband has wearied of my love."

This confidence loosed a thousand conflicting emotions in my breast. On the one hand, I wanted her to myself again, maid and mistress in our old loving world. On the other, I wanted her to be happy. Even if her happiness lay with the duc de Malvoeux? My silence lengthened and, "I'm right, then," she cried. "I'm dull and silly and hideous!"

To this, my answer came easily. "Madame is exquisite, as always," I said. "No sane man could weary of loving her!"

She cuddled her cheek into my bosom, and for a time I stood and stroked her until her sobbing dwindled into hiccups.

"I'll make thy tisane myself, madame, and then I'll brush thy hair just as I did when thou wert Mlle du Fourchet and Mme Ursule had birched thee for thy spelling. Here"—taking off her high-heeled shoes and tucking a stool under her feet—"sit and repose thyself."

Making tisanes clears the mind wonderfully. Bien sûr, I wanted my mistress to be happy, and where better for her to be happy than in Paris? Before long, her pride would surely carry her back to the Hôtel Malvoeux, to furnish it anew in gilt and rosewood and, like other women of her class, to settle down to a life of keeping abreast of the mode in dress, friends, and amusements. I need only have patience, I thought, and I'd soon have her to myself again.

Accordingly, over the next days all was fair weather with me. Until I'd some hope of leaving it, I didn't realize how Beauxprés, its many rooms, its many *things*, had weighed upon me. Each time I passed through the gallery of Depositions or the Hunt closet, I could hardly keep from singing aloud, knowing that soon I'd be far from those weeping Madonnas and moth-eaten rows of withered paws and tails.

Naturally, I scorned to betray my mistress' confidence, only hinting to a few intimates, to Marie and Artide, that madame and I might soon be returning to Paris.

I remember telling Artide about the house in the Marais. " 'Tis not like Beauxprés, Artide, but 'tis a very fine house all the same. All it needs to become the finest hôtel in Paris is some life in it and new furnishings. The season is beginning, and madame is anxious to get back and see her friends again. I must confess I'm puzzled at monsieur's continued residence here. What could possibly possess a duc, who is entitled to ride in the king's own carriage, to stay in the country while the court sits at Versailles?"

"Simple. The birds."

We were sitting in the drying-yard at the foot of the old donjon tower: a pleasant green protected by tall hedges which seemed to catch the sun and hold it longer than any other place in the grounds. I was mending a stocking; Artide was polishing a large silver salt cellar—a towering marvel of filigree and metal flourishes. He coated a blackened encrustation with an evil-smelling paste and began to rub at it vigorously.

"The birds," he repeated. I looked at him quizzically. "The birds, Berthe. You know: the present duc's answer to this monstrosity." He flicked his thumb against the salt cellar, which gave out a flat, metallic sound like a muffled bell.

"Ah," I said. "To be sure. The birds."

Artide sighed. "How blind a Paris-bred fille can be! Listen then, and I will tell you. 'Tis the curse of the ducs de Malvoeux that each is taken by some maggot of acquisitiveness that gnaws upon his mind all the days of his life. With monsieur's father, it was flowers, shrubs, and trees; with his grandsire, it was fans. With this duc, 'tis birds. His aviary is in Beauxprés, and so, therefore, is his heart." He hesitated. "I fear your mistress has no hope of attaching his interest for long unless she sprout feathers."

"Bon Dieu," I breathed—a prayer of enlightenment and horror both. "The man is mad!"

"Chut now, Berthe! You must not speak of monsieur so. He is a duc, the scion of an ancient house, and not like common folk. In you or me, such a quirk would indeed bespeak madness. In a duc, 'tis no more than a sign of nobility."

I glared at him. He winked broadly at me and we sat for a space in silence, he rubbing, I stitching. A curse! And here I'd thought monsieur's birds to be no more than the signature of idleness, like the gray Angora cats of Mme de Mirepoix that sat on her lotto table and pushed at the pawns with their paws. Why, every man of sufficient means had a craze. M. du Fourchet had money; M. Voltaire and Mme de Châtelet had experiments on the weight of fire; the marquis de Taillade-Espinasse had a vital ventilation machine; M. de Malvoeux had birds. As far as I was concerned, there was nothing to choose

among them. I wished with all my heart that M. de Malvoeux's craze
were one-half so harmless as that of M. Voltaire; so wishing, I shook
my head and sighed.

"It must be hard on the poor lady," said Artide kindly. "But
nobles are like that; 'tis in their blood. Take my advice, Berthe, and
encourage your mistress in a cheerful acceptance of M. le duc's little
ways."

"Ah, bah, Artide! You sound just like Dentelle. Why should any
wife cheerfully accept that her husband prefers the company of a flock
of witless birds to hers?"

Artide laughed. I'd never before that moment noticed that he
brayed when he laughed. "If she cannot accept it cheerfully, then she
must accept it miserably. Accept it she must; she cannot change it."

For a few days after this exchange I was in poor charity with
Artide, who'd presumed, I thought, far past the bounds of friendship
and decorum. What business had a mere lackey to talk about the
duchesse de Malvoeux as though he'd the right to pity her?

The question now was whether I should tell my mistress what all
the world, except us two, knew about her husband. Half a dozen times
I opened my mouth to speak. As many times I shut it again. My mistress
was, after all, no more than a child, and I an old toy she'd owned for
many years. The gloss had worn off me, as it were: I was no longer
new. Her husband, on the other hand, fairly glittered with novelty.
Furthermore, his aloofness made him hers but not hers: elusive, mysterious, desirable. In such a contest, I must always lose. I held my
peace.

In the event, it was as well that I did, for if madame had mastered
anything at Port Royal, she'd mastered the mirror's art of returning
to the gazer his own bright and pleasing image. The sudden change
of image—love-struck to bird-struck—had briefly clouded her surface,
that was all. Her husband loved birds to the point of madness. Bon.
So, then, did she. One morning she rang for me at cockcrow and bade
me dress her in a white gauze gown monsieur had once said gave her
the look of a white egret. Then she directed Pompey to supply himself
with a quantity of stale bread and await her in the vestibule. Dismissed,
I trailed her at a forlorn distance, reaching the great stair just as
monsieur emerged from his apartment, clattered down the steps, and
stalked purposefully towards the front door.

Madame stopped him upon the threshold with a hand upon his

wrist. "François, dear husband," she said. Monsieur gave no sign that he'd heard her. "François," my mistress repeated, shaking his arm. "Will you not take me to see your birds?"

Perhaps 'twas the shaking broke his trance; perhaps 'twas the mention of birds. In any case, I saw him blink, a slow hooding of his sharp black eyes, and then his other hand came up to grasp her fingers. "You are abroad monstrous early, chérie," he drawled. "My birds? They are nothing—a mere whim of mine: a few mangy specimens in a dirty glass house. You will spoil your pretty slippers for nothing."

"Not nothing, I am sure." Carefully, my mistress released him. "My cockatoo Bébé is a charming creature, as are the lovebirds you gave me on our betrothal. If your other birds are half so clever as Bébé or half so pretty as the lovebirds, then I will be well-rewarded."

Silence, and then, "Very well. You may come. But I will not have you fidgeting about. An aviary is no place for a chattering woman."

"Of course not, François," said madame indignantly. "Did I not sit quite still and quiet when you taught Bébé to take bread from my lips?"

"Hmph," said monsieur. "See that you remember." His tone was gruff, his words abrupt; but as they turned to the door, he took her hand and laid it within his arm.

Four hours later, my mistress returned. Her gauze overskirt was laddered by tiny, dirty claws and a malodorous white streak fouled her lace cap. Her forefinger had been pecked to the bone.

"Oh, Berthe, an emerald cuckoo took grain from my fingers, and I have learned to hold a bird's wings while monsieur my husband examines it, and he says that my hands are very delicate and that I may come with him every morning, and then he kissed me and said that I was a sensible little thing. The bird-handlers feed them, so I won't need the basket tomorrow. I do need an apron, and gloves, and a sunshade. I'm afraid that my pretty gown is all spoilt. Have I a plainer to wear tomorrow? Gray would do, like a wood-dove. Oh, Berthe, I am so happy!" And she embraced me.

Over her shoulder, I saw Pompey standing by the door with the covered basket still clutched in his small fist.

Now, the art of reading faces is early learned by servants, being as necessary to the proper execution of our duties as a discreet tongue and a pleasant expression. I've always prided myself upon my skill at the art, but Pompey baffled me. Because he was small and black and did not speak, madame treated him as she treated Doucette. I, too, assumed he understood madame only as Doucette understood her—from tone and gesture and animal sympathy. For the five months I'd known him, no reflection of emotion had troubled his small, round face; he might have been an automaton, cleverly crafted of ebony and ivory and dressed in rose satin for my mistress' pleasure.

Thus, I was astonished to see his placidity distort, as I thought, into a grimace of rage. The expression lasted only so long as he imagined himself unobserved. When he felt my eyes upon him, he composed himself immediately, so that almost I could think myself mistaken. Almost. It cost me a night's sleep, that almost, turned aside my thoughts that otherwise would have plodded their well-worn track between Paris and my mistress. The shock was so great, you see, like a lady removing her domino at a masked ball to reveal a beak or a muzzle underneath. It ran through and through my head that the most docile dog may run mad. Who can say that the most docile savage might not do the same?

It was with heavy eyes that I woke my mistress at lark-song next morning. Nor was I cheered by her insistence upon being dressed in a stuff gown that madame her mother would have disdained to wear to count the sheets, with one of my own plain linen caps to cover her hair. She looked in the pier glass and made a moue. "A wood-dove indeed," she said. "I look more like a penitent Magdalene. But monsieur my husband will be pleased. Now, Pompey, my gloves and the sunshade, and then I am ready."

A low murmur from the dressing-room, then Pompey appeared, sunshade in hand and a wild look in his dark eyes.

"Come, Pompey," called my mistress. "What a dull creature thou art, to be sure! Come here, I say!"

"Oh, mistress." At the sound of the soft, hoarse voice, I started and madame stared, first at the cockatoo Bébé, and then at Pompey. "Oh, mistress. I cannot."

Madame wavered for a moment between anger at being thwarted and surprise that Pompey had spoken. Anger won. "Cannot? Pray tell me, monkey, why not?"

"Oh, please, mistress." He dropped the sunshade and, running to kneel at her feet, plucked piteously at her apron. "Pompey does not want to go to the glass house again."

If his face had been silent before, it was eloquent now. Well I knew the language of quivering lips and wrinkled brow, shaking hands and welling eyes, for I'd seen them often enough in my mistress. The child was clearly terrified.

Madame, one eye upon the ormolu clock, snapped, "Silly baboon. 'Tis thy place to go wherever I go and obey my commands. Otherwise I'll send thee away, and although I do not know where disobedient black pages are sent, I fancy 'tis a more unpleasant place than monsieur le duc's aviary."

"Please, madame," I said. "The child is not disobedient but terrified. See how ashen his cheeks have grown."

"Don't be impertinent, Berthe. There is nothing for him to fear."

"No, madame. But I am reminded of how Doucette trembles and whines when she sees a broom, and how madame sends Pompey to check whether some maidservant may be sweeping the hall before he takes her outside."

My mistress pouted a moment, then shrugged. "Oh, very well, Berthe. If you think Pompey is afraid, then I won't insist he accompany me. I'm not a monster, after all."

"Mistress is an angel," said Pompey gravely.

"No doubt," said my mistress. "Berthe?"

I smiled at the boy, who smiled shyly in return and ran to retrieve the sunshade from the dressing-room and to snatch up a pair of gloves and a light shawl, which he presented to me with a little solemn bow.

Madame stamped her foot in an agony of impatience. "*Quickly*, Berthe, or 'twill all be for nothing."

I rolled my eyes at Pompey and was rewarded, as I hurried after madame, with the sound of a child's delighted giggling.

Because of the ducks, the aviary of Beauxprés had been built at the edge of a large ornamental water some little way from the château. Led by my master, we crossed the formal gardens, passed under a pergola, and followed a graveled path through a copse to a meadow in the center of which was set a lofty, sunny structure built of wood and glass. As we neared, I saw orange trees through the glass and bright forms darting through its upper reaches like colored lightning. Monsieur bent his head reverently to the lock and let us into an antechamber like a small cage with doors at either end, one to the outside, the other to the building itself. The outer door tightly closed, monsieur opened the inner upon Paradise.

Now, recall to yourself that I was a child of cobbles and tall houses and parks in which not a flower dares bloom without a gardener's permission. The only birds I knew were sparrows, pigeons, crows, and chickens. Bien sûr, I'd seen peacocks at Versailles, larks in pies, and pheasants roasted whole in their feathers. But the birds of M. le duc de Malvoeux were a higher order of being, the angels and fairies of bird-kind. Fire-breasted widow birds, all jet and flame, bright taffeta honey-birds, toucans with painted beaks, cranes and herons and storks. Parrots—hundreds of them, gaudy as whores and contentious as fishwives. Indigo buntings from the New World. Golden pheasants from Cathay. Black swans from the Antipodes. Their movement and color surpassed the most brilliant ball imaginable, and their calls made a music at once harsh and melodious that I found altogether enchanting.

A low chuckle at my ear brought me to myself. "Your Berthe is bouleversée, my love. I am glad she attends you and not that blackamoor page, whom I half-repent of buying. Ah, chérie"—to a small cockatoo with a top-knot like a coiffure poudrée that had alighted on his shoulder and was nibbling his ear—"Have patience, little one. Thy master has brought thee grapes."

Thus a ritual was established. Each morning at seven, I scratched at madame's chamber door and brought in her chocolate. Then I pulled back the crimson curtains to waken her and her husband, who slept beside her with his nightcap rucked over his ear and his arm thrown across her breast.

The first time I discovered my master in my mistress' bed, I thought I must die of chagrin. Before I could drop the curtain and back out of the room, however, madame yawned a tongue-curling yawn and opened her eyes. Seeing me, she blushed and smiled.

"Is there enough in the pot for two?" she asked. Speechless, I nodded. "Then take one of those little blue cups from the étagère, yes, the handleless ones, and set it on the tray. If monsieur my husband wishes for chocolate, he may just as well drink it from his great-grandsire's Chinese cup as from a French one."

Never let it be said that Berthe Duvet cannot acknowledge defeat. Monsieur had won my mistress, body and soul, and if I wished to retain her heart, I must needs take her master for my own. He was, after all, her husband. A necessary evil, like rain and doing penance.

So. Every morning I set down my tray, opened the curtains and made up the fire. At the rattle of the poker, monsieur would rise, shake himself like a bating hawk, and take himself off to Dentelle to be shaved and dressed. We were in the aviary by nine, and usually remained there until dinner at two.

In those hours madame busied herself giving the birds treats and whistling to them while monsieur went over the breeding records and checked the progress of any wounded or ailing specimens. They did no real tending of course, no cleaning, feeding, or physicking—that was all done after they were out of the way. Monsieur paid his bird-handlers handsomely and treated them almost as equals, in consequence of which they were all as proud as peacocks, if a measure less colorful. Even the seed-boy and the man who scraped the perches disdained to drink at the inn on market days, but kept their revels— if indeed they reveled at all—strictly among themselves. They were a dour lot, and I remember wondering whether their feathered charges had drained all color and animation from them.

So monsieur whistled and madame petted, and Noël Songis—the chief of the bird-handlers—lurked among the potted orange trees, making it clear he could do no real work while his master was present. My only duty was to sit quietly out of the way, holding madame's sunshade and a kerchief until she called for them. Often, watching the Second Estate work as the Third Estate idled, I fancied myself the great lady for whose sole pleasure the ruby hummingbirds flashed from branch to branch and the emerald cuckoos perched like enamelled bibelots among the polished leaves.

In Which the Future of the House of Malvoeux Is Secured

Home to Paris! I was transported by joy. Monsieur had business, madame stood in need of a new corset, and the long and the short of it was that we were to spend the winter in the rue des Lions.

"I shall be so happy to see Mme la baronne, and Stéphanie-Germaine, and Mme de Fleuru, and the marquise de Berline. The court is quite gay now that Mme du Barry has become maîtresse en titre to the king. She's nothing more than an adventuress, of course, but Stéphanie-Germaine writes that she is the most amiable of women and so beautiful that 'tis no wonder the king forgets his advanced age." My mistress sighed. "How I should like to see her! I love Beauxprés passionately, of course, but I must confess I have missed going out into society."

My "Yes, madame," was heartfelt. Our only company that autumn having been an aged naturalist and his no less aged wife, madame was feeling rather ennuyée, and I as restless as a caged lark. So high in the mountains, the first snow had fallen in October, curtailing my visits to Mme Pyanet and renewing my longing for the Comédie Française, for the back kitchens, the peopled streets, the whirligig modes and gossip of Paris. Even the prospect of monsieur's graceless town lackeys could not daunt me; now that he'd found his tongue, Pompey was a charming companion and Marie was to accompany us as laundress-cum-sewing maid.

Even in the midst of our planning and packing, we contrived to spend the greater part of each forenoon at the aviary. Monsieur had more to do there than ever, with a thousand details to attend to of fuel and furnaces, of grain and fruit and maggots and beetles. He was constantly with Noël Songis in anxious consultation over this or that, and madame obediently accompanied him although she must leave her jewels unsorted to do so.

One hard, crisp morning not long before we were to leave, we set off across the garden as usual. With the white of the snow, the black-green of the firs, and the hard, bright blue of the heavens, it was like walking through a Sèvres bowl, though amazingly cold; by the time we reached the aviary, madame was pinch-mouthed and shivering. Monsieur opened the outer door and glared back at us lagging behind. "Hurry yourself, Adèle," he said. "The air chills."

Madame stumbled over the threshold. I took her arm; unsteadily she smiled at me and I saw the sweat standing in drops on her brow. Just then, monsieur opened the inner door and the aviary exhaled a warm breath laden with the concentrated stench of charcoal braziers, potted trees, and the droppings of a thousand birds.

"Oh," said madame faintly, and brought up her morning chocolate and biscuits.

Monsieur held his lace kerchief to his nose and made a moue of disgust. "Why did you not say you were ill, Adèle? There is no need for you to accompany me if you are ill. What if the complaint be contagious? You know yourself how parrots are prone to fevers, particularly in winter."

Tears rose to my mistress' eyes. "Indeed, François, I'd not considered it. I'm very sorry. I was well enough when I rose this morning; I don't know what has come over me."

I bethought me of cholera, of typhus, of quartan fever. Did not the plague sometimes commence in cold sweats and vomiting? "M. le duc," I ventured, "these sudden purgings are not common with madame. Is there an apothecary in the village who might prescribe for her?"

Monsieur, who had already stepped through the inner door, lingered there looking over his shoulder like a blessed soul held back from Paradise. "Yes, yes, Duvet, I suppose so," he said impatiently. "Ask Menée or Jacques Ministre—one of them will know."

Well. In the past weeks, I'd managed to put myself in a fair way of liking the man, or at least of tolerating him. Now my most charitable thought would have earned me a beating. Even as I supported my mistress' weak steps homeward, even as I murmured soothing nothings in her ear, I raged inwardly. Madman (thought I). Feather-wit. Parrots can catch human fevers, can they? Then maybe she'd caught her death from one of them. Did you think of *that*, M. Bird-brain?

As we entered madame's bedchamber, I heard Pompey singing to Doucette, a strange, sad little chant like nothing I'd ever heard before.

Furious as I was, 'tis astonishing that I noticed it and more astonishing that I should recall it now, so many years removed. Truth to say, I hadn't recalled it until the words appeared on the paper in the wake of my pen. Magic calling to magic, perhaps? The garden, the paper, this inkpot that never runs dry, Colette herself—ghost and sorceress, magic to her marrow—all conjuring up memories of Pompey's childish chants and spells that I could not see or hear at the time, blinded and deafened as I was by Reason.

In any case, I remember clearly that Pompey chanted, and that he broke off with a start when we entered, took one look at madame's white face, and bundled Doucette off into the dressing-room, where we heard him murmuring to her.

"I'd swear Doucette understands him," said madame, sinking down into an armchair to let me remove her shoes. "When he speaks to her, she looks almost clever. Do stop fussing, Berthe. I feel quite well now, and will by no means go to bed."

Well, I need hardly say I'd not hear of *that*, and before long, I had her stripped and tucked up snugly and was off to Menée to inquire after a medical man.

Monsieur's maître d'hôtel was in the Armament room as always, deep in research into a bottle of monsieur's best vintage oporto.

In his person, Menée was florid, bigger of belly than of brain, with a drooping eye and a drooping lip and a nose like a blood-pudding. In his nature, he was lustful, suspicious, and bibulous, and ruled the household with a hand of iron. From his likeness to our Most Serene and Puissant Majesty King Louis XV of France, he was known among the household as LeRoi.

So there sat LeRoi Menée, red-nosed and smug, and there I stood before him, wringing my hands in my apron. Madame was unwell, I said, and monsieur would like to have a doctor to her. It was nothing, just a little chill on the stomach, but at this time of year, it always paid to be careful.

Menée leered. "Unwell, ye say. Ah, yes. Unwell. A chill on her stomach, ye say?" He winked broadly and rubbed his own fat paunch. "Then ye'll be wanting mère Malateste."

I was far from wanting any such person. "I'm sure monsieur will not want some country herb-wife dosing Mme la duchesse with le bon Dieu alone knows what potions and poisons, Menée."

"Now, Duvet, don't turn up that sweet pretty nose at mère Malateste. She knows a carbuncle from a fever-blister as well as any Paris quack, and can tell a tertian from a quartan fever merely by smelling the patient's bed-linen. Monsieur never lets another near him. She was his wet-nurse, y'know. Breasts to feed a village! Glorious they were, like a cow's dugs. One of them'd make two of yours, but ye needn't pout: I like small breasts, too, if they're white and unspotted. Are thy breasts white, eh, Duvet?" Unsteadily, Menée began to rise from his chair. "I'm sure they are, such a dainty Paris piece as thou art, but I wouldn't mind seeing for m'self."

I murmured, "Thank you kindly, I'm sure," and fled.

As it happened, I knew mère Malateste by sight. In those days, I didn't believe in witches, and even if I had, mère Malateste would not have suited my idea of one. She was a handsome, prosperous-looking woman: tall and big-boned, with the Roman nose, the proud, hurrying gait, and the cold, haughty eye of a well-fed goose. Her hair was astonishingly black and her teeth sound for a woman of an age to have given my master suck. The breasts Menée remembered so fondly still dangled full as a cow's udder when she bent to fill her buckets at the village well. She spoke to no one on these occasions, and the younger women always spat and crossed themselves as soon as she turned her back. Witch, they called her, making the old women laugh.

"She knows more than thee, that's why tha fears her," I remember one granny saying. "Witch or no, she brought thee into this world, and'll bring thy brats likewise, so tha's best be civil."

Inquiry among the other servants yielded the information that mère Malateste lived some little way off the village path, in a stone cottage tucked under a stony outcrop surrounded by fir and brambles. By the time I'd slogged and slithered there through the heavy snow, I was quite breathless and my skirts soaked through to the knee.

For Beauxprés 'twas a neat cottage as, for a Beauxprés peasant, mère Malateste was a neat woman. Yet I vow upon my mother's head that when she opened the door to my knocking, my hand twitched with the impulse to sign myself against evil. I thrust it firmly into my shawl, greeted her politely, and stated my business.

"Hmph," she said when I was finished, and closed the door in my face.

"Wait," I cried, and "Oh, *please*," and also, "the Devil damn you black," whereupon mère Malateste emerged again with a red shawl over her head and a small basket on her arm.

She eyed me down her nose, then set off at an astonishing pace up the path I'd made with me stumbling behind. In at the kitchen door she swept without a by-your-leave, and up the backstairs to the China apartment.

Upon reaching madame's door, mère Malateste didn't scratch or knock—no, not she. Mère Malateste simply walked into the bedchamber, stripped back the coverlet without a word, poked madame here and there on her belly, lifted her eyelids one by one and peered under them, smelled her breath, untied her chemise to look at her breasts, and asked her abruptly when she'd last had her woman's courses.

Madame blushed uncomfortably. "I . . . I'm not sure." And, bridling, "What need have you to know such a thing as *that*?"

"Hmph," said mère Malateste, and looked at me.

"Six weeks, perhaps seven," I said slowly. "Of course! How I am stupid!"

"What *is* it, Berthe? Mère Malateste? Why do you look at me so? Am I very ill? Will I die?"

Mère Malateste honked with amusement. "Bien sûr ye'll die, madame: ain't we all dust at the end? And ain't ye a daughter of Eve, doomed to birth your children in blood and pain?" She turned to me. "Tonnerre! Does the girl know naught?"

I shrugged. How very like Mme du Fourchet, I thought, to instruct her daughter on the sowing of the seed without mentioning the possibility of harvest. Gently, I took my mistress' hands and patted them. "You are to become a mother, madame. Your firstborn grows in your belly, and you will bear it forth in nine months' time or a little less."

"If all goes well," said mère Malateste darkly. "Narrow-hipped as a sparrow she is. Like as not it'll be born untimely. Tha, city girl. Thy name's Duvet?"

I nodded. "Berthe Duvet. I've served madame from a child."

"Well, Duvet, see that she keeps warm and has plenty of meat to her diet. And oporto before she sleeps."

"I don't like oporto," said madame.

Mère Malateste huffed out her bosom and stared down her nose at madame, whose lips began to tremble. " 'Tis to strengthen your blood, madame," I said hastily. "You must allow mère Malateste to know best what you are to eat and drink, for she has brought a goodly number of infants into the world, and you not a single one."

"Can I still go to Paris?"

"Go to America if ye wish, madame—'tis your baby, after all. I've known a woman rode a-horseback ten days before her time and her babe was born alive. Bien sûr," she went on thoughtfully, "it never thrived, and died of a convulsion ere ever 'twas weaned."

"Oh." Madame turned quite white.

I clasped my hands together under my apron to keep them from mère Malateste's cheeks. "We will consult monsieur," I said.

Mère Malateste snorted in answer, then picked up basket and shawl and marched off to the front hall to await her nursling. Feeling that madame would surely need an advocate, I accompanied her, and we stood louring at one another until our master came in, when she called out that monsieur would be the father of a son in eight months' time, providing he didn't do anything foolish. This trip to Paris, for example. Nothing could be more foolish than that.

I'd begun to object when monsieur himself forestalled me. "Nonsense," he said. "Of a surety we go to Paris. I will not have my son born a weakling from over-much coddling of his mother. Ah, Nounou, thou art as great a tyrant as monsieur our king," he added, smiling at her. "I know thee of old, but my duchesse does not, and I'll not have thee worrying her into an untimely birth."

Mère Malateste smiled slyly. "Not of your firstborn, M. François, that goes without the saying. But your duchesse is such a tiny thing —more bird than woman, with bones I might crack with a flick of my littlest finger. Monsieur knows what pains monsieur's mother suffered in his bearing, and how I brought the infant that would've been monsieur's younger brother out of her belly piecemeal, with my little hook."

"Yes. To be sure." Monsieur's look was bleak. "You have told me often enough."

"However, if only she keep warm and drink her oporto like I've told her, I think madame'll carry your get as long as she need. This body-woman of hers is a silly, townish slut. . . ." She glared at me with a challenging air; I shut my teeth and curtsied. "But I'll learn her. Ye'll see, monsieur, what tender care I'll have of your duchesse."

Mère Malateste shouted this last to monsieur's retreating back, for he was flying up the steps two at a time, shedding his cloak as he ran. Dentelle appeared as if by magic to gather it up off the stairs.

"What a brouhaha is this?" he exclaimed. "Mère Malateste! Is the mistress dead? Or"—a sly smile spread his fish's pout—"an heir! An heir to the House of Malvoeux!"

The happy news spread through the household like a blaze in a high wind. Marie was rapturous. "Heir to Beauxprés! Just think of it, Berthe. Who'll have the nursing of it, I wonder?" I made a scornful noise, and she looked at me curiously. "Why, what ails you, Berthe?"

I shrugged. "My mistress is hardly quickened; 'tis early days yet to speak of a wet nurse. Time enough for that when the brat is screaming for the teat."

Marie embraced me. "Dear Berthe. You mustn't worry about your mistress. For all that mère Malateste's the Devil's own dam, she's the best midwife in the district. Providing the child's baptized at once, there's nothing to fear."

"To be sure," I said, not at all comforted.

For, reasonable woman though I was, mère Malateste made my teeth ache, and not only with grinding them. The woman terrified me beyond all reason. In her face I saw bloody sheets; in her voice I heard the moans of dying women. For me, there was no comfort in her having been monsieur's wet nurse, and nursemaid too, judging from the intimacy between them. Duc and peasant-woman spoke together as equals—as confederates, I almost wrote, although I'd be hard put to say what cause their confederacy might further. Perhaps I caught in their attitudes some distant reflection of the first duc de Malvoeux and his evil nurse. Perhaps I now only believe I should have.

If there's one thing Beauxprés has taught me, 'tis that omens can be more real and true than death. Equally, they can be simple hindsight. The trick is in telling the one from the other. Hindsight is as good as a telescope for swelling small events into great prophecies. *How could I have been so blind!* we cry. *'Twas plain all along to those with eyes to see! The grange burned on the very day I turned the beggar from my door; my sister's daughter had a convulsive fit not an hour after I saw the screech owl in broad daylight.* And ever after, when we see a screech owl in daylight, we look about us for a child in convulsions, which is not so rare a sight that one cannot be found if needed. Thus I look back on monsieur and mère Malateste knowing the history of Jorre

Maindur and his nurse Barbe Grosos, and I find in that knowledge, which I did not then have, the cause of my dismay.

Even Jean, who is as superstitious a man as ever hid a Host in the stable against goblins, even Jean says that I was merely jealous.

Merely jealous! Well, perhaps, though jealousy seems too simple a word for my turmoil. I remember watching my mistress as she dreamed pink-cheeked by the fire, her hair about her shoulders and one hand upon her belly, and thinking that M. le duc de Malvoeux had not so much devoured the girl who had been Adèle du Fourchet as he had invaded her, set his stamp upon her within and without, filled her so full of himself that no corner of her was left either for me or for her to dwell in. My heart would draw tight as a stay-lace, and then I'd feel a touch on my hand and look down to see Pompey, all satin turban and jet eyes, nodding at me with a grave little air of sympathy.

Because of madame's queasiness, monsieur and Dentelle went ahead of us to Paris. We followed them three days later—madame, Pompey, Marie, Doucette, and myself, all packed together into a traveling sleigh. We were an interminable eight days upon the road, with madame and Doucette moaning and spewing, and Pompey as close to sullen as I'd ever seen him. Marie wept for Beauxprés before it was well out of sight, and if all that weren't enough, snow in the mountains kept the skies leaden and our pace to a weary crawl. In Châtillon, where the snow thinned, we changed to a berline, and after that made better time. Yet 'twas an age of the world before we reached the outskirts of Paris on the afternoon of December the tenth.

There needed no wall to divide Paris from its surrounds. One moment we were driving past leafless copses and gray fields stuck with windmills, their vanes sailless to the winter wind. The next, we were surrounded by black and ugly tenements that towered above the berline four stories or more. The horses' hooves clattered and slithered on mucky cobbles. A chilly reek trickled up the drains and gusted from the tanneries across the Bièvre. Madame, well-dosed with laudanum, slept in the corner.

Marie buried her nose in her muff. "Does all Paris smell of stale piss?" she asked plaintively.

I shrugged. "Give thanks to heaven 'tis winter, Marie, or it would smell of worse things than that. The reek is no more than the village on a hot day—you'll soon grow used to it."

Marie made a rude noise, but removed the muff so that she could see more freely out the window.

I've promised Colette to be as honest as possible in this account. Dearly as I'd love to paint a portrait of Paris as Heaven upon earth, honesty compels me to confess that a large part of it more closely resembled Hell. The outmost faubourgs were a maze of narrow streets clogged with dung, porters, beggars, ragged street-urchins, and crones of all ages hawking tisanes and old hats at each corner. Every face we passed was gray and peaked with cold, and the eyes within were hollow. Some cursed us as the berline crept through the crowd; some held up a bunch of withered herbs to sell, or filthy hands for alms. A tall man in a leather apron and a patched coat spat at the carriage, earning a curse and a flick of the whip from Carmontelle. And when the street began to widen and we could make greater speed, the berline rattled and lurched over cobbles heaved up by the frost and never reset.

Madame, thankfully, did not wake. Who knows what prodigy of nature might have resulted from her seeing, thus early in her pregnancy, the beggar-children with their misshapen limbs and weeping wounds and the cheap street girls with their faces painted red and white like barber poles and their noses gnawed by pox?

"I don't think I like Paris," said Marie.

At that moment, fresh from two months in the country, I was nearly as shocked as she was. But I'd rather have died than said so, and therefore: "This is not Paris," I declared. "This is only Saint-Marceau. Wait until we come to the better districts—to the Marais and the faubourg Saint-Honoré. There you will see such boulevards and gardens and houses as you've never seen before and lackeys dressed in silk and velvet like lords." And, when she still looked doubtful, "Come now, Marie. The folk in Beauxprés are nearly as poor as these."

"Yes," she said. "But that's different."

Pompey scratched Doucette between her ears. "How?"

"What knowest thou of poverty, baboon? It is—that's all."

Like most of the Beauxprés servants, Marie regarded Pompey as little more than an expensive and over-sized pet. I'd hoped that in traveling with him, she would come to know him better. And she might have, had he not taken it into his woolly head to cling to madame, who lapped him in a corner of her fur robe and made a great fuss over him. No doubt Marie would pinch at him the whole time we were in Paris. To the Devil with them all, I thought; and as we drove north-east through the slums of the Île, almost I wished us back at Beauxprés.

I began to feel better when we reached the wide boulevards of the faubourg Saint-Honoré, better yet when we entered the Marais, and by the time we turned into the courtyard of the hôtel Malvoeux, I once again knew that Paris was Heaven.

"Perhaps I'll like Paris after all," murmured Marie as we entered the foyer. "How this is elegant!"

Astonishingly, it was elegant. Fresh blue paint on the front door, rocaille cabinets displaying a collection of inkstands in the grand salon, woven carpets in the antechambers, gilded chairs in the halls—even in the first flush of impending fatherhood, monsieur would never of himself have spent so freely and to such good purpose. He must have enlisted help: Mme du Fourchet, I suspected. Mme la baronne's taste for opulence and à la modality was apparent throughout, especially in madame's bedchamber, where the long-case clock had been replaced by a small gilt écritoire that transformed into a reading-stand at the turn of a crank. The stark crimson bed-curtains had given way to billowing draperies of white satin, and a gilt pier-glass, fitted out with no fewer than four candles, reflected a rocaille dressing-table and an overstuffed chaise longue.

All in all, I calculated the transformation of the hôtel Malvoeux must have cost monsieur as much as a year's expedition to Cathay or Africa, without even a rare bird to show for the expense. Yet he seemed to think the gold well-spent in feathering a nest for his promised son. Nor did he forget to extend his joyful generosity to his son's mother. When madame entered her chamber, reposing upon her new lace pillows was a small casket that revealed, when she opened it, a splendid pair of pearl ear-drops.

"Oh, Berthe, I *am* so glad we have come to Paris," madame said rapturously. "Stéphanie-Germaine will be quite beside herself with envy."

Mère Malateste would certainly not have approved the life madame led in Paris: driving in an open carriage in the Bois, walking in the Orangerie, eating dinner with Mme de Mirepoix, playing at proverbs in the salon of the marquise de Livry. I dressed madame for the theater, the opéra, lectures at the Académie, balls, and masquerades. I accompanied her to Versailles, where I stood for hours in a draughty antechamber while madame curtsied to the dauphin and admired the du Barry's brilliant complexion. My mistress was as happy as a puppy with a slipper to chew, and monsieur also. In Paris, my master became a sensible man, interested in natural history and philosophy, apt to discourse fluently on the nature of Reality, the scientific method, the practical uses of electricity and the like. He was welcome at the salon of Mme du Deffand, conversed with Lavoisier and d'Alembert, and called frequently upon the duc de Luynes and the financier Boudin, whose collections of natural history rivaled those of Buffon himself. As for his habit of keeping canaries in his dressing-room, his bitterest enemy could not have called it worse than eccentric. Oh, they were the talk of Paris, the canaries of the duc de Malvoeux, and much imitated. Before evening parties, the lackeys would arrange their cages in the vestibule and cover them with heavy embroidered cloths that they pulled off when the guests arrived. The canaries greeted the candlelight with delighted rolls and trills, much to the enchantment of the guests, who imagined themselves the cause of the song.

Snug in a world where each magic had its reasonable explanation, I began to think of Beauxprés—its birds, its cabinet des Fées, and its mère Malateste—as a kind of living bibliothèque bleu of incredible tales and legends with which to regale my fellow servants. I was a child of the Enlightenment, me, educated and well-read. Witches were for ignorant peasants to believe in.

Being a devout atheist, M. le duc de Malvoeux did not himself observe the feast of Christ's Nativity. Neither would he accompany my mistress to Mass on Christmas morning, although he graciously consented to take dinner at the hôtel Fourchet, and even to refrain from arguing politics or economy with his father-in-law.

All the while I was dressing her, madame fretted and fidgeted. "I do not know what will be worse," she complained. "If madame my mother has told them I am increasing or if she has not. If she has not, I will be spared Pauline's jealousy. If she has, I will be spared Hortense's teasing about how stout I've grown. I protest I'm tempted to plead a migraine and keep my bed."

"If madame is absent, her sisters will while away the afternoon speculating on her health, and decide at last either that madame has miscarried or that the child is none of her husband's getting. And consider—if madame doesn't go to the rue Quincampoix, Pompey and I will be condemned to eating cold mutton in an empty house."

"Oh, Lud, so you must. Well, that won't do, I suppose," said my mistress playfully. "I indulge you, and you tyrannize over me. I should beat you, I vow, or stop your wages, or even dismiss you." She caught my hand, hovering with a comb by her ear, and held it briefly to her lips. "Instead, I'll brave Pauline and Hortense and their tiresome husbands, my father's gout, my mother's sharp tongue, and M. de Malvoeux's inevitable ill-humor, not to mention indigestion and headache, all that you may dance with my father's handsome valet de chambre. Just see you don't lose your heart to him."

"If madame permits, I shall take Marie as a chaperone."

"Poor Marie. Naturally, she must not be left to dine alone. She may ride on the box with you and Carmontelle."

This arrangement found more favor with Marie than with Carmontelle, who grumbled prodigiously at the crowding, vowed he could not drive so impeded by women and skirts, and cursed my panniers to hell and back every time we took a corner. But as the postilions had as much to do with guiding the horses as he, we arrived at the rue Quincampoix without mishap.

While the greater part of the household was occupied in serving up the Christmas feast, Dentelle, Marie and I retired to the back kitchen with the other femmes and valets de chambre: Saint-Cloud and Olympe for the du Fourchets, Louison and LeBeau for the de Bonsecours, and two I hadn't met before who belonged to the comte and comtesse de Poix.

Saint-Cloud greeted us warmly. "Joyeux Noël, Dentelle. Berthe, I'd swear you grow prettier by the day! Pray present me to your charming friend." He studied Marie until she turned scarlet. "I adore girls who carry the smell of the country upon their skin. It quite adds a year to my life to be around them."

"Ah, bah, Saint-Cloud," I said, kissing his cheek. "This is Marie Vissot, personal laundress to madame. There is not a blanchisseuse in all of Paris to touch her way with thread-lace, so pray you be civil to her. Marie, this out-sized piece of nature is Gilles Lasnier, called Saint-Cloud, who is valet de chambre to M. le baron and the most shameless gallant this side of Montmartre."

As Saint-Cloud kissed Marie's fingers, Olympe approached in a rustle of taffeta to embrace me. Saint-Cloud then opened a bottle or two of M. le baron's bettermost champagne, and before long, M. de Poix's valet, who was called LeFranc, was regaling us with the story of how his master had threatened to beat him for overheating the tongs and scorching his best peruke into a frazzle.

" 'Lud, monsieur,' says I to he. 'Indeed, you must thank me

instead.' And, 'Why, capon?' says he, though he's a fine one to be calling me a capon, he who is no earthly use to his wife or any other woman."

"Mon Dieu! Has he been gelded, then?" inquired Marie anxiously.

LeFranc spluttered into his champagne and began to cough. Amid great peals of general laughter, Dentelle reached over and thumped him smartly upon the back.

"Sacré Mère de Dieu!" Olympe managed at last. "I'll burst my stays! No, Marie, M. de Poix hasn't been gelded."

"No need," said LeFranc unsteadily. "His name alone tells all." And then we were all off again, Marie as well this time, until our sides ached and we could laugh no more.

"Aye me," said Saint-Cloud at length. "So, let us hear the rest, LeFranc. Why should your master have thanked you for ruining his peruke?"

LeFranc wiped his eyes and ventured another sip of champagne. "The story is not near so amusing as the prologue, I fear, but here 'tis, as perfect an instance of a fool setting the mode as you'd ever wish to see. 'Why, monsieur,' I says. ' 'Tis a full two weeks since monsieur set Paris buzzing with the scarlet hose he wore with the suit of purple velvet. All the world waits for monsieur's next daring fashion. Add but a dusting of blue powder to the frizz, parade it along the boulevards, and in two days, Paris will stink of scorching hair.' He thinks for a little with his eyes squinched up, so. Then, ' 'Pon my soul,' says he, 'thou art a Jacquard among valets, LeFranc.' And he bestows upon me the sapphire from his cravat, flings a pound of blue powder upon his head, and goes whistling off to the promenade, looking like nothing I have ever seen."

"He sounds like a heron," I said judiciously. "Especially when one considers his spindly legs."

"Ah," said Louison. "I've heard about your master and his birds. My mistress, she finds him peu sympathique, and declares 'tis a marvel to see him dine upon bread and flesh and not upon raw grain or beetles."

Dentelle, who'd been sitting a little apart from us, sneering to himself as he drank, set down his glass with a snap. "Thy mistress is a great cow," he said. "Does it therefore follow that she dines upon hay?"

Louison gaped at him, whereupon Dentelle descanted upon his

master's impeccable lineage until Saint-Cloud wearily bade him shut his jaw. There was an uncomfortable silence into which I said peaceably, "My master's no worse than many another, Louison. My mistress is mad with love for him, and he seems fond enough. Although"— with a sly glance at Dentelle—" 'tis my opinion she's barely even with his birds on that score."

"That's as may be," said LeFranc. "But I hear that Mme la duchesse is heavy of his child, and I'll warrant there's no bird can say the same." He laid a finger to his nose and winked. "To tell true, the half of Paris is privy to the news. Madame my mistress was storming up and down the house, shouting: 'Here's my sister enceinte not seven months since her wedding, and I still a virgin after four long years. I rejoice that she, at least, has wed a man and not a tailor's dummy.' Costerine, thou should'st advise thy mistress that a reluctant husband is not to be seduced by pelting him with candlesticks and hard words."

What Costerine would have answered I don't know, for just then Pompey appeared, looking small and very black in a suit and turban of white satin.

"Why, if 'tis not madame's little baboon, let off its chain for a Christmas treat," cried Marie, who had drunk her share of champagne. "Come hither, ape, and dance for us!"

Pompey shrank into his jacket and looked as though he would have fled the room if he'd known where to hide. "Shame, Marie," I said. "You shouldn't drink if you can't hold your wine." I rose carefully, crossed the room, took the child by the hand, and led him back to the fire. "Olympe, you know Pompey. Pray present him."

Olympe introduced Pompey civilly enough, and he ventured a shy smile which Louison declared most charming, like pearls against black velvet. He looked alarmed, but taking no notice of his shrinking, she drew him to her and commenced to stroke his hands, exclaiming on the pinkness of his palms and the softness of his black skin.

"Oh, let me touch," said Costerine and dabbed gingerly at his cheek. "Peste! You're right. Just like good felt. But he's so ugly, Louison. Have you seen such a face outside the royal menagerie? The duchesse de Grandcourt's blackamoor is not nearly so tarry and blubber-lipped as this. Duvet, are you sure he's not an ape after all?"

Pompey looked pleadingly at me. I could see that his chin was wrinkled with the effort of keeping his bottom lip still; his eyes swam with tears. "Apes don't weep," I said as levelly as I could.

Louison took Pompey's chin in her hand and turned his head to look into his face. "So he is weeping," she said, surprised. "I'd no idea he could understand me."

"He's a human child, Louison, and I who have watched him serve madame these seven months can tell you he's quicker in his wits than most children, and infinitely better behaved."

Well, this inspired Dentelle to a jibe about crocodile tears and Costerine to protest that the most mischievous ape was better behaved than most children, and then M. Dubedat the chef de cuisine entered the back kitchen followed by a chattering crowd of servingmaids and kitchen-boys bearing linen, china, and cutlery. Pompey was forgotten.

We ate as well as our masters above-stairs, I dare say, for M. Dubedat was one who did not shrink from shoeing his mule at his master's expense. Trout and roast larks and veal there were in abundance, as well as a large bûche de Noël and chocolate iced cream. With each dish came its wine, until we all grew merry as nuns on the sabbath. When we were done eating, the tables were pushed aside, Carmontelle produced a fiddle, and lackeys and maidservants, kitchen-boys and femmes de chambre, valets, coachmen, postilions and all commenced to dance.

After one particularly lively tarantelle, I collapsed upon a bench beside Olympe. Her color was very high, she smelled of lilac-water, sweat, and eau de vie, and she seemed wholly unconscious that her nipples were showing above the neck of her elegant English nightgown. Blearily she smiled at me and reached up to pinch my cheek.

"Thou art in truth charming, ma mie, a credit, I feel, to she who had the raising of thee." A sly look came over her face and she leaned closer. "Come," she whispered, "are thy mountain boys as lusty as we hear? Tell Olympe thine amorous adventures, and I'll swear upon my gold beads that thou shalt not hear them told thee again as the finest new on-dit."

"Of course I trust thee, Olympe, but upon my mother's blessed soul, I swear to thee I've nothing to tell. I return to Paris just as I left it: *virgo intacta*."

"Chut! Either thou liest or the men of Beauxprés are all capons like our dear M. de Poix. Never mind; if that's thy tale, then I will back it." She put her mouth to my ear. "Hear, untrustful one, how I trust thee. At the de Chardons' this autumn, no less a personage than the marquis d'Emplumer summoned me to his bed. Ah, Berthe, the pleasure of it! His lips like burning coals upon my breast, and his hands, and his mighty sword that thrust me through and through.

. . . If 'twere possible to die indeed of pleasure, I'd have given up the ghost upon the moment." I looked at her blankly. She leaned back and giggled. "His tool, silly child, his manhood. 'Twas prodigious large, and he wielded it with a will. I vow I didn't piss comfortably for a fortnight."

I felt myself blush scarlet.

"What an infant thou art, to be sure," said Olympe, and patted my cheek. "I begin to believe thee virgin indeed. After he'd sated himself, the marquis gave me a gold louis and offered to set me up in my own apartments in the rue de Rivoli with a carriage and a chain of sapphires. I was tempted, I vow. But I'm nearly thirty, though you'd not think it to look at me. You know how men are—he'd discard me at the first wrinkle. Having no desire to end my days in a ditch, I regretfully declined. Would you credit it, ma mie? He wept. Perhaps I should have accepted his offer after all."

That night, a little drunk myself, I examined my face in madame's hand glass, and wondered what I would say to such a proposal. The circumstance was not altogether beyond belief, for I was young and well-shaped, as well as having particularly good teeth. Handsomer men than Menée had stared at my breasts; Saint-Cloud himself had said I was a toothsome piece. Presumably he, and they, had imagined—how had Olympe put it?—thrusting me through with their swords. I could very well imagine dying of such a proceeding, but not from pleasure. I remember I felt quite terrified and sick—though that could have been the champagne—and calming myself with a fantasy of how 'twould play on the stage, where lovers grapple only with words.

The curtain would rise on a summer-house or a private salon, discovering me seated upon a sofa or a rustic bench, reading. Enter a handsome marquis or chevalier, who, upon seeing me there, would clutch his breast, fling himself at my feet, and reverently embrace my slippers.

"Thou art more beautiful than an angel," he'd exclaim. "Only let me hope, and the meanest of thy jewels shall be a chain of gold and amber."

Withdrawing my feet from beneath his brow, "Monsieur," I would reply. "Beg no more, I pray. Twenty golden chains would not suffice to draw me from my mistress' side, who has all my service and my love. You mean kindly, monsieur, I'm sure. But no." Then I thought

I'd give him my hand to kiss, and perhaps a tiny lock of hair pour mémoire.

Such nonsense! But I remember being moved to tears by my imagined lover's despair and my own noble chastity. Is there any greater fool than a virgin of twenty bung-full of sentiment and champagne on Christmas night?

After her morning-sickness passed off, madame's pregnancy proceeded without incident. She was only eighteen years old, after all, and (thanks to the meat and oporto) in stout health. So stout, in fact, that by March, Marie had let out her waists as far as they would go, and it became apparent to all that 'twas high time for Mme de Malvoeux to retire to the country. Accordingly, back to Beauxprés we posted, as soon as the roads became passable.

Once more monsieur disappeared into his aviary, and this time madame was glad enough to see him go. The more her belly and her ankles swelled, the more moody she grew, and snappish, and prey to odd fancies and hungers. One week, she desired all her dishes to be garnished with pickle even though mère Malateste warned her that such a diet must make the child hot-tempered. Then she took a fancy to be bled, and fretted until mère Malateste consented to put a leech to her arm and draw off a gill of blood. Though the treatment made her weak and more peevish than before, the witch-wife repeated it twice or thrice, saying 'twas likely to keep the baby small and the labor short, which would be all to the good, she was sure.

My part in all this was more work than a month of court presentations and far more tedious: back-massaging, foot-bath carrying, posset-fetching, listening to madame's endless speculations on the infant's sex, its name, its character and future prospects. I took some little comfort, however, in monsieur's continuing absence and in madame's need of me, which grew more anxious as her confinement approached. From the time she rose in the morning until she lay down at night, I must be by her side, keeping boredom and fear at bay. To be sure, 'twas no more than I'd prayed for only a year past, but now I found myself a little lonely and not so indulgent of her moods as I had been. And I missed Pompey, whom mère Malateste had forbidden madame's sight until she be delivered, lest monsieur's heir be born with a darker skin than is usual among the French nobility.

———

Madame's pangs began one sweltering August night, when a full moon hung swollen and red above the far hills. I ran to fetch mère Malateste with sweat running down my face and such a stitch in my side that almost I felt as though I too labored.

"It's begun!" I gasped, flapping my apron at the witch-wife's hissing geese. "Oh, pray make *haste*, mère Malateste. Madame dies with pain."

"Hmph." Very leisurely, mère Malateste began to pack bunches of herbs, an earthen jar, and a small jug into a basket. "Mme la duchesse had best accustom herself to pain," said she. "First babies are a mortal long time coming. I've known a girl labored three days and more, and brought forth nothing at last but dead meat and blood." Horrified, I stared at her, and she laughed. "Never tha fear: I've the delivering of this babe. Thy mistress'll bear a living child; I have sworn it. But don't tha be thinking 'twill be easy."

Indeed it was not easy. For upwards of sixteen hours mère Malateste, two old grannies from the village, Marie, and I sat in murk and heat while madame groaned and sweated under a featherbed. They'd called for it when they came in, as well as a knife, a comb, a bottle of brandy, a pot of water and the fire built up to a midwinter roar. The knife went under the bed to cut the pain, the comb was dragged through my mistress' hair to keep its tangles from binding the child in her body. When the pot of water boiled, "Nothing like heat to draw out a reluctant child," said mère Malateste, and put scalding clothes to madame's belly while I fed her warm brandy and one of the grannies rubbed her privates with a foul-smelling unguent mère Malateste swore would make the baby pop from her, when the time came, like a pea from its pod.

As the day wore on, she massaged madame's belly while the grannies enlivened our waiting with tales of infants strangled by their own birth cords, of midwives who had torn a foot or an arm from a babe while drawing it forth from the womb, of monstrous litters of hedgehogs or tiny devils that had leapt from between their mothers' thighs to scurry madly about the floor before flying up the chimney, blaspheming.

Towards late afternoon, while the grannies were bouncing her vigorously on their knees "to encourage the brat," madame gave a great moaning cry. Mère Malateste groped inside her, shook her head, and poured herself a tot of brandy. My mistress began to sob weakly, and I ran from the room like a madwoman. As I ran, the grannies' tales chased themselves through my head. Devils, hedgehogs, hooks, knots. Hedgehogs, devils, pepper, knives. Hooks, devils, knives, knots. Knots.

No longer enlightened, certainly no longer reasonable, I swept through the château from the Alchemical attic to the wine cellar, opening doors, smoothing fringes, unloosing knotted draperies. Why, when I found Dentelle mending a rent in monsieur's hunting-jacket, I snatched the work from him, ripped open the seam, and boxed his ears for good measure. 'Twas the Lace antechamber stopped me at last. For a moment, all I saw was thousands upon thousands of knots keeping madame's baby from being born, and then I saw Pompey curled like a dog in a corner with his hands over his ears and his eyes screwed shut.

At the sight of a pain I'd power to assuage, my madness drained from me. I knelt and rocked the boy in my arms. " 'Tis nature," I soothed him. "The child will come, in spite of mère Malateste. And when 'tis done, madame will forget all her pain—le bon Dieu has ordained it thus. Take comfort, little cabbage. All will be as it was."

"Never the same," he sobbed. "Oh, mistress, I'm sorry."

A strange thing for the child to say, to be sure—sufficiently strange for me to have recalled it through all the brouhaha that followed, and to have mulled it over. Years later the answer came to me. Having sniffed out M. Léon's character in his mother's womb, he must have been trying to keep the little limb of Satan from leaving it. Perhaps he did not realize, child that he was, how 'twould make his mistress suffer thus to frustrate nature, fate, and mère Malateste. In any case, he hastily uncurled himself, removed his hands from his ears, and clung to me a moment, then released me with a push. Moved and woefully puzzled, I kissed him and returned to madame's bedchamber.

Madame was propped at the edge of the bed, held there by the two grannies. Past screaming, she looked piteously on me when I entered, and I thought her lips shaped my name. The grannies exchanged wise looks over her head and mère Malateste grabbed my wrist with a bloody hand.

"Now, Duvet," she said. "Tha'rt a city wench, weak as water. That mare's turd Marie is weaker yet, and I must trust thee, foreigner or no. Climb up on the bed, kneel under her hips, grasp her so, under her breast, and squeeze when I tell thee. Do as I say, and we'll have her delivered ere the Devil can spit."

Thus it was upon my knees that the heir of Malvoeux was born, screaming lustily even as he emerged blood-smeared from between my mistress' thighs. He thrashed at the vinegared water as mère Malateste washed him, fought the swaddling bands with an energy that astonished us all, and never left off howling until one of the grannies gave him a teat of cloth soaked in warm brandy to suck.

"Behold the little demon!" mère Malateste said indulgently. "He'll sleep now, and when he wakes, Boudin should be here. He's one'll bite sooner than suck—I'd best make her up a salt-paste to toughen her paps. Duvet," she continued, turning to the bed. "We're not done here. M. François will want to see his duchesse and his son, no doubt, and his duchesse, at least, is not yet fit to be seen."

At last it was over. The afterbirth was fetched out and burned, madame washed in wine and milk, the sheets changed, mother and son sunk in a sleep of utter exhaustion. The grannies departed with Marie, who looked very pale and thoughtful. Mère Malateste followed.

After a few minutes, monsieur entered. Without a glance at the bed, he strode to the lace-hung cradle, thrust back the shutters, flung open the window, and scooped up his son. Cradleboard and all, he held up the infant to the light and gazed hungrily upon his son's tiny, folded face.

"Léon Philiberte Jorre Guillaume Maindur," he said at last. "Vicomte de Montplaisir. Heir of Malvoeux." He laid the child back among its pillows, and I thought I saw tears glitter in his black eyes.

For wet nurse, mère Malateste had chosen Guyette Boudin, she whose husband Marie had once told me was good for nothing. He'd been good enough to quicken her, however, for she'd been brought to bed a week or so before madame, though the baby had died on the eve of madame's confinement, making Boudin the best—in fact, the only—wet nurse in the district. Guyette Boudin was a bolster-shaped woman with round scarlet cheeks, and her chief virtues were the richness of her milk and her stolid indifference to the young vicomte de Montplaisir's furious screaming. She'd a strong conceit of her place in the household as nurse to the heir of Malvoeux and demanded white bread and veal and the best Bordeaux with every meal. But M. Léon thrived and grew fat on her milk, and monsieur often remarked that her family had been tenants of Malvoeux for so long that it seemed to him that the vicomte must be sucking Beauxprés itself from her breasts. So we were forced to abide her.

Madame's milk dried within a week, and her fever being past, she rose from her accouchement five weeks later, fully recovered if a little weak. Monsieur, delighted with the lusty infant she'd produced, became prodigiously attentive. He could hardly bear to be parted from her, even for an hour, and went so far as to abandon his birds to sit with her, mère Malateste having temporarily forbidden my mistress the aviary. He hung the China apartment with cages of canaries and lovebirds and sweet-voiced redpolls, and as soon as ever his old nurse gave him permission, returned to her bed.

Thus Justin Victor Antoine Nicolas de Malvoeux was born in July of 1765, barely eleven months after his brother.

In Which the Sorcerer Maid Is Born

When, in later years, M. Léon grew to be a libertine and his brother Justin a monk, my friend Mme Pyanet told me 'twas not to be wondered at. Bad crows lay bad eggs, she said. There was never a Maindur born knew the meaning of moderation. As for the bent of their intemperance, why, Mme la duchesse had only herself to blame. While carrying M. Léon, had she not disported herself in Paris? Had she not, although warned, consumed great quantities of pickled onions? And had not *he*, the cursed one, drawn his first breath when a blood-red moon rose over the chimneys of Beauxprés? These things being so, what choice had he save to be choleric, luxurious, and criminally disposed? And his brother was fish-natured by reason of his mother's remaining at Beauxprés all the course of her pregnancy, drinking milk-pap, and bearing him just as the moon sank under the horizon.

Although I'm sure I did not accept Mme Pyanet's explication without comment, I am equally sure I did not mock it. After all, there was no denying that madame's pregnancies had been conducted as Mme Pyanet had described. Nor was there any denying that Justin was a weak and doleful infant who wailed like a vielle day and night or that M. Léon was from birth an imp of Satan. Something—chance, mischance, curse, or fate—had cast their natures in just such a way as to wound their mother's fragile heart.

With her two sons, at least, my mistress was so far before or behind the mode as to trouble herself with her children beyond the bearing of them. In the face of mère Boudin's disgruntled mutterings, she insisted that her sons be brought to her apartment every morning to be dandled and cooed over for an hour or so, or until she could no longer endure their tantrums. Whatever she did with them—sing, prattle, dandle them on her knee—they'd yowl like tied puppies and squirm and push her away. Mère Boudin disdained to advise her, of course, and what did I know of the care and amusement of infants? I did venture, once, to suggest that M. Léon might not scream and struggle when she embraced him if only she would not squeeze him so tight or weep so loudly in his ear.

"No," she replied sadly, "he does not love me. Nor Justin neither. I do not know what I have done to deserve such unnatural children, to hate their mother from the womb—their mother, who so entirely and tenderly adores them. Bien sûr, I weep over them. What woman of sensibility would not?"

And weep she did. Where once she'd been as gay a companion as anyone could wish, now she sobbed and sighed from morning until night. In vain I plied her with all her old remedies—needlework, the bibliothèque bleu, Doucette, Mme d'Aulnoy, her birds. She only shook her head, smiled wanly, and murmured that next week perhaps she would be stronger. In vain, monsieur berated her for being spoiled and weak-willed. No doubt he was right, she sighed; only she was tired to death, and indeed she couldn't help it. He sent for mère Malateste, who gave her a purge that sank her into such depths of despair that he wrote to Mme la baronne du Fourchet to come at once and take her daughter in hand.

His letter was answered within a fortnight—not by madame's mother, but by the marquise de Bonsecours in person, accompanied by a Swiss nobleman and his wife, who, being on the way home to Lausanne, had kindly offered to carry Mme la marquise with them as far as Beauxprés. Quite in his Paris manner, monsieur courteously desired the comte and comtesse Réverdil to break their journey for a day or two, in the course of which he and the comte found so many common friends and philosophies to discuss that the Réverdils stayed with us for five weeks.

Thank le bon Dieu they did so! For my mistress was not so cheered by her sister's presence as she might have been. First, the episode of the mock-trial still rankled, even after so many years, madame holding her sister's ill-judged championship entirely to blame for the extremity of her own sentence. Second, Mme de Bonsecours, though well-intentioned, was a monstrous poor sick-nurse. Her own health was rude, her nerves comfortably cushioned. When she should have murmured, she bellowed; where she should have soothed, she braced. And whenever I was present, she insisted upon asking me what I thought of this play or that actress, as if my mistress could possibly be interested in my opinion on theater gossip. I was puzzled how to interpret her attentions. Was she trying to woo me away from my mistress' service? Did she think to make a friend of me? Neither prospect appealed; and yet I liked to hear her talk of Paris and Versailles, of the haut monde's flutterings, the philosophes' feudings, the courtiers' polite grapplings for power. Concerning Mme la marquise de Bonsecours, I continued to be hopelessly of two minds.

Concerning Eveline Réverdil, on the other hand, there was but one mind to hold. She was like a sheep—a very pretty sheep, to be sure, snowy of wool, mild of gaze, with a most gentle and mellifluous bleat. Herself a mother of four, she took pity on madame's ignorance and spent hours in reading the whole of M. Rousseau's *Èmile* to her and telling her tales of her own children, how they wept and laughed for no rational cause, like the little savages Nature had made them. Madame drank down her common sense like a tonic wine, and was soon sufficiently recovered to converse and eat with her guests.

What peaceful weeks those were, to be sure—a Saint-Michel's summer of the spirit, blessedly warm, serenely golden, and all too brief. In the evenings after dinner, the company would gather in the Miniature salon to drink coffee and listen to the comtesse play upon the clavichord. She was possessed of a delicate touch and a set of études written especially for her by the Austrian emperor's young Kappelmeister Mozart. I remember once when madame, in the first flush of M. Rousseau's views on family unity, insisted that both M. Léon and Justin be present at one of these impromptu concerts, with Pompey and myself in attendance to keep them quiet.

That afternoon hangs in my mind like a painting, a conversation piece by Saint-Aubin, for example: "Music at Beauxprés," or "The Clavichord." A soft autumn light falls through the windows of a noble salon hung with hundreds of miniature portraits. The left middle ground is occupied by a satin-wood clavichord at which is seated a plump blonde lady in green and pink plaid. Balancing the composition on the right is a chaise longue supporting a pensive beauty in a gown of painted silk. An Indian shawl covers her feet; her hand rests on a

small liver-and-white spaniel. Clavichord and chaise frame a group of
two men and a lady in the center background. The lady is large and
florid, but vastly elegant nonetheless in purple lustring and silver lace.
Her clever gaze is turned on a small, sleek man who gestures with a
lorgnon towards the painting's central figure: a dark, sharp-faced
gentleman in a cerise coat who, half-turned from the scene, gazes out
the window. In the foreground, off to the right, a small black page in
a feathered turban and a silver collar kneels beside a stout child wal-
lowing in an abundance of white satin skirts. Behind them, a pretty
young servant in a striped sacque holds a sleeping infant in a cradleboard.

What this pleasing picture fails to show is that M. Léon—who
was tied to my chair by his leading-strings—was beating his little
wooden cat on wheels against Pompey's leg. Pompey endured his
attentions stoically, although his jaw would tighten when M. Léon got
in a particularly shrewd blow. Neither he nor I made any attempt to
take the toy away. Better that Pompey's leg should be bruised than
that the will of the heir of Malvoeux should be crossed, especially in
company.

Falls and trills of notes, golden as the autumn light, spilled from
the clavichord. Please may M. Léon stay quiet, I prayed. Please may
Justin not awake.

There was a small commotion at my feet as the vicomte de Montplaisir, bored with trying to make Pompey cry, reeled in the silver
bauble tied to his waist and prodded it at my ankles. I shifted my feet
away. Encouraged, he hauled himself upright and brandished the bauble as high as he could reach, poking at his brother's face with the
well-chewed wolf's fang at its tip.

"Is it not sweet," said madame languidly, "that such a young child
should so dote upon his brother? See how he tries to share his favorite
bauble with him? When I see them together, I rejoice with M. Rousseau
in the unspoiled goodness of little children."

Pompey gave a soft whimper, which could equally well have been
of pain or mirth. Hearing it, M. Léon left off trying to poke out his
brother's eye and, clambering onto Pompey's thighs, thrust the bauble
in his face instead. Pompey flinched. M. Léon crowed and had at him
again.

"I wonder," said the marquise, "at seeing my nephew still be-
decked in satin and whalebone and wound about with leading-strings.

You are become such a disciple of Jean-Jacques, sister, that I would not have been astonished had young M. Léon sat before us barefoot and clad only in a linen smock."

Monsieur turned from his contemplation of the gardens. "My dear marquise, I beg you recall this discipleship you speak of is a thing of yesterday. Before our charming musician introduced them"—monsieur bowed gallantly to the comtesse—"Adèle was as ignorant of la methode Jean-Jacques as of the craft of carpentry."

"That is not so, husband," said madame indignantly. "I have often heard M. Rousseau mentioned in Paris, although, to be sure, no one took the trouble to explain his ideas to me as Mme Réverdil has done. I quite intend to direct mère Boudin to leave off Justin's swaddling-bands, at least at night when he can come to no harm."

"Do you really believe, sister, that leaving him unswaddled now will make a man of him when he is grown?"

Madame's face settled into a fretful sulkiness. "There's more to it than that, Hortense, as you very well know."

"I dare say. But Jean-Jacques is so *impractical*, sister. Consider his ideal tutor, for instance. Where does there exist such a prodigy of nature, who will teach your child for love of teaching alone? And if you did find him, would you not fear lest he might prove more naïf than his pupil? Furthermore, this wise and patient pedagogue who bids mothers suckle their own infants and fathers teach their own sons has sent *his* children to be brought up in a home for foundlings."

"No one likes testing his own theories, marquise," said comte Réverdil smoothly. "Besides, the children were bastards, and he quite unable to afford their keep. Considering the circumstances, we must not condemn him, but rather commend his charity in sending them to a home for foundlings rather than drowning them like puppies, which I suspect he would have preferred."

"You know the man, Réverdil?" asked monsieur.

"I dined with him twice or thrice before the affaire Saint-Lambert in '57. A suspicious, uncharitable man, with the imagination of a fasting saint and the humor of a rutting bull. To frown at him is to offend him; to jest with him is to make him your enemy for life."

"You are very hard, comte," said madame.

The comtesse, having come to the end of her étude, lifted her hands from the keys and folded them in her lap. "My dear," she said gently, "only consider that M. Rousseau has said harder things than that of men who call our husbands friends."

Madame's head came up and her eyes widened pitifully, like Doucette's when she's being scolded. "Oh, dear. Is he quite wrong then? And *Èmile*, is it all lies? I vow, I don't know what to think, I don't indeed!"

Temporarily in accord, Mme de Bonsecours and monsieur lifted their eyes to the ceiling while the comtesse hastened to reassure madame that a philosophe's private actions may safely be divorced from his abstract musings.

"Indeed, my dear duchesse," added her husband, "a philosophe's opinions may safely be divorced one from the other. For as many as prove pure gold, so many more will prove to be dross. Take that Italian, for example: Vico of the New Science. Have you read the book, marquise?"

"The man who believes our far ancestors to have been giants? Charming nonsense, I thought it."

"And yet that nonsense contains more than a grain of sense. That our far ancestors were giants I believe no more than you. That they might have deduced quarreling gods from the voice of the thunder, I think very likely. Do not our ignorant peasants to this day ascribe metaphysical meaning to simple natural phenomena?"

"Alas," said the marquise, "they do. And their evil auguries so far outnumber their benign ones that I sometimes wonder how they find the courage to set foot outside their houses for fear of encountering a hare or a magpie or some other sign of doom."

"Peasants are savages," said monsieur coldly. "Vicious, credulous, and wholly self-interested. My chief quarrel with M. Rousseau is this same fairy tale of man's natural goodness, which is no less an offense to the rational mind than the church's fairy tale of original sin."

M. Léon was beginning to pout. I exchanged with Pompey a look of purest anguish. Which would be worse, I wondered, to disrupt the debate by taking him away or by allowing him to howl?

"We all know of M. Locke's argument of the *tabula rasa*," Mme de Bonsecours was saying, "that a child's mind is as a blank white page upon which his teachers write their wisdom. How, then, can man be said to have a natural state at all?"

The comte answered her. "A child knows to suck at the breast and to weep if he is hungry. The natural state of man, then, is the same as a beast's. Like a beast, he is born neither good nor evil."

"Yes," said monsieur suddenly. "Yes, Réverdil, that's what I have always believed. Anyone who has ever observed an infant must know that man is born possessed of only his five senses. 'Tis education alone that distinguishes a nobleman from a peasant, a philanthropist from a thief, a physician from a murderer—"

Mme de Bonsecours laughed. "Nothing, my dear Malvoeux, distinguishes a physician from a murderer, excepting that the latter is hanged for his work and the former is paid. However," she said hastily, seeing monsieur offended, "your point is well taken. Pray continue— education."

Monsieur turned to look out over the ducal gardens. "I believe we owe nothing to our fathers save a certain cast of countenance, perhaps, a tendency to height or corpulence or weakness of sight. In that, a man is no different from a horse bred for its endurance. But character—by which I mean judgment and will—that is added on to a child by education, not set in his blood by nature. My son is heir only to my title and lands, not to my vices and virtues nor to the crimes and philanthropies of my ancestors. Once his reason is informed and matured, this child, this *tabula rasa*"—here monsieur flourished his hand towards the vicomte de Montplaisir, who was staring at his father with owl's eyes—"will be a new man, a disciple of Science and Reason, untouched by the false superstitions of religion and—"

At that moment, M. Léon lost patience. He opened his plump mouth and gave forth such a shriek as would have caused the Devil himself to clap his claws over his ears and flee to the relative peace of Hell.

For a moment, monsieur stood foolishly pointing at his screeching son, then shouted at Pompey to quiet him. Justin woke and began to wail; madame helplessly wrung her hands. Doucette jumped down and yapped at M. Léon, who swiped her across the muzzle with his bauble and roared again with infantile rage. I thrust Justin into Pompey's arms and picked frantically at Léon's knotted leading-strings. The comte Réverdil began to laugh. The last thing I heard as we made our untidy retreat from the Miniature salon was Mme de Bonsecours saying, "Ah, brother-in-law! Your *tabula rasa* seems to have opinions of his own. How does *that* fit into your theory, I pray?"

When the Réverdils at last resumed their interrupted journey, they invited my mistress to accompany them to Lausanne, which invitation she readily accepted. Monsieur, who'd a wide acquaintance among the scientists there, came with us.

Oh, how I loved Lausanne! And Bordeaux, where monsieur went

sometimes in the spring to visit the bird markets, and Brittany, with its gray stone villages and the gray sea beyond. I liked the sea, at least to look at: flat as the fields around Paris, as I remember, with a sheen to it like taffeta, and white birds crying mournfully overhead. Mountains are very well, but I'd like to see the sea again. And Paris. How I long to see Paris.

Two hundred years! Surely it has changed in that time. The last I heard, the customs walls were down, the monasteries and convents defaced, the Bastille demolished to its very foundations. What has risen in their place, I wonder? Does the hôtel Malvoeux still stand in the rue des Lions, concealing its splendors behind a grim, gray wall? What is sold in the shops along the Palais-Royal? Who buys there? Are there still bourgeois in France?

Jean says I wonder too much. This is Paradise, he says. I wished for it, and my wish came true. I'm warm and fed and safe, as I had asked. Why can't I rest content?

Why not indeed? Everyone else is content. Colette has her eternal quest for why and how, which she pursues through the myriad books and collections of Beauxprés. Sixteen lifetimes were barely sufficient to bring them together, she says. Twenty lifetimes are not sufficient to understand them. Especially when she devotes so much time to the writing and performing of plays.

Before Colette began to grow, Adèle and I found the time in Paradise hanging heavy upon us. My old tasks of making and mending were taken over by our dexterous servants, and while Adèle could still design and embroider, even the finest stitches and most astonishing designs must pall. So we beguiled a decade or so in wooing our little resident ghost down from the tree she'd been haunting with games and tales and a golden ball; another twenty years in watching her grow first more solid and then older, and in teaching her how to read and write.

And then, when she was fourteen or fifteen to look at, four hundred years dead and fifty years resurrected, she brought Adèle a play she'd written—a foolish scrap not two scenes long, cobbled together from an old hearth-tale of a peasant girl and a frog. Adèle read it through with cries of delight at the cleverness of it, praising Colette for having thought of it, for having invented, all out of her own head, such clever words for a frog and a peasant girl and her mother to say to each other.

"We must act it at once," said Adèle. "I shall be the mother, you, Colette, shall be the peasant girl, and Jean shall be the frog."

That was the beginning of Colette's plays. They've grown with her learning and ambitions, throwing out new characters and plots and conceits as saplings throw out shoots, and our skills have grown to accommodate them. I am dresser to our little troupe, which rôle tests my ingenuity more than a little. For Jean will not play women nor Adèle men, and so Colette plays both, wearing breeches under her petticoats as confidante or soubrette and stays under her jacket as messenger or young lover.

Justin too is content, or at least as content as his nature will allow. Beauxprés is for him a hermitage, an antechamber to Purgatory, and mightily does he labor to purify his soul. Each day he reads his daily offices, tends the enchanted garden, performs his rituals of meditation and contrition. By my reckoning, he's achieved about two-thirds of sainthood: his faith in the grace of le bon Dieu and the rule of St. Benedict is as unshakable as his hope of one day winning to a less earthly Paradise. Charity, though—he's somewhat lacking in that. Within the last few years, however, he's begun to watch Colette's plays with me, and has even consented to hold the book and hear his mother's lines. Of late, I have seen him smile at one of Colette's jeux d'esprit. I begin to have hopes of Justin.

And M. Léon—is he content, I wonder? He has what he wished for, just as we all do. Yet once in twenty years or so I see him at his chamber window, looking out over the enchanted garden, his face sharp and sour. Envy, it looks like, tempered with pride and wrath. His other look is lust, wet-lipped and leaden-eyed. When that gaze by chance lights on me, my skin crawls and shrinks as from a leper's touch. Haunted by the specters of Léon in his tower and M. le duc in his aviary, how can I be wholly content?

Jean, who is as sensible as any man could be after two hundred years in cloud-cuckoo land, Jean thinks me a great fool. He's said so, often and often. And now that I am writing this history, he thinks me a greater fool for setting my foolishness down where anyone may read it. Colette has asked for a history of Beauxprés, he says, not a sermon. And I answer that this sermon is part of the history of Beauxprés, and Colette wants to hear everything, doesn't she? And Colette, who is reading in the garden, leans in the window and laughs and agrees that she wants to hear everything, so long as 'tis true. Jean sighs and mutters about some things being more important than others, and why do I ask his advice when I've no intention of taking it?

To tell true, I wonder myself why I have asked Jean for his opinion, for to this point, he's done little but complain. I must learn to consider my audience, he says, and not simply my own tastes. I am writing for Colette. Bon. I must ask myself whether a maid, even a sorcerer maid, will find anything of interest in birds and birthing pangs. Youth, he says, craves excitement. What about the time monsieur went hunting with the king, and that quarrel between Saint-Cloud and Dentelle that ended with Saint-Cloud kicking the little valet ass over ears down the stairs? Now that's the stuff they like to hear, he says. And why have I left out monsieur's friendship with Mme la présidente de Baudeville that drove my mistress frantic with jealousy until she realized 'twas the lady's birds her husband lusted after and not the lady at all? At times I've been tempted to dump paper, pen, and ink in Jean's lap and tell him to write it himself, he who has never met Saint-Cloud or Mme la présidente, nor even so much as seen Paris. But Jean can neither read or write, and so is safe in his role of critic.

Now that I've come to the events he himself witnessed, he carps worse than ever. Tell about Marie and the beggar woman, he commands me. That is sure to make Colette's ghostly heart race. And surely she'll want to hear how I found the chests in the old donjon. Do I intend to leave out the magic altogether? Has all my reading taught me nothing of the art of telling stories?

"She'll be bored witless," he says, shaking his finger under my nose. "Mark my words, old woman. Tell the full tale of Beauxprés, and thou'lt be so long in the telling that le bon Dieu Himself would lack the patience to hear thee out."

Well.

Neither Jean nor Colette need fear an endless catalogue of gowns and balls and small domestic occurrences. To be honest, even the mnemonic powers of a magic inkpot cannot redeem from oblivion every event that befell us between 1765 and 1776.

To be sure, a great deal happened in those years. The library contains a dozen accounts of those events—the dauphin's marriage in 1770, for example, and the death of the old king in 1774—events, which though great in themselves, affected our lives not one whit. Parliaments might be dissolved and their members sent into exile, new taxes might be assessed and new alliances made, new ministers might rise and fall like comets, and the duc and duchesse de Malvoeux would continue to amuse themselves as always with their birds and their journeys and their evening entertainments. In Paris, the hôtel Malvoeux was bright with company. In Beauxprés, the seasons turned peacefully in their appointed rounds and the peasants paid their tithes without excessive complaint. Mme Pyanet had a son, her sister-in-law the in-keeper's wife died of a fever, Artide's mother became one of the village grannies. Monsieur sponsored a birding expedition to India that netted him a live pair of secretary birds, a clutch of eggs taken from the nest of a bird-of-paradise, and any number of honey-bird skins. Maidservants married; lackeys moved on to positions in Dijon and Besançon.

One incident I do recall is that Jean mentioned of the beggar woman, and to please him, I will recount it here, although I cannot imagine what Colette will make of it.

'Twas before the birth of Mlle Linotte, I'm sure, in chilly weather—say the autumn of 1771, then. Madame had had a sudden yearning for a tisane or a bowl of milk—pregnancy always made her monstrously thirsty—and sent me down to the kitchen to fetch it.

In the general way, the kitchen was quiet after dinner, with M. Malesherbes off in his closet pondering new dishes and the kitchen-boys off gaming or sleeping or flirting with the village girls or whatever it is kitchen-boys do when not turning spits. That day it swarmed with craning, pushing domestics, above whose jabbering I could hear a woman's hysterical whooping.

The woman was Marie. She was half-lying on the settle, drumming her feet and clawing at her hair like a madwoman while Jean knelt before her, swearing and grasping helplessly for her hands. I leaned over his shoulder and slapped her smartly across the cheek, whereupon she stopped whooping.

Jean launched himself at me, snarling.

"Peace, Jean," said M. Malesherbes, whom I'd not seen enter. "If Berthe'd not boxed her ears, I'd have done as much myself. Artide, brandy. Finette, a measure of sugar in the pot, and stir up the fire a bit. Jean, sit. The rest of you—out!"

Well, I knew he couldn't be addressing me, so I sat down by Marie and gave her a corner of my apron to wipe her eyes upon. Her own was liberally caked with what looked (and smelled) like dung. Straws peeked here and there from her clothes, her hair crept down her neck in raveled hanks, her bodice was half-laced, her smock was awry, and all in all, she looked like a girl who's been tumbled in a horse-stall. Jean looked no better, with a button torn from his breeches and horse dung smeared across his face.

"Well?" said Malesherbes. "What happened?"

Marie sniffled and gulped. Jean picked dung from his cheek and stared glumly at Finette, who was excitedly rattling pokers and pothooks.

Malesherbes sighed. "I presume 'twas not rape, or you, Jean, would be halfway to Champagnole by now."

"Oh, no," said Marie, tucking up her hair with trembling fingers. " 'Twas nothing like *that*! I wouldn't have been in the stable at all, only I needed fresh horse piss—for bleaching madame's sheets, you know—and Jean most kindly offered to help me get it."

"Yes, that's it," said Jean eagerly. "Horse piss. So there we were in Thunderer's stall with a bucket, waiting for him to oblige, and talking of this and that, passing the time. You can't rush a horse even when he's been recently watered, which is why I picked Thunderer in the first place, as well as him having the largest stall, where there's plenty of room for two people to stand without crowding and scaring the horse, like as not, when there's no telling what he'll do, but nothing to the purpose, you can be sure. . . ."

"Bon." Malesherbes stood up. "I'll not waste time or brandy on a tale of a cock and a horse. Either you, like the horse, produce something to the purpose, or come along with me to Philiberte Malateste and explain to him how you use his horse-stalls."

Although Jean's mouth worked comically, I was not tempted to laugh. Well, consider. Here my friend's been playing pluck-my-harp with an undergroom, and me with no hint of a liaison until this very moment. The silly cow! Although he was mère Malateste's son, Philiberte Malateste was a famous prude who'd often sacked grooms without pay and without a letter of character, only upon suspicion of fornication. Should Malesherbes make good his threat, 'twould be the road for Jean and the street for Marie, with branding or the galleys and an early grave for them both at the end of it all.

Marie, very white, looked up at Malesherbes and said with dignity, "We were in Thunderer's stall, M. Malesherbes, just as Jean told you. And we were . . . much employed."

"No doubt," said the chef dryly; but he sat down again. Artide came in with the brandy and Finette heated up enough brandy-and-sugar for six. We sipped and sighed; the lovers began to breathe easier.

"Well?" M. Malesherbes repeated.

"Thunderer's stall's at the back of the stable," said Jean sullenly. "All the doors were closed—why, I'd closed them myself. That's what got my attention: hearing the midden door creak, loud and slow, like someone didn't know 'tis noisy unless you throw it open smartly. I don't mind saying it startled me more than somewhat."

"I'll wager it did," murmured Artide, but Jean did not so much as glance at him.

"I knew it had to be a stranger, or he'd have known about the door, and what stranger'd be sneaking into monsieur's stables save a horse thief? 'Twas the work of a moment to take up the hay-fork and prepare to defend monsieur's horses with my life. I threw open the stall. The stable was empty. No, there by the door, a stranger. I lifted the pitchfork and advanced. Then the stranger stepped forward into the light, and I saw 'twas only a beggar woman, bony as a rat and worse clad, clutching a bundle of filthy rags to her bosom and dangling a half-dozen bare-arsed brats from her skirts. Naturally, I told her to fuck off. She said nothing, only fumbled about in her skirts and brought out a bit of paper so grubby I couldn't have read it even if I *could* read it, which I can't. I told her as much, and recommended her to get herself and her ditch-got bastards out of monsieur's stable. Marie, a true daughter of Eve, came up to look. When she saw her, the woman began to make odd noises and pushed me aside to get to her."

"It was disgusting," Marie wailed. "She was like a skeleton, fevered, I'm sure, and she kept shoving her paper and her bundle of rags at me, babbling all the while. I took the rags—why, she thrust them in my arms." Remembering, Marie threw her filthy apron over her head. "It was a baby, M. Malesherbes—a dead baby. Long dead."

Finette gasped. Artide frowned and shook his head. I felt a sympathetic thrill of horror chill my bones, so that I shivered and gulped hot brandy to warm them.

"A terrible thing," said M. Malesherbes solemnly, "and no less terrible for being common. The poor woman was clearly mad."

Finette gave an impatient bounce like a child listening to a conte des fées. "What happened then?"

Poor Marie being by now reduced to weeping and hugging herself, Jean took up the tale. "Marie screamed and dropped the thing as if it'd bit her, and then it was like all the devils had taken a holiday from Hell. The woman screeched—I could see she'd had her tongue clipped—and the brats too, and they went for us like rats. They knocked Marie flat on the straw, and 'tis a wonder Thunderer didn't step on her, all nervous and dancing about as he was. He did step on a child, kicked one or two more, and caught the madwoman a shrewd nip on her arm that cleared her out at last. Marie began to howl. I bundled her out of the stall, calmed Thunderer, threw a blanket over him and gave him a mouthful of grain. Then I tried to calm Marie, failing which, I brought her here."

"So what became of the baby?" asked Finette.

Jean shrugged. "Trampled? Retrieved by its mother? Who knows. There's naught in the stall save a few rags and a bone or two, but 'twas only bone and rags and a bit of hair to begin with."

"And the woman? What of her?" M. Malesherbes' voice was dangerously smooth. "Don't tell me; let me guess. You said nothing to Malateste or Jacques Ministre, but left a diseased, insane vagrant to run loose through Beauxprés, wreaking havoc and shedding children like fleas. Even now, those very children could be stealing sheets from the drying-yard or wheat from the granary, and not a soul to stop them. Have you not heard of the brigand Hulin, who sends his trollops on before as scouts? What in the name of all the saints at once were you thinking of, eh?"

For some minutes Artide had been tapping his foot and scowling. "A scout for Hulin?" he burst out now. "Quelle bêtise! Hulin is leagues from here, in the Beauce. Furthermore, if that paper is a passport, she's no more than an honest woman fallen on hard times. In any case, 'tis only Christian charity to give her bread."

"Bah!" Malesherbes threw up his hands as if tossing away beggar woman, Artide, and all. "Hear the savant now, the man of learning! I am the chef de cuisine, me, and my authority is second only to Menée and Jacques Ministre. Do you care to argue your points of law with them, M. Learned Pig? Do honest women have clipped tongues?"

Defeated, Artide gnawed his lip, and M. Malesherbes triumphantly folded his arms over his mountainous apron and turned to Jean.

"You must take your story to Jacques Ministre so that he may be on his guard, but I think you need not mention Marie's presence. 'Twas just as well you were there, after all—Heaven alone knows what harm they might have done the horses. You, Marie. Stop sniveling or I'll remember that your virginity is in doubt and have you examined by mère Malateste." He lifted his plump hands to Heaven. "A hundred thousand thunders! How can I contemplate a new sauce when I am surrounded by prick-proud grooms and laundry-maids screaming about dead babies? I am an artist, me, and I require peace! How I am tried, cher Dieu. How I am tried!"

When later I tasked Marie with her secrecy, she flared up at me like dry tinder. Whatever my life might consist of, hers would not be all lace and dirty chemises, not if she could help it. Her Jean was a jewel among men. He was stronger than my precious Parisian Saint-Cloud, she said, and handsomer, too, for all he wasn't decked out in silk and gold lace and fine linen hose. Her Jean was an honest man, one who'd make his way in the world, and he'd promised to marry her just as soon as she'd saved up a proper dowry from her wages, providing monsieur gave his consent to the match.

Well. I thought that only such a gaby as Marie would believe that any man was likely to buy a mare he could ride for nothing any time he wanted. And then there was the danger of her belly growing round sooner than her purse, leading to the streets and the branding I mentioned earlier. But a woman in love will not listen to sense, and so I held my peace.

After Justin, madame bore only one living son—Louis-Marie Timothée Antoine Charles—a quiet child who lasted a matter of four months before succumbing unexpectedly to a summer fever. Two more infants she slipped before their time and was delivered of another, dead, after a labor that all but killed her as well.

Now, 'tis very sad when a woman endures the pangs of birth with no babe to show for it after, but in the living world, that's the way things are. If every child lived that was born, the mightiest wizard could not conjure up sufficient bread to feed them all. And which is sadder, after all: to bury a babe that has never drawn breath, or watch it die a year or so later of disease or hunger? Grief and resignation—every woman must make her peace between them. But no woman so much as a midwife.

Now the midwives of Paris, who are more accustomed to hustle an infant untimely from the womb than to deliver it alive—the midwives of Paris have a name for hardness. Yet I vow and declare that mère Malateste's insensibility would have astonished even those bloody-handed viragos. A miscarriage at four or five months? Never mind, madame, it was bound to be born deformed or worse, and besides, it had no soul. Did the birth-cord strangle a full-term boy?

Never mind, madame, mère Desmoulins had the holy water to hand, and 'tis better he died with his soul bound for Heaven than later when it might rot in Hell.

"You must not worry my wife into an untimely birth," monsieur had said, and his nurse had answered him, leering, "Not of your firstborn, monsieur. No indeed." Not of the firstborn, nor yet of the second, for children die from time to time, be they never so healthy. Even the heir of Malvoeux. But the third-born and the fourth and the fifth? It beggars belief.

Here in the library of Beauxprés are many chronicles of great families, and from them I've learned that too many children weaken a great family as surely as too few. Dowries for daughters and portions for younger sons chip away at both land and goods until at last nothing is left of a mighty domain but a few pieces of plate and a hectare of stony pasture. Yet the ducs de Malvoeux endured sixteen generations in an unbroken line with their holdings undiminished. And no duchesse de Malvoeux ever raised more than four children to adulthood.

Now, although mère Malateste may not have been a student of history, like all peasants, she understood economy. Two children was a good number, and two children would madame raise: no more, no less. Louis-Marie was born when Justin had been sick for over a year—first a swelling in his neck, and then a series of fevers and coughs and purgings that left him weak, skinny as a starved kitten, and deaf in one ear. Eventually, Justin recovered his health, though not his hearing. Louis-Marie died.

Two children: no more, no less.

Mlle Linotte Héloïse Charlotte Jehanne de Malvoeux was born on May Eve, 1772. Had mère Malateste not died in '71, she wouldn't have been born at all. And since she had to be born for the curse to be broken, I can't help thinking that some good angel must have put it into monsieur's head to bring a male accoucheur from Dijon to deliver madame.

I confess that I didn't take to Dr. Patin or to his starched-up assistant, but his brisk and scientific air, however chilly, was vastly reassuring. A large, pale, smooth man with large, pale, smooth hands, he carried a leather case that clinked most importantly with each step he took, and while he examined madame he quoted from the writings of the learned physicians Delaroche, du Fot, and de la Motte, for all the world as if he were lecturing a class.

Although he employed a lancet instead of leeches for bleeding and smelled of Parma violets, in arrogance at least, Dr. Patin was mère Malateste's soul mate. No sooner had he set his neatly-shod foot in the door than he announced that he had his methods, and if anyone did not like them, bien, let them say so now and save him the trouble of unpacking. Monsieur hastened to assure him that his methods came highly recommended, and Mme la duchesse promised to follow them to the smallest particular. Docile as a pigeon, she drank the milk he gave her, submitted to judicious bleeding, and walked the length of her apartment twenty times a day. She did protest when he told her that only his own attendant might assist at her confinement, but was easily overborne. Thus it was that while modern science delivered Linotte, I held vigil outside with Pompey.

Pompey was by this time fourteen or fifteen years old, a handsome enough youth once you got used to his looks, with skin like dull ebony and high, round cheeks. During the last year, his voice had slid an octave, his chest had deepened, and Mme la baronne had written from Paris to suggest 'twas time he was sent to the stables. "He is no longer a Child," she wrote, "and I cannot think it convenable to keep a Grown Savage in yr House. Who knows when his Bestial Blood might not move him to some unimaginable Act of Violence?"

The peasants of Beauxprés have a saying: "Beware the anger of the dove," a saying that my mistress has proved the truth of more than once. My mistress wrote back that M. Rousseau had demonstrated that savages were gentle by nature and more loyal to those they love than any civilized man. She would not be so narrow-minded as to banish Pompey to the stables only to satisfy madame her mother's silly prejudices, indeed she would not. Besides, no one else in the household read with such expression and sensibility. She'd keep him by her, and that was that.

Some little time later, a packet arrived from Mme de Bonsecours, its contents a note complimenting her little Adèle on her independent spirit and a romance by M. Butini entitled *Les lettres Africaines*.

'Twas a very silly book. Madame enjoyed it amazingly. She would waddle dutifully from couch to window and back to the tune of Pompey's voice declaiming the romantic ecstasies of Abensar and his mistress Phedima. After a savage idyll among the mighty palms and wild tigers of the African jungle, the pair was captured by English slavers and cruelly separated to suffer innumerable hardships among the wild palms and mighty tigers of Louisiana. Apart, they composed long letters of thwarted love, the beauty of whose sentiments inspired madame to design a fire-screen portraying the pair, which sits in her dressing-room to this day.

Upon a large piece of silk, she sketched Abensar in breeches, turban, and waistcoat languishing at the feet of his dusky ladylove. A large, striped, catlike animal lurked in the bushes behind them; monkeys and parrots sported in the palm leaves above. Between walks, she plied her needle busily, and soon had reason to fear that she'd crowded the design with one monkey too many.

"Peste! It must be unpicked," she exclaimed, and had just taken up her stork-billed scissors to clip the thread when a look of terror, longing, and pain twisted her delicate face. She gasped, dropped frame and scissors; I knew her time was upon her.

While Pompey ran for Dr. Patin, I supported madame to her bed, every moment half-expecting mère Malateste and her cronies to totter in at the door, munching their gums and calling for the fire to be made up higher. Very glad I was when Dr. Patin bustled in with his clanking case instead, even when his starched-up assistant swept me from the room like so much dirt.

"Poor Berthe," said Pompey as the door closed firmly behind me. "Think of mère Malateste cooing over the dead and shrouding the living, and take comfort that she's gone." He shivered violently. "The air of Beauxprés grew sweeter when she died, but 'twill be long before the stink of her evil disappears entirely. That cottage of hers! Pah! I wonder how M. Malateste can bear it."

"She was his mother," I said absently, straining my ears towards the inner room. "Besides, he's so pious, she wouldn't dare haunt him. What nonsense you are talking, Pompey."

He picked up the *Lettres Africaines* and waved it at me. "No greater nonsense than I've been reading. Listen to this, if you please. *'To a man who burns with love, you offer friendship and gold? Friendship? There has never been, will never be such a thing between lovers. Hatred, cruel Phedima, hatred alone is the beginning and ending of love!'*

"The sentiment aside, tell me if you can, Berthe, how a savage African learned to turn his phrases as prettily as any chevalier in France."

I shrugged. "He's a prince, isn't he? African or no, why shouldn't he speak prettily? After all, you can turn a phrase when you've a mind to, and with far greater wit than Abensar."

"I'm not an African prince. I'm not an African anything, Berthe, for I seem to recall I was born in Haiti. There are no tigers in Haiti, and I doubt I'd remember them even if there were. Firs are more familiar to me than palm trees. I live in France, speak French, read French." He looked surprised, as though an idea had just occurred to him. "In fact, by every sign of culture and education, Berthe, I am a Frenchman."

Grasping his wrist, I waggled his hand before his eyes. "Is a Frenchman's skin black as a crow's wing? Is a Frenchman's hair woolly as a sheep's back? Haitian or African, you're still a blackamoor. If your descendants were to breed for ten generations under our pale French sun, perhaps your ten-times-great grandchildren would be white. If so, they'll be Frenchmen. However prettily you may speak, you are not. You are madame's noble savage, Pompey, and you'd best remember it."

"I know, Berthe. I know." His voice was so sad that I moved to embrace him, but he shook me off gently and went over to the sofa where Doucette snored on a cushion. She opened her eyes when he stroked her, and her stumpy tail gave a languid thump or two. Beyond the closed door, madame groaned; the little spaniel raised her head and whined.

"She grows old," said Pompey. "Time was she'd have scratched the door down trying to get to her mistress if I didn't keep her from it. Now look at her." Doucette dragged herself up onto all four feet, turned around, and with a prodigious sigh, lay down again. Another sigh, and she was asleep, one paw over her nose.

"We all grow old," I said sourly. "I myself am nearly twenty-eight. And you are a great lad of what, fourteen? Pompey, do you remember . . ." Thinking I had heard madame calling my name, I stopped abruptly.

"Do I remember what, Berthe?" Restless, he turned from Doucette to the lovebirds whose cage hung in the sunny window. The original lovebirds had died: one at the hands of M. Léon, who hadn't understood it wasn't a toy, the other of a broken heart not long after. Madame had wept until monsieur gave her another pair, with instructions to look after them better. They were pretty things, tame enough to perch on your finger, and except when her eldest son was present, madame left their cage door ajar so that they could fly about the room at will. One flew out now to light upon Pompey's shoulder and nibble at the pearl in his ear. He laughed delightedly and stroked the bird with a gentle finger. "Do I remember what?"

"When you were just a little lad," I said, "and we first came to Beauxprés, you wouldn't go near the aviary, no, not though you were threatened with beating. I thought at first you feared the birds. Since then, I've seen you touch birds—even feed Bébé from your lips when you thought no one was near. And I remembered that you weren't afraid of the birds we brought from Paris the first time we came to Beauxprés. So what—"

A series of rising cries brought me to my feet. Pompey put his finger under the lovebird's tiny claws and conveyed it gently back into the cage, then took up the embroidery from the floor. "Sit down, Berthe, and unpick madame's monkey. Waiting's easier if you're occupied: you taught me that."

Reluctantly, knowing he was right, I took the tambour frame from him, perched on madame's chair, and began to pull out her neat stitches. There was no use in wasting good thread, so I picked at the work with a silver needle while Pompey, sitting at my feet, sorted and smoothed the tangled silks in madame's workbasket.

"It wasn't the birds I feared," he said thoughtfully, "or at least not the birds themselves. I thought them very bright and pretty, but I remember they made me want to weep. When I heard a parrot scream or saw a redpoll losing its pretty colors in a cage, I'd grow sad and angry all at once. When we first went to the aviary, and I heard them all cawing and chattering and calling out in their wild voices, 'twas almost more than I could bear."

For the first time I wondered what Pompey remembered of the place of his birth, and whether he'd missed the heat and the jungles and the running about carefree and naked. "Did it remind you of your home?" I asked curiously.

"I don't know. My earliest memory is a ship's hold, very hot and stinking, and a hairy man with great golden rings in his ears. He was the first white man I'd ever seen, and except for the golden rings, I found him prodigiously ugly. His face was pointed like a beast's and of a most inhuman paleness, and he stank abominably of greed. When first I met monsieur, he smelled the same, and I feared all white men would smell thus of avarice, but I was wrong."

I laughed. "I should think so indeed! How could a duc smell like a filthy slave-merchant who's been at sea for months and has probably never come near a flagon of perfume in the whole of his life?"

Pompey shrugged. "People do have a certain—'smell' is not the right word, but there is no better. Artide, for instance, smells of damp hay. And Dentelle smells like a long-dead mouse. Madame, she smells a little like Doucette. Sometimes, when I smell rain or carry your linen to the laundry, I think I remember the scent of my mother. She was a good woman, my mother, and loved me."

The monkey was half unpicked by now, and threads in shades of brown and black and cream lay neatly ranged on Pompey's knee. Beyond the door, I heard my mistress grunting. I applied myself with a good will to the monkey's buttocks and tail.

"In that case, 'tis no great wonder that monsieur should smell like a slaver," I said idly. "According to your science, a duc with great collections might even smell the same as a peasant with a horde of golden louis under his mattress."

"More or less. And there's something else as well—some stink of old blood and . . . Listen, Berthe!"

Through the door came a strong, lusty wailing. Tears blurred my view of madame's embroidery, now monkeyless. "An hour," I whispered. "Less. And it sounds healthy enough. Que Dieu soit béni!" Reverently, I crossed myself as the door opened on the doctor's assistant, considerably less starched than she'd been an hour ago, and smiling in a most unscientific manner.

" 'Twas the easiest birth I ever attended," she said. "M. Patin is quite put about. You may tell M. le duc de Malvoeux that he is father to a handsome daughter. She slid into the world with no fuss at all, and there's no bleeding to speak of. Almost magic, it was. I've never seen the like."

In Which an Ancient Beggar Makes a Nuisance of Himself

Now I come at last to the horse I spoke of when I began: the beggar and his curse.

To tell of the beggar is a harder task than I had expected. Not that my memory fails me—what I intend to write is as clear in my mind as my catechism. No, I set these blots and scratched-out lines to Colette's account. After all, Colette knows—none better—who the beggar was and what cause he had to curse. And her sympathy, in the course of nature, must lie with him. In telling her this tale, Jean has always cut it to a childish measure, goggling his eyes like a frightened cow, inviting Colette to laugh at him, monsieur, me, the beggar—the beggar most of all. Yet the beggar was as he was, which was far from droll. And he did what he did, which was far from comic. Whatever Colette may say now about the beauty of a plain story, I fear she may not find it so beautiful when she comes to read what I am about to write. On the other hand, there's no use to my writing a history at all if I temper this, which is its matrix and its heart. For without the beggar and his curse, the events of the next twenty years had neither order nor meaning.

Jean says this is great nonsense. Things happen. Sometimes they make sense and more often they don't, but none of it means anything in particular. Once a good tale's bought its teller his fill of wine, it has served its whole purpose and might as well be forgotten. He's wrong, of course: he doesn't even really believe he's right. Our presence here in Beauxprés must convince even Jean that tales often do have meanings, and events, patterns.

Take the maze in the library—that happened the very morning we first saw the beggar, and a blind man might have seen 'twas an omen. The question is, an omen of what? Now its significance is plain as a pattern-piece. Then . . . I remember well how I turned it this way and that on the fabric of events until at last I discarded it as useless. I didn't believe in magic—more fool I—not as I believed in Nôtre Seigneur and the power of reason and madame's right to throw her pomade at me when she felt liverish. Bien sûr, there'd been magic once in France—the tales of the bibliothèque bleu, of Charlemagne and Mélusine and St. Denis proved it beyond doubt. Even in Mme d'Aulnoy's day, perhaps, fairies and wizards had meddled in the affairs of mortals. But in 1776? Bah!

As I recall it, the twelfth of April was a cold, blustery, dismal day both within doors and without. We'd just returned from Nice, where the trees were already greening and the air fragrant with spring. Monsieur had been attentive, his friends flattering—in short, madame had been happy in Nice, easy and bright as a rose in bud. Now the rose was distinctly frostbit.

"I'm a hag today," she complained, putting aside yet another lace cap. "Look here, Berthe, and here." She rubbed viciously at her brow and cheek. "Wrinkles. And my hair! 'Pon my soul, there's little enough need to powder it. To look at me, you'd think my oldest child to be twenty, not half that age."

"Twelve, madame."

"What? Twelve what, Berthe?"

"The vicomte de Montplaisir. He is twelve years old, madame, not ten."

My mistress began to rouge her cheeks in angry little dabs. "Ten, twelve—in either case, too young to have a crone for a mother. And far too young to go away to college among all those soldiers. Far better he remain at home, in the bosom of a family that loves him. I cannot bear to think of him marching up and down with a heavy sword, and taking orders and such. My Léon is a delicate boy."

"Yes, madame." What good would it have done to tell her that M. Léon would be much improved by a forced march to someone else's beat? In that mood, she'd have fallen into strong hysterics. As it was, she only complained of a migraine, of a ringing in her ears, a tingling in her teeth, and a thousand vague aches and pains which drove her to her chaise longue as soon as she was dressed. I put a hot brick to her feet and was sponging her temples with vinegar when there came a scratching at the door.

"Enter," she said weakly.

Artide entered, bowing. "M. le duc requires madame's presence in the library," he said. "At once."

Madame laid her wrist to her brow and winced delicately. "At once? When my head pounds so I can hardly lift it? Convey my regrets to monsieur my husband, pray, and tell him I am indisposed."

" 'Tis an affair of some moment, madame, concerning madame's children."

Madame surged upright with an energy I'd not have credited had I not seen such transformations before. One moment she'd be indolent, careless, her vital forces blocked with ennui like a forest brook with leaves and dirt. The next moment, she'd be in spate, freed by some appeal to her heart or her erratic sense of duty. Can a soul be at once generous and petty? Such was Adèle's soul, once upon a time.

"A shawl, Berthe, quickly. The library, was it? Oh, do make haste!" And she had snatched the shawl from my hand and hurried out the door before I could well gather my wits about me.

Artide and I followed her through the Fan room and down the Tapestry hall. "What's going on?" I whispered.

Artide shrugged. "Who can fathom the whims of an aristocrat? Today he returns from the aviary before two and holds court in the library. Tomorrow he may call us all into the stables at dawn. As to what's going on, who can say?"

Drawing near the library, I grew conscious of a quivering in the air. My teeth itched, and as I stepped over the threshold, my blood quickened and beat in my ears, insisting that something was about to happen, something perilous and strange. Yet at first glance all I saw was monsieur in a rage: perilous, bien sûr, but hardly strange.

As always, he'd taken center stage, in this case the mirrored pier between the long glass doors. His arms were folded across his breast in a froth of fine lace, and below his blue-powdered wig his face was white and beaky with rage. He looked like a high-tragic hero—Theseus, perhaps, confronting Phèdre with her adultery.

Madame picked up the cue with a speed Mme Dumesnil might have envied. "Husband," she gasped. "Why do you look so? What has happened here?"

Monsieur flung wide his arms. "Chaos," he answered.

His gesture encompassed the shelves, which had been denuded, and the floor, which had been crazily scattered with books. Some were propped erect and others lay flat, so that the room had the look of a hayfield after a heavy storm, with chairs and tables, globes and lectoires standing amongst the wreckage like bony cattle.

Monsieur pointed to a miserable huddle of children and servants cowering in a corner. "What has happened here?" he echoed her. "What has happened, madame, is that your children have run wild. They are no better than beasts, madame, and I must hire a menagerie keeper to keep them in order, since a nursemaid and a tutor cannot."

My mistress produced a handkerchief. "They're only babies," she pleaded. " 'Twas only an excess of spirits, depend upon it. What harm have they done?"

"What harm? I'll tell you what harm. I enter my library to consult my Brisson, and what do I find but that, that silk-and-satin ape of yours squatting on a desk while your daughter roots about like a pig on the floor. As I take my stick to the blackamoor, I hear Léon laughing behind the curtains. I drag him out, and he shows me where his brother is hiding in a cupboard. I send for their nursemaid, who is asleep in the nursery, and for their tutor, who is run to earth in the Silver closet with a half-empty bottle of Burgundy."

This tutor was one M. LeSueur, a rusty, weedy little man whose unenviable job was to teach the vicomte de Montplaisir and his brother the fundamentals of Latin, Greek, and mathematics. He'd been at Beauxprés for four years, and hardly a day of those years had passed without his finding his bed fouled with a dismembered frog, or his chamber pot filled with stable-sweepings, or his books scribbled over with rude verses. Remembering Stéphanie-Germaine and my mistress at Port Royal, I might have pitied him. But his nose was so long and drooping, his eyes so weak and small, his hair so lank and red that I confess 'twas all I could do not to add to his torments myself. Pompey said he smelled like one of those flea-bit curs you always itch to kick whether it's done anything to deserve a kick or not.

When monsieur's glare turned on him, M. LeSueur's head retreated nervously into his neckcloth. "Poltroon," said monsieur disgustedly. "Drunkard. Sot. Thou art no longer in my service, thou."

The vicomte sputtered with laughter. Monsieur darted out a long arm, seized his heir by the ear, and dragged him forward. "And thou, my son. What hast thou to say?"

M. Léon rubbed his ear and scowled. "Nothing, monsieur. Justin built it."

"Justin?" The duc's bellow drew his second son from behind Boudin's skirts as a magnet draws a needle—although, to be sure, there was nothing either sharp or bright about Justin as a child, especially with his face all slobbered with snot and tears.

"Well, Justin?"

Justin snuffled. "M. LeSueur was teaching us the Siege of Troy, that had streets like a ball of twine, and how that made it impregnable."

"And so you slipped away from him while he contemplated the impregnability of Troy?"

"No, monsieur," said M. Léon slyly. "He told us to go away. To Cathay. Or the Devil—he cared not which."

"Did he, by damn! And so we return to M. le comte d'Encre. Speak, thou! Is this how you teach my sons?"

From my little knowledge of him, I'd have expected this question of his master's to reduce M. LeSueur to blubbering and pleading. Instead, he shook his head unsteadily. "Ah," he said. "Your sons. Your sons, sir, are unteachable. Or rather your older son is unteachable, and your younger son too cowed to learn."

"You forget yourself, maggot," said monsieur. "You are drunk."

A tiny, reckless spark kindled in the tutor's bleary eye. "Bien sûr, I am drunk. How else am I to face the indignities to which the vicomte de Montplaisir subjects me?" His voice rose. "Do you know what he has done to me, to his own brother, to newborn puppies and flies? He puts their eyes out, is what he does, and he tears their legs off, one by one." He was shouting now, his eyes flaming madly. "He's not human, I swear it. He's a demon, an imp of Hell. He should be exorcised, or horse-whipped, or, better yet, burnt."

"Oh!" Madame knelt in a froth of lace and silk to gather her eldest son into her arms. "You're the one should be horse-whipped or burnt," she cried. "Horrid man! You shouldn't be let near decent children."

M. LeSueur, now thoroughly aroused, screamed that the vicomte was *not* a decent child, and then everyone was shouting at once—M. LeSueur, monsieur, madame, and even mère Boudin, who assured us loudly that M. Léon's blood was only overheated, and all he needed to make him docile as a pigeon was a dose of sulfur to clear his bowels.

In the midst of this brouhaha, Pompey sidled up beside me and touched my arm. "Here," he whispered. "Monsieur's forgotten her."

I felt a tug on my skirt, and looked down to see Linotte staring up at me, her black curls powdered with purple spangles. For all the world as if she and I were old friends and not mere nodding acquaintances, she took my hand. Pompey smiled, an ivory flash, and slipped like a shadow out the door.

"Enough," shouted monsieur at last. "Boudin, to Hell with your sulfur. Take the children away; take them out of the house—anywhere, through the park, to the aviary. Keep them there long enough for this man to pack his traps and leave." His eye fell on me where I stood in the door with Linotte. "Duvet, Mme de Malvoeux will spare you, I'm sure, to assist Boudin. Now. All of you. Out of my sight."

We scattered before him, all save my mistress, who turned her anxious face to him like a flower to the sun.

A matter of ten minutes later, the five of us were trudging against the wind through the formal garden, Boudin grumbling mightily at the cold and puffing great clouds of breath into the chill air. Me, I was glad to be outside under the clean heavens. Linotte and M. Léon ran shouting down the pebbled paths before us, and even Justin stopped sniveling and released Boudin's hand to trot along behind them.

It was the kind of April day all too common in the high meadows—more like late winter than early spring. Though the snow was mostly gone, the grass was still brown and livid clouds blew across a sky as pale as January. Before we reached the pergola, my feet were aching with the cold and my cheeks stinging.

As we entered the copse, a ragged ancient popped out of the bushes like an operatic demon.

For Colette's sake, I'd like to write that I gave him a sou and a kind word, or at least that I stood my ground. But I have sworn to write the truth, and the truth is that I screeched like a scalded hen and recoiled two or three paces. After all, beggars were not common around Beauxprés, where neither work nor charity was plentiful. And this beggar was so particularly repellent. His chin was disfigured with a sparse white beard, his mouth was a graveyard of blackened teeth, and he stank like a sick goat. He squinted from me to Linotte with diseased yellow eyes, then thrust out his hand and whined for alms. Had I not been so afraid, I might have pitied him, for the hand was blue with cold and wrapped in rags, and he leaned heavily upon an iron-shod staff.

Wide-eyed, Linotte shrank back against me, and I felt another small body pressing hard at my back. The beggar reached for Linotte and might have seized her for all I could do to stay him. 'Twas fortunate for us all that Boudin was cut of sterner stuff. Boudin never quailed. Boudin stuck her nose into the beggar's filthy face, thumped his skinny chest with one fat, red finger, and cursed him and his ancestors to the most noisome deeps of Hell.

"M. le duc de Malvoeux," she finished, "is accustomed to order all vagrants chopped fine and fed to his hawks. If thou, beggar, hast any love for that scrawny carcass of thine, I'd advise thee remove it."

"He'd give the hawks bellyache," piped the vicomte de Montplaisir scornfully. Behind me, Justin giggled nervously. Linotte, to my surprise, began to cry; moved by a sudden impulse of tenderness, I knelt down and hugged her to me.

The beggar laughed and spat thickly at our feet. "That's once," he said and, leaning on his staff, shuffled back among the trees, his cloak folded tight around him.

Boudin was all for returning to the château and complaining to monsieur. Justin, once again in tears, seconded her.

"Poltroon," said the vicomte in his father's lordly tone. " 'Twas only an old muck-worm, weak and harmless. We need not trouble monsieur my father with such." He turned to me with a graceful bow. "Take courage, Duvet. The heir of Malvoeux himself shall protect you." And he made a great business of cutting a withy from an arching shrub.

"Hoy, M. le mendiant," he shouted, whistling the withy over his head. "Tough as it is, the hawks of monsieur my father hunger for thy flesh."

Linotte, who'd been standing quietly all this while, struggled in my arms. "No, no, no, no! No hawks, you mustn't!" she cried, and would not be comforted even when Boudin assured her that hawks wouldn't eat man-flesh, and wouldn't she like Duvet to take her back to the house and make her some nice chocolate?

"No! Don't want to go back," Linotte wailed. "Want to see birds!"

"It'll be better so," I said, rising.

Boudin growled. "Why?"

"What do *you* think monsieur will say if we return almost before we've set out? Do you think he'll thank you for interrupting whatever he's doing to M. LeSueur to tell him that you've been frightened by an old beggar?"

She opened her mouth to blast me, hesitated, "But—" she said. "Well—" She shrugged, then bent to Linotte and none too gently swiped at her eyes and streaming nose with the corner of her apron. "Very well, mademoiselle. 'Tis forgotten. Come see the birds now."

That night, after I'd put madame to bed, I retreated to the kitchen, where I sat by the banked fire and listened to the comfortable snoring of the kitchen-boys asleep on their pallets under the tables. Thoughts of libraries, beggars, even of the hapless M. LeSueur, pushed and jostled in my mind.

"In all wide Troy, there is none to befriend me, none," mourned a low voice in the shadows. "For all turn from me with loathing."

"Name of a name! Pompey! Thou . . . monkey! I'm like to've bepissed myself!"

Contrite, Pompey stepped into the light and laid his hand on my shoulder. When I twitched it off angrily, he sank to one knee before me and clasped his hands to his brow. "A thousand pardons, Mlle Duvet," he said. "Behold me cast down at your feet, my head sunk to my breast under the mingled weight of my cruelty and your displeasure."

"Oh, bah," I said. "I'll forgive thee, monkey, if only to hear what happened in the library. 'Tis all a mystery to me from beginning to end."

He curled down on the hearth and busied himself removing his slippers and his white silk stockings. "Mademoiselle and I were in the cabinet des Fées," he began.

I nodded. Pompey and Linotte were always in the cabinet des Fées, at least when he was at Beauxprés and madame had no immediate need for him. From the time she could babble, Linotte had made it clear that she preferred Pompey's company to all other. Given the characters of her nurse and her brothers, this was not remarkable. That Pompey should have taken pleasure in the company of a girl-child of four was perhaps more so. Yet he did.

The cabinet des Fées was their favored playground, and the pair of them would crouch by the hour together sending the Princess Florine's tiny steel coach on quests across the carpet, coaxing milk and cake from the magic satchel to feed the violet rats that drew the coach, stroking the rainbow fur of the White Cat's sleeping dog, Toutou. The treasures came alive for Pompey as they did for no other, excepting the wand of the Fairy Friandise, which worked its magic only for Linotte. 'Twas a trumpery thing, that wand, fluttering with silk ribbons and crowned with a purple star. When waved, it would shower the air with marzipan pigs and trails of sparkling purple dust in which Linotte would dabble her hands until it swirled in glittering veils around her.

That (said Pompey, wiggling his naked toes in the warm ashes) was what she'd been doing that morning, and it had occurred to him to wonder, as he watched her, why the wand only produced sweetmeats and purple dust. Other wands conjured up practical things: meat pies, gold coins, cudgels, cars drawn by winged frogs. But marzipan pigs and sparkles? What use could they be, even to a fairy called Friandise? He thought the library might yield him an answer.

"You know no one enters it," he said, "not since Artide gave up thinking he'd go to Paris. Well, I heard bumping and voices, and thinking them to be the sounds of a lackey and a servingmaid . . . dancing a country dance, I told mademoiselle we'd come back another time. ' 'Tis only my brothers,' says she. So I tap. There follows a deal of scurrying and banging, and when I open the door, the room is as you saw it, save for two wooden horses lying among the books, and this by the window."

From the pocket of his coat he withdrew a largish object, which proved to be a lacquered egg about the size of a goose egg, snow-white.

"The swan's egg's missing from the case in monsieur's antechamber," Pompey said.

"Monsieur will be furious."

Pompey shook his head. "Monsieur won't notice 'tis gone if no one tells him. An egg is not a bird, after all."

"Granted. So. You saw all this and then what?"

"Mademoiselle laughs and claps her hands. 'A puzzle,' says she."

"A puzzle? To be sure," I said waspishly. "Two horses, an egg, and a welter of books make a puzzle indeed."

The kitchen was growing cold; Pompey took the poker and stirred one corner of the fire into flame. "It wasn't just a welter, Berthe—I saw that at once. The books defined a winding path, like a maze."

"Ah, bah, Pompey. I've never heard of such a thing! A maze of books? What is there in building a maze to catch the fancy of an imp like M. Léon? Is it a trap? An engine of torture? What could it gain him?"

"Well, it did trap M. LeSueur, though the vicomte more likely intended it for Justin. You misjudge him if you think him incapable of doing something simply for the joy of it."

I tweaked his hair playfully. "You defend his character, Pompey? You who have so often said that the vicomte de Montplaisir stinks of musk and blood?"

Pompey laughed and untangled my hand from his hair. "Oh, you needn't think I mean to praise him, Berthe. 'Tis only that you're foolish to think M. Léon a dull boy just because he won't learn Latin. He's sharp enough when it comes to his own pleasure or discomfiting others."

"D'accord. So M. Léon built a maze. What was he playing at?"

"The Siege of Troy, of course. Justin as much as said so."

"Did he? I don't recall." And I didn't at the time, although I do now. It must be the magic inkpot has improved my memory as my reading has improved my mind. For example, I'd never need to ask now, as I did then, what on earth a swan's egg had to do with a game of Troy.

Pompey smiled at me. "Helen, the whore of Troy, was said to be hatched from the egg of a swan."

"To be sure," I said, and pondered what he'd told me. It made a kind of sense, once I knew how to look at it. There would have been the fun of stealing the egg, pulling the books from the shelves, and the game itself—no doubt as complicated as its setting. All this, and the delicious thought that in time someone (not M. Léon, to be sure) would catch a beating for the whole.

"Very likely you're right," I said at last. "So. Linotte said there was a puzzle. Then what?"

"She bunched up her skirts and began to walk the maze, heel-to-toe. Some of the books had fallen when the boys fled, so the path was no longer clear. She came to the first horse."

I sighed. Pompey, who read the tales of others so beautifully, had no gift for telling his own. Hind-side-fore as often as not, and half of it left out. "Go on, Pompey," I said as patiently as I could. "What happened then?"

"She picked it up, and with all her might, she threw it from her.

When it fell, I felt something begin to gather in the air, bright and dark at once. Magic."

"Magic. Bah! Nerves, anticipation, impatience, anything might have caused such a sensation. Not magic. We live in an Age of Reason now. All that's left of magic in France are some antique curiosities like the pie of prophesying birds and the wand of the Fairy Friandise— pretty toys of no practical use whatever."

"You forget the seven-league boots, Berthe: those are useful. And this *was* magic, I swear it. Oh, at first I wasn't sure. But when mademoiselle reached Justin's horse and threw it after M. Léon's, the magic swelled and swelled until I thought I should burst. When monsieur interrupted her, she was within an arm's reach of the terrace doors and the egg." Pompey hugged his knees and shuddered. "Oh, 'twas terrible, Berthe. The air was ringing a thousand bells, and I felt somehow as if I were about to sneeze, but could not. Monsieur screamed when he saw me and plowed through the books, scattering them as he came. He caught me hard across the arm with his stick. I heard the vicomte laughing."

I pulled his head against my knee and burrowed my fingers in his woolly hair. "Dear monkey," I said. "For all your broad shoulders and deep voice, you're nothing but a child, after all. To be so caught up in a small girl's game that you come to believe in it as faithfully as she!" He shook his head and began to protest; I hushed him with a laugh. "I fear the purple dust of the Fairy Friandise has gone to your head. Now, 'tis past midnight, and my eyes are drooping from their sockets. Bank the fire, poppet, and go to bed. No doubt it will all be forgotten in the morning."

The beggar did not appear again until July. The day was very warm and clear, I remember. Madame was hard at work at a tapestry of Leda and the Swan. I'd opened the long windows to let the fragrant air refresh her when all at once a wild clatter of hooves and the shouting of an excited child rose shrilly from the court. Madame started, driving the needle into her hand. The sight of the blood beading on her palm turned her quite faint, and what with binding up her wound and burning feathers to bring her round, I quite forgot the fuss that had begun it all.

Had Marie been able to keep her counsel, I'd have thought no more about it. Jean had begged her to keep silent, having himself been warned to discretion by M. le duc himself. As well warn a cock not to crow or a hen not to cackle. At least Marie had the sense to tell only me, who knew how to keep a still tongue in my head.

It seemed that Jean had ridden out that morning with the young master, his brother, and two dogs, all set upon hunting rabbits. As they dismounted at the edge of Just Vissot's cornfield, a cloaked and filthy man appeared and begged for alms. The dogs took one sniff of him, whined piteously, and shrunk trembling behind Jean's legs. The vicomte, sounding most precisely like his father, demanded whether the beggar had forgotten the duc's hawks. For answer, the old goat laughed horribly, spat on the ground, said, "That's twice," and vanished back into the corn.

The incident was soon over, and Jean himself not particularly disturbed by it. After all (he told Marie) the man was only an old vagabond, not a pretty sight, perhaps, but hardly dangerous. He, Jean, was therefore astonished when the vicomte had flown into such a passion as is only permissible in a noble of an ancient house. He raged and swore that such a slight must be avenged, and ordered Jean to scour the field for the old man and whip him out to justice.

Judging this task at once useless and unpleasant, Jean was just considering how he might avoid it when Justin began to whine and snivel. The young master had shouted that Justin was a blot upon the name of Malvoeux and lifted his whip. For a moment, Jean thought he'd lash it across his brother's face, but he turned it upon the dogs instead, then flung himself on his horse and rode ventre-à-terre back to the château. Jean had followed more slowly with the sobbing Justin, to find Artide awaiting them at the mounting-block with the unwelcome word that the groom Jean Coquelet was required immediately in the library.

So Jean went to the library, reluctant but obedient, and scratched politely at the door. Monsieur himself opened it, wearing such a look as would curdle a man's blood like milk, vastly displeased that the impudent beggar of whom his son had told him had not been pursued and brought to justice. Leaning over a desk, his nose thrust forward and his eyes glittering, monsieur had informed Jean of his laziness and his cowardice and his striking personal resemblance to a turkey-vulture. Jean, recounting the scene, had added that monsieur had looked uncommonly like a bird himself, although Jean did not pretend to know exactly which one.

"He wasn't sacked, though," said Marie thoughtfully, "and he wasn't thrashed, and *that's* a riddle, if you will, given monsieur's temper and all. Such a fuss about a beggar, and he didn't even *do* anything, not like that horrible woman and her baby, do you remember, all those years ago?"

I exclaimed properly, but kept my own counsel on the subject of beggars and the past. Yes, I recognized my beggar in Jean's beggar, and yes, I fretted over it. Even in an Age of Reason some ancient rules hold true. "That's twice" promises "That's thrice" as a round apron promises a new mouth to feed by and by. However, I couldn't prevent the beggar's return by revealing that I'd seen him too, and such a revelation would bring up my having hidden it at the time: all in all, it hardly seemed worthwhile to mention it. So I held my peace and waited for the third time to wind up the charm.

I waited four months. The first month I looked about me constantly; the second and third, less often. By October, I was on the way to forgetting the entire incident. And then one chill November morning, monsieur burst into the China antechamber carrying Linotte in his arms, dropped the child into madame's lap, and stalked out again without a word.

Linotte was whooping and sobbing like a mad thing. "No hawks, no, no, no," she wailed, and my heart turned over in my breast. Pompey hummed soothingly, I chafed her hands with cologne to draw the heat from her brain, and still she sobbed and sobbed until madame began to weep in sympathy. I was nigh beside myself between them when Artide entered, as swollen with importance as the frog in the fable.

"Madame's servants are summoned to the forecourt," he announced shortly. "We are all summoned, from LeRoi to the bird-boy. Monsieur has a thing of the greatest importance to convey to us, and the stocks await any who absents himself."

"You'll be of no use in the stocks," said madame, wiping her eyes. "Go, go, both of you."

So Pompey and I hurried off to the forecourt to take our places among the uneasy throng of grooms, bird-handlers, gardeners, lackeys, cooks, laundry-maids, porters, and servingmaids already gathered around the fountain of Latona.

Pale as death, his wig askew, monsieur emerged from the front door and advanced to the top of the steps. He clutched the hilt of a sword under his cloak and declaimed the following in a pinched, harsh voice:

"If any one among you should see an elderly beggar-man, a cripple with a black staff, possessing peculiar yellow eyes and wearing a black cloak he's obviously stolen from a gentleman—if any one of you should find such a vagabond in the seigneury of Beauxprés, then he is to bring him without delay before M. le duc de Malvoeux. Furthermore, if M. le duc were to hear that any one of you have failed to bring this felon to judgment, he will consider that ingrate the felon's accomplice or familiar, and use him accordingly."

Then he stalked back into the château and we scattered, each one cursing the duc or blessing himself as the fancy took him.

Pompey and I returned to our mistress to find Linotte asleep upon her knee and madame herself aglow with triumphant motherhood and in no need of either our help or our company. Annoyingly, Pompey retreated to his closet with a volume of Mme d'Aulnoy, forcing me to go in search of someone else to talk to.

The laundry was empty and, as far as I was concerned, the kitchen also; for I was not on gossiping terms with the sous-chef grumpily directing two kitchen-boys in the preparation of dinner. The occasion of his ill-temper was not far to seek: all the world had decamped, leaving him alone with no one to help him save two idiots who'd as soon drool into the soup as stir it, and what did I make of the scene in the courtyard, hein? I shrugged and exclaimed sympathetically and hurried out.

All the world—or that part of the world in the service of the duc de Malvoeux—was at the inn, of course. If decorum forbade the discussion of monsieur's peculiarities under monsieur's own roof, where else could they find a fire, wine, and reasonable privacy? 'Twas their good fortune that this was not a market day, when the place was packed to the walls with belligerent peasants. No sensible domestic would risk his head in Yves Pyanet's inn on a market day. No sensible servingmaid would risk her virtue there any day of the week, though it was not uncommon for the village women to take a mug of mulled wine there with their husbands of a Sunday after Mass. I'd gone in once with Mme Pyanet and her husband Estienne: once, and never again. The chimney smoked villainously, the food wasn't fit for pigs, and the wine would've burned your gullet raw had Yves Pyanet not watered it down to nothing.

Hesitantly, I pushed open the door and slipped into a thick fetor made up of equal parts of raw wine, turned cheese, damp smoke, and filth. Through the gloom, I made out a crowd gathered around the fire, ten or so men, I thought, and a few women, looking as uncomfortable as the subject that had brought them there.

"Ah, Mlle Duvet," said Yves Pyanet. "You were expected. Right devil's Mass it is, and no mistake. Wine?"

I shrugged acceptance and picked my way through the maze of crazy benches towards the crowd. A devil's Mass? Why, the only devils present that I could see were Menée LeRoi and mère Boudin. Surely Philiberte Malateste considered himself a God-fearing soul, and the rest of the company were no more wicked than any child of Adam. Artide, Jean, and Pierre Arroseur the head gardener looked very much at home, as indeed they ought, having been drunk in that tavern every Sunday since they'd been weaned. M. Malesherbes' lip was drawn up with disgust, and Jacques Ministre's eyes dwelt uneasily on the baker Estienne Pyanet, who was the host's brother and the only villager present besides père Boudin—who, living off his wife's milk, hardly counted for a man—and the host himself.

"M. le duc de Malvoeux is a fair master," Menée was saying. "But once he stands to a thing, he's harder to shift than a bull at stud."

He gave the pretty girl on his knee a lewd wink and held his cup to her lips. She sipped, sputtering when he tipped the cup too far.

Marie beckoned me to sit beside her. "LeRoi's new hobby-horse," she hissed in my ear. "Peronel Mareschal. A week in the laundry, and she still don't know a sleeve-ruffle from a fichu. She's well-shaped, though. I'll give her that."

I wasn't interested in Menée's little friends. "That was a fine scene monsieur played us in the court this morning, eh, Jacques Ministre?"

The steward sighed. "I was just telling friend Pyanet, here, that old man's likely to get a short shrift and a shorter rope should he show his face again."

"Not only the old man." Pierre Arroseur took a pull of wine and made a wry face. "Anyone shelters him'll hang alongside 'till the pair on 'em drop from the tree like rotted plums."

"Ah," said Jean boldly. "But who'd protect such a one as that? A sorcerer, beyond doubt, who's sold his soul to the Devil in exchange for unclean powers."

"What do you know of it?" demanded Malateste. "Beware how you boast, boy, and remember that bearing false witness is as great a sin as fornication."

Jean looked pained. "By my hope of salvation, M. Malateste, my witness is true. For I, Jean who speaks to you, was present when this very demon threatened the lives of the vicomte de Montplaisir and his noble brother."

"Noble, my ass," mumbled mère Boudin. "The boy's a milksop, wouldn't say boo to a goose. Wets himself when I look at him cross-eyed."

"I don't doubt it, ma mère," said Jean, and took a gulp of his wine to give her time to think about it. We all laughed, père Boudin like a maniac until his wife clipped him over the ear with her cup. Then he moaned while Menée bellowed for silence, after which Jean began his tale.

"Mesdames, messires, this was the way of it. We're in the corn-field, out after rabbits, y'see, when all of a sudden, this sorcerer comes out of the corn, cloaked in a thunder-cloud and shooting fire from his goatish yellow eyes. The young sieur challenges him, whereupon the sorcerer curses to sear the air and spits a flaming gobbet like a dragon. The spit withered the grass it landed on, and left a bare spot where nothing grows. You can see exactly where he stood, too—the earth's gone gray. Anyway, the horses shied like nuns passing a whorehouse, and the dogs tucked their tails between their legs and whined like— like M. Justin." There was a little laughter, but Jean only shrugged and went on. "I cannot blame any of them, me, for I myself was so afraid that every single hair upon my body stood up at attention."

Menée made a sly remark that caused Peronel to giggle and blush. Malateste clicked his tongue like an old biddy hen, and M. Malesherbes said primly, "I thought you dragged me down to this midden to parley, Menée, not to wallow in bawdry."

Estienne Pyanet stirred upon his bench and opened his mouth, no doubt to object to the chef de cuisine's description of his brother's inn.

"Even so," said Jacques Ministre hurriedly. "Let us return to our muttons."

We all sat in silence, and then I said, "Jean's beggar appeared three months ago. What inspired monsieur to speak of him today?"

Pierre Arroseur cleared his throat. "I were pruning the espaliered apricots," he said, and stopped.

"Go on, grandpère," said Menée. "Spit the dirt from thy mouth and speak up."

Like all gardeners (at least like all gardeners I've ever seen), Pierre Arroseur is as brown and wrinkled as a tree and only a little more conversable. He mumbled his lips, rubbed his crack-nailed hands against his culottes, and sighed deeply. "Monsieur went out with the little lass, then came back through the pergola carrying her," he said at last.

"Yes," said Jean. "But what happened between the time he went out and the time he returned?"

Pierre Arroseur shrugged.

"He met the beggar, of course," I said, having long since lost patience. "And we'll never know what passed between them, not if we sit here until our bellies rot and our bottoms grow into the benches. The question, it seems to me, is what it all *means*."

"Sorcery," said Malateste.

"Buggery," said Menée. "No one sells his soul to the Devil nowadays—y' don't get enough for it. What else?"

"Poverty," said Artide, so loud that we all started. He'd been brooding over his sour wine, his brows a brooding knot over his eyes. "Hunger is what it means, and injustice."

Pyanet banged his tankard on the bench. "Desmoulins has got the right on it, livery or no. Since they brought back the corvée in '76, we've known what to expect from the likes of the seigneur, and 'tis all of a piece, I tell you, all of a piece."

"Aye," said Artide. "When the duc de Malvoeux hunts down a starving cripple, 'tis not to feed him and give him a place by the fire, you can be sure of that."

"Softly, Desmoulins," said Philiberte Malateste. "Remember that the duc de Malvoeux feeds you."

Artide glared at him so fiercely that a fight seemed inevitable until Peronel burst out, "My grandam said," and threw her apron over her head like a duck dabbling for weed.

"Speak up, little cabbage," said Jacques Ministre. "What said thy grandmother?" We all encouraged her, and Menée pulled the apron down from her face and held her hands so that she couldn't replace it. Finally she realized that she'd get no peace until she spoke.

"My grandam was laundress in the days of M. le duc's grandsire, he who liked fans. Anyway, once grandam was approached by a beggar in the lane between the château and the village, and she sent him about his business—as well she should, he being toothless and sore-ridden and plague-ridden too, like as not, for that was in '20, you know, when the plague came to Marseilles."

"Thy grandam," said M. Malesherbes between his teeth.

"Very well. Grandam said she'd sent the beggar away with a flea in his ear, and was walking on her way when she was stopped by the duc on his brown horse. 'And what was that man I saw thee a-talking with, my dear?' says he, and 'a beggar-man,' says she, and 'dids't thou give him alms?' says he, and 'no,' says she, thinking the answer please him. Well. Down with his riding whip across her shoulders and a look on his face, said grandam, like there was a hound of Hell at his horse's feet and not my grandam at all. So she screams and cries for mercy, and he draws back the whip and wipes his face with his kerchief and says that no beggar is ever to be turned from his door, but fed and warmed and offered whatever'd please him."

Philiberte Malateste nodded heavily. "My mother once told me a like tale concerning monsieur's father. Louis-Alexandre François Guillaume Maindur de Malvoeux was a godly man, a saint among men. 'Tis said that he wept when his carriage ran down a peasant's child and gave the father a whole livre in compensation."

"The old duc," said Pierre Arroseur suddenly. "The old duc was a great man for plants." He sighed again, a sigh of such longing as Adam might have sighed when he held little Cain and Abel on his knee and told them tales of Eden. "Ranunculus," he said. "Tulips."

"There," said Jacques Ministre. "Perhaps, Artide, monsieur means well by this beggar after all."

"Buggery!" Menée blew his nose into the fire. "I'm with friend Desmoulins here: our duc means to hang him, even if the old cow-skin's the prince of sorcerers in disguise."

Mère Boudin sat up very straight. "Happen he is. The Forêt des Enfans is thick with fairies and spirits still. Why not a sorcerer? Happen he's kin to that ogre lived there once, who ate his way through six villages—the one our own Jorre Maindur cut into pieces four hundred years since."

"Aye," said Jean eagerly. "Maybe he's a loup-garou with a taste for noble flesh."

"An old wives' tale to frighten babies," sneered Artide. "More likely he's monsieur's old tutor, turned off like M. LeSueur, and fallen to begging in his old age."

Philiberte Malateste tutted. Jacques Ministre threw his hands aloft, and Malesherbes remarked acidly that if Artide kept talking like that, 'twas even more likely that he himself would be begging his bread before he was much older. Artide called Malesherbes a damned Italian eater of mushrooms, and the parley turned into a mêlée. At last Pierre Arroseur stood up and stalked out of the tavern, followed by Estienne Pyanet, who left the door open behind him. Yves Pyanet ran to close it, but not before a chill wind fluttered the fire to a flame and set us all shivering.

The Curse

When I was a little child, my mother told me that the man in the moon had been sent there by le bon Dieu because he would not cease his labors, even on Sundays and feast days. God taxed him with his sacrilege, whereupon he replied that he was a poor man and had all he could do to keep his family in radishes and black bread when he worked every day in the week. Nevertheless, he promised to try and keep the sabbath. And try he did; but things just kept turning up that had to be dealt with. Three times God pardoned him: when he hoed the weeds that were choking his cabbages; when he mended a hole in his hedge; when he wandered the fields in search of his goat.

Then one cold Sunday God caught the man gathering a faggot of thorn for his fire instead of attending Mass and lost His divine temper. "For that thou hast not obeyed Me," He thundered, "I will remove thee altogether from the face of the earth. Thou shalt live in the moon, thou and thy faggot of thorn, and roll her each night across the sky. When rest was lawful did'st thou refuse it; thou shalt not rest again until the Day of Doom." And so it came to pass.

The man's name, maman said, was February.

This tale made little sense to me until I spent a winter in Beauxprés, when I came to feel a deep sympathy for M. Février and his faggot of thorn. Winter in the mountains is as different from winter in Paris as chalk is from cheese. In Paris, the cold lasts only from December to March, and there are balls and entertainments and theaters and salons to distract you from the weather, and plenty of wood and coal (if you can afford them) to keep the fires burning high. In Beauxprés, the first snow falls at the end of October and the last in early April, if we're lucky. Out of doors, there's wind and storm and roads frozen hard as stone, so that we must go about in sleighs if we go about at all. Within, draughts fairly whistle among the tapestries, and the constant damp makes the fires balk and madame's gowns slick and musty. The days are short and dark, and to brave the steep path to the village is to risk a broken leg or worse, so that monsieur's servants sicken of one another's glum faces and bicker like children.

Jean always laughs when I complain about winter in Beauxprés. I should've come out to the stable, he says. Then I'd know what cold and damp really are. 'Tis not so bad sleeping with the horses—you always know where you are with horses, and they make quiet, warm bedmates. Undemanding, too. But mucking out frozen straw and tearing the skin from your fingers on the icy metal of the harness buckles—musty gowns are nothing to that!

That's as may be. Stable and château, indoors and out, each one of us was tried in his own way. But among monsieur's household, none was so sorely tried as the bird-keepers, whose task it was to keep monsieur's tropical birds from dying of the cold.

Le bon Dieu had cause, if He'd a mind, to send the bird-keepers to help M. Février with the moon; for they worked like ants, Sundays and Saints' Days and all, hauling wood from the great stacks among the outbuildings and feeding it to the Gargantuan furnaces, the stoves and wheeled braziers that heated the aviary. Come February, with two more months of cold still ahead, they were out in the forest daily, eking out their damp and dwindling fuel with windfalls while Noël Songis nursed a pack of unhappy, molting, wheezing birds whose blood God had made for warmer climes.

Although 'twas the same every year, I did not witness it often, for of habit madame and monsieur lived in the rue des Lions from Christmas until Lent. In January of 1777, however, the damp that threatened the parrots with pneumonia seeped into Linotte's chest as well, striking the child so dangerously ill that Jacques Ministre wrote monsieur that his daughter was dying. Monsieur, wig-deep in scientific discourse, referred the matter to madame, who sighed once for Mme de Bouffler's rout and bade me pack and order the berline.

Despite fur robes and a brazier in the sleigh, our journey to Beauxprés was anxious, protracted, and prodigiously cold. Madame could neither rest nor eat for worrying that we'd not arrive in time, although how she intended to help her daughter once we got there was no clearer to her than to me. In any case, we made it at last, hungry, weary, and chilled to the marrow, to find that Linotte's fever had broken the very day Jacques Ministre sent his letter. Nevertheless, the child was very weak still and touchingly glad to see my mistress, who declared her intention to nurse her daughter back to health with her own hands. Which vow, to my deep astonishment, she mostly fulfilled, making such ado with lap-robes and broth and lavender-water 'twas a wonder the child did not fall ill again. At the end of a week, Linotte was beginning to grow fractious and madame herself to cough.

Madame fell ill at the end of January. As the days wore on towards the feast of St. Valentine and her coughing worsened, monsieur rode down to Beauxprés at last, bringing with him one M. Berthelemy, a famous physician who'd bled the gout from half the philosophes in Paris. Having studied my mistress' water and felt her pulse, M. Berthelemy let a pint of blood from a vein in her ankle and prescribed for her a tisane of saffron and the kernels of pine-nuts, mixed with a little wine and calomel.

Nursing madame naturally fell to me. I couldn't be with her every moment, of course—M. Berthelemy said I'd fall sick myself if I did not take some rest. So Pompey sat with her during the day, or mère Boudin. Monsieur, he wouldn't come near her, even though illness had made my mistress more birdlike than ever, with flat, bright eyes, scaly claws, a pink and pointed beak, and a staccato cough like a water-bird's call.

At night, I sat my vigil alone. Fever had weakened madame's eyes—she couldn't bear even a shaded candle near her—so I sat in the firelight listening to her breath whistle and creak in her lungs like a leaky bellows.

This illness of my mistress' was hard for me to bear. Not only did I fear for her life, but there were long hours when she did not know me. The sick may be free to say whatever they like, but what madame liked was to berate me. Even as I sat wiping the fever-sweat from her face, she would mutter that I had deserted her, that I hated her, that I was spiteful, jealous, managing, sly. Twenty times I planned to leave, to walk down to the village and beg Jacques Charreton to give me a seat in his cart as far as Besançon. I'd some money laid by—almost two hundred livres—a respectable dowry, and enough to start a business on. I'd be a modiste, I thought, or even a lingère like my mother. I even thought of taking passage to America. There was war there, I'd heard, but also great riches and freedom for all, and no law against hiring a servant with no letter of character.

And why didn't I go? I asked myself the question a thousand times or more. Was it that ancient vow of constancy, sworn by a child to a child weeping in the night? Bah. I'm not so much a sentimentalist as that. Greed? Well, 'tis true that my wages were good—twenty livres a year, paid regularly upon the Feast of the Assumption. My mistress was generous, too, in the matter of castoff gowns and petticoats, ribbons and trinkets. But these were not enough to keep me, had I truly wished to go.

The real answer to the question, then, is that I did not want to leave her. Leave Beauxprés, yes. Leave monsieur, his birds, and his collections, a thousand times yes. But leave madame my mistress? I could not. Habit, need, and affection bound me to her with the strongest of gossamer threads, and in the end I stayed because my place was at her side. I stayed because I could not leave her and still remain Berthe Duvet.

On the night following St. Valentine's feast day, the beggar appeared to us for the last time.

I'd asked Peronel to come at midnight and sit with madame for an hour or two while I took some rest in the dressing-room. Peronel wasn't quick, not like Marie, but she was gentle-handed, quiet, and very pretty. Besides, I pitied the girl. Menée had brought her into the laundry, warmed his bed with her for a few months, and then set her aside. The other servingmaids, naturally enough, made her life a misery, which she didn't really deserve, poor cabbage. Madame seemed to like having her about, and she got on with Pompey. So I let her help with the nursing.

Just before twelve o'clock, Peronel scratched at the door and entered, balancing a tisane on a tray and yawning prodigiously. Madame had fallen asleep. I rose from my chair, stretched, took the tray, and carried it to the fire, which was burning very low. When I'd mended it, I knelt upon the hearth to set the tisane in the coals to warm.

The clock on the mantel began to chime the hour, and the air splintered with a clamor like iron bells.

At first, it seemed no more than a harsh, metallic raving; then, one by one, words clanged through my head: "François Marie Baptiste Armand Maindur, duc de Malvoeux. Come thou forth to thy judgment."

Again the call, drawing me as surely as if 'twere addressed to me. I knelt by the fire in a puddle of tisane and cast an anxious eye toward the bed. Thanks be to la sainte Vierge, madame still slept, though she frowned and whimpered restlessly. Peronel, silly slut, had her eyes screwed shut and her fingers stuffed into her ears.

I rose, took her by the shoulders, and gave her a good shaking. "Watch madame," I told her when her eyes opened. "If she wakes, hold her hand and talk to her."

"About what?" whispered Peronel, panic draining her cheeks.

"Anything—laundry!" Releasing her, I rose and tiptoed out the door and across the stair-head to the little panelled door that gave Dentelle private access to monsieur's dressing-room. I opened it and slipped into a murk that smelled of eau de cologne and birds. A sullen, uncertain glow illuminated the window. My ears rang with fear and something more—the clamor of a thousand bells, bright and dark at once.

Magic?

As I have come to look, look I must, though my legs will hardly bear me to the window. By the fountain of Latona stands the beggar, so translated that I'm hard put to recognize him. His eyes are ablaze, and his staff gouts a scarlet fire in whose flickering light the fountain's half-frogs grimace and contort. The rags of his black cloak flutter in a sourceless wind; his hair and beard writhe about his face like smoke. He's no longer bent or crippled, nor does he look particularly old. The air trembles under the iron lash of his voice.

"Three times have you and yours refused me charity. Three times have you and yours reviled me. Three times have you and yours taunted me. The prophecy of which your father told you being fulfilled, a new prophecy ariseth to take its place.

"I say to thee, François Marie Baptiste Armand, François called L'oiseleur, that, great as it is, thy collection lacks the one bird it must have. Without it, thine estate will dwindle, thy herds slacken, thy wheat rot in the fields, thy ventures miscarry. Without it, thou wilt grow old, solitary, bitter, mad. Without it, thy wife will know no peace upon this earth. Without it, thy sons will have no inheritance and thy daughter no dowry. Without it, the family of Maindur will wither and die."

The beggar fell silent. I waited for monsieur to answer him, to laugh and tell the old goat that curses count for nothing in an Age of Reason. But the duc de Malvoeux only leaned his hands upon the balcony railing.

The beggar—the sorcerer, I should say—lowered his voice, so that I must strain to hear him. "As thy daughter hath shewn some impulse of kindness towards an old beggar, so will the old beggar shew some pity for her sake. The bird is the Porcelain Dove; look for it in the Fortunate Isles." He laughed, showing sharp white teeth; above them his yellow eyes stared expressionless. Then, like a snuffed candle-flame, he was gone.

As if the sorcerer's words had turned us to stone, monsieur stood on his balcony and I in my window. Like the afterimage of lightning, the sorcerer's form was emblazoned on my eyes, and I could no more turn from it than I could sprout wings and fly up to where M. Février trundled the moon across the sky. Then I became aware of the stars again, and the courtyard lying cold and still in the moonlight. And I remembered madame and what monsieur would say if he caught me spying.

I groped my way blindly through the panelling, and was stumbling across the stair-head when monsieur threw open the door of his apartment. So pinched and set was his mouth and so fierce his eyes when they fell upon me that I feared at first that he'd heard me in his dressing-room. Expecting a blow, I cringed when he raised his arm; but he only put me blindly aside and stalked past me down the stairs.

Trembling, I returned to madame's chamber to find my mistress asleep with Peronel sitting beside her, holding her hand and murmuring.

"Now, you starch thread-lace with sugar-water," she was saying. "But sugar-water doesn't work at all on blond, which takes—"

I must have made some noise, for Peronel started violently and clapped her free hand over her mouth to stifle a scream. When she saw me, she crossed herself. "Why, Berthe! You're white as your fichu. In the name of le bon Dieu, what have you seen?"

Although two hundred years later I can quote the beggar's words as he said them; although I can describe quite accurately how monsieur's peregrine eye fixed upon and dismissed me; although these words and events were even then fresh imprinted on my senses, I could not answer her.

In Which the Quest
for the Dove Begins

The next morning when M. Berthelemy came into madame's chamber, I endured two minutes of his airs and graces before I excused myself to break my fast, leaving poor Peronel as chaperone.

The kitchen, not remarkably, was as frantic as a hen-coop when the fox has been and gone. M. le duc de Malvoeux employed upwards of a hundred and fifty souls to serve him at Beauxprés, and I vow every one of them was in the kitchen that morning, waving his arms and getting under the feet of the cooks. I was pushing my way to the hearth in quest of porridge when Marie seized my arm.

"Did you see him, Berthe? Did you see the sorcerer? To be sure, 'twould be a wonder if you had not—all the rest of us did, including the dog-boy and Dentelle, though none of us saw anyone else seeing him. Well, how could we? We were so frightened, you see, except for Jean, who'd seen him before, though not like *that*, bien entendu, and was not so thunderstruck as the rest."

"Well . . ."

"I've heard of sorcerers, of course, who hasn't? But I never dreamed they still walked under the sun, or rather the moon." She shuddered delightedly. "To think that I'd live to see such a thing!"

"Did you say everyone saw the sorcerer?" I asked stupidly. "I don't understand. How could they?"

Marie shrugged. "Magic."

"Magic."

There 'twas again, and however much I might want to deny it, I could not. With my own ears I'd heard the sorcerer's iron voice; with my own eyes I'd seen the bale-fire in his eyes. And these others had seen and heard him, too. The sorcerer must be real. And if the sorcerer were real, then the wand of the Fairy Friandise, the White Cat's dog, the superstitions of the villagers, even Mlle Linotte's maze, these might be real as well. And where did that leave our Age of Reason?

"Ah, bah, Marie," I said, and shook off her hand, thinking that the reality of magic is not a subject to be contemplated on an empty stomach. Mine was as empty as a lover's vow; and what with the cooks too distraught to light a fire, I despaired of finding anything to fill it with. Yet I managed to unearth the end of a wheaten loaf and a sup of milk at last, and retreated with my booty to the back kitchen, hoping for solitude. Instead, I found M. Malesherbes eying a large, fluffy omelette with intense loathing.

"Ah, Duvet," he greeted me sadly. "I do not know whether I shall ever be able to eat again. First, monsieur descends upon me in the dead of the winter without any manner of warning, bringing with him a physician who pronounces my sauces too peppery and my meat undercooked. Bloody meat heats the blood, he tells me, and heated blood produces fevers. No doubt he has told monsieur 'tis my cooking has driven Mme la duchesse to death's door, so that from minute to minute I expect to be hauled in chains to prison. And if that is not enough, a madman spouting flames and prophesying doom rousts me out of bed at the unholiest of hours. I am an artist, Duvet, a man of great sensibility," he said simply. "I do not think I can bear it."

Things were indeed come to a sad pass if M. Malesherbes had lost his appetite. I patted his hand and gently relieved him of the plate. "A great artist," I agreed, and cut into the omelette. It had mushrooms in it, and a sprinkling of fine herbs. I'd not swallowed more than a mouthful when Menée LeRoi came surging into the room attended by Philiberte Malateste and Jacques Ministre, both of them long-faced as mourners at a funeral. Behind them was Dentelle, looking, if possible, more dismal still.

When he spotted us, Menée bellowed triumphantly. "Malesherbes! Berthe Duvet! Well met, well met indeed. High and low we've been looking for ye, to talk things over, y'know."

I'd thought to finish M. Malesherbes' omelette in peace and quietly seek my bed. Yet I was curious, too. So I kept my seat.

Menée opened the proceedings by spitting into the fire and saying,

"As long as we're here, we might as well stay, hein? Now, what's to do? Beauxprés crawls with wizards, madame our mistress knocks at the gates of Heaven, and monsieur our master sulks in the library. An owl flew over me this morning when I went out to piss. Soon the cows will go dry and the rats desert the granary. Beauxprés is done for. The only question that remains is: When do we follow the rats?"

Dentelle's thin lips twitched. "You please to jest, Menée, but I assure you this is no jesting matter. A curse upon our duc and his house is also a curse upon us, who are, as 'twere, the blood and bones of Beauxprés."

I sputtered over a mouthful of omelette. Dentelle cocked his nose and glared at me. "Trollop," he sniffed. "Parisienne."

"Leave her be," said Jacques Ministre. "Duvet, you're a sensible girl. What do you think?"

I swallowed hastily. "You speak of wizards, M. Menée. Are you certain 'twas a wizard we saw last night?"

"Foutre! What else could he be?"

"A clever mountebank," I said, "with a grudge against monsieur. Or hired by someone with a grudge—M. LeSueur, for example."

Jacques Ministre nodded thoughtfully. " 'Tis possible, I suppose. Tell us what you saw."

Obediently, I recounted the scene in the fountain court, taking care to tell it as undramatically as possible, explaining that the flaming staff could have been a torch, the clangorous voice produced by a mechanical device, the snuffed-candle departure achieved by a theatrical trick. When I had done, there was silence.

LeRoi stirred in his seat. "A whoreson theatrical trick, eh? I don't know."

"That would account for the stink of old fish," said M. Malesherbes more cheerfully.

"Sulfur and brimstone: the stink of Hell," murmured Philiberte Malateste.

Dentelle blessed himself.

"Such a trick must cost as much as a good bull, or more," said Ministre, ignoring them. "Where would M. LeSueur find the money?"

I shrugged. "He's one single example. Monsieur has made other enemies, I'm sure."

"That don't amount to the fart of a dead mule," said Menée. " 'Tis a curse, depend on it. All old families have these curses. They're like public alms-giving: part of the burden of the title. Without a curse, the ducs de Malvoeux would be no better than plain monsieurs Maindur."

Dentelle bristled. "What do you know of curses? My family has served the house of Malvoeux for centuries. You're a foreigner, a Savoyard, hired a bare thirty years ago. You know no more of this affair than Duvet—which is to say, nothing at all!"

In my current state of nerves, I might have flung my plate at his head had not Jacques Ministre chanced to come between us on his way to the fire. He put his back to the flames, hiked up his coat-skirts, and said, "Calmly now, Dentelle, Menée."

"Sit down, peacock, before ye singe yer tailfeathers," snapped Menée. "I am the maître d'hôtel of Beauxprés, and I say the beggar was a wizard. I've given the matter serious thought, me, and I see no need to carry on like the hen who thought the world was ending. A sprinkle of holy water, a livre or two in the alms-box, and I wager monsieur'll be able to dismiss the whole."

Philiberte Malateste shook his head. "No, Menée, I can't agree. Did ye not hear what the sorcerer said? 'Three times have you and yours denied me charity.' Lack of charity's a heavy sin, Menée, a heavy sin, and seldom goes unpunished. In Lanvaux, where my mother's cousins live, there are barren acres that once were green and prosperous, and all because one M. Richard turned a beggar from his door."

"We've all heard the story, Malateste," said Menée. "That beggar was Our Savior Jesus Christ Himself, and the damned miser must've been blinder'n a mole not to have seen it."

"Nôtre Seigneur came to him in disguise," said Malateste.

"Bugger!" said Menée. " 'Tis the Son of God we're talking of, not some demi-sou saintling y' couldn't tell from a common sinner without a direct sign from Heaven! M. Richard was a mole, I tell ye, and ye're a mule-brained sot if y' think this beggar was Nôtre Sauveur in disguise."

"Saint or devil, 'tis all the same," said Malateste. "Beauxprés is doomed."

M. Malesherbes, who'd sunk into gloom once more, roused himself enough to say, "Unless monsieur finds the Porcelain Dove."

"Unless monsieur finds the Porcelain Dove," echoed Menée. "Just so. And he knows where to find it—the sorcerer himself told him. All monsieur need do is find the Fortunate Isles. A little trouble, a little expense, and monsieur'll have learned to be more charitable in future. A whoreson neat curse, by Christ."

"A neat curse?" screeched Dentelle. "A neat curse? Ingrate! You are unworthy to rule monsieur's dung heap, far less his house! A neat curse indeed!"

A dry voice addressed him from the outer door. "Ah, Dentelle, but it *is* a neat curse—very thorough, and thoroughly unpleasant. Yet it may be averted." As one we started and turned to stare at Noël Songis, who'd entered without our noticing. "Jacques Ministre," he said when he had our attention. "I'd have a word with you."

Menée looked prodigiously aggrieved. "*I* am maître d'hôtel here. Ye ought to speak with me."

"Bon. I'll speak with you all." And without further ado, the bird-handler perched himself upon the settle. Perfectly calm, perfectly self-possessed, he sat upright with his hands upon his wide-spread knees. There was something about Noël Songis—some air of nobility despite his face like an old boot, his frieze coat streaked with droppings, and his hands laced with a thousand souvenirs of beak and talon. Looking at Noël Songis, I knew I was in the presence of a man who thoroughly understood himself and his world.

"Jacques Ministre, you know something about fowl," he said.

Ministre looked more than somewhat puzzled. "A little about chickens. I was born in Bourg-en-Bresse; chickens are in my blood."

Noël Songis nodded gravely. "When do you set the clutch under a broody hen?"

"Mondays, Thursdays, or Saturdays. Never on a Friday, or the chicks'll all be cocks."

"If there's a storm when the hens are sitting?"

"An iron nail in each nest, to ward off the thunder."

"A broken horseshoe works better," said Songis. "Well, you know enough not to embarrass yourself, and my men know everything else." He rose. "Come to the aviary after dinner—we'll talk further."

A thousand questions rushed up to my throat, crowding it so I could not speak. Noël Songis slept with birds and waked with them. Noël Songis knew everything there was to know concerning souimangas and Bengal redpolls. Why not Porcelain Doves?

The hope was not mine alone. Regardless of bird-droppings, Dentelle reached up and clutched the bird-handler's sleeve. "M. Songis," said he. "Can you tell us anything of this Porcelain Dove?"

For the first time in a dozen years, I found myself in harmony with the little valet. "Yes," I said. "Please tell us."

Songis looked at me, at Dentelle (who hastily released his sleeve), at Malateste and at Menée.

"The Porcelain Dove," he said thoughtfully. "I've heard tales of a Porcelain Dove."

This did not sound encouraging. I asked, "At least can you tell us whether the bird is real?"

The bird-handler almost smiled. "Real? Who can tell, these days, what is real and what is not? To lay the curse, how real must the Porcelain Dove be? As real as the rainbow? As real as the beggar? If 'tis sufficiently real to be tempted by grain, I will bring it back to Beauxprés."

Menée laughed angrily. "A philosophe, upon my orbs and scepter. The bird-man is a philosophe."

M. Malesherbes looked up from contemplating the hearthstones. "Are you, too, a sorcerer?" he asked.

Philiberte Malateste's long face darkened. "A sorcerer! Le bon Dieu help us." He crossed himself. *"Vade retro, Satanas!"*

"Yes, Songis, get thee behind Malateste so his farts can blow thee back to Hell. So yer going after the Dove, eh? Well, I wouldn't be astonished, me, if Duvet weren't right after all, and the whole weren't a trick ye and yon beggar compounded betwixt ye just to travel in foreign parts, all expenses paid by M. le duc de Malvoeux. Ye'll be back in a year, I wager, carrying some flea-bit white pigeon ye'll swear is a genuine Porcelain Dove, and retire a rich man."

I'd not slept all night, you understand—had not slept soundly for days. My ears sang with weariness and my patience was a dry well. "I don't doubt that's what *you'd* do," I heard myself say. "You should be ashamed, Menée, and you, too, Philiberte Malateste, with your talk of sorcerers, as though we were no better than superstitious peasants. M. Songis is a man of learning, and he deserves our respect."

Noël Songis smiled outright, while Menée's face went from red to scarlet to royal purple. Malateste said that he would pray for my soul. Dentelle put on his best river-pike face; even Jacques Ministre frowned. I began to regret my outburst. What if Menée exploded from affronted pride, or Malateste from an excess of Christly restraint? Would that make me, I wondered, the first instrument of the beggar's curse?

"Your pardon, M. le maître d'hôtel, M. l'oiseleur, gentlemen all.

Mme la duchesse is asking for Berthe." Pompey's voice, flat and colorless, went through me like an electric shock.

The cheek of a savage cannot pale, the deep hue of the skin concealing the ebb and flow of the blood beneath it; yet Pompey gave such an impression of pallor that I could have sworn that he'd blanched. I remember thinking this—about skin and blood and savages—even as I rose, curtsied blindly to the company, and followed him to the China apartment. I dared not think what might await me there.

When we reached madame's antechamber, Pompey said, "Remember, Berthe. The sorcerer did not say that madame would die."

I could not imagine what he was trying to tell me, unless . . . My heart stopped, then fluttered painfully. "She is dead, then?"

"No." He touched my hand gently. "No, Berthe, not dead, but burning with fever. M. Berthelemy is bleeding her again."

"I remember well enough what the sorcerer said. 'No peace on this earth.' That's what he said, Pompey." And I ran into madame's bedchamber.

Though the sun was risen well above the hills, the room was dark as midnight, the shutters locked, and the curtains pulled tight against M. Février's chilly breath. The fire burned high and hot, nearly smokeless for once. Its flames glinted in M. Berthelemy's lancet as he held it up before his eyes, examined it, gave it a loving rub with a stained cloth, and tucked it back into its leather case. Peronel, looking a little green, was binding up madame's ankle with a length of white linen. A basin of blood was pushed half under the bed. The only sound to trouble the silence was a low railing that might equally have been the fire or madame's difficult breathing.

I heard a low, hoarse murmur from the bed. "François l'oiseleur, bird-man, man-bird. Look hard, yes, hard. . . . Find her, poor child. Oh, look there—*poor* children. So young. So fresh. So . . ."

A cough like the rattling of bones shook her, and M. Berthelemy turned her so she'd not choke on the effluvium. Snatching up a clean basin, I pushed him aside and held it under her mouth.

"Well, girl. 'Tis time you got here," snapped M. Berthelemy in a furious undertone. "Where is all the world? I shouted out the door until I was hoarse, and after a goodly while, was answered by a blackamoor that fled when I addressed it. Tell me, where are the lackeys? Where is M. le duc?"

The doctor's voice was like the ghost of Doucette's barking in my ears—a noise without a trace of substance. I'd removed the basin and tucked another pillow under madame's shoulders before I even understood he'd spoken. "Where is M. le duc?" I repeated. "Did you not hear the beggar?"

"Beggar?" M. Berthelemy's voice rose. "I inquire of ducs and you answer with beggars! What beggar?"

"You slept soundly last night?"

"Bien sûr, I slept soundly—I am in perfect health, me, unlike the inhabitants of Beauxprés. What has my sleeping well or ill to do with M. le duc?"

I opened my mouth to explain and shut it again helplessly. "M. le duc de Malvoeux is in the library," I said at last. "I beg your indulgence, M. le médecin. Ill news came in the night, and the household is disarranged."

"Disarranged? Deranged! Where is this library, girl?"

I looked at Peronel, who was standing at the bed-foot with her knuckles pressed against her mouth. "Peronel, M. Berthelemy wishes to speak with monsieur. Pray have the goodness to lead him to the library."

Peronel's eyes went wide as a frightened horse's before she bobbed an obedient curtsy and trotted out of the room. At the door the physician turned and shook his finger at me.

"My patrons will hear of this, you mark my words. My faith! Beggars!"

"Beggars," echoed madame weakly. "Famine. Pestilence. War. Death."

I leaned over her. Her eyes gazed over my shoulder, filled with tender welcome. I looked behind me to see who might have entered and saw only the flickering shadows cast by the fire brushing the walls with small dark wings. I heard a low twittering. Had madame's lovebirds escaped their cage? Surely lovebirds do not fly in the dark. And lovebirds have no reaching hands, no pain-filled eyes. Lovebirds do not weep.

The room was full of children. I blinked; I shook my head. When I looked again, they were still there, thronging the shadows: nurslings and babes old enough to creep and stand; little girls and boys no bigger than Linotte. They beat the air with beseeching hands, and their cries were like the singing of a thousand nightingales.

"Poor babies," murmured my mistress. "Poor little birds. Yes, yes, I shall stand godmother to all of you, every one. Stop crying now, mes petits, or my heart will break before 'tis done."

She sketched a cross in the air with one shaking finger. *"In nomine Patris, et Filii, et Spiritu Sanctu."* She reached into vacancy and groped frantically over the coverlet, searching for I knew not what. When I took her cold hand in mine, she looked at me at last. "What shall I do, Berthe? There's no holy water."

"No, madame." Panic and grief were thick in my throat. "Pompey," I called over my shoulder. "Pompey, come quickly!" And when he appeared in the doorway: "Pompey, run at once for M. le curé, and tell him madame requires last rites. Hurry!"

As though he'd not heard me, Pompey stepped over the threshold into the midst of the ghostly children. A shadow among shadows, he crossed from door to bed, the children parting like a dark mist before him. Between his hands he held a wine glass filled with black liquid.

"Pompey! Bête! Imbécile! Can't you see madame is dying? Go for the curé!"

Solemn and absorbed as a priest at Mass, he came towards the bed step by step until his foot hit the basin of blood, which slopped a little, releasing a salt-sharp perfume. The children stilled their weeping; their presence weighed heavy upon me and heavier still, a rock upon my breast. Madame gripped my fingers.

"The blood will do," she whispered. "Let them approach."

"Their time is not yet, Adèle," said Pompey gently. "Nor thine. Thou hast sworn and blessed them. For now, 'tis enough."

"No."

"Yes." He brushed past me, lifted my mistress upright with one arm behind her shoulders, held the wine glass to her lips. "Drink, Adèle," he said, and to my amazement, my mistress drank what he gave her, sip by sip to the very dregs. He laid her back upon the pillows, then squeezed my arm and nodded towards the antechamber.

I heard the outer door open. A voice—M. Berthelemy's—shouted: "Softly, M. le duc! Softly, I say!"

Pompey scooped up the basin of blood and faded into the shadows.

Monsieur strode into the room. "Pah! What a stink of blood." He jerked back the curtains and, with a great rattle of bolts, threw open first the shutters and then the casement to the cold, clean air.

"Have a care, M. de Malvoeux," wailed M. Berthelemy. "A

draught is of all things the most injurious to the health of an invalid."

Monsieur spun on his heel. "An invalid? You told me my wife was dying, perhaps already dead." He was pale and red-eyed, clothed in a cream silk gown over yellow velvet breeches, with a black nightcap over his shaven poll. Confronting the doctor with his chin in the air and one hand cocked on his hip, he might have been own cousin to the African cranes stalking under the orange trees in the aviary.

"Not dead, but certainly dying. Pray close the window, m'sieur, and call a priest, if you believe in such things. Medical science cannot save her."

"Medical science has killed her."

M. Berthelemy drew himself up as tall as he'd go, which brought his eyes almost level with monsieur's nose. "I'll not bandy insults with a man bereaved," he said. "Neither will I burden a house of mourning with my entertainment. Pray order a carriage for me—or a sleigh, or whatever vehicle may safely hazard these mountain roads in winter. I wish to be in Besançon before nightfall."

"Out," said monsieur.

M. Berthelemy bowed and left.

Rubbing his face wearily, my master came to stand by the bed and looked down upon my mistress. Me, I studied him. He'd a rigid face, not like madame's, which reflected the complexion of her heart and mind like a glass. For all the emotion my master showed, he might have been watching a dull play; and yet I felt an energy of rage and grief in him that might, had he released it, set off a storm of fire. I'd opened my mouth to say something, le bon Dieu knows what, when he frowned and touched my mistress' wrist, then uttered a noise like a bark. Reluctantly, I lowered my eyes to the woman lying between us, and my heart emptied.

As I knew myself mortal clay, I knew that my mistress was dead. She lay among the pillows just as Pompey had left her, her face calm and young, with no furrows of pain to age it untimely. Her cracked lips were parted, their low muttering stilled, and her breast no longer heaved with labored breathing. Was she with the children now, I wondered, comforting them? I'd pray for them too, when I offered my prayers for her soul.

A strand of hair that had escaped the nightcap lay lank across madame's sunken cheek. I smoothed it back gently; she sighed and turned her head into my hand.

Tears welled in my eyes. I looked up at my master, who threw

back his head and laughed. "Alive, by damn! No thanks to our fine
M. Berthelemy, who cannot distinguish a sleeping woman from a
corpse. I'm minded to pay him half his fee, and let the other half be
forfeit to his unseemly haste. But then he would stay to argue, and
I've no time for arguments. No time, no time at all, if I'm to find the
Porcelain Dove."

And out he went.

Pompey popped his head around the dressing-screen and said,
" 'Either the patient will turn up her toes or she'll return your love.
I'll stake my reputation as a doctor on it.' " Then he flourished me a
bow and began to caper about the room.

I gaped at him. Here I'd been weeping for a tragedy. Had the
play been a farce all along? Hastily I stooped to my mistress' mouth
to assure myself she breathed. A faint warmth touched my cheek. I
stood upright.

"What did you give her?" I asked.

At the open window, Pompey halted his dance in mid-spin to
pull the casement shut. "The fresh air smells sweet, but enough's
enough: no need to freeze the poor lady's blood."

"Nom de Dieu!" I whispered furiously. "I asked you what you
gave her, Pompey."

"Oh, nothing out of the way. Just a glass of red wine laced with
three drops of blood from the left ear of a black cat."

"Nothing out of the way! And why did you not bleed this cat
before and save madame the torment she's been suffering? Did her
coughing amuse you, hein? Was it revenge for wearing a silver collar
like a dog and being called ape and baboon? Madame the mother of
my mistress was right: you belong in the stables!"

By this time I was trembling in every limb as though madame's
fever had leapt from her veins into mine. Sobered, Pompey answered
me gently. "I learned of the physick only yesterday, from an old man
I met in the Forêt des Enfans."

"Another sorcerer, no doubt," I snapped. "You're a kind of
wizard too, aren't you? Tell me, M. le sorcier, what do I smell of now,
eh?"

Pompey shrugged. "Grief and peppermint. You are very tired,
Berthe. Go to bed, or lie down in the dressing-room. I will watch by
madame."

All at once I was on the edge of tears. "I don't understand what's
happened here. I'm not even sure I know what's happened. Beggars,

doves, black cats, curses, ghosts: 'tis more than I can bear, Pompey. By Saint Colette and all the angels, 'tis more than I can bear."

To my great astonishment, the boy put his arms around me. To my greater astonishment, I laid my head against his shoulder and wept there as comfortably as if he'd been my own son. He said nothing, did not hum or rock or pat my back, just stood and held me until my sobs grew less. Then he released me and went to madame's bedside.

How present and near that scene is: as present as the books and tables of this library, as near as the cramp in my hand, or as Colette, reading with her dark head inclined towards the page and her dark eyes blind with concentration. Watching her, 'tis hard to credit that she was one of those same ghostly children I have just described.

What does she recall of that scene, I wonder? Did she take comfort from madame's blessing? Did she rejoice at monsieur's ravings? Did madame's return to life enrage her vengeful soul? Did she observe these things to remember them, or was she insensible to all save her own animating pain? I feel it is indecorous to ask her outright. Yet I long to know what memories we share; if among them is this vision of Adèle asleep, her wasted hands and face bone-white against her pillows, and my lost Pompey watching tenderly over her, still and precious as an ebony statue.

I slept for a day and a night. When I woke the second morning, much restored, I sent for Peronel to help me change my garments from the skin outwards and brush out my lank hair with flour. She was agog to talk over M. Berthelemy's sudden departure and madame's no less sudden return from the foothills of death. I fear she had no joy of me, for I had as little to say as I had much to think on.

In the sober light of a new day, I found I could not believe in magic. I know better now, bien sûr—I know many things I didn't know when I was young and pig-headed and reasonable. Then, I discovered twenty explanations for my vision of the ghostly children —lack of sleep, fear for madame, the close, fetid air of the sickroom —all of them very, very reasonable. As for Pompey's tincture of cat's blood, madame's fever had run its course, and 'twas surely chance that caused it to break just when he gave her to drink.

And the beggar? Well, the beggar remained. Pig-headed as I may have been, I could believe in one sorcerer, particularly when I'd seen him twice.

Of a surety monsieur believed in him. Like St. Paul upon the road to Damascus, his eyes had been dazzled by faith, and he lived by the beggar's gospel from that day forth. Oh, he called it scientific curiosity and common prudence, but you may trust me 'twas nothing of the kind. Is it prudence to send a groom posthaste to Marseilles in the middle of February when the roads are deep in snow over treacherous ice? Is it prudence to offer a reward of ten thousand livres for the capture of a single bird? Of course not. Nor is it any kind of science to consult a pie of prophesying birds and a homunculus in a glass jar about where that bird might be found. Yet while he waited for Jean to fetch his most favored bird-hunters from Marseilles, monsieur did both. I can't remember whether I was surprised or not when Artide told me that the birds had refused to prophesy. As for the homunculus, although monsieur fed it the bloody heart of a black hen, all it did was laugh and laugh until he shut up its jar again.

A week passed, then another. Madame grew a very little stronger. Monsieur sent lackeys scuttling upstairs and down to gather this thing and that from the collections of Maindurs long turned to dust: sextants, celestial globes, an orrery, obscure charts of the seven seas, books of natural philosophy and travel and venery—anything, in short, that might help find a Porcelain Dove. He arranged these things in the library in orderly rows and waited impatiently for the bird-hunters.

There were three of them, the best that money could buy, celebrated throughout France and Spain for their tight nets and their clever traps. Guided by Jean, they arrived in the teeth of a storm, cloaked in snow and shod in ice and mud. Monsieur embraced them in greeting like brothers and drew them into the library before they'd even had time to put off their soaked garments. And in the library they remained, mysterious as wizards, while those of us who had no call to wait upon them took turns squinting at them through the keyhole.

I was among the squinters, I do confess it, and remember thinking the bird-hunters monstrous villainous types. Pompey told me they smelled of sea wind and pride, which made me laugh and answer that I imagined them more likely to smell of horse dung and tobacco. Yet I understood what he meant. Monsieur's bird-hunters cared not a pinch of snuff for M. le duc de Malvoeux and his sixteen quarterings. They didn't even really care for birds, only for hunting them. They spat upon the Aubusson and cocked their mucky boots upon the inlaid tables. They emptied their pipes into their half-eaten food and their bladders into a Sèvres vase. They had only contempt for science, philosophy, beauty, and wealth.

Artide was fascinated by them. "You'd think them princes," he said once, "the way they call for blood pudding and tripes and declare monsieur's green Jura wine poor, thin stuff. And when all's said and done, they're nothing more than rogues in cheap wigs." He shook his head admiringly. "They can't even sign their own names."

For two days, monsieur (still in his nightcap and gown), Noël Songis, and the three adventurers sat arguing over old tales and poring over old maps, plumbing legend and history and rumor for news of the Fortunate Isles. 'Twas Artide's jest that they should be called the Elusive, or perhaps even the Illusive, Isles for not one of those far-traveled men had the least idea where they lay. What they'd more than enough of, however, was theories.

The oldest of the bird-hunters argued that, most northern birds being white, the Porcelain Dove was likely from one of the tiny uncharted islands under the Arctic Circle. Another had hopes of the abundant archipelagoes of the Southern Seas. A third, more mystical, spoke of the fabled lands of the West: Hy Brasil and Avalon.

Noël Songis took no active part in this grand parliament. According to Artide, he was the only one of the lot who behaved like a sane man, quietly studying maps in a corner, leaving the library to take his meals, to make water, and to sleep. When monsieur appealed to him for his opinion, Songis replied simply that he would journey east.

For two days, the bird-hunters shouted and belched and fouled the air with their heavy tobacco. On the third day, the library stood empty—except for a monstrous litter of ash and mud and fragments of bread and meat—and the bird-hunters, their pockets heavy with de Malvoeux gold, were scattered to the north, south, and west. A day later, with no fanfare, Noël Songis rode east, accompanied by Jean Coquelet.

All the household was astonished that Jean went to Cathay. Jean, who before he went to Marseilles, had never ventured further afield than Besançon, and that only seldom. Oh, the fairy tales he told when anyone questioned him about it! He'd dreamed of a beautiful Eastern princess; Noël Songis had enchanted him; he'd eaten opium in Marseilles. Such tales were amusing, and served their purpose, which was to confound the curious. To me, who has known him longer than any living soul, to me, Jean has told the truth.

He asked Marie to marry him and Marie accepted. This was just before the beggar's curse, you understand, when madame was at her worst—not at all an auspicious time for a betrothal, but what would you? That's when Jean made up his mind to marry, and that's when he went with Marie to ask permission of Jacques Ministre, who sent them to Menée, who sent them to monsieur, who looked down the length of his nose and said they were welcome to do as they pleased. Their marriage had nothing whatever to do with him. He'd keep no married servants in his house.

Jean vows upon his mother's soul that he was prepared to risk the world outside, set himself up as a carter perhaps, move to Besançon or even Dijon. 'Twas Marie, he says, who demurred, who argued that her savings were too small and the city too cruel a place for country folk—for that, I fear her trips to Paris were to blame. She might have given over in the end, married him in monsieur's nose and died a carter's wife. But before she could screw up her courage for the change, Jean, heart-sore and angry, had ridden east with Noël Songis. He was gone for seven years, braving hardships and dangers among men who were yellow as jaundice and chirped when they spoke. At least that's what he says. Not having been there myself, I can't call him a liar.

After the bird-hunters had left, monsieur's first act was to visit madame. Fortunately, I was there to prevent him. Fortunately, I say, for after three sleepless days and nights, the duc was a wild man. His cheeks were dark with stubble, his eyes red-rimmed and wild, his nightcap smeared with some foul-smelling liquor, the cream gown cream no longer, and the shirt under it might have been used to wipe up after the sacrifice of the black hen. In short, his appearance alone was enough to throw a more robust woman than my mistress into strong convulsions. As soon as I set eyes on him, I closed the door of the bedchamber and barred it with my body. Monsieur, hands twitching impatiently, came inexorably on.

"Stand aside, girl." Monsieur's voice was low and harsh.

I shook my head stubbornly; in truth, I doubt I could have moved, my belly and legs were quaking so. "Madame is still very weak," I said. "She must not be alarmed."

Monsieur glared at me with a bloodshot eye. "Bien sûr, she's weak—that's why I've come, to strengthen her. Beware how you presume on my good nature."

Monsieur's good nature! As well presume on a wolf's lack of

appetite or a hawk's short sight. He stepped very close to me, so close that I could smell the blood and stale perfume upon him.

Heaven alone knows what indignity he might have visited upon me had not Dentelle appeared just then at the door and whimpered, "Oh dear, oh dear. Will m'sieur not let me shave him? Or put on his wig? May I bring m'sieur fresh linen, at least? Please, m'sieur?"

Monsieur turned to stare at him, then rasped his long nails over his cheeks and chin, said, "The razors, and swiftly," and stalked from the room with the little valet wringing his hands at his heels.

A good three hours later, the duc de Malvoeux presented himself a second time at his wife's chamber. He was bathed and shaved and smelled of lilies, resplendent in a freshly curled wig and an azure satin coat over a peach-colored waistcoat embroidered with bluebirds. His breeches were a shade deeper blue than his coat and his stockings were primrose yellow. At his elbow a lackey bore a covered basket and a heavily gilded folio volume, which he carried into the bedchamber and arranged on a table by the bed before bowing himself out. I withdrew to madame's dressing-room where I could be out of sight and yet within call should madame need me. Out of monsieur's sight, that is: I made sure I had a clear view of the bed.

The covered basket contained a bunch of grapes that monsieur peeled one by one and popped into my mistress' mouth. More magic, I thought, to command grapes in February. But this was the magic of wealth, a magic easy to understand; after all the mysteries of the past week, I found it oddly comforting. I was comforted, too, by the mildness of monsieur's voice inquiring after my mistress' health, begging that she would forgive his late neglect and explaining that he'd been preoccupied with fitting an expedition for a particularly rare specimen.

"The search will, I fear, be costly, for I am not sure of the bird's range and must therefore mount several excursions. In truth, until two weeks ago, I'd thought it a chimera, no more susceptible to trapping and caging than a gryphon or a cockatrice. Now that I'm sure it exists, I shall spare no effort to procure a specimen. 'Tis quite a lovely thing. Look—I've brought a painting of it."

He laid a pillow upon my mistress' lap, opened the folio, and propped it there. She glanced at the picture and said languidly, " 'Tis indeed enchanting. I do not wonder, husband, that you thought it a traveler's tale. 'Tis almost too beautiful to be real."

Monsieur's voice sharpened. "The bird is not yet caught. It will be long and far to seek; we must not expect to see it this year, or even two years hence." He clapped the folio shut and madame started nervously. Ready to do battle, I half rose; but he himself was rising to leave.

"When you are a little stronger, Adèle," he said, "you must go to Switzerland, to Lausanne. I've already written to Réverdil to engage a house and servants. You've always said the air of Lausanne agrees with you, and I've every confidence that the Swiss physicians will soon make you strong and rosy again. You must spend the summer there, and the children as well. 'Tis time they saw something of the world outside Beauxprés."

This news so pleased madame that she began to cough again, sending me to her side and monsieur from the room. By the mercy of God, the relapse was brief, and by April she was well enough to sit on her chaise longue for an hour or two at a stretch and take an interest in her embroidery.

The journey to Lausanne was planned for the beginning of May, which left me little time to prepare. Madame's wardrobe was a shambles. Bodices that had once fit snug and smooth hung loose upon her wasted frame. When she put on her court gown—apricot silk taffeta, trimmed with painted bands and boasting a décolleté that barely covered her nipples—she resembled a little beggar-girl en masquerade. How could she hold up her head before Eveline Réverdil and the fashionable ladies of Lausanne? How could I hold up my head before their maids?

Accordingly, a letter was dispatched to Mme du Fourchet, who responded with a dozen fashion plates, twenty ells each of lustring, Lyon silk, and calamanco, lengths of point d'Espagne and Brussels lace, twenty-five ells of silver galloon and three hundred violet silk tassels for trimming. With these I was able to make do, along with dimity, ribbons, and ordinary blond bought from the peddler. Peronel and Marie assisting me, I remade the court gown and two robes à la française, cut, boned, stitched and trimmed a new polonaise, a petticoat and a caraco, and made a robe chemise for Linotte and a suit of clothes apiece for M. Justin and the vicomte de Montplaisir.

M. Léon was now twelve years and nine months old, a handsome lad very much in the mold of the Maindurs, which is to say that his face was long, his hair black and unruly, his nose fine-drawn, and his lips thin. His eyes were of an older stamp: deep-set, pale, lambent as moons among his dark lashes. If the portraits were to be believed, such wolf's eyes hadn't appeared in the family since Jorre Maindur himself. A handsome lad, as I said, and twice as wicked as the Devil.

M. LeSueur had not been replaced, and the boy was let to run as wild as he would, which by all accounts was as wild as the wolf he resembled. Tales of disemboweled hares and headless cats traveled among the grooms and gardeners, and all within-doors went in fear of his rages and his malice. Poor Justin was his chief victim, and was forever being fished out of the ornamental pond, helped down from trees, rescued from roofs, released from cellars, or untied from wherever his brother had dragged and forgotten him in the course of one of his elaborate games. Me, I saw M. Léon only when he visited his mother, upon which occasions he conducted himself as prettily as anyone could wish. 'Twas otherwise, however, when I measured him for his new suit.

Stripped to shirt and breeches, he stood in madame's dressing-room on a stool and held out his arm for me to take its length, contriving as he did so to brush the back of his hand down my breast. I was startled and a little annoyed, but thinking it a piece of childish mischief, snipped marks at elbow and wrist without remark.

When I held the paper tape across his back, "Are not my shoulders grown astonishing broad, Berthe?" he asked me, squaring them proudly.

"Astonishing broad, M. le vicomte," I agreed coolly, and indeed they were broad for a child, and his chest also.

I passed the tape about his waist, marked it, and moved it down around his hips. Then I knelt to measure his inside leg, whereupon he turned and displayed, not three inches from my nose, a most unchildish bulge in his breeches.

"Pretty Berthe," he leered. "How you blush, just like a little virgin. But then, you are a virgin, or so I've heard. Tell me, ma belle, do I hear truly?"

I primmed my mouth and averted my eyes. "If the vicomte will please to turn around, I can proceed with my work."

The vicomte caressed the bulge. "Here's other work for you, ma belle."

I wished Marie were present, or even better, mère Boudin. If ever there lived a woman who could, with a single glance, stem the rise of a young sprig's sap, Guyette Boudin was that woman. "If you'll not be a good child and stand still, vicomte or no, I shall call your nurse to hold you."

I spoke at full voice, and from the bedchamber, madame called out querulously, "Léon? Only be patient for a little minute, and 'twill be soon done."

M. Léon pouted. " 'Twill not be done at all, ma mère. I don't like her clumsy hands upon me. Tell her to stop touching me."

"She cannot take thy measure without touching thee," said madame reasonably. "Berthe, do make haste. I want your advice on this head. Shall the ribbons be soupir de Vénus, or cheveux de reine? I vow, I cannot decide betwixt them."

Hard as I tried to keep my countenance, my lips began to quiver with laughter and the threat to my virtue abruptly subsided. Swiftly I took the remaining measurements, rose, and curtsied. "That will be all, M. Léon. When the suit's ready, Dentelle will fit it for you. In matters of the mode, a valet's a better adviser to a young man than a femme de chambre."

The vicomte de Montplaisir bared his teeth at me, then snatched aside my fichu and pinched my breast so cruelly that tears of pain rose in my eyes. 'Twas a childish revenge; but his smile when I gasped was not childish, nor the leer with which he said, "Pretty Berthe," before taking up his coat and leaving the dressing-room.

"Your Berthe is as clever with her tongue as she is with her fingers, maman," I heard him say. "Such a girl might have risen to the top of her profession, had she only stayed in Paris."

I came around the dressing-screen in time to see my mistress pat her son's smooth cheek. "Sweet child," she murmured. "Yes, my Berthe speaks like a lady, and is far cleverer than her silly mistress, are you not, Berthe? Now, the ribbons. The cheveux de reine is more à la mode, but do you not think the yellow makes me look sallow?"

After madame had retired to dream of ribbons, I sat late in the Fan room with Marie and Peronel, cutting M. Léon's new coat and breeches out of plum-colored broadcloth. Reflections of our work-candles flickered in the glass cases, so that you might almost swear the mounted fans waved again while the ghosts of coquettish eyes peeped around their lacy or feathered edges, searching in vain for new hearts to enslave.

Snip, snip went the scissors along my chalked lines.

"You'd best make it larger than the measure, Berthe: boys that age grow monstrous quick," said Marie.

I finished cutting a sleeve and handed it to Peronel to baste in a silk lining. The broadcloth was soft and tightly woven, 10 écus the ell at least. "Such fine stuff, to be squandered on a child," I sighed. "He's sure to outgrow it within the six-month, if he doesn't spoil it first."

"Very like," Marie said. "Would you have him therefore go naked? Or dress in leather and russet like a peasant boy?"

"Bah, Marie! What a great silly you are! He'd be known for a Maindur no matter how he was dressed."

Marie took up chalk and tape to mark out the breeches. "He'll be taller than monsieur, I think; his hands and feet are like a giant's. There's no telling how much he's likely to grow when he starts his beard in another year or so."

I snorted. "Another year or so? I wouldn't wonder if he were shaving daily by this year's harvest, and the father of a brace of bastards besides. Our vicomte is a forward lad."

Snip, snip, snip around the little pocket at the breeches front. Marie laughed. " 'Tis you who are the great silly, Berthe. Any peasant boy in a haystack can make bastards. All the world knows that a Maindur proves his manhood by making a collection."

"I shudder to contemplate what this Maindur's collection might be. Dismembered frogs? Wingless flies? Wait, I know. Maidenheads!"

"Berthe! For shame," exclaimed Marie, vastly diverted. "The vicomte de Montplaisir's a wicked child, to be sure, but he's the heir to Beauxprés for all that." She giggled. "Maidenheads! What an idea! I know how he'd collect them, but oh, Berthe—how would he display them?"

"Blood-stained sheets?"

"No," said Marie. "I fancy a bed would be too ordinary for our M. Léon. He'll have a taste for stables and hay-cocks and empty stairways."

"Blood-stained petticoats, then. And a snip of the chevelure mounted beside it, with the date and time collected written out in crimson ink. They can call it . . ."—helplessly, I began to laugh—"they can call it the Bloody chamber."

Peronel, who'd kept very quiet through this exchange, made a sound, almost as though she were going to be sick. I laid down my scissors and turned to see her face puckered and her plump lower lip caught between her teeth. "Why, Peronel," I said. "Never say you're a prude?"

"No prude she," said Marie nastily. "Not LeRoi's precious hobbyhorse. She's only jealous that she didn't think of the jest."

"No," said Peronel. "Maidenheads and Bloody chambers—'tis not a fit matter for a jest, indeed 'tis not."

Marie gaped with astonishment. "Hoity-toity! Pray tell us, demoiselle whore of LeRoi, why not?"

In answer, Peronel threw her apron over her head and began to sob, whereupon Marie flew at her to shake her. I stepped between them; for although Peronel was goosish and had undoubtedly been Menée's mistress, she was also gentle-hearted, and I'd a kind of affection for her from the night of the beggar's curse, when she held my mistress' hand and talked to her of laundry. So I glared Marie down, then knelt by Peronel and pulled the apron from her face.

"Now, now, little cabbage, dry up thy tears," I said gently. "What is it in our fool's talk has distressed thee so?"

Peronel gulped and clutched her apron. "A week ago, or perhaps 'twas two—a fast day, at any rate, for we had salt fish to our supper, I remember. Anyway, I was on the stairs, carrying eau de vie to mère Boudin, and there I came upon M. Léon just below the landing, where the stair is straitest. I stood aside for him to pass me, but he put up one foot to the step above and barred my way with his arm. 'I am a troll and this is my bridge,' he says, smiling with all his teeth. 'Pay the toll or I'll not let thee pass but eat thee up, hair and bones and all.'

"Well, when I ask him what toll I must pay, he answers, 'A kiss.' 'Very well, M. Léon: a kiss will not break me' says I, and lean down, thinking to buss him on the brow. And what do I get but his lips, and they open, and his tongue lapping and his teeth nipping my underlip until it bled, and his hands upon my paps. . . . Oh!" And up came the apron again, while Marie and I stared at one another open-mouthed.

I put my arm about Peronel's heaving shoulders and gave them a hearty squeeze. "What horror, Peronel! Yet a kiss is not a thing to distress oneself over."

"Oh, Berthe, the shame of it! I hardly dared struggle for fear of dropping the tray or waking mère Boudin, who might have stopped him, and might equally have not, or blamed the whole on me."

With an exclamation of impatience, Marie pulled down Peronel's apron and peered eagerly into her face. "Well? Did he? Only twelve years old! Could he?"

"Let the girl be, Marie," I snapped, but Peronel was already sobbing that he could have and he would have, save for the awkwardness of the stairs. "He would go at it hindside before, like a dog, and so I escaped, though I did spill the eau de vie."

"There," said Marie. "What did I tell you? However eager, a child can't do a man's work until he's fourteen. I'll wager he didn't even know what he was doing."

Peronel wouldn't have it so, but wept more heartily than before, and declared she'd even thought of leaving Beauxprés, so fearful had she grown of meeting M. Léon. "And I'd not have you think I'm alone, neither. Elizabel won't stir a step without Eve or Oudette to accompany her, and we all sleep together, though 'tis very cramped."

I soothed her with promises of a new ribbon for her hair and freedom from the vicomte's attentions if she'd only persevere for a month. 'Twas no more than high spirits, I told her, and being mewed up in the country all winter with nothing to occupy him.

"Isn't natural for a boy to be left so completely to his own company," I said. "In Switzerland he'll have more to think about than the arses of servingmaids. Mark my words, Peronel. Two weeks in Lausanne, and he'll be changed out of all recognition."

In Which Madame Adventures Far from Home

On the first day of May, 1777, we set off for Lausanne. There was nothing so unusual in either journey or destination that I should recall the date so particularly, save that monsieur did not accompany us and madame's children did.

I was glad enough of the change, you may be sure, after the alarms of the winter. Although I'd done my best to dismiss it from my mind, the beggar's curse lay heavy on my heart, so that the prospect of Lausanne seemed to me like the promise of Heaven to a soul in Purgatory. There is something about Lausanne that steadies even the flightiest imagination—the clear air, perhaps, or the mineral baths, or the mountains that are more enduring than the most powerful wizard's curse. There are no mysteries in Lausanne, save the mysteries of clock-making and Swiss government, no ghosts, no omens, no Porcelain Doves. And this time there would be no monsieur either, to come between my mistress and me. There were, however, the children.

I cannot expect Colette to understand how very little I knew or cared for my mistress' children—after all this length of time, I hardly understand myself how I had wandered so far from the little femme de chambre who pitied Mlle Adèle because her mother had no time for her. If I thought of madame's sons at all, 'twas with a kind of impatient distaste. They were such a tiresome pair, after all: wolf and hare, devil and martyr. M. Léon existed to torture; Justin existed to be tortured. C'est tout.

And Linotte? Linotte was a very infant still, pretty in the way of infants, with her mother's black hair and velvet eyes. Pompey loved her, itself a recommendation of some weight, and she was a lively little thing, full of strange snippets of tales and fancies. I remember rattling along the precipitous mountain roads towards Lausanne to the accompaniment of Linotte's clear pipe exclaiming over each alpine meadow, each chalet, each beetling cliff and shadowy gorge. She was particularly excited when we came in sight of the snowy cliffs of the high ranges, visible from Beauxprés only on the clearest of days and at the edge of vision. "Magic castles!" she crowed. "Is that where the good fairies live, Berthe?"

"Hearken to the child," sneered M. Léon, who was riding with us. "Magic castles! Have you ever heard such nonsense? Madame my mother, pray tell her to be quiet. Her prattling makes me quite ill."

Linotte thrust out her tongue at him, precipitating a quarrel and a migraine and a rearrangement of the party so that the children all rode with mère Boudin and the sous-chef in the second carriage while Pompey and I bore madame company in the first. Afterwards, the journey proceeded more quietly, and I had leisure to close my eyes and feel the blessed leagues unreeling between me and Beauxprés and the curse. Soon, all would be as it had been, I thought. I'd have madame to myself, and I'd be happy.

The Réverdils had taken a house for us near the north-west edge of Lausanne, in the quiet but not unfashionable rue Devant de la cité Dessus. The house was called Bellevue, and its hire included a garden, a laundry, and a goat-shed stocked with a little herd of milch goats and a strapping red-cheeked goat-girl who giggled when she saw Pompey. Within were ten pleasant chambers, two servingmaids, and a half-dozen boys to serve as grooms or scullions as the need arose. The rooms were well-appointed, and from the salon windows we could see Lac Leman and the white peaks of Mont Billiat and Mont Ouzon beyond. Comte Réverdil had done well by us, I thought. So had Mme la comtesse, who'd made the place quite homelike with a pot of early roses on the writing-desk and a dozen cards of invitation upon the mantel.

Madame blanched upon seeing the pasteboard array and declared herself too exhausted to read even one. She was here to rest, she said, to gather her strength in tranquillity, not to amuse herself. Nevertheless, she took up the largest card, read it through, and held it out to me with a weary sigh.

I searched out the card this morning, and found it jumbled in a drawer with unpaid bills, ancient billets-doux, and long, crossed letters from Mme Réverdil and Mme de Bonsecours. The pasteboard's a little yellowed now with age, the ink a little faded, but I felt as though that long-ago visit to Lausanne—grand mountains, butterfly society, heart-felt pain and all—had been inscribed upon a card a hand's breadth wide, decked with nymphs and shepherds, the whole scribbled edge to edge in Eveline Réverdil's childish hand.

> My very Dear and Beloved duchesse. I am giving a journée—nothing so Stylish as you might attend in Paris, yet I remember your ancient Love of our Swiss Simplicity, and Dare invite you nonetheless. You've no conception how you've been looked for. Adorn my garden tomorrow, Sweet Friend, and you will be sure of meeting any number of your old Acquaintance. Do not Disappoint them, or me, your Ever-devoted—Eveline, Comtesse Réverdil.

"There," said madame. "How can I refuse such kindness? I cannot. If I do not go and drink a cup of coffee at her journée tomorrow, I will appear sadly ill-mannered. Now, not another word, Berthe. You mean well, I know, but the duties of friendship must come before a selfish desire for solitude. 'Tis a certain contempt for her own wants makes a lady amiable, Berthe, and you'd do well to remember it."

"Yes, madame," I said so fervently that she chid me for mocking her, yet smiled as she scolded, gay as I'd not seen her for many a long week. Her spirits rose even higher when she turned to the other cards, all bearing similar messages. Some expressed the writer's earnest wish to divert the so-charming French duchesse from her recent sufferings, some gave her sage advice on physicians, diet, clinics. All were kind. Prodigiously kind. Too kind to be refused. Before I'd so much as unpacked her dressing-case, madame had written to accept, in addition to the journée, an assembly, a musical evening, and a lecture on the history of the cantons.

Next morning, however, when it came time to leave for the journée, she sang another song. "Ah, Berthe, I look a *hag*!" she exclaimed and then, "Mme de Charrière's bound to be there and M. Deyverdun. What on earth am I to say to them?"

To hear her, you'd have thought she'd never been to court or taken tea with the redoubtable Mme du Deffand. And so I told her, somewhat sharply, to which she answered that 'twas not the same thing at all. Then, she'd been in excellent health and looks, supported by her beloved husband. Now, she was alone, weak, dizzy with weariness, and hideous beyond description.

Stifling a sudden desire to shake her until she was weak and dizzy in very truth, I perched a fetching chapeau tambour atop her towering coiffure and said that the paleness of madame's cheeks set off the luster of her large, dark eyes—most women, I reminded her, must suffer themselves to be bled in order to achieve that fashionable pallor. She demurred, she sighed, and at length—as I'd known she would—she agreed to appear at the journée, if only to please Mme Réverdil, who'd been so prodigious kind.

The comtesse had indeed been kind, even to sending a chair to carry my mistress up the hill to her house, which was called Portsûreté. She was awaiting us at the door and affectionately embraced my mistress, when she alighted, upon both cheeks.

"You cannot conceive," she bleated, "how I am enchanted! I hardly dared believe you'd come, dearly though I desired it. I myself am always prostrate with exhaustion for at least three days after the journey from France, and entirely unable to face a soul. Never fear; the entertainment this afternoon is of the simplest—just a few intimates who are equally amenable to a hand of whist, a game of lotto, a charade, or whatever pleases you. You've brought your Berthe, I see, and Pompey. Splendid." The comtesse smiled upon us warmly and took madame's arm in hers. "Now we may all be quite comfortable."

Mme Réverdil's intimates proved to be numerous as the stars of Heaven. Her gardens were like the Palais-Royal on a Sunday, filled with Swiss card-players sitting on rustic benches, French charade-players posturing on the close-clipped grass, and English gossips wandering among the rose beds in twos and threes, sipping coffee between confidences. I gawked at the sight like a grisette at her first play.

"M. le comte is in Geneva," Mme Réverdil was saying, "and half the household gone to attend him. We are therefore amazingly short-handed. Berthe, do you have the goodness to help LeGrand at the sideboard. And Pompey, you will pass a tray, will you not? Come, Adèle. Mme de Charrière has been asking for you."

I was glad enough for a task to occupy me; gladder still of this cozy world in which sorcerers were only to be found in hearth-tales.

I hungered for news beyond Beauxprés; Mme Réverdil's guests hungered for strawberries and cold roast tongue. Between their gossip and the comte's chef, there was plenty to satisfy all.

As I took my place behind the sideboard, a tall, florid woman in a feathered turban fell upon the strawberries with a cry of, "Ah, M. Deyverdun! Look, here are strawberries, 'pon my soul, and as red as a soldier's coat. I vow I know not how Eveline finds them so ripe at this time of year!" She scooped up a handful, regardless of the dark stains they left upon her gloves, and popped one into the mouth of her companion, a stout man of middle years. " 'Tis a pity M. Gibbon's not here to share them with us."

M. Deyverdun swallowed the strawberry and touched his lips with a kerchief. "A pity indeed, Mme Bell. He has been much occupied of late in Parliament, subduing America, he says. What a wretched piece of work the British are making of America, to be sure. The naval strength of Great Britain is not sufficient to prevent the Americans— for do you not agree, dear madame, that they can no longer be called rebels?—from receiving every assistance from the French."

The lady paused with a second berry halfway to his mouth, "They can indeed be called rebels," she said frostily, "for they *are* rebels, rebels against the authority of His Most Gracious Majesty King George. And the sooner they come to realize that, the sooner my husband will be able to return home. To England, M. Deyverdun, which is my home also." And laying the strawberry in her own mouth, she flounced away.

"Tea, Deyverdun, tea," said a slight, fair man at his elbow. "With all the tea those English drink, there's little wonder that they're all mad. Ah, Duvet, Berthe Duvet, is it not?" I curtsied and smiled with a good will. Everyone knew M. Tissot: a neat, nervous man in a plain gray coat with eyes made sad by gazing on misery. The darling of society, he was not above doctoring common folk as well. Once he'd lanced a boil on my thigh and couldn't have been more courteous had I been the queen of France.

"I'll take some of the tongue, Berthe, if you'd be so kind," he said, and then, ever the doctor: "I trust you've been bathing often. Boils are not to be sneezed at, you know, and regular bathing is the only way to avoid them."

Well. A journée is no place for unwelcome truths, so I assured him that I'd bathed head to toe only last night. He smiled, then turned his attention to a plump girl who was tapping his arm with her fan, crying, "Maître docteur, a word if you please!" He nodded politely and she embarked upon a litany of palpitations, lethargy, and melancholy that might have lasted the afternoon had not M. Tissot interrupted it to inquire whether she were accustomed to drink tea. She was just telling him that she fairly lived upon tea when a young man came up behind her and tweaked a hanging curl.

The plump sufferer squealed and jumped. "'Pon my soul, Étienne, I wonder how you can be so cruel, to startle me knowing how the least upset brings on my palpitations."

"A thousand pardons, sister," said the young man cheerfully. "Shall I fetch your salts, or perhaps a dish of tea?"

"No, no tea," said M. Tissot earnestly. "Teapots are evil things, worse than the box of Pandora, from which all evil issued. For teapots do not even leave hope behind but, being a cause of hypochondria, disseminate melancholy and despair."

The girl pouted. Her brother promised the doctor that his sister's teapot should be thrown onto the dust-heap without delay, then bowed and retreated, towing her behind him.

I remember that I thought him an insolent young puppy, though pretty as a watercolor. One may meet a dozen such in an afternoon's promenade through the Bois, all of them alike as whelps of a single litter. I'd not have thought of him again if 'twere not for what happened an hour or so later, when I was going through the gardens pouring coffee from a silver pot for Mme Réverdil's guests.

They were very famous, the gardens of Portsûreté, and I'm sure they are famous still; for beauty is beauty and must remain so, however many years come between. They are laid out in the English manner, with numerous grottoes and arbors overhung with climbing roses cleverly arranged to create an illusion of solitude even in the midst of the most crowded assembly. Perhaps now they shelter great artists or sages contemplating the joys of perfect liberty, equality, and fraternity. In my day, they were commonly used for flirtations.

Under roses and among fragrant ferns, lovers sat or knelt by their mistresses' sides, murmuring verse into delicate ears and searching lowered eyes for some spark of desire returned. Some were glad of the coffee I offered them; some bade me go drink it myself. Others were too engaged to notice me. Among these latter was the melancholiac's pretty brother, whom I discovered on his knees in one of the fernier grottoes fanning a reclining woman.

My first thought was professional curiosity. Where in Lausanne had the woman come by the same striped stuff I'd used to make my mistress' gown? My next was embarrassment, to be thus peering and spying upon an amorous assignation. I was just on the point of turning away when the woman sat upright and patted the lace at her bosom. It was madame.

Well. My heart gave a thud or two, and I'd hardly the wit to step behind a bush and conceal myself among its leaves. The hushing of an artificial waterfall masked their words, but I could clearly see the tear sparkling in my mistress' eye and the sigh swelling the young man's narrow chest. He caught her hand and pressed it to his lips. Blushing, she withdrew it, upon which he looked downcast. She paused, then addressed him animatedly, leaning a little towards him as though scolding him for his impudence. He snapped shut her fan and held it to his white forehead in an attitude expressive of despair, peeping at her as he did so, very like a puppy indeed.

Madame laughed. My mistress—newly risen from a bed of pain, haunted by a sorcerer's curse and the weeping ghosts of children— my mistress laughed aloud, snatched the fan from the young man's grasp, and coquettishly tapped his wrist with it.

I need hardly say I'd no desire to watch the dumbshow's denouement. I prefer tragedies to comedies, with their single, tedious, unvarying plot of attraction, misunderstanding, and consummation. Lovers on the stage are always foolish, save when their passion is tried by unimaginable hardships and glorified by poetry. Lovers off the stage are foolish, tout simple. All that blushing and simpering—bah! Even now it sickens me to write of it.

The journée dragged on as 'twere for three days, until at last the sun began to set and the guests to disperse. Pompey went to alert the chair-men while madame made her farewells to Mme Réverdil. The puppy was beside her, his arm under her hand, and when the chair came, he helped her into it, gazing upon her with his infant soul in his eyes. As I trudged back to Bellevue beside the chair, I caught glimpses of her through the glass, twirling a pink rosebud between her fingers and smiling vaguely, for all the world as if she were stupid with drink.

Knowing she must long for me to tease the story out of her, I declined to mention the puppy, and talked only commonplace as I prepared her for bed, about the beauty of the comtesse's garden and the excellence of the comtesse's table. I might as well have held my tongue, for my mistress was too preoccupied with her mirror to answer me. By the time she dismissed me to my pallet, I was agitated beyond description.

Clearly the puppy had captured my mistress' fancy. More than thirteen years of absolute fidelity to her mad husband, and now to entertain the blandishments of a boy ten, perhaps twelve years her junior! What could she hope to gain by such an affaire?

Even to my sand-blind eyes the answer was evident. Admiration, after all, was the breath of life to my mistress. Doubtless the puppy had compared her to Venus, praised her arching eyebrows and her lithe, white neck. They were worthy of praise—why, time and again I'd praised them myself, trying to distract her from the faint lines her illness had graved between her brows. Yet when I told her she was as beautiful as the dawn, she only protested that she more resembled the twilight and bade me veil her mirror. Not two hours in the company of a pretty young man and she was preening at her naked image in a long glass, dreamily folding up her black hair and then unfurling it over her pearly breasts, her sloping belly, and her round, soft thighs.

"Is this the body of an old woman of thirty?" she had asked me archly. "Would you believe I'd borne seven children, Berthe, had you not seen me brought to bed of them?"

I'd thought her, as always, more beautiful than the Princesse Printanière. But I'd be damned, that night, if I'd tell her so.

Lying on my pallet, listening to the straw rustle with my movements and the patter of the wind through the trees, I chewed the cud of jealousy whose taste was even more bitter than it had been on madame's bridal-night. I'd always known I must share her with a husband. A lover was a different matter.

I arose next morning late and unrefreshed, dressed in blind haste, and hurried so with my mistress' morning chocolate that when I reached her door at last, the tray-cloth swam with it. A faint and tuneless tra-la-la-ing reached me through the polished wood. I scratched for admittance; Pompey opened to me and lifted an eyebrow.

"Berthe?" caroled madame from within. "O Berthe, dearest Berthe. Come hither at once, sweet Berthe, and see what Pompey has brought me."

Twitching my ribbons and my smile into place, I entered. My mistress was sitting by the window in a stream of sunlight with both casement and curtains flung wide and the fresh mountain air stirring the lace lappets of her nightcap. In her hand she held a small scarlet object which she gazed upon with a hungry amazement that wrung my heart like a mangle.

"Look, Berthe," she said. "Only look what the chevalier de Faraud has sent me."

The object she held up for my inspection was a heart, fashioned out of scarlet satin and stuffed plump with cotton wool. A scrap of paper was skewered to it by a long silver pin. The whole reeked most vilely of attar of roses.

"You may read the verses, Berthe," said my mistress, blushing. "They contain no word I need scruple to show all the world."

Unfolding the scrap of paper, I read the following.

> *The sovereign art of inspiring love is thine,*
> *With handmaid arts of gentleness and ruth.*
> *Thy wise heart knows the gaiety of youth*
> *And eke the weight of philosophy divine.*
> *No wonder thy heart falters, when the tooth*
> *Of mortal illness gnaws fast at its root.*
> *Ah! Friendship then, looking before, behind,*
> *Must faithful prove in its fond endeavor*
> *To ease the path this fainting heart must tread*
> *And enlist Art to make it beat forever.*

"Very pretty, madame," I said when I could trust my voice. "I confess the silver pin puzzles me."

"You are laughing at me, Berthe," said madame reproachfully. "Or else you haven't really grasped his meaning at all. The silver pin is me. I've transfixed his heart, you see, like the pin, and he intimates that Love is the cure both of my illness and his pain."

I glanced at her doubtfully, then reread the verses. They might support such an interpretation, I supposed, if the recipient brought sufficient art to the reading of them.

"There's also a note asking if I will allow him to escort me to the musical evening at Mme de Charrière's. He writes that his happiness depends on my acceptance, Berthe. Deprived of the light of my eyes, he strays benighted. What shall I answer him?"

With a fine attempt at carelessness, I shrugged. "Were I madame, I'd tell the impudent puppy that I was a duchesse, me, and not to be won with a few trinkets and a little indifferent verse."

"Indifferent verse? I cry shame on you, Berthe, for making sport of the poor chevalier, who's done nothing to deserve your scorn. Jealous creature."

Though I felt the traitor blood in my cheeks, I shrugged again. "Jealous, madame? I've no right to be jealous, me. Madame might think of her husband, however, before squandering his good name upon a pretty boy barely seven years her son's senior."

I was sorry as soon as I'd said it—not that I didn't mean every word from my heart, you understand, but that my tongue had betrayed my good sense.

My mistress' lips thinned. "Never think, Berthe Duvet, that I cannot find another femme de chambre," was all she said. But coupled with her tone, which I vow I'd never before heard from her, 'twas enough to bring tears to my eyes. Whereupon she bade me not to be an idiot and desired me to bring her lap-desk at once that she might compose the chevalier an answer.

"Replying to a billet-doux is a most delicate matter, don't you think?" she said lightly. "Not too warm, not too cold. Friendly, easy, just a little distant. As you say, Berthe, he must be reminded that I am a duchesse."

An hour or so later Pompey conveyed her note to the chevalier's lodging and shortly returned bearing a brief note tied around a posy of dark blue ribbons.

Madame read the note, smiled, and stroked the ribbon posy with her forefinger. "Such a lovely color, don't you think, Berthe? I believe they're the exact color of his eyes. I shall wear them on my skirt tomorrow."

Over the next weeks, my mistress revealed a gift for coquetry whose existence I had never so much as suspected. She who had always seemed so wholehearted in her passions, so artless in her desire to please those she loved, toyed now with her chevalier as a cat toys with a wounded bird. Now she allowed him to kiss her inside wrist, now she sent him a note informing him that today she was indisposed to see him. She received him lying in her bed—but only when half a dozen friends were present. Worst and cruelest of all, she required me to witness the whole. As once she'd prattled of her husband to me, now she prattled of the chevalier de Faraud, the difference being that this time she knew very well how I hated to hear her speak of him. Each night I tormented myself with waking dreams of his mouth upon her breasts, his ink-stained fingers rifling her most secret treasures while she stretched and sighed. Each night I swore I'd leave her, only to discover the prospect even less supportable than that of seeing the chevalier in her bed.

My only relief was complaining to Pompey.

"How can she not see that he loves her not at all? He loves his bad poetry, the exchange of notes and trinkets and gewgaws. How he smiles and preens when a friend or a mirror tells him that he and she make a prodigiously pretty pair! Though he wears his heart on his sleeve, I wager he locks it up at night with his rings and watch-fobs!"

'Twas spleen made me rant thus. Yet Pompey agreed that the young man stank of self-love. One day he came to me with his mouth primmed up as though he'd eaten alum.

"This is the chevalier's latest gift." He held out a box—silver filigree, with the inevitable slip of parchment tucked under its amber latch.

I shrugged. " 'Tis pretty enough."

He slipped the parchment free, unfolded it, and declaimed aloud:

> " *'While my love from me is parted,*
> *Cruel hours, swiftly flow.*
> *But, that time's law be not flouted,*
> *When I'm with her, journey slow.'* "

"No worse than usual," I said. "What has upset you so?"

Gingerly, Pompey opened the box, revealing two dead spiders on a bed of salt.

I poked one of the little corpses curiously; a threadlike leg broke off. "What grotesquerie," I said. "What could he mean by it?"

"I asked the same of Mme Réverdil's coachman, who informed me that the haut monde has contrived a language of flowers and objects for the purpose of sentimental communication. In that language, salt signifies 'I love you night and day.' "

"And the spiders?"

" 'I love you until death.' Dear Berthe," he said, shutting up the little coffin. "I am sorry for thy pain."

I did not know whether to rage or to weep. So I pulled his woolly hair and sent him away.

———

'Tis clear enough, I suppose, why my memory of that sojourn in Lausanne remains so sharp when other, happier journeys have faded like watercolors in the sun. Jean laughs when I swear that I've forgiven madame her chevalier, and speak of him only in illustration of the change that came over her after the beggar's curse. I'm still angry, he says, like the beggar himself, cherishing my grudge through more than two hundred years, and for nothing more grave than a few silly gifts, some bad verses, a kiss or two, perhaps a brief embrace. I record his opinion because I've sworn to be honest: Colette must judge which of us is right. And while she's judging, she should take into account how strangely madame's children comported themselves in Lausanne. For 'tis my opinion that the family de Malvoeux took advantage of the absence of monsieur to step one by one upon the stage and, like the persons of a harlequinade, declare their characters and their destined rôles: Coquette, Rake, Monk, Sorcerer Maid.

M. Léon, of course, was the Rake, although his dissipations were limited by his tender years. He bought himself an arbalest, with which he shot at every cat, dog, and goat unlucky enough to cross his path until mère Boudin took it from him. Then he took to disappearing for hours at a time, walking, he said, exploring the beauties of the natural world. Entranced with this evidence of her son's sensibility, madame never questioned his absences, and we'd never have known what he was really getting up to had not Linotte run into the garden one midsummer's day to tell us that Léon was fighting with Bernarde in the laundry.

"Bernarde?" asked madame blankly.

"The goat-girl, madame," I answered her, and on the instant, madame started up and ran towards the house. Scattering her silks, I hurried after, calling for mère Boudin to come and remove Linotte, who was trotting curiously behind.

We all reached the laundry at once—Boudin, Linotte, and I—ten steps behind madame, who was clutching the lower half of the door and staring in through the open top. I caught Linotte and thrust her, protesting loudly, into Boudin's arms, then looked over my mistress' shoulder into the laundry.

I scorn to soil this paper describing what I saw. All I'll say is that Marie was wrong. Child as he was, the vicomte was able to do a man's work. As for how he chose to address his mistress, I can only conclude that he'd learned his technique from her goats.

"Oh, my son," moaned madame. "What will monsieur your father say?"

At the sound of his mother's voice, the vicomte started and groaned, and Bernarde gave a great shriek and buried her head in a tumble of sheets. Madame flung her arm across her eyes. The vicomte disengaged himself, did up his clothes, and floundered out of his nest of linens. His cheeks were scarlet with exertion; his expression was half-proud, half-sullen, and wholly unrepentant. Bernarde turned over onto her back, pulled down her skirts, and howled.

Madame lowered her arm. "Slattern!" she cried. "Putain! To seduce an innocent child!"

Bernarde commenced to wring her hands so hard I thought she'd wrest them from her wrists. M. Léon laughed aloud. "Ah, ma mère," he said. "You must not call my Bernarde hard names. For all of me, she's a virgin yet. And as for being a whore, why, I offered to give her five livres towards her dowry, but she'd not take a sou."

Well, that put the cat among the pigeons and no mistake. Such a weeping and a calling upon the saints and a praying for death to end her torments I'd not witnessed since Boudin had felt a swelling in her armpit and imagined it the plague. The vicomte soon had cause to repent his sauciness if not his lechery, for within two days, he was on the road back to Beauxprés, chaperoned by two stalwart Swiss grooms and the comte Réverdil's own secretary.

'Twas mère Boudin had the last word about M. Léon. "Boys'll be boys," she said as we packed his clothes. "The less fuss made about such games, the sooner he'll forget 'em. All that shrieking and moaning's more like to set him on than put him off, if you take my meaning." She lowered her voice confidentially. " 'Tis not as though the slut can charge him with a bastard, come March. Mère Languelonge salved Bernarde's back when her da thrashed her, and mère Languelonge told me that Bernarde had told *her* that the vicomte knew all sorts of pretty tricks. She'd not catch a round belly from any of 'em, she said, though to be sure 'twas a little painful at first. Ah, he's a fine lad, the vicomte de Montplaisir. A Maindur to the bones."

After that, things grew quieter for a while. Madame announced her intention of devoting herself to her children's education and received the chevalier less often, and more coolly, than she had. Whenever she was at home, she required Linotte and Justin to attend her, though she hardly knew what to do with them or how to instruct them, or, indeed, what to instruct them in. She was so awkward in their company, so intolerant of Justin's inattention and Linotte's restlessness, and so snappish when they questioned her, that I was almost relieved when the chevalier, in a brilliant change of tactics, began paying court to her through them.

Suddenly when he called, 'twas for Linotte and Justin he asked, and spent his calls in finding out their studies and their plays. When Justin admitted sulkily that he liked Latin, the chevalier gave the boy a volume of Catullus and lectured him on the essential purity of passionate love while madame sat by listening with her embroidery in her lap and the tears standing in her black eyes. Then he teased from Linotte the information that she liked birds, and next day brought her a mechanical nightingale made of silver-gilt and studded with bits of colored glass masquerading as sapphires and rubies. It sang only one song, but it sang it very beautifully and glittered blindingly all the while. Linotte stared at it open-mouthed while it chirred and twitched, and when called upon to thank him for it, silently hid her head in the beribboned billows of madame's skirts.

The chevalier contemplated the pretty picture they made together in a kind of rapture. "Petite précieuse," he exclaimed fondly. "I beg you not to scold her, madame. Her wonder is thanks enough. See how she peeps at me, the darling! The image of her beautiful mother."

"Ah, chevalier, I protest you flatter me. I am no more than an ordinary woman, whose growing children announce her own advancing years."

"Never say so, my jewel. Aphrodite, too, was a mother. Like her, you will never age, but remain a goddess of love and beauty when your daughter is faded and gray."

Madame smiled and stroked Linotte's silky black curls. "Do you wish on me an early death, then, chevalier?"

"O madame," he cried and fell to his knees beside her. "Eternal life! Eternal happiness! Your beauty and virtue deserve nothing less."

"Silly boy," said madame tenderly. "Linotte, my love, do thou take thy pretty bird and show it to thy brother. Here, 'tis heavy for thee; Berthe will carry it, will you not, Berthe? And, Berthe, you may stay within and mend the vive bergère gown."

You may imagine that I listened to this exchange with something less than perfect joy. Indeed, I sat locked in a rage so profound 'twas almost calm. Had madame required an answer of me, I'd certainly have thrown the workbasket at her or smashed the nightingale to bits.

As she did not, I only heaved the ugly thing into my arms and stalked off with it, stiff as clockwork and as cold about the heart. That was the first time she'd been alone with him.

Next morning, madame received an invitation from Mme de Charrière for a pique-nique at her chalet, an intimate affair of ten or twenty old friends in honor of the chevalier de Faraud's coming of age. He'd particularly requested that Mme la duchesse bring her two enchanting children on the outing.

As I dressed her, madame plotted nervously. "You'll come to look after the children, Berthe, for mère Boudin is quite impossible and it won't do to have them underfoot all day. They cannot be left behind, for the chevalier has said that he particularly wishes to see me with Linotte in an alpine meadow gathering flowering grasses, like Demeter and Persephone. 'Tis a pretty conceit, is it not? The chevalier is such a dear boy." She smiled at her reflection and tilted her chin to a more becoming angle.

"I shall wear the painted silk caraco, and the English hat trimmed with roses. Pink stockings, I think—the ones clocked with flowers will do—and the rose satin slippers. The party is to gather at the Charrières', and we'll all leave together at ten o'clock precisely. I've commanded a pony cart for half-past nine. Tell Boudin to see to it that the children are properly dressed and at the front door. The blue for Justin, no lace on his shirt, and a simple robe chemise for Linotte, with a rose, no, a blue sash."

When I relayed madame's message, Boudin's nose glowed an indignant red. "Half-past nine!" she cried. "The Devil fly away with half-past nine. I'll be until half-past nine catching Mlle Linotte, never mind getting her brushed and dressed."

"Start chasing her at dawn, then. They must be ready at half-past nine, or you'll wish the Devil had flown away with *you*."

At sunrise, mère Boudin burst into my closet. "He's not there!" she squealed.

"Chut," I said. "You'll wake madame."

She lowered her voice to a thick rumble. "He's not in his bed. Nor not in anybody else's bed either, nor the garden, nor the goat-shed, and somebody's let out all the goats."

"Bugger the goats," I said, none too patiently. "Who isn't in his bed?"

"Justin. The little toad. More girl than his sister, for all he's a prick between his legs. I'd not be astonished for M. Léon to stay out all night. But Mlle Justin?" She shook her head in wonder.

"They're both Maindurs," I said. "I must think what to do. Sit down and hold your noise."

While I pinned a lace cap on my hair, Boudin grumbled gloomily to herself like a sow that's overlain her last piglet. Were the occasion not so serious, I could have been amused. She'd always been so proud of being nurse to Malvoeux: so high with mère Malateste's old gossips, so mighty with the servingmaids. A careful nurse indeed to let her charges run wild, I thought, one to debauch the goat-girl in the laundry, another to stay out all night, le bon Dieu only knew where. And the third . . .

"Ah, mère Boudin," I said sweetly. "Have you checked upon Mlle Linotte this morning? If you cannot produce at least one of her children at half-past nine, madame may begin to wonder whether another nurse-maid might prove more vigilant."

"Cent mille bougres!" Boudin exclaimed and lumbered out of the room, Justin for the moment entirely forgotten.

As it happened, Linotte too was nowhere to be found, although her bed, unlike Justin's, had been slept in. More annoyed than worried, I sat down on a chest to think where she might be. If 'twere madame missing, I'd know where to look. But Linotte was only five years old. What was there to know?

Well, I knew that she stuck to Pompey like a leech. And I knew that Pompey was likely to be in the kitchen at this hour. Which is where I found him, eating cheese and drinking ale in the company of the French sous-chef.

Without preamble I announced that M. Justin Maindur had dis-appeared from the house during the night, and Mlle Linotte as well. "You'll need to find them quickly," I said, "or madame will be horribly put about. Mlle Linotte's too little to have gone far, and I doubt M. Justin's done anything very terrible, but we don't want either one of them drowning in Lac Leman or falling down an Alp."

"The boy's in no danger of falling down an Alp," the chef assured me through a mouthful of cheese. "The poor half-wit may have run afoul of a cow, though, or been frightened by a pigeon or some such foolishness. Someone will have to go fetch him."

I could hardly believe my ears. "A cow? Fetch him? From where?"

"Sant'âme, of course."

"Of course? What's in Sant'âme? Answer me posthaste, fool, or I'll give you Sant'âme, and painfully, too."

The sous-chef swallowed and took another bite. " 'Who,' Duvet, not 'what.' Père Michel is who."

"And who the great horned devil is père Michel? And what has M. Justin to do with him?"

"Ah," said the chef, wiping his lips. "That I've sworn not to tell."

I glared at him, my ears buzzing with fury. Pompey caught me by my sleeve-ruffle and drew me down on the bench.

"Softly, Berthe," he said. "M. Justin has made us swear, the cook and I, that we wouldn't tell a soul where he goes at night. I think his carelessness releases us from our oath. Père Michel is chaplain to an elderly Catholic gentleman who lives on the rue de Faubourg Saint-Laurent in a house called Sant'âme. Most evenings in the week, M. Justin goes there for instruction in Greek and Latin. Usually he's home by midnight."

"Mon Dieu," I said weakly.

"Exactly," said the chef. " 'Tis freakish and foolish both, but 'tis a freakish and foolish child, after all, the second son of the mad duc de Malvoeux. I'll send a lackey for the prodigal as quick as may be, but I doubt he'll be in time for madame's pique-nique."

I turned on Pompey. "And what about Mlle Linotte? I suppose the baker has taken her on as an apprentice, with your signature upon the articles?"

Pompey frowned and shook his head. "She's in no danger, that I'm sure of, but I do not smell her in Lausanne. Never fear. I'll find her soon enough." He smiled at me then, mischief and compassion mingled in his face. "Yours is the harder task by far."

Telling madame is what he meant: a hard task to be sure, and one I was in no hurry to perform. I put it off as long as I could, but when madame had drunk her chocolate and neither Pompey nor the lackey had returned, I told her how matters stood.

She slammed the cup down on the breakfast-tray with such force that the thin porcelain cracked. " 'Tis too bad!" she exclaimed. "I vow and declare, Berthe, 'tis too bad of them to serve me like this. Here's the chevalier counting on them being at the pique-nique, talking of bringing the fables of Aesop for Justin and how sweet I looked with Linotte in my arms, and now it will all be spoiled and he'll *never* come to my bed, and I'll have endured listening to all that silly verse to no purpose!"

I stared at her. Her children lost, whom she professed to love, and all she could think of was her precious chevalier! Was this some working of the beggar's curse to harden her heart?

"It won't come to that," I said coldly. "The children will soon be found."

"No, no. 'Tis spoilt, Berthe, and were they both miraculously to reappear this very minute, I still should lack the heart to go. No. I must write to Mme de Charrière immediately and send my regrets. I'll say I have the headache, or better yet, that Linotte is sickening for a grippe and I must stay home and nurse her."

"Yes, madame. That's best, I think. You won't enjoy the pique-nique if you're all in a worry."

"Just so. I can't think how the child could be so selfish. I've always been a good mother to her. And Justin, the sly creature. Have I not always said, Berthe, that he was a sly creature? He's at Sant'âme, you said. What's Sant'âme?"

"I've made inquiries, madame. Sant'âme is the home of an elderly Catholic gentleman who keeps a chaplain to say Mass for him, Mass being a hard thing to hear in Vaud, which is a Protestant canton, as madame knows."

"Yes, yes, Berthe. Do come to the point, if you have one."

"Certainly, madame. Pompey says M. Justin scraped acquaintance with this père Michel and persuaded him to instruct him in Greek and Latin. He also persuaded him to keep the whole a secret and to give him lessons in the evenings."

Madame had grown increasingly agitated as I spoke. "Pompey says! And why does Pompey know all this when I, Justin's mother, do not?" Madame's voice rose hysterically. "Why is my son sneaking off to study with some strange gentleman's chaplain? Why are my servants conspiring with him to keep it from me? I can't bear secrets, Berthe, and I can't bear conspirators. Pompey must be dismissed at once, without a character. And you. You knew, did you not? Of course you did. And kept it from me out of spite and jealousy. There's no one here wants me to be happy. And to think I believed that you loved me!"

Well. I stood with my mouth stupidly ajar and my blood freezing in my veins. What I might have said when I recovered, I'm sure I don't know—something unforgivable, I fear—had I not been saved by a scratching at the door. I opened it to one of the Swiss lackeys, he who'd been sent after Justin.

"Please, madame," he said blandly. "A priest, madame. In the blue salon with M. Justin. Requests the favor of an interview, madame."

Before he'd quite finished speaking, "Peste!" screamed my mistress, and pelted out the door, clothed only in her corset and petticoat and a white taffeta négligée that left her white bosom largely exposed. I snatched up a long India scarf from the armoire, and pelted after.

Somewhere between her chamber and the blue salon, madame must have bethought her that she could hardly berate a gentleman's chaplain as she would a cook who'd burned the roast. When I entered the salon, she was giving her hand to a broad man in a black cassock and smiling on him with chilly graciousness. Any French priest would have known to kiss the hand and tremble at the smile. Père Michel only held the one gingerly between his thumb and forefinger for a moment and briefly returned the other. He was a lumpish man, all pendulous jowls and eyes that retreated under his brows from the sight of so much bare flesh.

I laid the scarf around my mistress' shoulders. Impatiently, she shrugged it off again. "My servant informs me you have kindly brought home my straying son. Where is he, I pray?"

Père Michel produced Justin from behind his back and gave him a little push towards his mother, who gaped at the boy as though he were a prodigy of nature. Indeed, I was gaping on my own account, for the child more resembled an anchorite than a French noble's son. Somewhere he'd acquired a rusty black coat that a carter would have disdained to wear, and his shirt was cobbled together out of coarse sacking that must have chafed his skin unbearably. In his bony hands he clutched a missal and—most startling of all—his weak chin was thrust well forward in a stubborn pout.

My mistress found her voice. "Justin!" she cried. "What demon of naughtiness has possessed thee to go creeping out at night like a common thief? Dost love thy mother so little that thou would'st shame her before a stranger? And what"—this in a wail, a true cri de coeur—"what on earth has become of thy clothes?"

Justin lowered his eyes and hugged the missal to his narrow chest as though he feared she'd snatch it from him.

"Justin, I have asked thee a question. Where camest thou by that . . . that hair shirt?"

Père Michel, his eyes sternly averted from madame's heaving breast, came to Justin's rescue. "He made it himself, madame, in penance for breaking the Fifth Commandment."

Madame crossed herself, then fell to her knees beside Justin and tried to gather the boy into her arms. Justin pushed her away, whereupon she flung herself weeping over the seat of a nearby chair.

The priest, who'd been observing this display with stolid distaste, raised his voice to carry over madame's sobs. "There is no need for Mme la duchesse to distress herself," he said. "Madame's son is a good mind and a sensitive spirit, zealous, and apt to learning. Such a mind requires quiet and order and careful nurturing. A monastery school would most conveniently provide all three, madame, and, as I have good reason to know, the Benedictine school at Einsiedeln is among the finest. I myself, madame, am a product of that school."

My mistress pulled herself up on the chair and dabbed at her streaming eyes with the hem of her négligée while père Michel expanded upon Einsiedeln's myriad virtues as a place of learning. At least that's where he began, moving by degrees as he spoke from the nurturing of Justin's mind to the nurturing of his soul, and from the possibility of Justin's making a fine scholar to the probability of his making a fine monk. Monsieur would have wrung the priest's goiterous neck before he'd uttered a dozen words, but madame only shrank back in her chair and stared at him piteously.

"Enough, enough," she cried at last. "Let him go to Einsiedeln, then, only do stop *talking* at me."

For the first time, Justin spoke. "God will reward you, madame," he said. His voice was thoroughly smug.

I've lived in Justin's company for upwards of two hundred years, now. He is not a simple man, to be sure—no Maindur is simple. Nor is he an easy man to like. Yet he is no longer that sorry, sniveling child who was adamant as only the weak are adamant, who declared that God would reward madame for giving her son his heart's desire. In his own way, he was as proud as his brother. For what is it but pride, to do penance for a sin one fully intends to go on committing? Almost I preferred M. Léon's cheerful impenitence. But there: between his brother's attentions and everyone else's indifference, Justin had led a dog's life. Who would blame him for wanting to get as far from Beauxprés as the width of Switzerland and the height of the Alps could take him?

While we were still goggling at Justin, Pompey entered the blue salon, muddy to the eyebrows and with pine needles starting from his hair. In his arms he bore a grubby urchin clad in a filthy, torn nightdress that smelled strongly of goat. One small, bare foot ran with blood; but she was smiling, and so was Pompey. Linotte was found.

When madame caught sight of her daughter, her hands flew to her cheeks, her mouth gaped wide in an ugly "O," and she began to shriek aloud.

Père Michel hastily withdrew to the window and turned a wide black back upon the proceedings. For a futile moment, I wished that I could do the same, for my mistress' shrieks took on a mechanical note, and she began to drum with her heels and flail with her arms in a perfect frenzy of hysteria. In twenty years of serving her, I'd never seen her so unconscious of how she looked. The next minutes were a chaos while Pompey and I labored to get her laid down quietly on a chaise. Once there, she promptly fell asleep.

"Pompey, you'd best run for M. Tissot," I said softly. "He can see to Mlle Linotte's foot at the same time, so we can kill two birds with the one stone. Mon père?" I looked about me for the priest, though what I thought he could do, I don't know. To my profound relief he was gone, and Justin with him, hair shirt, missal, and all.

Pompey had set Linotte upon the nearest chair, where she sat quietly bleeding over the straw-colored silk. "Brother's gone with the black man," she said unnecessarily. "Is my mother dead?" She sounded only mildly interested at the prospect and not in the least upset.

I rounded upon the heartless chit. "No, she is not dead, gypsy, small thanks to thee. Where the devil hast thou been in thy nightgown and bare feet?"

Linotte's face set in a stubborn pout. "I was only looking for a bird," she said.

"To be sure. Thou art thy father's daughter for birds," I said, "with thy father's cold heart in thy breast, and not a thought in the world for the trouble thou'd'st bring upon thy nurse. Only regard thy foot! 'Tis cut to the bone. What bird could repay all this pother?"

"A nightingale," she said.

"Did not the chevalier du Faraud give thee a nightingale only yesterday?"

"That stupid thing?" She waved away the mechanical bird with fine disdain. "I only wanted to see if 'twere true, as Pompey told me, that real nightingales sing all the night long without once stopping or singing the same song two times over. So I asked the goats, and they said there were nightingales a-plenty in the high forests and they'd take me there if I liked, but they went too fast and I got lost, and then I fell down and then they found me, but I couldn't walk anymore, so I sent them to find Pompey and they did."

"Ah, bah," I said. "Dost think me as great a fool as the chevalier? I will not believe such lies."

" 'Tisn't lies," she said. " 'Tis truth. Ask Pompey."

Which I fully intended to do. But then M. Tissot arrived at a trot, examined madame, pronounced her overtired, prescribed a tonic and a week of solitude, and assured her that he'd make her apologies to Mme de Charrière himself. He bathed Linotte's foot with hot brandy, sewed up the wound with a length of clean silk, and told Boudin that if she so much as thought of anointing it with stable litter to prevent putrefaction, he'd have her ears for watch-fobs.

"Filth" he declared. "Filth breeds filth, and putrefaction is filth. Change the bandages daily and wash the wound with wine and I warrant the child'll be running about within a week. Mlle Duvet, keep your mistress in her bed for two days, no less, and then let her take some gentle exercise. She may eat what she likes, but as you value her health, let her not drink tea."

We tarried in Lausanne only long enough for madame to recover her strength and for M. Tissot to pronounce Linotte's foot fully healed. We occupied the time with packing and arranging two journeys: M. Justin's to Einsiedeln and ours to Beauxprés. You can't conceive of the letters to monsieur, to the Father Abbot, to the elderly Catholic gentleman who was père Michel's patron begging him to allow his chaplain to convey Justin to Einsiedeln. I played secretary, for madame's nerves were still quite overset. One letter, however, she wrote herself and showed to me, by way of apology.

The letter, to the chevalier de Faraud, was a masterpiece of its kind. The chevalier had been prodigiously amiable, she wrote, to serve as her escort while she was in Lausanne, and she'd vastly enjoyed his company. Equally vast was her regret for the imminence of her return to France, the preparations for which must command all her attention between that time and this. She was confident he'd kept copies of his delightful poems, but in case he had not, she was returning the originals. She beseeched him to display them before a wider audience, and to believe in the continuing good wishes of his grateful friend, Adèle de Malvoeux.

This missive madame instructed me to pack up with the chevalier's poems and gifts—the filigree box, the ribbon posies, the satin heart and all—and convey the whole to the chevalier's lodgings, with the information that she'd not be at home to him when he called.

He called anyway, of course, sent notes and flowers and haunted the rue Devant de la cité Dessus at all hours hoping to catch her as she went out or came in from some necessary errand. It took one week of her returning his notes and gifts unopened to make him go away.

Just before we left, my mistress gave a small soirée, during which Mme de Rivière mentioned that the chevalier had returned to his father's house in Vevey and was rumored to be engaged to marry a rich widow.

"She's fully forty years old," said Mme Bell the Englishwoman, "and plain as a grisette's apron. But all the world knows marriage to be the surest antidote to lovesickness."

"Better to marry than to burn," said Mme de Rivière slyly.

My mistress flushed and the comtesse Réverdil patted her hand. "I hope you do not think yourself ill-used, my dear. We are only congratulating you on your escape. I have it from a reliable source that, as bad as his poetry is, his lovemaking is worse."

In Which Monsieur
Fouls His Nest

When we returned to Beauxprés, 'twas more than six months since the beggar had shown his beard, yet the rumor of loups-garous still lurked behind each tree in the Forêt des Enfans and omens of plague and famine fouled every breeze that blew. Unsure whether to fear for their lives or their souls, monsieur's servants went about in groups of three or four armed with cudgels and pieces of the Host wrapped in clean linen while the villagers hung wreaths of Saint-Jean's wort over their doors and kept a sharp eye out for omens.

Now, curses batten on omens as maggots on spoiled meat, and no man can tell whether the maggots rot the meat or the meat spawns the maggots. A cow dying, a new tax levied, a summer hail-storm, martins flying south before harvest: were these signs of the curse, or signs of the seigneur's uncharity that had inspired it? And if the misfortunes were curse-brought, could a bowl of milk or a consecrated Host left in the byre protect the cows that remained, or were they doomed whatever a man did or left undone?

In the tavern and the church-porch, by the well and in the bakehouse, Estienne Pyanet, Just Vissot, Claude Mareschal, their kin and their wives and sisters argued the point until they were hoarse. Most of them stuck to the old wardings. If a Lenten egg placed on the roof protected it against hail, they reasoned, then well; if it did not, what was the harm? Even Mme Pyanet, who I'd always thought a sensible woman, took to baiting her kitchen garden with a little dish of ashes balanced between the rows of beans, just where a malicious imp would be sure to knock it over. For (she told me when I asked her why) if an imp scatters ashes, he can't do anything else until he's picked them all up again.

When I heard *that*, I hooted with laughter and said that imps of Hell must all be Maindurs, thus to be enslaved by nothing.

"Could be," said Mme Pyanet. "Many's the true word spoke in jest, they say. Laugh if it pleases thee, Duvet. I'm a practical woman, me. Owls mean storm and crows mean famine, and a person can't deny there's been more of both about since the beggar's curse."

To each horse his own stall, as Jean always said. Like the ancients, the villagers sought their auguries in the erratic flight of birds. I sought mine in the erratic moods of M. le duc de Malvoeux.

I'd always thought my master mad, but in the early years of his marriage, the glass of his madness had generally hovered at fair-to-changeable, with only occasional drops to storm. Now he seemed set at rainy-to-foul, and the quarter he blew from varied from hour to hour. If he swept my mistress off to the aviary to nurse a clutch of fledgling widow birds in the morning, at noon he was likely to sweep her out again.

"I vow and declare, Berthe, 'tis too bad," madame exclaimed one morning. "Only see how he uses me, his own faithful wife!" She shook back her sleeve-ruffle to display five purple marks imprinted upon her arm. "He said my voice would curdle new cream, and then he thrust me out, Berthe, flung me out the door so that I all but flew into the duck-pond, and all because I'd walked too close to a souimanga's nest. 'Tis too bad, I say. I should have stayed in Lausanne, where there are those who value women over birds."

"Yes, madame," I said, and almost wished it true. Le bon Dieu knows I'd not wanted to remain in Lausanne. Yet no sooner had I caught sight of Beauxprés glittering at the crown of its green mound than I'd been moved to leap from the berline and flee—to Paris, to Lausanne, to I cared not where, so long as 'twas far from that rank and gilded midden. But Paris was a long walk. And I couldn't leave my mistress.

Madame turned her attention to a bleeding scratch upon her shoulder. "What does he think I am?" she asked me bitterly. "A dog, to be called and dismissed at will? No, not a dog—M. le duc de Malvoeux has no use for dogs. I remember when Doucette died, how he laughed at my tears. I do believe he loves me not at all."

" 'Tis only one of his freakish starts. Madame will recall he's had them before, and madame has always been most understanding."

" 'Tis no more than my duty. And surely you must acknowledge that Louis-Marie's death was ample cause for agitation."

"Bien sûr, madame, although I think beating the mother a curious way of mourning the child. But I refer to the time when the vicomte de Montplaisir dismembered the popinjay, and two years past, when that bird-merchant sold M. de la Varenne the American bluebird he'd promised to monsieur. On both occasions, madame suffered most cruelly."

Madame rubbed her bruises and sighed. "Yes," she said. "What you say is true, Berthe. My husband is indeed given to freakish starts. After being so happy alone in Lausanne, I'm of half a mind to leave him forever. 'Tis only that I cannot bear the thought of packing my things again when they're barely unpacked, not to mention jolting for hours in that horrid carriage. And there are so many things to consider besides! Where would I go, for example, and would monsieur allow me to take Linotte? And what of you, and Pompey, and mère Boudin? How could I afford to keep you? Who would pay your wages? Not monsieur, surely. No." She sighed again deeply, clasped her hands piously at her bosom. "Although he may use me ill, François de Malvoeux is my husband still, and I will do my utmost to be a good wife to him."

How could one breast contain so many contradictory sentiments? Did my mistress love her husband or did she hate him? I think, me, that she herself knew only that she craved attention as a sot craves wine. And if the wine she drank was poor and sour, well, it brought her oblivion as surely as a finer vintage. Time has educated her palate, and circumstance, and the air of our enchanted garden in which untruth cannot live. In those days, however, monsieur's beatings and beratings gave madame's life definition and form. Without a man to reflect, she'd have been as blank as a mirror in an empty house. As I would have been without her.

Despite her bruises, therefore, madame was content to be home. I have already said that I was not. At every step, memories rose to torment me: of madame's rasping coughs; of the beggar's amber eyes; of mère Malateste and her coven of grannies; of the ghostly children. In the village and the château, signs of magic confronted me at every turn, and I had no talisman to avert them. My rags of philosophy didn't cover ghosts; my tags of tragic verse didn't comprehend wizards. I came close to hating, not only monsieur, but every male creature on the face of the earth. And how did I contend with my unease? I found routes through the house that avoided the cabinet des Fées. I laughed at poor Nicola Pyanet and her ashes. I was cool to Pompey and distant with Artide. I quarreled with Marie.

'Twas not a thing difficult to achieve, a quarrel with Marie. The rosy young laundress who'd embraced me so kindly when I'd first come to Beauxprés was rising thirty now, rather plumper than she'd been and not quite so kind. Well, 'twas no wonder, all betwixt and between as she was, neither wife nor maid nor widow, and Jean's departure gnawing like a rat at her heart.

All winter long she lamented, mournful as an owl, and always hooting the one note. "I'll never hold a baby to my breast," she would sob. "I'll live barren and die alone, without chick or child to weep my passing."

One night some imp of misery inspired me to challenge her. "You might have held a baby to your breast any time these last twelve years. I'd say you've gone to some pains not to. Be honest now, Marie: what you really want is a husband. I can't imagine why."

This brought up Marie's head. "What are you saying, Berthe? Any woman must prefer the company of a man to any other. And what is a woman without a man, after all, but a poor, lone, stunted sort of creature?"

"Even as I am?"

"No, no," she protested. "I didn't mean that at all." But her sidelong look suggested that she'd meant just that, though she'd never say so outright.

With an effort I curbed my anger. "Only consider, Marie. If you put what you've saved for your dowry out in the rents, the interest will assure you of a respectable old age. In the meantime, you've a full belly, a roof over your head, all the male companionship you could wish for, an undemanding mistress. What more could a husband give you?"

"Why, a house of my own, naturally. A little warmth in my bed at night. Children. His name, so that I'd no longer be called Jean Coquelet's whore."

"Oh, Marie," I said pityingly. "You'll never get that in Beauxprés. Monsieur has made it more than plain that he won't keep married servants, and the village dirt-arses will take none save a virgin to wife. If you must have a husband, look for him in Paris. A laundress of your skill must always find employment, and in Paris, a man doesn't care if a woman's common as the public way, provided she's well-dowered."

Marie's cheeks grew white as paper, then scarlet. "Cow," she shouted. "Hedgehog! You're no friend of mine, Berthe Duvet. I pray your soul may roast in Hell!" Then she slapped me, burst into a fury of tears, and stormed away, leaving me hang-jawed with shock. After that, she'd not say a word to me, not so much as "iron" or "starch."

I soon repented of my cruelty in speaking so to Marie, for Peronel, though a sweet child, was too young and silly for a confidante, and Artide was beginning to affect an air of philosophical discontent that I found most tiresome. I'd made an enemy of my only friend without even the poor comfort of knowing myself to have been right. For in March of 1778, Marie achieved her heart's desire in marrying monsieur's head groom, the pious Philiberte Malateste. The Devil alone knows why a man who'd been known to whip the stable-boys for watching a stallion cover a mare would take to wife a woman he knew to be . . . well-used. And if the Devil has an answer to that conundrum, perhaps he'll also vouchsafe the reason monsieur bestowed freely upon Philiberte Malateste the blessing he had denied Jean Coquelet.

Jean, to whom the subject is a wound long healed, is of the opinion that Malateste charmed monsieur with some remnant spell of his witchy mother's. Perhaps he's right—surrounded by magic as I am, I can hardly deny the likelihood of such a thing. Yet, I think it more likely that monsieur was inclined to favor his milk-brother over ordinary domestics. And I think also that the shadow of the Porcelain Dove so overcast the duc's mind that had his dog-boy desired to wed a hound bitch, he'd have given the couple his blessing and a silver écu as a bride-gift.

When Marie Vissot became Mme Malateste, I was in Paris. To my vast surprise, monsieur had insisted that we winter there as always. Once there, however, he proved more restless than usual, more inclined to quarrel than to argue reasonably, less gracious about squiring madame to balls and popular lectures on phlogiston. Furthermore, he took to clutching his sous as close as Molière's Alceste.

Bien sûr, this new meanness of my master's was not without real cause: the vicomte de Montplaisir's gaming debts, for example, and the cost of his new school, which was twice again as dear as La Flèche. A fine school, La Flèche, but altogether too serious and dull for the vicomte, who had tried to enliven it with private entertainments for his particular friends. It was one of these revels—among whose celebrants were two young harlots—that inspired the director of La Flèche to write the duc de Malvoeux desiring him to remove his son from his establishment without a moment's delay. Monsieur raged and swore to banish his wayward heir to a Cistercian monastery until he came of age. But the end of it was that M. Léon suffered no worse a punishment than to be moved to the fashionable académie L'Epieu.

Jean, of course, holds that this disastrous party of the vicomte's was a direct consequence of the beggar's curse. The wizard foretold (he points out) that monsieur's sons should have no inheritance. Monsieur was no prince de Conti or baron du Fourchet, whose fortunes were an ocean that no expense could drain. Monsieur's wealth lay in his lands—which brought him little income—and in his collections—which brought him none. As for madame's dowry, he must have spent its sum at least on the four expeditions for the Porcelain Dove. And here was Justin, a postulant in an order that demanded a generous dowry, and M. Léon enrolled in a school as costly as 'twas fashionable.

Again, Jean may be right. Whether 'twas the curse or simple common sense, monsieur must have foreseen gold pouring from his coffers like blood from a severed vein, for he bound the wound in anticipation. When my mistress and I returned to Beauxprés, he stayed behind to shroud the hôtel Malvoeux in linen, to shutter its windows inside and out, to tie up its knocker, nail boards across its doors, and dismiss its servants down to the maître d'hôtel and my old friend the pie-faced lackey. Only then did he follow us to Beauxprés, and not a word about it to madame until a letter came from Mme de Hautebriande innocently inquiring of her dear Adèle if 'twere true what she'd heard, that the hôtel Malvoeux was to be sold.

Madame, not remarkably, took monsieur to task for his secrecy, whereupon he struck her senseless to the floor and retreated to the aviary before she'd regained her wits. When I brought her to, she crept into her bed fully dressed, and for all my pleading, did not stir for the rest of the day. Thereafter, the marital comedy embarked upon a new act in which my mistress' role was to shrink against the wall when she chanced to encounter her husband, and his was to bow and inquire politely after her health.

"What ever will I do?" she mourned one night as I brushed out her hair. "Monsieur grows stranger day by day, rejoices that he'll never have to converse with Parisian fools again, and forbids me to order a new toilette because I'll never have occasion to wear it. If I must remain mewed up here in Beauxprés for the rest of my life, I shall die of boredom, Berthe, I know I shall."

Inwardly, I agreed that 'twas very like she would, and me with her. Then a happy thought struck me. "Quelle bêtise, madame!" I said. "Madame has only to write Mme la baronne, and we may be back in Paris within the week."

She took no persuading. Before I blew out her candle that night, she'd written to madame her mother, who responded, some ten days later, that Mme la duchesse de Malvoeux was welcome to stay with her. Armed with this letter, my mistress sought out monsieur in his aviary, returning shortly with a bruised cheek and the happy news that her husband didn't give a pin whether she stayed or went, so long as she never entered the aviary again without an invitation. Two days later, we departed.

Linotte remained with her father at Beauxprés.

This was the subject of some little heart-burning on my mistress' part, and I myself thought it a pity to leave the child behind. But monsieur would not allow that Paris was a fit place for a child of tender years, and madame, when all was said and done, could not imagine what she'd do with her there. She comforted her conscience with bestowing Pompey upon her daughter as a kind of valet à tout faire, and the pair of them seemed so content with the arrangement that I felt mean-spirited for wishing that he were to accompany us as usual. After all, I'd be at home at the hôtel Fourchet, with Olympe and other old friends to gossip and go about with. Yet I expected to miss him, and I did.

I began to miss him no later than the second day upon the road, when madame began to regret her show of independence. Twenty times she ordered Carmontelle to return to Beauxprés; twenty times she whirligigged him back towards Paris, all the while fretting and weeping and wringing her hands until I thought I'd go mad. Once ensconced in her old suite in the hôtel Fourchet, however, she recovered her spirits. It made her feel a girl again, she declared, to live under her mother's roof with only me to wait on her.

La baronne du Fourchet smiled to hear her say so—rather a wary smile, not to crack her maquillage. At more than three-score, my first mistress suffered from rotten teeth, falling hair, a seamed throat, and a shrunken bosom. Olympe was now forced to celebrate her Rites of

Pride behind closed doors; for the baronne's toilette required such a deal of padding and painting and powdering and polishing of false teeth that no man could reasonably be asked to witness it.

My mistress' toilette, now: that was another matter altogether. A word dropped in Mme de Hautebriande's ear, another in Mme de Fleuru's, and the fashionable young men came flocking to my mistress' chamber like pigeons to a hilltop cote. Within a month, the levées of the duchesse de Malvoeux were one of the sights of Paris, like Mme de Choiseul's salons and the Théâtre Italienne. Chevaliers on their way to fight the English in the West Indies begged her for locks of hair to wear over their hearts in battle. Marquises quarreled over the privilege of choosing her ribbons and placing her patches. Vicomtes made up parties to the Bois de Boulogne and taught her to ride a-horseback. My mistress, impartial as the sun, smiled on them all.

Squired now by one cicisbeo, now by another, she trotted from lecture to concert, from ball to masque. She ordered a mannish riding costume in flea's-head brown and displayed it on a rented hack at the fashionable Thursday promenade. She undertook the soubrette in a farce presented in the private theater of the baron d'Esclapon. She furnished her carriage and her mother's box at the Opéra with a succession of pretty chevaliers. Oh, she never admitted any of them to her bed—her lips, I'm sure, were all any man had of her. Yet her adherence to the letter of her marriage vows was no comfort to me. Where once I'd had a single rival for my mistress' affections, now I had a dozen, and each of them was a separate and unique torment to me.

Ah, how I suffered! Two hundred years, and the recollection of my silent rage still knots my throat and clenches my fist so that my pen sputters and blots. 'Twas stay-laces I broke in Paris, and hairpins, and once a costly bonnet au berceau d'amour, which I crushed when madame handed her haresfoot to one of her swains, directing him to powder her décolleté. Then I missed Pompey indeed, for Olympe only laughed when I complained, called me fool and dog in the manger. Without the theater, I think I must have died.

'Twas not quite like the old days, to be sure. Some of my mother's former clients were dead, others had forgotten me, and my special friend Mme Dumesnil had retired the previous season upon the admiration of all Paris and a pension of 5,000 livres. Mlle Huys still trod the boards, and LeKain also, and the plays I watched them act were as familiar to me as my mistress' face and far less variable. Twice or three times in a week I'd sit in a loge paid for from my wages and let my tears flow freely for Médée, for Bérénice, for Zulima, whose woes were so much greater, and so much easier of comprehension, than my own.

Since madame was determined to stay in Paris until her husband should think to recall her, we remained in the hôtel Fourchet for almost a year.

Now, I've sworn to be honest, and I'd not have Colette think, when she reads this account, that I was so poor-spirited as to nurse my suffering through every moment of every day. No. Paris is Paris, after all, and 'tis impossible for anyone to be wholly miserable there. I drank chocolate in the Palais-Royal with Olympe and her friends, I walked in the Tuileries, I spent my savings on scent and kerchiefs and ribbons to make myself fine.

One day in my wanderings I found myself upon the rue Saint-Denis where I was born. 'Twas dusk, I remember, and the street was crowded with porters and watersellers, with grisettes leaving their day's work and children returning from their petits écoles. The grisettes carried baguettes of fresh bread wrapped in their shawls; the children carried slates. As I passed the door of a millinery shop, a small girl darted in front of me so that I stumbled and she fell to her knees in the mud. Before I'd steadied myself, she picked herself up and, single-minded as a donkey, made for the milliner's door.

"Petite maman!" she shrilled as she pushed it open. "Guess what?" And the door swung to behind her.

Curious, I peered through the elegant display of heads in the window at the child, who was burrowing in the arms of a pretty bourgeoise. As I watched, the bourgeoise released her daughter, smiled down into the small, vivid face, and wiped a smut from it while the child babbled and waved her hands as though relating some momentous news. Her mother laughed and smoothed her tumbled hair. The street noises faded from my ears, and I seemed to hear my own mother exclaiming over my muddy apron and asking whether I'd conducted myself like the wise infant she'd sent from her in the morning or like the little hoyden I looked now. The voice was maman's, was Olympe's, was madame's, as were the arms I felt around my shoulders. For a moment, I was a child held warm against a loving breast, embraced and embracing in perfect understanding, and then I was myself again, the femme de chambre of the duchesse de Malvoeux, standing at the window of a stranger's shop with my skirt trailing in the muck and my eyes awash with tears.

Having wiped the tears away, I tapped impulsively at the windowpane. All smiles and curtsies, the bourgeoise opened her door to me. Even though she must have known from my apron that I was no great lady, she gladly showed me any number of elegant hats, from which I chose a beaver of puce felt trimmed with spotted ribbons and feathers dyed rouge de sang. 'Twas a most pleasing and modish hat, and the small girl watched wide-eyed as I tried it on, agreeing that it became me well. 'Twas very dear—a full ten livres—but I opened my pocketbook and paid for it, at which the mother grew quite as wide-eyed as her daughter. I kissed the child, who, unprompted, hugged me about my neck while her mother packed the hat in a round box.

If I were to close my eyes this moment, I know I would see them—mother and daughter, candlelit, smiling hand in hand against a background of silk and bright plumage. The bourgeoise was, I remember, my age or only a little younger, dark-haired as I was, animated, piquant, slender. Had my mother lived, had I succeeded her, had I wed and survived the midwife, had I successfully raised a daughter to the age of discretion, we might have stood and smiled so as we bade a client farewell. 'Twas a pretty enough scene: Chardin would have done it justice, I think. Honesty compels me to confess that I would not.

Among the countless ways in which our sojourn on the rue Quincampoix differed from madame's girlhood, one thing remained the same. Mme du Fourchet still never spoke of her children. 'Twas Olympe told me that Mme de Poix had left her petit-maître husband at last and gone to London to console herself with the English milords. As for Mme de Bonsecours, she was grown most respectable, the mother of three sons and highly placed at court by reason of her husband's office. Why the baronne commonly denied herself when the marquise called, I do not know; unless 'twas that as she grew older, Mme Hortense grew more like her father to look upon, more outré in her opinions, and more forceful in expressing them.

Given her reception there, Mme de Bonsecours called at the hôtel Fourchet with astonishing fidelity. At least once a week, and sometimes twice, a lackey would announce the marquise de Bonsecours a bare moment before that lady surged into the chamber like a silken wave and broke irresistibly over madame's unwelcoming silence in an affectionate froth of greetings.

"Ah, Berthe," she'd say, patting my cheek. "I'm enchanted to see you. You shall make the chocolate. When I tell her how lovely you look, Louison will be jealous, but never mind. However spiteful she grows, she can do me no more harm than God and my cook between them have done already."

In reply, I'd curtsy and murmur that Mme la marquise was, as always, trés élégante, which would made her laugh. My mistress, sighing, would send a lackey for chocolate and petits fours while Mme de Bonsecours subsided on the sofa and asked her how she did.

Then would my mistress commence chattering away at a great rate—about Dr. Mesmer and his magnetic tubs, for instance, or the towering heights to which fashionable coiffures were rising—while the lackey set out the chocolate service and a small mountain of iced cakes. By the time I'd whipped hot milk and chocolate in a basin, poured the frothy liquid into two porcelain cups, and set them on an elegant ormolu table, she'd be well into an account of her latest conquest.

"Of course, I told the silly boy I could not accept such a gift, were he ten times the king's cousin. He answered that I was right to reject it, that my price was indeed far above rubies, and next day sent me a most astonishing necklace, all diamonds of the purest water. 'Twas brought to me as I dined at Stéphanie-Germaine de Hautebriande's, and I vow, sister, I cannot conceive how he came to know where I was. Figure to yourself my blushes and confusion! We were twelve at table, and I barely acquainted with ten of them. How Stéphanie-Germaine contrives to collect such a crowd of notables, I don't know. Why, Mme de Genlis was there, and Mme Necker and her English friend M. Gibbon. But Stéphanie-Germaine's triumph, her pièce de résistance, was—no, sister, I will not tell you: you must guess. A beauty but lately come upon the town, at least as witty as she is fair." My mistress looked roguishly down at her fan. "She dresses most daintily, too. For a man."

Mme de Bonsecours laughed. "Do you refer to Charlotte Geneviève Louise Auguste Andrée Timothée d'Eon de Beaumont, formerly the chevalier d'Eon? I hear he has taken the haut monde by storm, like a grenadier in long gowns."

"A grenadier in long gowns! La, sister, that's very apt! The creature is prodigious dowdy, to be sure, though 'tis rumored that when she proclaimed herself a woman last year, the queen sent Rose Bertin herself to make the trousseau."

The two sisters smiled at one another, united in their opinion of the soi-disant chevalière. Then Mme de Bonsecours, unable to leave well alone, said thoughtfully, "I can imagine a woman wishing to be a man, but never a man wishing to be a woman. 'Twas easy enough for d'Eon to declare himself a female, but I wonder how 'twill be when he tires of corsets and petticoats and seeks to reclaim all the rights and privileges of manhood? He'll sing a new tune then, I vow. Men may do as they will. Women, like lap-dogs, must trail after men in the hope of snapping up some small scrap of knowledge or power."

Madame frowned delicately. "How can you say such a thing, Hortense, you who will give place to no man? And how can you say that women do nothing of themselves? Are you not a mother?"

"I didn't become a mother without my husband's help," said the marquise impatiently. "Nor do I think motherhood so high a calling as, say, politics or philosophy or war. Certainly 'tis not so highly honored. Tell me, Adèle, can you imagine any king granting a woman land or title for her service to her children? Why, illiterate nursemaids execute all the duties of motherhood with as much reward, or more, than the ladies who have borne the brats they nurse and dandle."

Madame commenced fanning herself with an offended air. "To listen to you, sister de Bonsecours, one would think you'd rather be, oh, a common soldier than a marquise."

"Bien sûr: a common soldier may hope for advancement. Were I younger, or thinner, or less attached to my comfort, I vow I'd cut my hair and put off my skirts and prove myself a more manly chevalier than Mlle d'Eon."

The marquise had spoken with a kind of passionate lightness. Madame, puzzled how to respond, made a great show of picking up her cold chocolate, sipping at it, making a tiny moue, and putting it down again.

Mme de Bonsecours observed this byplay with an amused air. "Pray," she said after a moment. "How are my excellent nephews? I hear of the vicomte from time to time—his parties are quite the rage, you know, among a certain circle of young men. M. Justin, now— how does he go on with the Benedictines? And Linotte must be growing old enough for school. Do you intend sending her to Port Royal?"

Madame glared at her. "No daughter of mine," she declared,

"will be subject to a flock of sour, barren virgins with never a kind thought or a gentle word amongst them."

"You will then educate the girl at home?"

Worse and worse. Madame nibbled at an iced cake, pronounced it stale, then said in a tone that dared argument, "M. my husband is not willing to engage a tutor for so young a child."

What monsieur had said was that there was no reason to cast away good money upon the education of a girl. All the chit needed to know was that she was a Maindur of Malvoeux, which wisdom would have to serve for her dowry also, as he'd not a sou to spare.

Mme de Bonsecours must have guessed something of this, for her color rose alarmingly. "So the girl is doomed to spend her life as ignorant as mud, without the means of learning better," she exclaimed. "Lud, Adèle! If you will not send the child to school, then send her to me. After three boys, I'd enjoy raising a girl."

"You need not trouble yourself, sister," said madame icily. "I myself have taken steps to ensure that the child's education will be in all ways superior to Port Royal, except, perhaps, in the study of pranks and intrigue."

In the general way, I would not have said the sisters much resembled one another, but now the pair of them sat stiffly on their chairs, their faces identical masks of suppressed rage. The visit did not look to survive the exchange, and I was preparing to break the chocolate-basin to give them some common cause for their anger when Mme de Bonsecours' face softened.

"I beg your pardon, Adèle. I'd cause to hate Port Royal myself, though not, bien sûr, so great a cause as you. Am I to understand that you intend to teach Linotte yourself?"

"Pompey will teach her," said my mistress.

"Ah," said Mme de Bonsecours. "Rousseau triumphant. I approve."

In September, a letter arrived from Beauxprés bearing M. le duc de Malvoeux's wonder at his wife's long absence. If the first snowfall did not find her home at Beauxprés, he'd be forced to consider himself a widower and his children motherless.

"Poor heart," was madame's response to this chilly missive. "I must go to him at once. How he misses me."

So it was that when next Mme de Bonsecours called, she found

us in a chaos of trunks and hat boxes, baskets and cases. She surveyed
the bed piled high with gowns, the corsets wrapped in muslin, the
stacks of gloves and folded chemises, and arched her brows.

"So your falconer has whistled you to his fist at last," she said.

Madame raised her chin. "I have but remembered my duty as a
wife," she said.

"Ah," said Mme de Bonsecours. "Still, I expect you'll miss Paris
sadly, after your succès fou. I don't know how a certain prince will
contrive to survive your absence."

My mistress blushed. "If he does not, 'twill not be for lack of
ladies willing to comfort him."

"Bien sûr. But how dull 'twould be not knowing which among
them he chooses. Shall I write and tell you?"

Though she seemed to tease, something in her tone drew my
attention, some echo of the yearning I'd often heard in my mistress'
voice when she addressed monsieur. Coming from so formidable a
woman, it surprised and touched me. Madame, of course, was deaf.
She smiled at her sister—a formal, chilly smile—and said, "If it amuses
you, Hortense, of course you may write."

I have them still, twenty or more of the marquise's letters, which
provide a running account of the bedrooms and salons of Paris and
Versailles. They sit beside me now, worn with reading, stained with
ashes and rouge and wax, breathing a faint perfume of vanished in-
trigues. The first of them arrived at Beauxprés before I'd quite finished
unpacking madame's things.

October 1779

"Mlle" d'Eon has been arrested. Just as I predicted, the
creature soon tired of being a woman and petitioned the king for
permission to wear breeches on week-days, saving petticoats for
Sundays and feast days. Not remarkably, the petition was ignored,
whereupon d'Eon wrote to Maurepas complaining of the king's ill-
treatment of a loyal subject who was both a gentlewoman and an
officer of the Royal Army. Though the letter was prodigious rude
and ill-writ—I've seen it myself—the creature was sufficiently
proud of it to print it up and circulate it among the ladies of the
court as a kind of Declaration of the Rights of Women. The fruit
of this idiocy was six grenadiers calling with an arrest order at the

chevalière's lodgings in Versailles. The delicate creature resisted (manfully, I had almost wrote), stunning two of them with a carbine charged with grapeshot, but was overpowered at last by the survivors. Now the chevalière languishes in prison, the nuns of Auxerre having refused sanctuary to a supplicant whom only the king, and not God, had created female.

In my memory, a small voice cuts through these final words like shears through silk—Linotte's voice, crying, "This chevalière, is she a hare?"

We were in the China antechamber, as I recall, madame at her embroidery, Linotte at her sampler, me reading Mme de Bonsecours' letter aloud to them as they worked. Madame had returned from Paris fired with determination to teach her daughter the maidenly pursuits she herself had learned at the convent. I cannot say she taught her well, having no more idea of how to proceed than of how to write a book of philosophy. Yet these lessons were not unpleasant.

The day of Mme de Bonsecours' letter, for instance. When we stared at her interruption, not knowing what to answer, Linotte repeated her question: "Is the chevalière a hare?"

"Of course not, mignonne," said madame, rather snappishly, "nor is she a she at all, but only a silly man dressed up in petticoats. Why should she—peste!—he be anything other?"

Linotte clearly found this question as silly as the chevalière. To my surprise, she answered it nonetheless.

"Well, madame, when le bon Dieu let the waters come down in the great flood, all the animals had to get on the ark in a great hurry. The hares, being very fast, were among the first to enter, but so were the tigers, and the tigress was very hungry, for she was carrying cubs. It took a very long time for all the rest of the animals to get on the ark, and when Noë came at last to feed the tigers and the hares, he found the male hare mourning over a pile of clean bones.

" 'Mme la Tigresse has eaten my poor wife,' cried the hare. 'Who will now bear leverets to run upon the new earth le bon Dieu prepares for us?' But Noë could not answer him. So the hare fell to his knees and called upon le bon Dieu, who told him that when the waters had departed, the hare would turn female and bear a litter, also male, who would turn female in their season and bear other litters, and so there would always be leverets and hares. And then le bon Dieu turned to the tigress and He marked her beautiful golden hide with black bars in punishment for her crime, though He forbore to make her all black because she was only feeding the children within her.

"And that is why I asked if the chevalière is a hare, madame, for that's the only creature to be male one season and female another. Unless"—here her face brightened with revelation—"unless by chance she has walked under a rainbow, right under the center of it, and changed from man to woman in the space of a step?"

Madame sighed and shook her head. "Petite idiote!" she said. "All the world knows that hares are born male and female, even as tigers and horses and chickens are. Are they not, Berthe?"

I glanced at Linotte. She'd offered up her nonsense with such a pretty air of solemnity, as though 'twere Gospel, and now she looked so cast down that I pitied her. "Well, madame," I said carefully. "It seems likely. Yet I have never seen a female hare, nor has M. Males-herbes, in all his years of roasting, stewing, and sautéing them. So we must either believe that all female hares are so much quicker and smarter than their husbands and brothers that no one ever catches them, or else we must believe that Mlle Linotte's story has some grain of truth in it after all."

"Peste, Berthe, thou'rt as great an idiot as she," was all my mistress had to say. But I was rewarded by Linotte's smiling at me—a secret smile, the smile of one initiate to another. I smiled in return, though I could not imagine what mystery she thought we shared. That was the moment I decided to ask madame to give Peronel to Linotte as her femme de chambre.

It seemed a good idea at the time, not only to me, but also to madame, who remarked sentimentally that Linotte was almost the age she'd been when I entered her service. "And how much happier they'll be than you and I, exiled to Port Royal. We must close the nursery and give her her own rooms, of course. Do you think the Cameo apartment would suit?"

As the Cameo apartment opened out of the cabinet des Fées, it suited Linotte very well, as did her official elevation to young ladyhood. Peronel, however, was oddly reluctant.

"But I *like* the laundry," she said when I told her of her good fortune. "I know nothing of rouge and head-dresses, Berthe, nothing of serving a great lady. And what if I want to marry someday?"

"Oh, Peronel. She's only a child as yet—you've time and enough to learn about the mode. And as for your marrying. . . . Listen to your Berthe, now. The bonds forged in youth are strong. The younger your mistress, the more events you both will witness and suffer together and the closer you'll grow, until a single heart beats in your two bodies. And if that prospect does not move you, consider that if you attend the child, mère Boudin will not. At a stroke, we'll all be rid of an unpleasant old hag, and you'll gain an extra five livres a year for your purse."

A year passed, a year of false peace in which monsieur once again welcomed madame into his aviary, Peronel learned to dress hair, Marie bore her first child, Pompey taught Linotte her letters, and mère Boudin set up in the village as a seller of secondhand linens. She did very well for herself, the château laundry-maids being glad to sell the worn sheets to her rather than wait on the peddler, who came by only twice or thrice a year and was a great thief besides. No one spoke of the beggar, though his shadow could still be discerned in monsieur's continued economies and the bowl of ashes in Mme Pyanet's garden. Then one summer's day, Artide came into the back kitchen waving a letter like a banner above his head. It was creased and stained and directed in an illiterate scrawl to M. le duc de Malvoeux.

"Jacques Charreton brought it this morning," he said. "It came from Nantes, he said, and the carrier who brought it had it of a sailor on the warship *Belle Poule*. I take it no one'll object if I open it?"

For answer, M. Malesherbes heated a sharp knife, and a crowd of assistant chefs, scullions, and servingmaids gathered around as Artide gently pried up the wax, unfolded the single sheet, and read it aloud.

March, 1778. M. le duc de Malvoeux. Expedition impressed into the navy. Have seen many islands, none of them Fortunate. Besides my ship, only birds common gulls and terns. C'est la guerre.

Yr. obedient servant, Gouberville

Artide laughed. "So much for Hy Brasil and Avalon. If the Dove's in the Indies, some Englishman has undoubtedly shot it and stuffed it by now. The English are like that, they say."

"Think you monsieur will rave again?" Finette asked breathlessly. "I missed it last time."

"Idiote!" snapped M. Malesherbes. "Imbecile! I see it now. Monsieur in an uproar, madame unable to swallow more than a spoonful of soft custard. I know not why I remain here, cooking for a madman and a malade imaginaire, when a prince of the blood royal has offered me a place in his kitchens. Par Dieu, I must be as mad as our master, me."

The sous-chef suggested that we burn the letter on the grounds of monsieur's heart not grieving over what his eye did not see. Artide shrugged. "What do you care whether monsieur grieves or not, eh? He cares nothing for your feelings. Besides, 'twill do him good to know that there are matters in the world more pressing than his jean-foutre bird."

So we sealed the letter up again and Artide took it to monsieur, who read it and flung it upon the fire. He did not rave, did not so much as frown, and for all I know to the contrary, spoke of it to no one, neither then nor later. I can only conclude that he decided there was no letter, and therefore no war, and that a bird-hunter still searched the West for a Porcelain Dove.

In the summer of 1780, the baron du Fourchet succumbed to a meal of port and lobster and went to learn how taxes were farmed in Heaven.

Monsieur made no objection to madame's attending her father's funeral. Indeed, he said he'd accompany her, and Linotte as well. Although the weather was charming and the journey an easy one, to my dismay Peronel was quiet and sullen the whole while, hated the inns and the changing land, and pronounced the Seine valley flat and tedious. Paris was a pigsty, the Tuileries not so handsome as the gardens of Beauxprés, and the elegant ladies in their barouches and diligences wore their hair too high and their gowns too low. She pronounced Olympe and her friends a flock of hens tricked out like peacocks, and the handsome Mlle Raucourt an over-painted virago who squealed like a pig. I began to think Peronel an ungrateful chit.

The house on the rue Quincampoix was more crowded than usual. Mme de Poix had returned from England to pay her last respects to her father, and her husband seized the opportunity to demand the return of her marriage settlement. I couldn't take three steps outside my mistress' chamber without running into her or her new English maid, or M. de Poix, or M. de Poix's handsome secretary, or M. de Poix's lawyer, or the young vicomte de Montplaisir.

Two years at L'Epieu had polished M. Léon to a high gloss. His neckcloths were astounding, his coats a second skin, his boots like glass, and he wore his own unpowdered hair tied back in a velvet band. He drawled when he spoke, sprawled when he sat, and dangled a lace kerchief from his finger's ends as daintily as any petit maître. His shoulders were still broad and his eyes pale and cold: a wolf in dandy's clothing.

And like a wolf, he had an attendant fox—a thin, sandy manservant called Alain Reynaud. When monsieur first became aware of him, I thought there would be murder done. 'Twas in madame's chamber as she dressed for the baron's funeral and the subject of her gown arose—how much it had cost and who was to pay for it. M. Léon agreed with monsieur that it had been very dear and madame returned the betrayal by inquiring whether the scrawny boy loitering at the door were another of L'Epieu's numerous amenities?

Monsieur turned his cold eye first upon the boy and then upon his son. "This lout belongs to you? Take care, Montplaisir, how you spend my gold without my leave. Begone, you," he told the boy, who cowered against the door. "And be grateful I don't have the public hangman count out your wages across your back."

M. Léon looked black for a moment, then laughed. "Come, m'sieur. 'Twill be a savings to ye, I declare. Here's laundry and personal services twenty livres *per annum*, not counting the odd silver for the carriage of messages and suchlike. A manservant costs no more than half that amount, outside of the livery, which may be sent from Beauxprés at no expense."

Monsieur looked thoughtful. "Ten livres, hein?"

Madame was clearly regretting her attack. "Let the vicomte keep him, François. He looks a sober lad."

"The boy's name is Alain Reynaud," said M. Léon, "and he's as sober as rain water. He's clever as well, and monstrous deft with a razor."

"Ten livres," said monsieur, rising. "And a suit of clothes. If we wait until the New Year to pay him, I make it thirty livres saved. I begin to hope for you, Montplaisir."

The farming of money being a highly civilized pursuit, the funeral of the baron du Fourchet was consequently a highly civilized affair, and the bankers and politicians crowding the church of Sainte-Catherine were solemn rather than grief-stricken. Mme du Fourchet may have shed a tear or two behind her widow's veil, but if she wept, she wept alone. Me, I felt only so much grief as any mortal creature must feel in the presence of a coffin and a grave.

After the funeral, certain mourners accompanied Mme la baronne back to the hôtel Fourchet, where over wine and cake they gossiped and flirted as usual. Before long, M. and Mme de Poix had begun exchanging their usual shrill pleasantries, the abbé was pale drunk, and I was seeking refuge in the lavender-scented quiet of the linen-room.

When I opened the door, what should I see but Peronel struggling in the vicomte de Montplaisir's embrace?

"M. Léon!" I exclaimed.

Grinning with all his teeth, he released her, pushed me aside, and loped away down the hall, leaving Peronel backed up against the cupboards, her face flushed, her bosom heaving, her breath ragged.

"Pauvre petite." I went to her and drew her into my arms. She shook her head and pulled away.

Overcome with shame, I thought. Poor girl. "He should be ashamed, not you," I scolded her gently. "And ashamed he shall be, when I tell madame how her son forces his attentions upon her servants."

She seized my hand in both of hers. "Oh, no Berthe! Oh, *please*, no! Not a word to madame, I entreat you. Why, she could decide that the best way to protect me is to send me away, and I couldn't *bear* that, Berthe, indeed I could not! Besides, 'tis all my fault for coming to Paris."

"Never blame yourself for M. Léon's goatish ways," I began, but Peronel interrupted me with her arms about my neck and her voice in my ear.

"Dear Berthe," she murmured. "Thou canst not be mother to all the world." Then she kissed me upon the cheek and fled, leaving me entirely bewildered.

Next morning, she was nowhere to be found. She left behind all her small possessions, with the exception of a silver cross and the little scarlet purse in which she was storing up her wages.

Madame was furious. "Wretch," she exclaimed when I told her of Peronel's disappearance. "Ungrateful. I always thought the girl both shifty and sly. You, you saw some promise in her, and I entrusted her with my daughter's well-being. Le bon Dieu be thanked she's stolen nothing."

Because I was coming to know this mood in my mistress better than I liked, I saved my breath to inquire after Peronel among the servants of madame's friends. I even ventured to visit a house of accommodation in Saint-Antoine whose matron, as a young whore, had bought peignoirs of my mother. No one had heard of a fresh young country girl newly taken into service or gone upon the game. And when I came upon Reynaud lurking by the closet where the maidservants slept and demanded of him where Peronel might be, all the answer he gave was to stare at me with sly, bright eyes, lick his white teeth, and slink away.

In Which the Vicomte Proves Himself a True Son of Malvoeux

Soon after the funeral, monsieur returned to Beauxprés, taking Linotte with him. Madame and I remained in the rue Quincampoix, this time at her mother's request. Mme the widowed baronne du Fourchet felt old and tired and desired her children about her. Pauline had become a trollop and a harpy; Hortense was, as ever, impossible. Surely Adèle knew that she had always been her mother's favorite child.

Had I been my mistress, I'd have laughed in her nose and taken myself elsewhere. Madame wept and stayed.

During the six months following the baron's death, madame could not go abroad, nor did that part of society she loved best care to call upon a house of mourning. Our only company was M. le baron's cronies—Farmers Général, officials of the Contrôle Générale, bankers, financiers—who came to the hôtel Fourchet to console their old friend's widow and stayed to eat her excellent dinners and gloom over the everlasting war with England and the upstart Necker's draconian reforms. 'Twas all as dull as hemming sheets.

If the winter of 1778 had been a whirligig of cicisbeos and entertainments, the winter of 1780 was an altogether more staid affair. Black did not become my mistress, convention barred her from balls and soirées, and there were now beauties on the town more piquant, more complaisant, and far more witty than she. I'd no cause for jealousy—quite the opposite. 'Tis the nature of a glass to reflect, and if there's no belle or beau present, then it must reflect whoever is—

crêpe-faced mother or whey-faced banker. 'Tis not astonishing that my mistress preferred to reflect me.

Save that we were older, she and I, we might have been back at the convent. A quiet, close six months, like a meadow among mountains of activity; a time of sitting by the chamber fire, she in an armchair, I on a low stool, she embroidering, I mending, she writing to Mme Réverdil, I reading aloud to her from popular pamphlets of art and science, favorite fairy tales, chapters of *La Nouvelle Héloïse* and the comtesse de Malarmé's new *Mémoires de Clarence Welldone*, a cleverly naughty broadside. Dressing and undressing, planning new heads for when she was out of mourning, and the sweet nightly ritual of brushing her hair while she sat, eyes closed and smiling, sighing gently now and again as I drew the brush through and through the springing ebony mass.

Sometimes I'd wake in the night from a dream of wizards or dunghills or beaked and feathered children and take comfort from the familiar rumble of cart-wheels upon the cobbled street. I'd even smile to think myself so far removed from cursing beggars, bird-mad ducs, and the cries of ghostly children.

What a fool I was, to be sure.

'Twas three o'clock of a chilly spring night. Madame, now in demi-mourning, was at a soirée. I was awaiting her return in the back kitchen, half-dozing over a poem on gardens I'd bought of a peddler just that morning. The hôtel Fourchet was very silent: I could hear the rain rattle when the wind caught it like pebbles thrown against the windows. Once the wind whipped up hard, and the pebbles rattled so fiercely I thought the glass must break. Then the wind faded, and I realized that what I heard was not the rain at all, but a hand tapping, tapping at the kitchen window.

I hesitated—only a fool would act without hesitation on such a night, at such an hour—then took my candle to the window. A figure like a drowned corpse stood without, white-faced and staring. The figure raised its hand to tap again, the mouth shaped my name, and I saw 'twas Peronel, wet as a rat and thin as famine, but alive.

In less time than it takes to tell, I had her in the kitchen with the fire stirred up and a blanket around her shoulders, her feet to the blaze, and a chunk of bread and cheese in her hands. She was dressed in a green-striped polonaise with a fichu covering her bosom—not new, not à la mode, but respectably clean. For twenty minutes or so, she nibbled at the cheese and stared silently into the fire. Fearing my mistress would return, I asked, "Where hast thou been, child? I half-thought thee dead."

"Dead? I've wished to be dead. Death could be no worse than the Hell I've suffered."

"Hell?" I echoed, bewildered, and bent to look into her face. No, this was indeed Peronel, a little puff-eyed and bruised about the mouth, but beyond doubt the same goosish girl who had talked to madame of laundry while the beggar cursed outside.

"A very particular ring of Hell disguised as a pleasure-house in the Bois de Boulogne. O Berthe, how I am stupid!"

In this judgment I concurred, though I did not think it kind to say so. "Softly, softly, petite," I said. "The vicomte de Montplaisir, did he steal thee away?"

"Yes. Well, no. I went with him willingly. He was so handsome, you see. And he promised me jewels and fine gowns and exquisite pleasures, and vowed that he loved me. He took me up in a closed carriage, just like a fine lady, and made love to me as we drove, paying me pretty compliments on the slenderness of my neck and the round-ness of my buttocks. Unless you've labored under the attentions of our so-dear maître d'hôtel, Berthe, you cannot imagine the pleasure to be gained from a sweet breath and smooth hands and a perfumed body.

"We might have driven so forever, fondling and kissing like true lovers. Yet all good things end at last, they say, and after a space, we alit. He led me through a garden into a little house—a cottage, almost, no more than a vestibule and two salons, with two chambers above. 'Twas vastly elegant."

I thought she sounded wistful, and said shortly, "This is not Hell, but the Elysian fields you describe. I wonder you troubled yourself with escaping."

She turned her red-rimmed eyes to me as gently as the silly Peronel of old. "A devil may wear a beautiful face, Berthe. May not Hell also?"

"Yes, yes: I suppose it may," I answered, a little shamed. "So. The vicomte de Montplaisir took you to a petite maison, and where he came by the gold to pay for it, the Devil alone knows. Oh, how monsieur his father will rave when he hears of it!"

Peronel fell forward upon her knees and seized my hands. "No one must know of this, Berthe, or I shall die of shame. You must promise me to keep what I say secret, or I'll say no more. Upon thy mother's salvation, Berthe."

How could I swear any such thing? I know how to keep secrets, me, but there are burdens that, borne alone, may crush the bearer's heart. Peronel's secret promised to be such a burden—already I felt my heart stagger under it. I considered a moment, then, "Very well," I said carefully. "Upon my mother's salvation, I swear to repeat no word of what you say this night to a Christian soul."

She nodded but did not rise, nor did she relinquish her hold upon my hands. "His valet brought in food and wine to us, and while I ate, he told me of his conquests. He'd had a dozen women, two dozen, fifty; he'd had them perform every amorous trick known to demon or man. This one swooned from pleasure, that one near died of it, another called for a priest. 'I shrove her myself,' he says, and describes her penance to me until I weep with fear. And every so often he stops and shakes his fist in the air and, 'Lord God, I defy you,' he cries. 'Strike me dead if you dare, O Lord raper of virgins!' "

"Just heaven!" I cried. "And what happened?"

Peronel shrugged. "Nothing happened. God answered neither his prayer nor mine, not then, and not when the vicomte took me upstairs into a room like a chapel, hung in black and furnished with such paintings and statues as I blushed to look upon. Do you remember how you and Marie once jested how the heir of Malvoeux would collect maidenheads? The truth is nothing so innocent as maidenheads, which interest him not at all. He collects whips, Berthe, and silken ropes, and little, sharp razors. And with them he pursues his true vocation, which is collecting cries of pain."

"Stop!" I cried. " 'Tis more than I can bear. The monster must be complained of, brought to trial, imprisoned!"

"Hush, Berthe," she patted my hand. "I am resolved to tell all, and you must resolve to bear it."

And so I heard it, held both by her tale and by her fingers stroking my hands. That chilled me more than her words, I think, that gentle, absorbed caress.

"I've learned a new language from him, Berthe. That member Menée called his scepter, *he* named with a dozen more ungentle names: Cupid's arrow, engine, lance, rifle. My body was the altar of Venus; my secret places were the gates of Heaven. No saint ever stormed Heaven more zealously than he. Day and night he celebrated his rituals of rope and flail and knife, his valet assisting him now as acolyte, now as surgeon. Many and varied were his approaches to bliss, but of all my gates, he favored the postern."

The fire snapped and the rain tapped at the windows. All else was silent as the grave, except my heart beating in my ears and Peronel's quick breathing. I could think of nothing to say.

"Do you know the penalty for sodomy?" asked Peronel at last. "He taunted me with it, should I dare to expose him. *He* would not burn—nobles, as all the world knows, are fireproof. The valet might die, and that would please me. But not enough to burn at his side with my sins unshriven. There were other girls, too, whom I would not betray."

"Bien sûr," I said, or croaked. "How long did this continue?"

Peronel released my hands and folded her fichu higher on her throat. "A week. Two weeks. I don't remember."

"But that was more than a year ago," I said.

"We escaped, my companions and I, down a rope made of the chapel's hangings, all knotted together and hung out the window. We fled to a place known to one of the girls, where the matron cared for us until we were healed, then took us into her employ. The work is easy enough, after *him*. Though you'd be astonished, Berthe, how many gentlemen cannot raise their noble rods without a touch of the lash upon their noble tails." As she spoke, Peronel had risen and shaken out her skirts, and now took her shawl from the settle where I had spread it to dry and wound it around her head and shoulders.

"I shouldn't have come here, Berthe; whores don't call on decent women. But I thought you might fret over me, and I only wanted to tell you there was no need. Keep the servingmaids away from him if you can. But do not betray me. I wish to go to Hell in my own way, not his."

'Tis difficult for me to remember her voice, and her pretty, foolish face. Not that I cannot recall them: her bitter words and hopeless look are etched upon my mind as though with acid. No, what is difficult is the memory of sitting by the dying fire with my mouth ajar like a Christmas pig, without a kiss for her, nor a word of farewell, nor any sign that I did not judge her soiled beyond redeeming. I'm ashamed, too, to think of my vow of silence, and how I made it intending to break it, or at least to bend it, in relating the whole to Pompey, whom a flood of holy water would never make Christian. Now I make what amends I may. Beg he from now until the Trump of Doom, Jean will never hear this chapter of my history. Colette, however, will read it. And she will shed a sister's tears for Peronel and in her name forgive my broken oath or else set me a penance for it. For not le bon Dieu Himself has Colette's right to judge me in this matter.

By the autumn of 1781, madame my mistress was finding Paris sadly flat. The haut monde was chewing over the same tired subjects like a particularly indigestible cud: the Compte Rendu, Necker's resignation, Fleury's taxes, the price of salt, Mesmer's animal spirits, the infant dauphin, the war with England, the price of grain, the latest satires, the new robes-chemises in which the queen of France could not be distinguished from a grisette on her way to bed. There was nothing new to talk about, no one new to talk to. Parisian society was eternally the same, she complained, and the Parisian streets stank worse than the aviary in August. Unsummoned and unannounced, we returned to Beauxprés.

After so long an absence, I'd almost forgotten how mountains can loom over one, how fir and brambles overshadow the road on one side and open to a long and rocky drop on the other. The farmhouses like great stone tents, the church steeples tiled like snake skins, the villages playing cache-cache on the rocky hillsides—mile by mile, they grew more familiar. I found myself thinking fondly of Estienne Pyanet's crusted bread and the back kitchen at Beauxprés with a fire in the hearth, a hot brandy-and-sugar in my hand, and M. Malesherbes, Artide, the sous-chef, Jacques Ministre, even Dentelle regaling me with the small happenings of the year past.

And Pompey, the child of my heart. Pompey most of all.

The fire and the brandy-and-sugar and Artide and M. Malesherbes were all just as I'd imagined them. Pompey, on the other hand, was nowhere to be seen. I wasn't too astonished—he was Mlle Linotte's only servant, after all, and not one to take his duties lightly. Yet I thought he might have come down to greet me.

"Oh, Pompey's a great man now," sneered Artide when I inquired after him. "He's playing Abélard to our little Héloïse and has no time for us."

M. Malesherbes shook his head over his steaming cup. " 'Twas one thing when he was small, to make a pet of him and laugh at his barbaric ways. But to give a grown savage governance over a Catholic child! I cannot think it right, me."

"Nor would I think it right," I said, "were Pompey in truth a savage."

Artide laughed. "Give it up, Malesherbes. You know how Berthe dotes upon our dusky ape." I looked daggers at him; he threw up his hands as though to ward against a blow. "Peace, peace, Mlle Amie des Noirs. I'll admit that Pompey is as civilized as you please, if you'll admit that there are more suitable tutors for a French noble's young daughter than a full-grown male blackamoor."

"Ah, bah!" I said. "He's as suited for the job as any Frenchman of a like age, and more suitable than most."

"Enough!" said M. Malesherbes. "I see, Berthe, that Paris has done little to mend your temper."

Artide leaned forward and pinched my chin. "Go seek your monkey in the cabinet des Fées, my cabbage. I wish you joy of your reunion."

Dismissed and deflated, I mounted the stairs to the hall of Depositions. Absence—or perhaps the sour taste of the scene just past —must have made me more than usually sensitive to the gloomy influence of bleeding Christs and weeping Virgins, for by the time I'd reached the Snuffbox antechamber that led to the cabinet des Fées, I felt myself close to tears.

Reluctant to greet Pompey in this maudlin state, I stayed where I was and tried to compose myself.

The Snuffbox antechamber is a good room for distracting the mind. The boxes are arranged in a kind of crescendo—plain enamels nearest the Fan room, moving through beaded and cloisonné and jeweled and painted to the most artful, the most precious of all, housed in two cases flanking the door of the cabinet des Fées. These are a hundred oval boxes bound in vermeil, each bearing the miniature portrait of some renowned fairy, wizard, or princess. In the left-hand case, the Yellow Dwarf scowls ferociously, the White Cat lifts a dainty paw, the Fairy Magotine flourishes her wand of serpents. In the right-hand case nestles a clutch of golden-haired princesses, one as like another as hen's eggs. Perfect beauty is perfect beauty, after all, and doesn't vary much.

I'd just reached the princesses when Pompey's voice sounded through the door. "No, no, mademoiselle," he said, amused and indulgent. "Don't you remember? The roses were Prince Lutin's, and their virtue died with him. They are curiosities only. Now, I ask again.

You wish to make a long journey. Which of these objects would you choose to take?"

Half-ashamed of my stealth, I applied my eye to the keyhole. A broad table occupied my field of vision, and upon it I could see a small green cap ornamented with scarlet feathers, a good-sized walnut, three roses, and a worn leather satchel. Mlle Linotte had her elbows on the table and was studying the objects before her with knotty concentration. She was then ten years old, not nearly so pretty as her mother at that age—thin and tall and sharp-faced like her father. The resemblance was so strong, I wondered how I'd not noticed it before. Her black hair hung in elf-locks about her narrow shoulders, and her white gown was spotty and smudged. I thought her a repellent child.

"The walnut holds a dress," she said suddenly, "and would be of no use to me unless my journey were to Versailles. The satchel gives food, which would be useful on a long journey. I think I'd rather have something to make the journey short." She squinted up—at Pompey, I suppose, though she seemed to be looking straight through the keyhole at me. As I drew back discomfited, I heard her say, "I can't remember what the cap does. If the roses are curiosities only, then I should take the cap."

Pompey laughed. "Well reasoned! When you are grown, if sorceresses are not à la mode, you may call yourself a philosophe. Now, go and read 'Prince Lutin,' which you were to read yesterday, and learn about the cap—yes, and the roses, too. And when you have done that, we will go to the aviary and help Jacques Ministre feed the birds."

Hastily I unbent myself, knocked smartly upon the door, opened it, and stepped inside. "Ah, Pompey," I said briskly. "Artide said I should find you here. Mlle Linotte"—I dipped her the smallest of curtsies—"your mother is returned home from Paris. Pray go and welcome her." I looked her up and down, from beggar's skirt to unkempt hair. "I see mademoiselle has no one to attend her. Shall I find a comb for her, and perhaps a clean gown?"

If I'd hoped to daunt the child, I was to be disappointed. She tilted up her chin at me, tossed back her hair, and sailed out the door as proudly as one of the snuffbox princesses.

Linotte gone, I held out my arms to Pompey. He came into them readily enough, and lifted me clean off my feet in a mighty hug. I'd forgotten how big he was—tall as monsieur and a span across the shoulders, with beautiful long hands beside which mine were small as a child's.

"You intend to stay this time," he said as he put me down again. "I'm glad. There is no one here to talk with save mademoiselle, who is still very young." His soft voice deepened. "You weren't very kind to her, Berthe."

I drew myself out of his arms. "The child is a disgrace. Are there no laundresses at Beauxprés? And surely she's not so young that she cannot comb her hair now and again."

"Ah, Berthe," sighed Pompey, and turned away from me to gather up the enchanted hat and other things from the table and return them to their proper cases and drawers. Stitch by stitch, I felt our old easy friendship raveling into tangle of petty jealousy and broken loyalty. Pompey was no longer the little page I'd comforted in my arms, the soft-eyed youth I'd teased and protected. In this year of absence, he'd grown into a hulking stranger: a savage, alien. The tears I'd banished among the snuffboxes welled up again.

"I've missed you, Pompey," I said. "Olympe grows old, and all her conversation these days is of old lovers and new aches. I love her still, bien sûr—she is my mother's blood. But I cannot trust her discretion."

"You have something to tell me that torments you past bearing. I could smell it through the door, like rotting flowers. Poor Berthe."

Poor Berthe indeed! How dare he snuffle at my emotions without my leave? "Can'st then sniff out what torments me?" I snapped. "Sacré tonnerre, boy! 'Twould become thee better to let me tell my tale in my own way!"

Pompey bowed his head and waited as I asked until the silence grew thick and heavy between us. He waited while I seethed, while I considered flouncing out of the room, while I considered throwing a magic nut at his inky face. He waited until I began to grow exceedingly perplexed and somewhat ashamed. Then he asked quietly, "You have found Peronel Mareschal?"

"How do you know?"

He shook his head. "I only guess. Is she well?"

"She's alive and she's not ill, at least not yet, though I'd hardly call her well. Our Peronel's a Parisian whore, and Parisian whores seldom keep their health for long, especially in such a house as she inhabits."

Silently, Pompey came to me, took my arm, and led me into the Fan room, to a window furnished with a deep, cushioned seat. There he sat me down and listened gravely while I told him of Peronel and the vicomte and of his valet Alain Reynaud and their curious, distasteful pastimes. When I was done, I found I could not look at him, so I looked instead at the dusty fans in the case behind him and remembered how I'd cut out M. Léon's breeches in this very room, and how Marie had teased Peronel because a young boy had stolen a kiss of her.

"Musk and blood," said Pompey from a long silence. "All the Maindurs smell of old blood—even Mlle Linotte. But Léon! Even in the womb he stank of shit."

Confessed, I felt lighter. "Well," I said, giving his hand a pat. "Now there's two of us to keep an eye upon the servingmaids, should the vicomte take it in his head to come visiting."

"Yes," he said. "But if servingmaids begin disappearing one by one, how are we to prevent it? Monsieur is unlikely to believe his son a monster."

I thought of M. LeSueur and of Justin's being whipped, more than once, for some misdeed of his brother's. "To be sure. 'Twill end, I fear, as it always ends with M. Léon—with others paying for his crimes. Yet forewarned is forearmed. We'll think of something when the time comes."

In the life of a village, a year is longer than this eternity we have dwelt in Beauxprés. That Sunday when I went to Mass, I was astonished to hear all that had transpired. The old curé had died, and a foreigner from Bugey had taken his place—a baron's son, godly, learned, and timid. He preached a sermon on the blessing of life in honor of Marie Malateste, who was being churched after the birth of her fourth child in three years, the second child having been twins. I nodded to her courteously at the church door and was rewarded with such a look as I'd give a cat who'd kittened on my Sunday petticoat. Dentelle stood godfather to the brat, and to hear him brag, you'd have thought he'd fathered it himself.

Mère Boudin was dressed in black, and told me when I greeted her that she was a widow now. Mme Pyanet whispered in my ear that 'twas said that she'd lost her husband's balls to the Devil at dice, whereupon the poor man'd had no choice but to die of shame. All in all, 'twas as good as a play.

I was not displeased to be home again. Yes, home. Jean says my brain must be going soft. As far as *he* recalls, I never liked Beauxprés, never ceased for a moment to long for Paris, to praise its theaters, its boulevards, its shops, its pleasures. Well, he's right. I didn't. None-theless, Beauxprés had come to feel like home to me. Colette, wiser in the ways of grief than Jean, may understand what he does not: that I was linked to Beauxprés by what I'd suffered there. And the quiet of Beauxprés was not so different, after all, from the quiet of Port Royal and of the hôtel Fourchet, where madame and I had been so peaceful together.

Madame, on the other hand, had had her fill of peace. As the days drew in, so did her restlessness increase, until she was like a bitch in heat, forever on the wrong side of the door. We hardly saw monsieur, who had not troubled himself so much as to greet her upon her return, and Linotte all too clearly preferred learning magic and mathematics from Pompey to learning embroidery and the clavichord from her mother. Finding nothing to distract her in all Beauxprés, madame turned to the state of her health.

I will not dwell on the rheums and agues, the languors and irritable fits of that long winter. She wrote for advice to every quack in France and spent all her ribbon-money on nostrums, potions, and powders. One physician counseled her to eat fowl fed on vipers. Another advised her to take a tincture of gold in milk to strengthen her heart. She bathed every day—even days in water so hot she was in danger of scalding, odd days in water so cold 'twas a wonder she escaped pneu-monia. M. Malesherbes complained of her diet, the lackeys complained of the countless cans of hot and cold water they must haul up to her room and down again. Even Dentelle complained, for my mistress called upon him in his role of monsieur's barber to bleed her once a week. In short, not a soul in Beauxprés but rejoiced when M. Tissot wrote from Lausanne suggesting that all madame needed to maintain perfect health was a regimen of regular equestrian exercise. Not a soul, that is, except monsieur.

Not that he minded madame's riding—he'd hardly have noticed had she taken a fancy to tramp the hills with a pack, like a gypsy. His objection was that his stable did not include a horse trained to a lady's saddle, and M. le duc de Malvoeux would not squander a hundred livres on a beast that boasted neither wings nor feathers. If madame his wife needed exercise, he said, she could walk in the garden.

'Twas once again a case of inciting a dove to wrath. Next morning my mistress was up betimes, stealing a rope of pearls from her own jewel box, and ordering an undergroom to accompany her to Cham-pagnole for the purpose of buying a horse. Having failed to argue or flatter her into a prudent docility, I washed my hands of the affair, and when she returned that evening with a pretty brown mare tied behind the dog-cart, I fled to the aviary. When parrots scream abuse at one another, I cannot understand their insults.

As I'd predicted, monsieur was angry enough to spit iron. Le bon Dieu be thanked, I didn't see it, though Artide was glad to give me every detail of how my master had broken a riding-whip across my mistress' shoulders and sworn he'd have the groom hanged and the mare butchered for hawk-meat. So much was monsieur's way and only to be expected; madame's response was another thing altogether. According to Artide—and to Philiberte Malateste and the groom as well—my mistress boldly declared that the pearls were hers, given her by her father, and the horse she'd bought with them her own personal property.

"Keep the nag, then," monsieur said. "May it break your neck."

Thereafter, madame rode the mare Fleurette every day, and though she swore the exercise gave her little pleasure, she abandoned her nostrums and her chaise longue and ate with an appetite to bring joy to the fainting heart of M. Malesherbes.

The spring that saw madame riding Fleurette ventre-à-terre through the fields to the grave peril of wayfarers and stray chickens also brought the vicomte de Montplaisir back to Beauxprés.

I'd expected—well, hoped—that the vicomte would follow the usual path of fledgling nobility into the army or the court. But the vicomte de Montplaisir, as always, followed his own path. Upon completing his fifth year at L'Epieu, he wrote that he could no longer bear to be away from his ancestral home. He wished to hunt and learn husbandry and to be a comfort to his father and mother.

The letter, alas, is lost. I remember it as a work of art, false as an abbé's compliments and twice as fulsome. Yet what could I say? It told madame what she wanted to hear—that her eldest son loved her. And monsieur . . . Well, monsieur was so far moved as to await his son's arrival by the fountain of Latona and to kiss him on either cheek when he alighted from his horse. He bore him straightway to the library, and shortly thereafter summoned Menée and Jacques Ministre to confer with them.

Only figure to yourself how curiously we awaited their report! By we, I mean M. Malesherbes and Artide and Dentelle and some few younger servants who'd wormed their way into the inner circle while I'd been gone. Of them, I remember only Clauda Boudin, mère Boudin's niece whom I'd been training in Peronel's place as madame's laundress. I did not make new friends so easily at thirty-seven as I had at eighteen.

So there we all were, talking of this and that, when in came Menée LeRoi and Jacques Ministre, both of them with the faces of men who've just dined on rotten meat. Between them was the vicomte's manservant Reynaud, and his face knew where the meat came from.

"This is the valet of M. le vicomte de Montplaisir," said Jacques Ministre. "Pray you all make him welcome."

Reynaud caught sight of me. "Mlle Duvet, is it not? Berthe, dear Berthe! Mere words cannot express how comfortable it is to discover thy dear countenance amidst this crowd of strange faces!" He plumped to his knees on the flagstones and kissed my hand while the rest of them stared—Menée with fury, Jacques Ministre with astonishment, the maidservants with varying degrees of envy. I dare say they thought him good to look upon.

Snatching my hand from his lips, I applied it smartly to his cheek. "Impertinence!" I said.

"Oh, unkind," he said, and his water-green eyes glowed as if with tears. He lifted them to Clauda. "You are too . . . young, demoiselle, to know the pain of love forsworn, of passion denied. Take a warning of me, my dear, and never trust a lover's vows, lest your innocence, like mine, be betrayed."

Clauda, who was as plain and thick as a wooden sabot, squinnied at him. "I don't know what you're going on about, M. le valet, but ye'll be wanting a bit of meat to put to that cheek, or it'll turn black on ye sure as hedgehogs."

This artless speech inspired Reynaud to a jest about raw meat pointed enough to make Clauda thrust her large, red hands under her apron and stumble out of the kitchen with real tears in her eyes.

"You are a rude fellow," said M. Malesherbes when she was gone. "I tolerate no rudeness in my kitchen."

Reynaud hopped up from the floor onto Clauda's stool. "M. Menée told me the girl was a great-uddered cow with a wet lip and a wetter—"

"I deny every word of it," sputtered LeRoi. "You, M. Smart-Mouth, are a lying, jumped-up, lace-eating, powder-pissing, buggering remover of boots."

"Like Dentelle?" inquired Reynaud brightly.

Well. In less than a second, Menée was bellowing and spluttering, Dentelle's eyes were bulging from his head, Malesherbes was imploring Heaven for patience. Even Jacques Ministre was shouting and gesticulating. And there sat Alain Reynaud looking unhappier and smaller and more and more frightened until everyone started to feel uncomfortable, and even Menée fell silent.

"I want to be friends," said Reynaud, very small.

"Pooh," said Dentelle loftily, and waved his hand.

The boy flinched away from him. Dentelle looked startled.

"You've an odd enough way of showing it," said Jacques Ministre.

Reynaud turned to him a face candid as a puppy's. "I'm from the street, you see, my master picked me starving from the street, and that's the way life is in the streets of Paris. We often call a friend salopard or vieille vache in all love."

The household of the duc de Malvoeux exchanged glances that said: the boy knows no better, he's young, the streets of Paris are strange and unknown territory, the service of M. le vicomte de Montplaisir could not possibly be much better. A servingmaid—Finette, it seems as if there was always a Finette in M. Malesherbes' kitchen—mixed a mug of hot brandy-and-sugar and handed it to Reynaud. Artide ruffled his hair. Dentelle offered to teach him how to mend a lace jabot. Thus, at the cost of a scolding, Alain Reynaud bought himself a place in the kitchen, which was the living heart of Beauxprés. 'Twas as pretty piece of cony-catching as you'd wish to see outside a thieves' market.

Soon the talk turned to what had passed in the library.

"The boy's to set up his collection," said Menée. "We talked of where to put it, mostly. There's precious few rooms in Beauxprés left unnamed and unfilled."

Dentelle sighed. "Time passes so quickly! 'Twas only yesterday, or so it seems, that monsieur was begging his father to build a mews to house the haggard falcon he'd snared in the Forêt des Enfans. Ah, how his father was proud! Well I recall my distress to find he'd used his stocking for a snare and his shirt for a gamebag! Pray heaven, boy, that your master's fancy is not hard upon his clothes."

Through his sandy lashes, Reynaud gave Dentelle a laughing look that said as clear as words that valets share jests beyond the understanding of less privileged mortals. Dentelle, vain fool, beamed besottedly.

"So what is it?" asked Artide. "What strange and deadly thing has captured the noble vicomte's heart? Puppies' tails? Wingless flies? Peasants' hides?"

Reynaud remaining silent, "Bugger a word of what," said Menée. "Solid gold chamber pots, for all I know. Truth to tell, there won't be much reason to call the chamber anything, for 'tis stuck all by itself in the old donjon. Opens from the gallery of Swords—you know, overlooking the drying-yard?"

Artide chucked Reynaud on the ear. "I'll stake my soul on it *you* know something. What's your name—Reynaud? A good name for a gamin, I vow. Now, Reynaud. There isn't a fox alive doesn't know more about the wolf he follows than he lets on. To the wolf, that is. We're all foxes here."

"I swear, I know nothing—or very little. He keeps his counsel, does my master, and would not thank me for giving it away. There are some books, some few boxes of a middling weight. Please. I can say no more."

No fox with feathers on his lips could have been more vehement in denying all knowledge of goose-flesh. We understood that he knew the contents of those books and boxes to an item, yet would not, or could not, reveal them. The other servants thought him too afraid; I thought him too clever. He was certainly clever enough to call up pity in one servingmaid's black eyes, compassion in another's smile. Before my mind's eye swam the vision of a chapel hung in black, and Finette plucked naked and trussed upon the altar like a hen on a salver. My heart sank into my slippers. No more than Reynaud could I say what I knew; still, two may play at innuendo.

"I'll warrant 'tis no great thing, this collection of your master's," I said. "Little *knives* for gutting frogs, is my guess, or perhaps horse *whips*."

He grinned at me. "I can't say, I'm sure. I am not so intimate with my master's tastes and pleasures as you, dear Berthe."

"Yes, Duvet, how come you to speak with such authority?" That was Dentelle, with such a leer that LeRoi near pissed himself laughing. I told Dentelle to take care lest his lip grow permanently curled beneath his nose, but my heart wasn't in the exchange.

When the roads were dry enough, Jacques Charreton conveyed the few boxes of middling weight from Besançon, and lackeys carried them up to the round chamber in the donjon tower. The carpenter built shelves for the books, several glass cases, and a pair of mounting boards set with small hooks in patterns of the vicomte's devising. Then the vicomte unpacked and arranged his mysteries while lackeys and servingmaids polished the blades in the long-neglected gallery of Swords to wires and prayed for him to leave the door to the unnamed chamber unlocked.

This was not a safe pastime; the vicomte might turn up at any hour and he had no patience with spies. One lackey he surprised with his eye to the keyhole he might have choked to death had not Reynaud pulled him away.

I succeeded where the rest of them failed, me. I entered the forbidden chamber, unveiled all its secrets, and came away scatheless. I had the key.

I didn't steal it, exactly: 'twas not an easy thing to steal, that key, being as long as your palm with a great chased grip. Furthermore, the vicomte wore it on a length of blue ribbon like a lorgnon, and never removed it, except, perhaps, to sleep. Try as I might, I couldn't come up with a colorable plan for taking it, or even its impression. At length, I carried my dilemma to Pompey, who treated me to an incomprehensible discourse on locks and keys, the sum of which was that I'd no need to touch the key at all, only coat a blank with wax and stick it in the lock to get an impression of the wards. To me, this sounded no easier than procuring the original, and I was still trying to puzzle it out some days later when Pompey handed me a heavy, handkerchief-wrapped packet and told me the blacksmith would know what to do with it. To my astonishment, the blacksmith did. And charged me twenty sous for a clumsy iron rod with a flat "N" stuck on one end which he swore would fit that lock as a plow its furrow. After that, I could only wait with what patience I could muster for M. le vicomte de Montplaisir to get safely out of the way.

Before I'd quite gone mad with waiting, a pair of rare Muscovy ducks arrived from South America, and monsieur took it into his head that all his family must go pay homage to them. A pretty picture they made: handsome father and pretty mother, tall son and little daughter, strolling in the brilliant sunlight through the brilliant gardens of Beauxprés. They hadn't reached the pergola before I was threading the maze of rooms, drawing the key from my pocket, inserting it in the lock, and enduring the tortures of the damned while it caught and snagged in the wards.

Finally, it turned. I slipped inside, closed the door, and with some reluctance, locked it again behind me.

The chamber was round, thick-walled, and dark. A little sunlight filtered through the shutters, barely enough for me to see what was to be seen. No black draperies and no profane altar, le bon Dieu be thanked, but whips and knives in plenty. My first thought was that there wasn't much to see, and my second that there was a great deal, considering how little time the vicomte had had to collect it.

My third thought, as I examined the contents of the cases, was that here were represented all the collections of Beauxprés: weapons, snuffboxes, fans, miniatures, tapestries, china plates, etchings, a chamber pot. There was furniture in the shape of a low sofa and a curiously constructed chair. There were statuettes and an oil painting, figured lace, a lacquered ostrich egg, and, strangest of all, a pair of animal skins stuffed with straw: a fox and a hare posed in such a manner as to defy nature, gravity, and belief all at once.

What united this motley of objects into a single collection was their common—their very common—theme. In pairs, alone, in groups of two and three and more, men, women, and children danced countless variations of an old and simple dance. How ingenious were those variations! Many looked comical, many more painful, and all of them monstrous hard on the back. I was puzzling out the number of celebrants in one particularly crowded fan-painting when I heard the unwelcome scrape of a key in the lock and the voice of the vicomte de Montplaisir saying, ". . . of all kinds, *much* more curious than those musty wands in the cabinet des Fées."

Well. My face went numb with the cold of absolute panic, and I was barely able to slip behind the sofa before the door opened and the vicomte entered, shepherding a small figure before him. So befuddled was I and so dim the light that it took me a moment to recognize Mlle Linotte.

"My magic rituals are far more interesting than Pompey's," he was saying. "And 'tis far more convenable that you learn them from your brother than from a black savage."

Shrugging his hand away, Linotte went to stand before the hare and the fox. "Interesting indeed, brother. What is the purpose of this object, for example?"

"To put the viewer in a frame of mind proper to the working of my magic. Contemplate it, ma soeur, examine it closely. Touch it if you like. There. Is't not soft and yielding to your hand? Are you not moved?"

Linotte giggled. "Yes, brother, in a manner of speaking. The hare has moths, I think."

"Come look at this picture. Shall I lift you up to see it?"

"No need—here is a footstool for me to stand upon." A long silence ensued. Unable to see what was going on, I began to think I'd have to make my presence known. Imagining the vicomte's reaction, my belly quaked within me. Nevertheless, I'd eased my skirts from under my feet and was preparing to rise when I heard Linotte say, "What sillies! Aren't they cold?"

"No." The vicomte's voice was sharp. "Their sport warms them." He paused, then said more softly: " 'Tis chilly in here, is it not? I thought I saw you shiver a moment since. Come here, dear sister, and let me warm you."

"I'm quite comfortable. But 'tis kind of you to ask."

"Here, look at this wand, sister." I thought the vicomte's voice was taking on a desperate tone. "It masters a most potent magic. Shall I teach it you?"

In the silence, I heard a soft intake of breath that might have been a yawn. "I suppose," said Linotte, very ennuyée. "If it pleases you. 'Tis monstrous ugly."

The vicomte's red-heeled shoes minced past the sofa and out of my sight. "Take it in your hands, thus, and stroke it. Yes, like that. And while you stroke it, I touch you here and here, to wind up the spell."

His voice had thickened, and again my heart began to labor. Linotte giggled.

"You tickle," she said. "And this stupid wand, see how it bends and flops. Is that part of its magic? Or is its virtue used up, like Prince Lutin's roses?"

She was fortunate, Linotte. Another man might have forced her. The vicomte simply lost his temper.

"Get out," he shouted, sounding very young. "You've spoiled it all, you bitch. Go play at snakes and holes with your filthy blackamoor, just get your hands away from me, and quit laughing, damn you!"

"I'm sorry," said Linotte, not at all contrite. " 'Tis only that you look so droll that I can't help it. Thank you for showing me your collection, though. I'm sure 'tis very interesting. Has monsieur our father seen it?"

"Out!"

She left the door open behind her. The vicomte slammed it shut. I heard the key turn in the lock, saw his shoes march towards the sofa. My heart began to thump and pound so 'twas a miracle he didn't hear it. Muttering, he threw himself down upon the sofa, and presently I heard him grunting and thrashing close by my head. After a space he gave a sob—I thought of pleasure until I heard him curse Linotte anew, and with a kind of fear, as a damned witch. Then he rose and fled, I suppose buttoning his breeches as he went.

Well. My heart slowed at last, and I made haste to leave that Bluebeard's chamber, lock the door behind me, and drop the key in a narrow-necked urn where I prayed it would never come to light. I told Pompey about the scene, of course, in payment for the key. He nodded when I told him how his pupil had sprung her brother's trap.

"She's a wise child," he said, "cool-headed and sensible beyond her years. I've lately learned a spell to unman him—'tis only a matter of killing a wolf and taking its foreskin. He won't be easy to live with after. I'll have to put some warding upon the maids."

So M. Léon's lust was shackled, and you may be sure that he shortly grew as ill-tempered as a bear roused at midwinter. Reynaud's countenance became strained and nervous, and noises were heard at night from the donjon tower as of animals in mortal pain. The rumor went about the château and village that the young master worshipped the Devil, or was possessed of the Devil, or was an incarnation of the Devil, which last, you must agree, was closest to the truth. I hardly dare think what pleasures he might have turned to in his frustration —rituals and enormities to rival those of his ancestor Jorre, I've no doubt. 'Twas by the grace of le bon Dieu that he left Beauxprés again two months later.

The 12th of September, 1782, began as usual, with my dressing my mistress in her favorite bottle-green riding costume. I remember she looked very well in it, her slender body encased in a coat of military cut, the shape of her legs visible through her skirt and single petticoat. I buckled her spurs, pinned her mannish hat securely atop her coiffure, and followed with her whip and gloves as she jangled down the great stairs. As usual, when Artide opened the door to her, madame paused upon the threshold to draw on her gloves and breathe deeply of the morning air. As usual, Fleurette and the groom pranced by the fountain, fresh and eager for a run.

Then the vicomte de Montplaisir came galloping up the chestnut drive, and that, at ten o'clock of a fall morning, was not usual at all.

He pulled his horse up on its haunches, flung himself off before it had stopped plunging, and pushed past us into the château, calling loudly for monsieur. Madame, as if drawn by a magnet, followed.

From the forecourt, Roland shouted that two strange horses were coming up the drive. As they drew near, I could see they were muddy, weary, and burdened with wide, covered platforms built over their haunches. In addition to all this, they carried two villainous-looking men, scarcely less muddy than their nags, who dismounted at the fountain. The taller of them stalked up the steps and through the open door, leaving the groom, Artide, and me to stare at his companion, who was spinning around and around with his arms outspread in ecstasy and the beatific smile of a man who, beyond all hope, finds himself in Paradise.

"You, dirty fellow," said I. "Do you know where you are? What business have you here?"

"Don't you know me, Berthe? Have I changed so much?" He stopped his twirling and cocked his eye at me. "You have changed not at all, except for being a little fatter."

Quite apart from being entirely untrue, this remark was sufficiently offensive to strike me speechless. We stood confronted like two dogs, he grinning broadly, I first glaring, then gaping as I realized that all the matted hair, three-days' beard, and mud-stiffened leather hid none other than Jean Coquelet, back from the dead.

"Marie has married Philiberte Malateste," I said stupidly. "Have you found the bird?"

Laughing, Jean ran up the steps and embraced me regardless of the groom and Artide, who goggled at him as though, like the unfortunates on the fountain, they'd been translated into frogs. He turned from me to Artide. "Well met, mon vieux! I see you haven't yet run away."

"Salopard!" said Artide, and kissed him heartily on either stubbly cheek. "And where would I go? I am content to see you, Coquelet." The groom, who'd been a stable-boy when Jean left, came bounding up the steps to clap him on the shoulder. In short, 'twas a riotous homecoming, and we were still chattering and exclaiming when monsieur burst through us and down to the horses.

Tearing the covers from the panniers, he emptied them, taking cage after woven cage from the harness, lifting it, examining it, and casting it upon the ground, until at last the horses were unburdened and he surrounded by cooing, twittering cages. He turned to Noël Songis, who had followed him from the château.

"What are these birds?" Monsieur spread out his hands, pleading. "Why did you bring back all these birds? Which of them is the Porcelain Dove?"

"Whichever you will, monsieur," answered Noël Songis dryly. "The birds are all doves, all rare, all unknown to modern naturalists. None of them is quite like the Porcelain Dove you have described to me. We collected this pair"—he knelt and picked one cage out of the mess—"upon an island the natives call Koshima, which in their tongue is Luck Island. And these"—he picked up another—"are china doves." He opened the cage, gently removed a snowy, fluttering bird. "One china dove. The other is dead."

Monsieur stared at the bird-handler. "China doves," he whispered. "Luck Island."

"I swore to you, monsieur, that, if it existed, I would find your Porcelain Dove. I have not found it, monsieur. I fear it does not exist."

A profound silence descended upon the courtyard as everyone— Jean, me, the groom, even the horses and the despised birds—held their breaths to hear what monsieur would say.

"Does not exist?" he inquired mildly.

Noël Songis shrugged. "The Porcelain Dove is a fabulous creature, monsieur, a chimera not to be seen outside the pages of the bibliothèque bleu."

"A chimera. I see. I own a painting of the bird—you yourself have seen it. Is that, too, a chimera?"

Once again, Noël Songis shrugged. "I have seen a painting of a gryphon also, monsieur. I am nonetheless confident that if I sought a gryphon to capture it, I would seek in vain."

"Ah," said monsieur. "I thank you, M. Songis, for your advice in this matter. You are a wise man, much traveled, and 'tis plain to see that you know better than I, than Horace and Brutus and the Venerable Noreas, all of whom speak of a white bird whose feathers are smooth and hard as glass. The English naturalist Fowler saw one at the court of the king of Russia, where 'twas kept in a golden cage tied up with scarlet thread, and anyone who was sick or melancholy had only to come in sight of it to regain his health and happiness. Is Fowler a liar, then? Are you wiser than the ancients? Beware, birdman, how you tell me to my face that my Porcelain Dove is a chimera!

How can the life and fortune of the duc de Malvoeux depend upon a thing that does not exist? Just tell me that, chevalier l'oiseleur! How?"

By this time, monsieur had his hand upon his épée and Noël Songis, still cradling the china dove, had risen to his feet.

"Answer me, man," shrilled monsieur.

He'd asked so many questions, and they so unanswerable, that I'd be puzzled where to begin. Songis, it seems, was not. Calm as deep water, he gentled the dove with his finger. "I fear the world has changed since Brutus described the Websti, who spin thread out of their bodies like spiders and weave it into fine cloth upon their own feet. Nor could I find any trace of Pliny's baromezus, though we journeyed in Southern China where he found it and I showed the natives an engraving of it."

I whispered to Jean, "What did they say?"

He quirked his brow and smiled. "They laughed," he whispered back, "and said that only a fool would believe that ferns grew on the backs of lambs."

"Shut your jaw," hissed the groom. "The seigneur's running mad."

True enough. For as Noël Songis spoke, monsieur had drawn his épée and now began to lay about him at random. Step by slow step, the bird-handler retreated towards the fountain. Fleurette, who'd been snorting nervously, shied and bolted; the vicomte's horse and the muddy nags followed whinnying after. Some of the cages were trampled in their charge; monsieur himself trampled the rest. He slashed at the woven rushes, thrusting at the birds inside. Spittle and curses flew from his lips; white feathers and blood flew from the cages.

I don't know when madame had come outside. "O Berthe," she breathed now, and hid her face in my shoulder. As I put my arms around her, I saw that the vicomte de Montplaisir had come out of the château and was standing beside me staring down at his father with narrow and glittering eyes. His hand was locked over Reynaud's shoulder. Both faces—the vicomte's and Reynaud's—were unreadable, which, if you ask me, was just as well. Neither one of them looked quite human.

Monsieur shook the last bird from his épée and glanced about for new prey. During the slaughter, Noël Songis had remained by the fountain, stroking the china dove with the tears runnelling down the seams of his cheeks. Catching sight of him, or the dove, monsieur screamed. Noël Songis stood very still. Monsieur feinted with his épée, threw back his head, and screamed again. Noël Songis moved not an eyelash. Uncertainly, monsieur peered at him with one eye, then the other. When the prey still did not move, monsieur dropped the épée and stared fixedly at him. The bird-handler stared back.

They might have stood there forever, eye-locked across the carnage, had not Pompey and Linotte come round the west wing from the stable-yard, leading a sweating and trembling Fleurette between them.

"She was trying to get into her stall," Linotte said, then saw her father and stopped.

"Isn't that M. Songis?" she asked in her piercing child's voice. "Did he find the Dove?"

Monsieur jerked about to face her, his mouth working. My mistress raised her head. I clasped her tighter. Let Pompey look to his charge, I thought, and I will look to mine.

For a painful moment, the tableau held, equally poised between melodrama and tragedy. Then the vicomte de Montplaisir dashed helter-skelter down the steps and, throwing himself at his father's besmottered feet, at one stroke turned the scene into romance.

"Father!" Slowly, monsieur's eyes turned from his daughter to his eldest son, down on one knee in the mud before him. Madame sighed and sagged against me. Gently as I could, I let her down on the doorstep. 'Twas all too much for her, poor lamb. She'd be better as she was until the scene was played out.

"Father! No longer can I endure the sight of your high spirit thus bowed to the earth by chains of want and woe."

I looked up at Jean, who'd shoved a hand between his teeth. Romance? Farce was more like it. I bit my lips to stifle laughter and wondered who had taught the boy to talk like that. Monsieur, however, did not laugh.

"Father! Would you send a maître d'hôtel to lead an army, a chef to plead in court, a groom to negotiate policy? Is it any less vain to send a lackey upon a hero's quest? If the honor of Malvoeux is dependent upon one white bird, is it not the duty of the heir of Malvoeux to find that bird and bring it home?"

"My son," said the duc de Malvoeux. "I . . ."

"Monsieur my noble father, I pray you bless me in this my endeavor; for, with your blessing or without it, I will set forth upon this quest, to journey through the vasty oceans of the deep, to sail far and wide for a year and a day, to, uh . . ." The vicomte's brow knotted and his voice trailed off. He seized monsieur's hand and kissed it.

"I have one son worthy the name of Malvoeux," said monsieur. "You have my blessing, Montplaisir. When will you leave?"

The vicomte glanced uncertainly up towards Reynaud. "Uh. Next week, perhaps? The preparations will take some time."

"I have a store of nets and snares. You may take those, and my horse Branche d'Or, and"—here monsieur pressed the bloody épée into the vicomte's hands—"my best sword to protect you.

"For I burn, Léon, you cannot conceive how I burn to hold her, that Dove with feathers as hard and smooth as glass. I shall not rest until I hold her, Léon. I shall know no rest until I hold her in my two hands and cut my fingers upon her glassy wings."

The vicomte de Montplaisir seemed dumbfounded at this speech, and I heard Reynaud tutting disgustedly as he trotted down the steps and knelt in the mud by his master. Taking the épée into his own hands, he bowed his sandy head. "Monsieur's bag is packed, as monsieur has directed, and I stand ready to ride at the rising of tomorrow's sun. Five long years has monsieur's noble father suffered, and 'tis cruelty to let him suffer one day more."

"To be sure, Reynaud," snapped the vicomte. "We must not dally. With the rising of tomorrow's sun, eh?" He must have caught our incredulous looks, for he flushed painfully. "All unaccoutered as I am, I burn to go this very hour. Yet, if you wish it, I will wait, and accept your sword, your horse, your nets, and your gold to speed me on my journey. And while my faithful Reynaud gathers these necessaries, I will slay you this proud peasant, this Noël Songis, and embrace my mother and my sister in farewell."

At the sound of his bird-handler's name, monsieur's brow began to cloud again, but Noël Songis had very wisely removed himself and his one china dove from the forecourt of the château Beauxprés. While M. Léon postured and declaimed, I'd watched him slip away around the north wing past Linotte, who touched his arm and smiled. That is the last any of us saw of him.

I've often wondered what became of Noël Songis. Nothing bad, I think. He was a man who knew what he wanted, and taking care of birds is not a hard thing to achieve. There were at least five men and one woman in France alone who would have accepted his china dove as a more than sufficient letter of character.

Though the scene in the forecourt was clearly at an end, the principal actors seemed reluctant to quit the stage. I loosened madame's waistcoat and sent Artide for her salts-bottle, and still father and son lingered by the fountain as if waiting for a prompter to give them their lines. As I chafed my mistress' cold hand, I saw Reynaud raise the vicomte from his knees and chivvy both him and his father in the direction of the aviary. I suppose they were going to look for the nets.

Jean took no notice of them, or of me, or of madame insensible on the ground. Slowly he descended the steps, squatted amid the pathetic remains of his Eastern quest and, taking up a broken cage, extracted from it a handful of bloody feathers. Linotte went to him and put her hand on his shoulder. "Did you love them very much?" she asked.

"No, mademoiselle. But I worked very hard to get them, and sometimes it amounts to the same thing."

In Which Accounts
Are Cast Up

So the vicomte de Montplaisir rode away upon monsieur's best horse with monsieur's most expensive sword at his side and a hundred golden louis in his purse. Shortly thereafter, the aviary furnaces broke down, the bird-handlers demanded their wages, and the roof over the Alchemical attic began to leak. To meet these expenses, monsieur desired Jacques Ministre to levy a tax on his tenants under the ancient feudal law of guet et garde. The peasants refused to pay, and led by Just Vissot, took monsieur to law over the matter. Monsieur raged that he'd burn the village to the ground, but settled for hiring a lawyer expert in the ways of legal rebellions. Although the peasants would of a certainty pay up in the end, monsieur expected to be considerably out-of-pocket over the affair.

"You must write to Mme Eloffe for me, Berthe," said madame, "and tell her I'll not be requiring the brocade caraco. Monsieur has told me we must make economies. To be sure, 'tis no more than the queen herself must do, yet I protest the price of one new caraco could make little difference to the coffers of either France or Beauxprés."

"No, madame."

"Little frivolities like new caracos add up, he says, so that there's no money left for necessities."

"Yes, madame."

This sounded like excellent sense to me, and more like Jacques Ministre than monsieur, who'd squander his last sou on corn to feed his birds. As for madame, why, the idea that caracos must be paid for at all was as foreign to her as idol worship. In her world, one attended Mass and put off one's creditors, who, enjoying the patronage of the nobility, ought not to expect silver as well. And if a time came when they must be paid, one could always borrow.

I can't swear I thought all this then, yet I do remember that something—perhaps the thought of debt—put me in mind of M. Léon, so that the next words from my mouth were: "Has madame any word of the vicomte de Montplaisir?"

She stared at me, startled, then rummaged among the papers on her écritoire and handed me a letter bearing the stigmata of a cheap tavern. Who can tell why I saved it? Yet here 'tis, with the ink all faded into the winestains so that I can barely make out the message.

November 1782

Chère Mme ma mère la duchesse de Malvoeux—

I have found a type—a villainous ugly man, but honest as a butcher, I vow. He's seen the Porcelain Dove with his own eye (he has but the one) and has promised me a map to the Fortunate Isles and a letter of introduction to the king of the place, but the Devil's in it that he wants 100 gold louis for 'em. M. my father has already been so generous that I cannot ask them of him. Do you, mère adorée, act as the agent of your loving, your most dutiful son. The "Lion d'Or" in Marseilles will find me.

Léon Philiberte Jorre Guillaume Maindur,
vicomte de Montplaisir

"One hundred gold louis!" I said. "The vicomte requires madame to ask M. le duc for one hundred gold louis? He's not lacking in gall, he!"

"I've already asked him," said madame with simple pride. "Monsieur says the vicomte must have anything he wants. Jacques Ministre is to sell a meadow or some such to raise the sum, but we shall lose the income from it, so I must frump about in last year's gowns and tell Eveline Réverdil that she cannot break her journey to Paris at Beauxprés as she intended, for we can't afford to feed her. A noble of sixteen quarterings, and can't afford to feed a guest! There's no accounting for it, Berthe. Unless Ministre has been stealing monsieur's feathers to soften his own nest."

Bah! As well suspect a turtledove of infidelity as Jacques Ministre of false accounting. And so I told madame, who laughed and said that I must then be wiser than her husband, who had demanded of that same faithful Ministre a strict accounting of all the duchy's wealth, both income and expense.

The compte rendu of the seigneuries of Beauxprés and Malvoeux made nearly as bulky a document as M. Necker's, for Ministre took a bitter joy in tracing the fate of every sou for ten years past. Here were the profits from selling monsieur's cattle and corn in the markets of Besançon; there were the peasants' payments for the use of monsieur's mills, his ovens, and his wood. There were whole pages for tolls, more for magistrate's fees, more for the interest from certain loans monsieur had made to the king. Set against these sources of income were the expenses of the estate, covering page after page of closely written lines. Meat, wax candles, linen for sheets, a new bull to serve monsieur's small herd of milk cows, seed corn, glass, salt, sleigh-runners, harness, oil, rope—oh, the list of things needed to keep Beauxprés from crumbling about our ears was endless.

As monsieur himself had predicted, his income was indeed sufficient to pay for all, including the upkeep of the hôtel Malvoeux, but only just sufficient, and only when times were good. Taking into account the recent bad harvests, M. Fleury's new taxes, the fees for Einsiedeln and L'Epieu, and the vicomte's allowance, not to mention four—no, five—birding expeditions, Jacques Ministre's figures revealed M. le duc de Malvoeux to be teetering at the edge of noble penury.

Monsieur's response to this news could not, perhaps, be heard all the way to Besançon, but 'twas more than loud enough to penetrate the library door to the ears of Artide standing without.

"Impossible? By hell, Ministre, I do not believe it. Beauxprés is a rich domain. Its cheeses are famous and its cows are fat. My father was too easy on his peasants, yes, and my grandfather, too."

Artide could not make out Ministre's answer. He must have been standing across the room by the window.

"Dismiss two bird-handlers? Shut up the glasshouses? Ten thousand thunders, Ministre! I'd sooner dismiss my wife and my daughter and shut up Beauxprés."

Jacques Ministre's voice again, in the cadence of a man pleading the case of reason. Monsieur interrupting, further from the door now, so that only some detached words and phrases reached Artide's straining ears: ". . . Mareschal . . . a hundred livres . . . hanging offense . . ."

"No, M. le duc." Ministre spoke so near and loud that Artide scraped his ear on the doorhandle in his fright. "No, I cannot do what M. le duc asks of me."

"Cannot? Will not!"

"Very well, monsieur. I will not. It does not make good sense for monsieur to hang Claude Mareschal for his father's bad debt. The land would revert to monsieur, bien sûr. But who would monsieur find willing to farm it for him, hein? And if no one farms it, where then is the profit? If monsieur insists upon every tithe, right, and levy due him as seigneur of Beauxprés, monsieur's tenants will starve. How will a full churchyard further monsieur's quest, eh?"

"Pah!" says monsieur. "Let them starve. I care nothing for them, lazy dirt-eaters."

The handle dipped. Artide leapt back from the door like a flea just as Jacques Ministre threw it open. "I am no philosophe, monsieur," said Ministre. "Yet I believe 'tis the part of a legitimate government to respect the rights and the needs of the people it governs. You, monsieur, respect nothing." And then he stalked away, and Artide said that his jaw was so bunched with fury he might have been storing nuts in it.

That same night Jacques Ministre left Beauxprés. He embraced us all in farewell, and we all wept. All except Menée, who caroused to his ancient rival's rout and pranced unbuttoned in the kitchen, waving his pizzle before the servingmaids and inviting them to pay his scepter homage—one at a time or all at once, he cared not which. To be sure, their virtue was in little danger, an excess of brandy having soaked him quite limp. Yet after several weeks of similar scenes, we were overjoyed to hear that monsieur had engaged a new steward.

Our joy was shorter-lived than a whore's bastard. Never have I clapped eyes on a stingier, stringier man than Gilles Sangsue. His eyes were close-set, the better to peer into ledgers and rent rolls; his fingers were long, the better to pry into pockets and purses. He'd been a collector of taxes in the north.

What a horror the man was! Bien sûr, I've seen greater evil at Beauxprés—M. Léon and mère Malateste, why, even Menée was more wicked than Sangsue, his misdeeds more open and shameless. But if the sins of lust, anger, gluttony, and pride are no less mortal than avarice and envy, they are at least sins of passion, and therefore more easily forgiven—by man, if not by le bon Dieu. Avarice and envy are cold sins, and the men who commit them, like giants, have no hearts.

Sangsue's first act as M. le duc's steward was to sack the greater part of M. le duc's domestic staff. When I complained of this to madame, she recalled to me one of Mme Hortense's letters of the previous year, in which she had described Necker sweeping through the king's household like Samson through the Philistines, felling battalions of royal cup-bearers, companies of royal stocking-folders, divisions of tax-collectors, and legions of venal office-holders of every rank. She reminded me how I'd laughed and sworn it served them right, the overdressed do-nothings. Now, watching lackeys and servingmaids turned out—and just before the first snow, too, when field work was impossible to come by. . . . Well, I found myself close to pitying those unemployed hasteners of the royal roast.

The economics of the case were undeniable. The duc de Malvoeux employed many more servants than were needed to run Beauxprés. The lackeys especially worked too little, ate too much, and were plaguey arrogant besides. Fewer servants cost less, eat less, work harder, and have no time for arrogance. I suspect that in the depths of that withered purse he called a heart, Gilles Sangsue cherished the image of a household trimmed to a single servant, infinitely hardworking, infinitely thin, infinitely humble.

Bread, onions, gruel and vin du pays—that's what he fed us, who'd been accustomed to share monsieur's sauced meats and fine Burgundies. Menée took these economies as a personal affront, threatened Sangsue with mayhem and murder, and died of an apoplexy just after the turn of the year. M. Malesherbes, who'd been melancholy as an owl, grew more melancholy still, until his entire conversation came to consist of belly-deep sighs and wistful moans. As for the rest of us . . . Well, we grumbled mightily, but ate what was set before us. The villagers would have been glad to have had so much.

I remember Mme Pyanet standing in the bakery door, glancing over her shoulder at her husband within, whispering that she didn't know how they'd pay their taxes, she didn't indeed.

"M. Pyanet, he has a big heart. The blacker the loaves he's brought and the worse they smell baking, the more eager is he to extend credit.

They're our neighbors, he says, we pray with them and we drink with them. Let them keep their copper for their tithes, he says. What about *our* tithes, that's what I want to know."

I gave her the basket I'd brought, packed with pork rind and scraps and a few pieces of silver wrapped in a rag at the bottom. Well, I'd no need of silver, stuck out in the high meadows of the Jura with nothing to spend it on save some rags of coarse lace when the peddler chanced by, and no one to see me wear them save monsieur's birds. And I had always liked Mme Pyanet.

In early spring, the vicomte de Montplaisir wrote saying he'd procured the one-eyed sailor's map, and 'twas all he'd hoped. Now he needed fifty livres to defray the immediate expenses of the journey. The letter's gone, but I remember its being more sober than the last, more neatly penned, more respectful: Reynaud's work, of a certainty. It inspired monsieur to send straightaway to a bank in Besançon for a loan of fifty livres, which he dispatched posthaste to Marseilles. While he was borrowing, he borrowed a second fifty livres to buy a pair of rare African birds-of-paradise that he'd news of from a southern bird-seller. They were very beautiful—like phoenixes, white with breasts so pink you'd think the magic flame burned them still. Madame was in ecstasies over them. The rest of us found them a poor enough substitute for our wages.

'Twas at about that time, as I remember, that Justin returned to Beauxprés.

After five years' absence, I'd all but forgot that madame's younger son was still alive. I suppose he had been dead, in a manner of speaking—dead to the world and sepulchered, first on the heights of Einsiedeln and then in the gray valley of Baume-les-Messieurs, two days' ride west of Beauxprés. Jean, who has been there, says that Baume-les-Messieurs is a sight to behold, a rocky, chilly place down at the bottom of a gorge with the wind whistling down from the heights above like the wrath of God. Just the place for a Maindur monk whose taste ran to the ascetic.

In any case, one day he turned up, unheralded and unaccompanied and riding on a fat white mule. Artide showed him into the Sèvres salon where the family sat at dinner. I remember how we laughed to hear Artide tell how Mme la duchesse had choked on her quenelle, how M. le duc had ordered a cover set and bade his son be seated for all the world as if his sudden appearance were in no way out of the ordinary.

"So I sighed with relief—LePousset, here, sighed also, and went for the cover while I pulled out a chair. Did M. Justin then sit down like a human man and help himself to Malesherbes' good quenelles? He did not. M. Justin clapped shut his eyes and folded his hands and commenced to mutter Latin while monsieur looked daggers at him and Mlle Linotte was seized with a fit of giggling, which she pretended was coughing. Monsieur roared at her to hold her noise, and madame said she hoped she wasn't falling sick. And all the while, our monkling kept up his *pater nostering* and *gaudeamusing* as though he were alone in his cell. Mademoiselle laughed until she coughed in good earnest and monsieur flung the seethed mushrooms at her head. After that, M. Justin consented to seat himself at last and dinner proceeded quietly."

"Quietly!" M. Malesherbes shook his jowls sadly. "I'd hoped to hear they'd dined on theological argument, for 'tis sure they dined on little else."

"You may blame our precious eremite for spoiling their appetites," Artide said. "The only thing to pass His Asceticship's lips—saving Latin, of course—was bread and water. Pah! 'Tis enough to make a man weep, to watch them turning up their aristocratic noses at a meal any peasant would sell his firstborn for."

Dentelle threw his hands to Heaven and implored the saints to grant him patience. "Ah, Artide, Artide. Peasants eat what they can. Ducs eat what they will. That is how the world wags. You who are so learned, so deeply and widely read in things that are not at all your affair, you should know *that*, at least."

"Not my affair?" Artide's cheeks mottled. "Was that not what Cain said of Abel?"

"Quote not scripture to me," snapped Dentelle. "I've heard you say often enough you believe not a word of it. Atheist!"

"Lick-arse!"

Dentelle sprang to his feet, ruffles quivering with rage. Artide stood more slowly, raised fists like hooves, and told the little valet to come on. M. Malesherbes, who'd been slumped over his evening brandy-and-sugar like a figure on a tomb, roused himself to shout with something of his old authority: "Regulate yourselves, the pair of you! Artide, your mouth is a midden. And as for you, Dentelle, nobles may eat while peasants starve, but as far as I know, 'tis not by divine law."

They glowered, grumbled, and as they subsided, I remarked that M. Justin was no doubt come to announce his intention of taking final vows.

"A blind man might see as much," said Jean loftily.

"Leave her alone," said Artide. "She's not seen M. Justin. I'll give the boy this—he won't be one of those fat monks whose spotless habit hides a spotted soul. If dirt and bony wrists be holy, our Justin bids fair to be a saint."

"Nothing fair about him," said the lackey LePousset. "A bird of ill-omen, if you ask me. A real magpie, in fact."

Dentelle muttered into his cup that some people had no respect for their betters. Jean laughed and slapped LePousset on the shoulder. "Very good, mon vieux! A magpie—ha! That's Brother Justin to the life, save that magpies are cocksure birds and Brother Justin seems set upon teaching a church mouse humility. You know that white mule he rode? Well, he led it to the stable himself and wiped it down with his own hands. Did a poor enough job of it, too, and you could see the mule wasn't happy, but put up with it like a God-fearing beast."

I sipped my brandy thoughtfully. "Magpie, mouse, or saint, monsieur won't like him going into holy orders."

"Pooh," said Dentelle. " 'Tis as natural for second sons to enter the church as for doves to flock to a cote."

M. Malesherbes shrugged. "The boy must go somewhere, after all. What else could he do, poor deaf stick that he is? Would you have him buy a commission and take up a musket against the English?"

The thought of M. Justin taking up a musket at all nearly undid us, even Dentelle. When I'd wiped the tears of laughter from my eyes, I said, "Ah, me. Of course not, poor boy. But only consider. The vicomte de Montplaisir is enduring God only knows what dangers in God only knows what foreign land. And if you have forgotten the little matter of the Porcelain Dove, you may be sure monsieur has not. He'll see to it our monkling stays in the world at least until his brother comes home, with or without that accursed bird."

Artide said, "In the world? He's never been in the world, any more than the rest of them. They're all alike, these aristocrats. They care only for their own pleasures and their own occupations, and everyone else may starve or go to Hell."

"Come now," said Dentelle. "This has not been a perfect world since Eve ate the apple."

"Foutre!" shouted Artide, and flung his cup clanging upon the flagstones. "I beg your pardon, M. Malesherbes, but Dentelle speaks like a fool. The world would be less imperfect if the likes of monsieur were forced to pay for what they took."

This outburst shocked even Dentelle into silence. Somewhat shamefaced, Artide shrugged and knelt to retrieve his cup and mop up the spreading brandy. A log broke and settled in the hearth, birthing a litter of spark and flame. That I remember clearly, and the crimson streaks the fire splashed across his broad face. Did I shiver and cross myself? I think I did.

The very next morning, madame declared that Linotte was running wild and must be taken in hand. She was right, bien sûr—the child had been running wild these three years and more. I was only surprised she'd noticed.

Jean, who likes things to be clear, says that Colette will never tell from my account of her whether I liked Mlle Linotte de Malvoeux or loathed her. His confusion is not in the least astonishing; I myself share it. Some days I'd see her in the formal garden, skipping through the paths in some intricate, private game, and 'twas as though the years rolled back to show me Mlle Adèle playing alone in the garden of the hôtel Fourchet. Then my heart would go out to her as it had to her mother, and I would resolve to mention to madame that the time had come to find a new maid for her.

On other occasions, I'd pass her in the cabinet des Fées or descending the Unicorn stair from the Alchemical attic, her black eyes fierce with thought, the air around her tingling like the magnetic spirit in Dr. Mesmer's tubs. Then she seemed to me her father's daughter from beaky face to long, narrow feet, indifferent to all save her own arcane pursuits. So I pendulumed between pity and dislike. And all the time I knew nothing of the Linotte de Malvoeux who was neither her father's daughter nor her mother's, but herself alone.

I was writing about madame.

Even though you'd think Justin's return would be uppermost in her mind, 'twas Linotte's ill manners and Linotte's ill looks came between my mistress and her chocolate, and not her son at all. Well, monks and their manners were far beyond her ken. Young girls, now, she knew exactly how young girls should dress and act.

Twice or thrice she lifted the cup to her lips, only to put it down untasted as another of her daughter's imperfections erupted in her memory. "Oh, that hair of hers! I'd be astonished if it's so much as seen a comb since the turn of the year. There's nothing for it but cut it all off. And her clothing! Why, she's ragged as a beggar's child. You'll make over something of mine, won't you, Berthe? The blue silk, I think, and that sprigged polonaise—the one that never became me."

When she sipped her chocolate at last, her mouth wryed. "This is cold, Berthe, and quite undrinkable," she said, thrusting the cup into my hands and throwing back the covers. "Well, why do you stand there gawking? We've not a moment to waste—my corset, at once, if you please, and the mauve lace powdering-gown. When I'm dressed, you may send for Mlle Linotte, oh, and for Pompey as well. He can read to us as we work. 'Twill be quite like old times."

In less time than I'd have thought possible, madame was dressed, and Linotte and Pompey were standing bewildered before her.

Madame bent a severe eye upon her daughter. "Linotte, thou art an object of disgust," she said. "Remove that, that *rag* at once, and Berthe will cut thy hair. Pompey, read to us." She took up her tambour frame. "I'm in a mood for fairies, I think."

"Yes, madame." Pompey opened a glass-fronted case and ran his finger over the books within. "What is madame's pleasure?"

"I don't know, I'm sure. Anything, so long as 'tis romantical." She waved a vague needle. "The one with the clever princess."

" 'Finette Cindron'?"

"Clever monkey! C'est ça!"

While Pompey leafed through the well-worn *Fées à la mode*, I unlaced Linotte's gown. To call it a rag was to overstate the case, though 'twas certainly not new, and far too tight for the girl. Pompey had done his best to comb her straggling hair and dress it, after a fashion, in a plaited tail down her back. Shivering in her skimpy chemise, she looked like a charity child, shamefaced and uncertain, and my heart, like a cracked tooth, ached with her chill. 'Twould not have been proper to embrace her, so I winked and whispered that if she stood still while I cut her hair, I'd make her a petticoat, yes, and a new gown as well.

She smiled at that. I fetched a pair of scissors from my workbasket and a sheet to spread on the rug. By now Pompey had found the place, and while I combed and snipped, he began to read aloud.

"Once upon a time there was a king and a queen who had managed their affairs so badly that they were driven out of their kingdom. In order to live, they sold their crowns, then their wardrobes, their linen, their lace, and all their furniture, piece by piece."

He glanced up under his brows at madame, who was holding her embroidery up to the light and considering it, her lips a little pursed. "Poor things," she said absently. "They must have been prodigious careless. Go on."

"When the king and the queen were truly destitute, the king said to his wife, 'We are exiled from our kingdom and have nothing left to sell. We must earn a living for ourselves and our poor children. Consider a little what we can do: for up to this time I have known no trade but a king's, which is a very agreeable one.' "

The queen's answer was rudely interrupted by the door of the China antechamber's slamming open and Justin stumbling into the room with monsieur stalking upon his heels.

"Madame," said the duc de Malvoeux. "Behold thy son."

Our eyes turned to Justin, who stood firm before our scrutiny. I remember thinking that LePousset and Jean had been right: the boy was very like a magpie in his novice's habit, all black and white with a cowl up to his chin, and his sharp, pasty face and his dark, cropped hair. In the five years since I'd seen him, he'd grown tall and bony, and his eyes burned with a martyr's passion.

Madame lowered her embroidery to her lap and sighed. " 'Tis ill-done, my son, to disturb thy father when he has so much to worry him. I'd have thought the monks might have taught thee consideration, at least."

Justin lowered his eyes to his sandaled feet.

"He professes a vocation," said monsieur in a voice of loathing. "I ask you, madame. A monk! I cannot imagine where the boy came by such an idea."

"He's been living in a monastery for six years," said my mistress reasonably.

"Madame!" Justin's voice broke and slid. He cleared his throat and tried again. "Madame my mother, I am eighteen years of age . . ."

"To be sure, Justin, I of all people need no reminding how old thou art. When I bore thee, I was little older."

Monsieur ground his teeth. "Hold your tongue, wife, and listen. The boy is eighteen. By law, no novice may make his final vows until the age of twenty-one. My consent is withheld by law, not whim. So I have told him and so you must tell him, madame. He will not believe me."

"Shame upon thee, Justin! Why should thy father lie to thee?"

Justin muttered into his cowl.

"If you'd speak," said monsieur, "speak. 'Tis bad enough I've spawned a monk without he be a coward as well."

Rage cracked Justin's face.

"My father would lie to me," he said passionately, "because he hates me, because he thinks me unfit to bear his name. He would lie to spite me, madame, and above all, to make divorce between my God and me. Believing in nothing, madame, he begrudges me that I do believe, and would murder my faith as he has murdered everything else I have loved."

He looked accusingly at monsieur. "What of my rabbit, monsieur, my pet rabbit that you took from my apartments and gave M. Malesherbes to cook into a pie? And what of my tutor? What of poor M. LeSueur?"

During his son's outburst, monsieur had frowned, then settled into an expression of bored distaste. "M. LeSueur was still in health when last I heard of him. Of the rabbit I have not the slightest recollection. Doubtless I thought it unsuitable for a Malvoeux to sleep with animals, like a peasant's child." He turned to madame. "Did I not know otherwise, I'd swear this eunuch was none of my getting. Mère Malateste warned me your seed might yet be weak from bearing Léon. If Justin is a bloodless turnip, I've only my impatience to blame."

In his chair by the window, Pompey sighed, just a little too loudly. Monsieur's bright gaze fixed upon his wife's servant. Identically black, identically contemptuous, their eyes met. Monsieur's chin lifted; his sallow cheek flushed.

"My son shall not return to the black monks of Baume-les-Messieurs," he said, speaking as to empty air. "In three years, if he still wishes to take the cowl, I cannot prevent him. Until then, he is still my son, subject to my authority by duty and by law. Until then, let him live as a son should, under his father's roof and under his father's eye."

He turned to madame, who was clutching her embroidery help-lessly. "See to it."

As soon as the door shut behind his father, Justin sank to his knees and commenced to beat his fists upon the floor and cry aloud to God.

There are few sights less pleasing than a grown man howling like a wounded beast, and if I'm no saint now, I was certainly none then. I'd a sudden urge to kick the boy where he lay, especially as madame had added her voice to his, and Pompey, who might have quieted them, sat staring into space like an obsidian statue. A howl rose in my own throat, and just as it was threatening to burst from my lips, Linotte tapped me on my shoulder. I spun around to face her, my hand upraised for a slap.

Unperturbed, she reached out and took my hand in hers, gave it a reassuring squeeze. "Don't fret, Berthe. I'll see to my brother."

I fetched a deep breath. "You're welcome to try, mademoiselle," I said, and went to madame to shake and pet her into some semblance of calm. Under her sobs and Justin's, I heard the rise and fall of Linotte's voice, singing tunelessly, repetitively, a few notes up, a few notes down, a drone like bees in summer or the hushing of blood in my ears in the night when not even the rats are stirring. Even after madame fell silent, I had to strain to hear it.

My eyes drifted shut. My chin came to rest upon madame's lace cap. Then Pompey was shaking me and pulling me to my feet and bidding me help carry my slumbering mistress into her bedchamber. Once we'd disposed her on her bed, loosened her stays, removed her shoes, and drawn the curtains closed, my head was clear again, and I followed Pompey into the antechamber where Linotte was sitting tai-lorwise with her hand upon a gently snoring heap of rags.

"I sang the sleep spell," she said proudly. "We can do anything we want with him now."

Pompey smiled. "Wise child," he said. "We'll wash him, I think. Will mademoiselle consent to stay and let Berthe make her fine while I tend to her brother?"

Linotte pouted at that, but was wise enough to know she'd little choice in the matter. So Pompey hoisted the heap of rags over his shoulder and bore it away to be bathed and clothed like a duc's son. I returned to cutting Linotte's hair.

When that was done, I bathed her and rinsed her thick black

curls with oil and comfrey water. At last she rose, a knobby Venus, and paused before stepping from madame's copper bath to consider her dripping form in madame's long glass. I remember how thin she was and long-wristed, and her naked limbs as bony and angled as a marionette's.

"I'll be as tall as Justin when I grow up," she said placidly. "Poor Justin. He won't find the Porcelain Dove."

In Which Wild Birds
Are Caged

Madame and I embarked upon our last journey from Beauxprés in August of 1783. We didn't know, of course, that it was to be our last journey, any more than we knew what had become of the vicomte de Montplaisir. Had we known, would we have spent it as we did, with the marquis and marquise de Bonsecours in Versailles?

For myself, I've never liked Versailles. Its chambers are built for titans, so that mortal men and women must pad themselves out with wide-skirted coats and panniers and elaborated rituals just to cast shadows in them. Wherever one looks, there are mirrors to mock one and gilding to blind one and paintings of gods to keep one in one's place. And should all this splendor seduce some ambitious noble into desiring it for himself, there are warnings in the shape of allegorical fountains. Latona is one. Another is a figure of the titan Enceladus, who sought to climb Olympus, half-crushed beneath a flooded tumble of stone. "We are gods," says Versailles. "You are vermin. And so shall you ever be."

Yet on that journey to Versailles I saw gods and vermin gaping in astonished equality at the phenomenon of a cock, a duck, and a sheep sailing through the air in a straw basket, and that was a sight I'd not have missed for a year's wages. 'Twas like one of Jean's hearth-tales come unexpectedly to life, and in its own way as great a magic as the removing of Beauxprés from the circle of the world.

The spectacle had been touted with much fanfare, and a

Judgment-day hodge-podge of ranks, professions, ages, and sexes were gathered in the Great Court to watch it well before the appointed hour. Between the terrace and the gilded gates, ministers and water-sellers, whores and shopkeepers craned and elbowed for a glimpse of the platform from which the balloon would ascend. Of the balloon itself nothing was yet to be seen save a great wad of azure material surrounded by any number of scurrying men. They were all dressed in black and looked very like mice from where we sat perched high upon the stone balustrade of the Minister's wing. Or at least madame, Linotte, and the marquise de Bonsecours were perched on the balustrade. I stood behind it, wedged between the marquis and the vicomte d'Anceny.

The vicomte was the marquis' oldest son—he who had attended my mistress' wedding in his mother's womb—grown to be a soldier and a veteran of the American War. A pleasant young man, with something of his father's placid temper and his mother's quick wit. I remember him undertaking to explain to me the mysteries of the scene before us.

"Do you see the tall man, Mlle Duvet, the one all dressed in black? That is M. Montgolfier himself, the inventor of the aerostatic globe, whom they call the Benjamin Franklin of the stratosphere."

To my other side, the marquis shook his head in solemn wonder. "We have discovered the secret for which the centuries have sighed." Poor M. de Bonsecours. With age, his hunchback had become more pronounced than ever and gave him an air of being forever on the point of glancing over his left shoulder. "Man will fly," he went on, "and, appropriating for himself all the power of the animal kingdom, become master of the earth, the waters, and the air. A heavy responsibility, is it not, my son?"

"Mountainous," agreed the vicomte amiably. "Look, Mlle Duvet, where the balloon inflates."

The heap of material stirred, subsided, billowed, and with infinite stateliness, blossomed into a monstrous azure mushroom decked out in swags and ruffles and golden fleurs-de-lis like a court gown. As it rose slowly above the platform and bobbed against its restraining cords, the crowd gasped and exclaimed.

"Look. Something's going on." My mistress pointed across the yard, where a wave of activity was rippling through the crowd. The marquis de Bonsecours, with characteristic prudence, had brought along a spyglass, which he now applied to his eye.

"What do you see, Bonsecours?" asked the marquise after a space.

"Yes, Bonsecours, what do you see? 'Tis monstrous unfair of you to keep both glass and knowledge to yourself, I vow." Thus my mistress, pouting.

"Patience, patience. I have not yet adjusted the focus." M. de Bonsecours peered and fiddled and twisted his neck into painful cricks, and, "Enfin, I cannot make it out," he said regretfully, and folded the instrument to replace it in his pocket.

The vicomte reached across me, plucked the glass neatly from his father's hand, extended it, and clapped it to his eye. "They're bringing animals onto the platform," he reported. "A sheep, a cock, some other bird, white—a duck, I think. Now they're putting them into a cage, or making the attempt. The sheep seems to have recollected a pressing engagement elsewhere. I can't blame it, poor thing."

"Poor thing indeed," said Mme de Bonsecours. "They say the king wanted to conscript a pair of convicts as the balloon's first passengers. This is much more humane, should the experiment miscarry."

"It will not miscarry," said the vicomte.

" 'Tis hardly an experiment, my dear," said M. de Bonsecours. "There have been many flights before this, not the least of which was a year since, in the Champ de Mars. I paid a demi-livre for seats in the stands. You do not recall it because it rained that day and you did not attend. On that occasion, the balloon ascended notwithstanding the inclement weather. You will observe that the sky is quite clear today, so that I have every confidence . . ."

Mme de Bonsecours laid a plump hand upon her husband's arm. "And so have I, Bonsecours, and so have we all."

"Look," exclaimed Linotte. "It rises!"

The drums rattled in a crescendo of excitement, M. Montgolfier's assistants cast off the ropes, and to my vast astonishment, the great azure mushroom wobbled ponderously upwards. All the clerics, aristocrats, bourgeois, and canaille gathered their breaths in a gasp of wonder, which they let out again in an exhalation that might have swept the balloon all the way to Paris had not a violent gust of wind dipped and scudded it westward instead. Against the sky a loose triangle of taffeta could be seen flapping wildly. Another gasp—of fear, this one.

"Oh! 'Tis torn!" shrieked madame. "It must come down! We'll all be crushed!"

"Don't be a goose, Adèle," said Mme de Bonsecours. "See, there it goes towards Vaucresson, high as ever." She put her arm about Linotte, who sat between them. "And what dost thou think, petite? Is it not a pretty sight?"

Mouth O'ed in rapture, Linotte watched the balloon glide over the roofs of Versailles, trailing its barnyard aeronauts in a wicker basket. Not until the gaudy équipage was out of sight did she turn to her aunt. " 'Tis splendid, madame. I should like to fly like that."

Knowing Mlle Linotte, I thought she very well might, someday. The vicomte, who did not know her, laughed indulgently and M. de Bonsecours patted her black curls.

" 'Twould be a strange thing for a little cabbage like thee to fly in a balloon," he said with ponderous levity. "Yet, if such flights grow common, one might say with Ovid that things are now done that hitherto have been regarded as completely impossible."

"Yet 'tis no stranger for a woman to fly than a man," objected the marquise.

Over my head, son and husband glanced at one another with a martyred air and forbore to answer her.

Owing to the press, it took us upwards of an hour to traverse the few streets between the palace and the de Bonsecours' apartments in the rue Sainte-Geneviève. Almost I thought myself in Paris as we edged our way down the terrace and across the Great Court, shoved and jostled by wearers of silk coats and frieze coats, phrygian caps and bonnets à la Montgolfier, elbowed by petits-maîtres with daintily curled wigs and laboring men with their heads tied up in dirty rags. Was that hand pawing my skirts an impertinence or a clumsy attempt upon my handkerchief? Such was the throng that it might have been either, or even an accident. Madame, who had never liked crowds, locked one hand around my arm, the other over Linotte's shoulder, closed her eyes, and endured.

You must recall that Linotte had not left Beauxprés above three times in her life, had been to Paris only once, and then was kept as cloistered as a nun within the walls of the hôtel Fourchet. Yet she threaded the crowd as deftly as a Parisian gamin, and, when a foul-mouthed carter loudly shook the fleas from a shabby cleric who'd had the misfortune to step on his foot, listened to his railing with grave interest and wondered aloud what a "salopard" could be. Mme de Bonsecours laughed; madame blushed and scolded. Later Linotte took pains to find me alone so that she might ask again. I told her, of course—it wouldn't do to have her use it when we returned to Beauxprés not knowing what it meant.

We were upwards of two months with the marquise and her husband; two months of dinners with financiers and soirées with diplomats from which madame returned heavy-eyed with boredom. We often walked in the gardens among the grottoes and the myriad fountains behind the palace, nodding to such of Mme de Bonsecours' vast acquaintance as might be walking there also, talking of scandal and money and how far the new treaties with England would redress the great wrongs done to the French economy in the treaty of '63.

Once, I remember Linotte asking, as we rested by the fountain of Winter after a game of cache-cache, whether 'twas true what her uncle de Bonsecours had said, that the Devil had spawned Englishmen in answer to the Frenchman of le bon Dieu as He had spawned crows in answer to doves.

Mme de Bonsecours laughed. "What a droll little cabbage thou art, to be sure. Thine uncle was only making a kind of joke, ma mie. Although they are our enemies, Englishmen are creatures of le bon Dieu no less than Frenchmen are."

"Then why are they always sinking our ships and taking our islands?"

Madame frowned. "It does not become thee, child, so to cross-question thy aunt. I'd have thought shame, when I was of thy years, to be so pert and forward."

"Don't scold the child, Adèle," said the marquise placidly. "The question is a fair one. Now attend, Linotte. This war with England is not a matter of good and evil, but of trade and commerce, the buying and selling of such things as cotton, rum, and slaves. The country commanding the greatest number of ports commands the greatest profit. Having so lately lost their American colonies, the English seek West Indian colonies to replace them. The Spanish and the Dutch are helping us to protect our possessions. C'est tout."

There was a little silence while Linotte considered this. "These colonies," she said, "they have people living there?"

"Bien sûr, my child: growers of cotton and sugarcane and other things that do not grow in Europe."

"Do they grow slaves, too?"

Madame laughed. "See how she teases you, Hortense. Indulge her, and you'll soon be out of countenance. Grow slaves, indeed! What a thing for a young girl to ask."

"I ask only because of Pompey," Linotte explained.

'Twas the turn of Mme de Bonsecours to frown. "There are no slaves in France, Linotte. We love freedom too well, we French, to deprive even a savage of the right of living freely upon French soil. Pompey is a servant whose wages are paid by monsieur thy father, like Berthe."

Linotte twisted on the iron bench to look up in my face. I'd just been thinking how neatly these sentiments sprang from one who was accustomed to complain of the slavery in which Frenchmen kept their women. Linotte caught my eye and winked as though she'd read my thought. Annoyed, I blushed. She smiled, turned again to her aunt, and said, "Like Berthe. I understand now, madame."

My last journey to Beauxprés was as little like my first as it could be. The cold weather had come on early that year, and we bounced over a frozen road between fields in which the corn stood stiff and black. The vineyards too were grim, and the grapes as frostbit and shriveled as the faces of the peasants who tended them.

As always, we slept the first night at Fontainebleau. Early the next morning, our courier, one Gousse, presented himself to madame with a rumor of desperate men murdering travelers upon the road. He, Gousse, feared to go on without protection, and begged the duchesse's leave to procure a musket or hire an armed guard. Madame, very alarmed, declared she would not stir another step, with or without a guard. For what was there to hinder an armed guard from robbing her himself? Gousse fetched a deep sigh and inquired whom the duchesse expected to inform M. le duc de Malvoeux of her decision to take up residence in Fontainebleau? Madame did not know, she was sure, and was Gousse being impertinent?

At this point, I took it upon myself to hustle Gousse out the door, winking and nodding as I shooed him away. Later, I slipped out to the inn yard, gave him a louis out of my own purse, and told him to arm himself as he saw fit.

That afternoon, Gousse returned brandishing a long pistol. Madame was vastly impressed when he put a ball through one of the innkeeper's chickens, agreeing, as she averted her eyes from the chicken's torn carcass, that even the boldest brigand might be reluctant to court a similar fate. Accordingly, we packed ourselves into the berline at lark-song next morning and once more set off towards Beauxprés.

The rumored brigands failed to show themselves either that day or the next, though I remember noticing an unusual number of vagabonds abroad. Trudging along by twos and threes, heads bowed and ragged coats flapping about their heels, they were as pitiable a straggle of walking scarecrows as ever sought work where there was none. When my mistress caught sight of one ahead, she'd down with the back window and shout to Gousse to make sure his piece was charged and ready to fire. Gousse would shout back reassuringly, which would silence her until we passed another group of poor sots wading through the mire.

A dull journey, dogged with little pieces of ill-luck, the last of which was the offside leader's picking up a stone in its shoe and slowing us so that sunset found us still climbing through the Forêt des Enfans, far from the nearest inn and farther still from Beauxprés.

In the course of writing this history, I have felt certain scenes and memories rouse as from long sleep to the scratching of my feather pen. Some events I cannot say that I have truly recalled until I've written them down and read them over to Jean, who says yes, he remembers something of the sort, though that's not how he'd have told it, him. This memory, however, this scene I am about to embark upon, is all my own.

The library is warm around me, a shaft of morning sun pierces the long windows to pick out the books' gilded titles and the furniture's rocaille flourishes. I'm fed, comfortably seated, a glass of wine to my hand. Yet when I close my eyes, I seem to feel myself swaying along a mountain road, rocky, narrow, and dim in the twilight. The shadows are long and dark. Madame drowses nervously in one corner, Linotte in another. Myself, I am too cold to sleep, depressed by thoughts of Sangsue and porridge for supper. The berline rattles and creaks, the horses clop and snort, stiff branches scrape the window.

All at once Carmontelle shouts. The berline lurches, bouncing Linotte to the floor and tossing madame from side to side like a tennis ball. Have we lost a wheel? I cling to the hand-strap as the carriage gives a final bound and stops, canted a little to one side, but upright. Not a wheel, then.

Angry voices without: Gousse, Carmontelle, others—how many I can't tell for all the noise within. Mlle Linotte, jolted from sleep, whines like a puppy; madame wails aloud.

"Ah, my heart!" she moans. "Berthe! My salts! I am shaken all to pieces!" And to Linotte: "Be still, naughty girl: thy noise goes quite through me! Does no one think of my nerves? Carmontelle must be drunk, or mad. I'll have the idiot turned out upon the street!"

"Yes, madame. Shall I tell him so?"

"Yes. No—I know not, Berthe." Irritably, she snatches the salts from my hand and sniffs at them. "I pray the fool has not run down a pig or some such nonsense. Do look out, Berthe, and see."

I'll do better than that, I think, and slip from the carriage on the uphill side. As soon as I'm out, I want to be in again, for the road swarms with wild-eyed faces and fluttering rags. Night is falling: I can barely see. There might be twenty brigands attacking us or thirty or a hundred, pouring out of the undergrowth like a pack of starving wolves, clawing at the horses' heads, yarring and whurring with rage. Their voices are shrill and their accents incomprehensibly rustic, but their cadence speaks clearly of our death.

"Blood! Blood!" I hear them cry.

I cling to the carriage door, my legs turned to wood and my bowels leaping with a thousand fleas. I'd give much to fall into a swoon, but I can no more faint than climb back into the berline. As Gousse swears at the failing light, I close my eyes, commend my soul to my Lord Jesu Christ, and wait for brigandly hands to rend me.

Behind my head, the window rattles open. "Imbecile!" Madame shrills. "Coward! *Do* something! Shoot!"

Gousse's pistol explodes.

For a moment, all is still—mob, madame, groom, horses, all shocked into silence by the shot. Then a single voice cries out, "Janneton!" and a chorus of wails and sobs splits the evening air.

Madame screams, "Drive on!"

The berline jerks forward, scraping across my back. I am thrown off-balance, falling under the wheels to be crushed, when I hear an imperious young voice cry, "Stop!"

The door flies open, knocks me sprawling into the road. Someone leaps from the berline with a rush of skirts and a light thump.

"Light," demands Mlle Linotte. "He's not quite dead, I think, but I must have light."

Cursing steadily, Gousse lights a flambeau, clambers down from the rearward seat, and lights the carriage lamps. I pull myself to my feet.

The scene revealed by the light was pitiful and strange: Mlle Linotte on her knees in the mud cradling the fallen brigand's verminous head in her lap. He was very skinny, that brigand, very ragged, and very young—younger, or at least smaller, than the girl who supported him. His shoulder and neck glistened darkly. The mob, clustered fearfully at the road's edge, was a handful of children—beardless boys and hollow-chested girls with grubby infants clinging to their skirts.

Untying my apron, I moved towards the boy, knelt, and wadded it against his gaping shoulder.

A leathern bottle appeared by my cheek. "Give him a drop of this." Gousse's voice shook in concert with his trembling hand. " 'Tis brandy from my lord's cellars, strong enough to raise the dead."

Linotte took the bottle and, pushing my hand and bloody apron aside, poured a dollop of strong brandy into the wound. The boy writhed and cried out. The children on the verge answered him.

"Leave be! Ain't ye made sorrow enough without ye torture him too?" A young girl, snaggle-toothed and scrag-necked as a crone, dashed the bottle away and raked the boy into her own arms.

Linotte sat back on her heels. "Let us put him into the carriage," she said quietly. "We'll bind his shoulder, give him a warm bed and food. You can come, too."

The girl hesitated. "Will you give me bread?"

"All you can eat," said Linotte.

"Sausages?"

"And wine and milk and porridge."

The girl jerked her head over her shoulder, where a dozen hungry eyes gleamed in the shadows. "For them?"

"Yes, yes, there's plenty for you all. Now, let Gousse lift him into the carriage. Is he your brother?" The girl shrugged, bewildered. "It doesn't matter. Brothers aren't anything special. Quickly, Berthe; make a bed for him."

Well. In less time than it takes to tell, I was folding lap rugs on the floor of the berline while madame wrung her hands and babbled at me. I'm sure she inquired what I was about, ordered me to fetch Linotte, her salts, a hot brick, brandy, but I did not hear her. My ears were echoing with cries for blood, with a beloved voice commanding Gousse to shoot and the pistol's prompt reply. My hands were dark with blood. I scrubbed them in the deep fur of the lap rugs.

When I'd made a kind of nest on the carriage floor, Gousse took up the wounded boy and laid him tenderly in it. The beggar-girl crept up the steps and crouched at his head; Linotte climbed in after and curled herself at his feet. And all the while madame never ceased exclaiming. "What are you doing? What is this? Get it out at once, do you hear me? Who is that amazingly filthy girl? Whatever will M. le duc say? Is that blood? Oh, I shall surely faint!" and so on and on in staccato counterpoint to the boy's sustained groans.

The contents of Gousse's leather bottle were soaking into the mud of the road, but a little silver flask of the same spirit was kept in a pocket on the carriage door. I found it, uncapped it, and tipped a few drops into the boy's mouth. He coughed and opened his eyes.

"Bread," he said. 'Twas no more than a hoarse whisper, but I heard it clearly. "For the love of God, give me bread."

Bread. Blood. Not so very close in sound. Fear had made of them a single word; shame declared them different tongues. The boy's eyes fluttered shut.

"He dies," said the girl coldly. "The lady has killed him."

" 'Twas the groom shot him," objected Linotte.

The girl shrugged. "Servant, lady—all the same. Poor Janneton. Still, 'tis faster than starving."

We had begun to move, slowly, to spare the wounded child. He fell into a swooning doze in which he seemed to feel no pain, except when a wheel jolted over a rut, when he'd whimper a little. Madame had fallen silent. Hoping that she, too, had fainted, I looked up to see her staring helplessly from the bloody child to the filthy beggar-girl to her daughter and back again to the child. Her muff was jammed against her mouth and her eyes were shadowed gorges. She neither stirred nor spoke—not when the boy Janneton died; not when Linotte tearfully vowed to give him Christian burial and make the girl her maid and take care of her forever; not when the girl spat in Linotte's face and demanded to be let down.

"I'll starve rather than eat bread bought with blood," she said fiercely.

I remember thinking how young she sounded. Pride makes a poor meal, I might have told her. Bread bought with blood will nourish you as well as cheaper fare. Take it for yourself and your friends. Then the boy won't have died for nothing.

All this I had in mind to say, indeed, half-thought I'd said it. I must not have, however, for next thing I knew, the girl had opened the door of the berline and tumbled out into the night, dragging the boy's body with her.

Naturally, Carmontelle stopped the horses at once, and naturally Gousse asked what the devil was going on now?

The beggar-girl picked herself up and laboriously tugged the corpse out of the road. Lulling it in her arms, she turned ancient eyes upon us. "Drive on," she commanded, mocking.

Carmontelle hesitated. Linotte leaned out the window. "Do as she says," she screamed, then brought her head in again and buried it in her arms. Obediently, the coachman whipped up the horses and drove through the black night to Beauxprés.

It must have been nearly dawn when we pulled up in the stable-yard and Jean opened the door of the berline to find the three of us sitting within, stiff and bloody and silent. He says at first he thought us dead. He says he touched my hand—gloved in blood, and cold, he says, as the hand of Death himself—whereupon I started, and awoke, and rose, and commanded fires and food and bed warmers like a sensible woman. He has told me all this, and has sworn upon the bone-white fountain that 'tis the truth. And I must perforce believe him, for I've no memory of any of it.

Even this magic pen cannot arouse the slumbering memory of those days. Was I entranced for two days? For three? Jean, of course, does not recall, nor does he understand why the loss of a day, or even a week, of my life in the world should chafe me so. They must have been ordinary days, given to unpacking, mending, washing, a walk to the village, confession, absolution, Mass, a gossip in the church porch, a cup of wine with Mme Pyanet. I ask him why I can't forget Janneton's shoulder, all torn flesh and chips of bloody bone, or madame's transformation, or what the peasants did to Sangsue, or Jorre de Maindur's hideous collection, or any other unpleasant thing, if I must forget? Jean answers that life is not fair, that if it were, beggars would all eat their fill and men like monsieur go hungry. I say that's no answer.

So. For a day (or two or three) I went about my business with my eyes open and my senses shut, and when at length I came to myself, I was standing in the stable-yard, holding a pair of fur-lined gloves, as I recall, and a riding whip. Beside me Mlle Linotte, dressed in a sky-blue riding costume, watched Fleurette mincing towards us behind a groom—a new lad, tall, strong-built, whose dark face and hands faded to invisibility against the mare's dark hide. Mlle Linotte gasped.

"Pompey!"

Belatedly, my mind awoke and gave my still-sleeping spirit a shake. "Pompey!" I cried.

"Why are you leading Fleurette?" asked Linotte. "That's what the grooms are for."

Pompey's onyx eyes, expressionless, moved from my face to Linotte's, then sidelong to Fleurette. "I am a groom now," he said. "Does mademoiselle wish me to help her mount?"

"Don't be silly, Pompey. I've missed you. I've been looking for you and asking for you, and no one will answer me. Is this another test? Have I passed it? May we go riding now?"

"I beg mademoiselle's indulgence. My duties prevent me. M. le duc has ordered Jean Coquelet to attend mademoiselle if it pleases her to ride."

"Well, it doesn't please me," Linotte said hotly. "I don't know why you won't look at me, Pompey, or why you're talking such nonsense. You are my tutor. Madame my mother has said so. If monsieur my father has made you a groom, he can unmake you again. And so I shall tell him." And she threw the tail of her habit over her arm and ran back into the château.

In my dizzy and bewildered state, this was altogether too much for me. Clinging to the gloves and the whip, I turned to Pompey and pleaded, "What passes here?"

Pompey shrugged. "M. le duc has decided that his children are unruly, disobedient, stubborn, and in sore need of trained minds and strong hands to control them. He has engaged a master of mathematics and a master of philosophy to teach them."

"That doesn't explain why you're suddenly a groom."

"M. le duc has declared that he will have no animals living in his house." Pompey's voice was bitter, his eyes sorrowful. The sorrow was an old thing, the bitterness new. Once I could lighten his grief with a jest or an embrace. Now I had no comfort for him. I had little enough for myself.

He smiled. "You don't have to weep for me, Berthe. The stable is not a bad place. I am out of monsieur's way, and Jean doesn't care if my skin is black or roan or dapple-gray, providing the horses like me. And you and I may still meet in the kitchen."

"Bien sûr," I began, "but—"

I was interrupted by a commotion at the door.

"Traitor!" monsieur shouted as he strode towards us. "Turn my daughter against me, will you? Take your baboon's face out of my sight, and be grateful that I don't have your black hide flayed from your back."

Fleurette blew and backed uneasily. Pompey patted her neck.

"Art deaf as well as half-witted? Have I not told thee to go?"

Pompey did not take his eyes or hands from the restive mare. "Monsieur's servant heard him clearly. But monsieur did not say where he desired his servant to go."

"To Hell!"

At monsieur's scream, Fleurette snorted and danced and would have bolted had it not been for Pompey's hand upon her bridle. Monsieur snatched the riding whip from me with such violence that I fell down in the dust, and cut it across Pompey's face, leaving a garnet chain of blood beaded upon one black cheek. Pompey struck the whip from monsieur's hand, Fleurette reared, and then all was shouting and plunging hooves and dust and a great confusion of booted feet, so that there was nothing for me to do but curl up in the dust and wait to be trampled. Someone kicked my wrist; a foot or a hoof caught me on the buttocks. For the second time in what seemed to me as many days, I commended my soul to my Savior.

Suddenly, the brouhaha ceased, and all was quiet save for the mare's panting and a soft murmur of men's voices. I ventured to uncurl a little and open my eyes. Mare and duc each stood splay-legged and trembling in the aftershock of passion. Jean held Fleurette's bridle, Philiberte Malateste held monsieur's arm; each poured honeyed nonsense into the ear of his shivering charge. After a moment, monsieur shook off his milk-brother's hand and commanded him to find the blackamoor. Once found, monsieur instructed Malateste to flay him, hang him, and pin his carcass to the stable door like a rat's.

Malateste bowed and swore the deed already accomplished, which oath made him at once a liar and forsworn. For Pompey had disappeared as utterly as a dream at waking. The servants whispered of witchery, of a wig compounded of hanged man's hair and lark's blood that allowed its wearer to walk unseen. Had he returned to Beauxprés, I fear he'd hardly have escaped burning. But he did not return, that day or any day thereafter.

The months following Pompey's flight from Beauxprés were unspeakably dreary. Hard cold came in November, with wind and snow and sleet, and fires forbidden in all rooms save the library and madame's apartment and the kitchen. The cold seeped into my bones until I thought I'd never be warm again, and images of the scene in the Forêt des Enfans were constantly bobbing up in my mind like drowned corpses. Dressing madame's hair, I saw the shadow of the pauper girl's haggard face in the glass; folding her gowns, I felt the boy's sticky rags between my fingers. I couldn't unstopper a vial of scent without smelling blood. And whether madame asked for her ribbon or her rouge-box, all I heard was her command to Carmontelle: "Drive on."

After so many years of painting it, studying it, washing it, stroking it, my mistress' face was more familiar to me than my own. Yet that winter, whether I saw it reflected in her mirror or turned to me in inquiry or bent over her tambour, I saw a stranger's countenance. This dark-haired, rose-mouthed woman who dressed in madame's clothes and smelled of madame's perfume—this woman was not madame, but a changeling, a demon. Only a demon would command a groom to fire upon starving children. Only a stranger would have been so ready to throw me to the wolves—when she still thought they were wolves, before we saw that they were coneys instead. It all went around and around in my head, and the longer I brooded upon it and her, the angrier I grew.

I said nothing to her, of course. Femmes de chambre do not comment upon the morals of their mistresses, be they unchaste as she-wolves or evil as cats—not if they wish to keep their places. A thousand times, I decided to follow Noël Songis and Jacques Ministre to freedom. A thousand times, I bit my tongue. Where (I asked myself as I tugged the brush through her graying hair) would I go?

As many plans as I conceived, so many objections rose like mère Malatestes to abort them. Paris? Upon the boulevards of Paris, lady's maids are as common as brambles in the Forêt des Enfans. It went without saying I'd get no letter of character, and without a letter, I'd end up like poor Peronel, or worse, being older and unsuited to the work. Not Paris, then.

Lausanne? I knew the comtesse Réverdil, and she knew any number of bankers' wives. I needed a change of scene, and Lausanne would be most pleasant. Ah, beautiful Lac Leman, I told myself. The mountains! The air! The damp, myself answered glumly. The cold! The snow! As well stay in Beauxprés. And mon Dieu, the Protestants! Lausanne was in the middle of a Protestant canton—not a priest for miles. Where would I hear Mass? And bankers' wives are fat and vulgar. Not Lausanne.

As far as I could see, all roads leading from Beauxprés ended, sooner or later, in Hell. For a practical woman of middle age, the choice between unhappiness and starvation is not a choice at all. I was miserable, bien sûr, but I was also passably well-fed, well-clothed, well-housed. And when I tried to imagine life without my mistress . . . Well, my imagination failed me, and that's the truth of it.

So there I was, feeling like a prisoner in the Bastille, and there were Artide, and Jean, and M. Malesherbes, and Dentelle, and Malateste, and Carmontelle, and Clauda, and the rest of them, all fretting and cursing and bemoaning their lot, but only when Sangsue wasn't by to hear them. There were Mlle Linotte and M. Justin, the one too young, the other too closely watched to run away. There was monsieur, who'd no desire to leave Beauxprés. And there was my mistress, who could not, though she tried.

In November, Mme de Bonsecours sent word of the death of the baronne du Fourchet. The weather had cleared a little, the roads were passable in a sleigh, winter traveling was hardly new to us—of course madame would attend her mother's obsequies. In less time than it takes to tell, the boxes were packed, the sleigh at the door, and we tucked into it with furs and a brazier, gliding over the milk-blue snow towards the chestnut drive.

The bare limbs of the chestnuts arched around us, black filigree against the pale sky. My mistress peered suddenly upwards. "There, Berthe," she exclaimed. "Did you see it? No, 'tis gone. But there *was* something: I know it."

"Madame has seen a bird," I said. "There are always birds around Beauxprés."

She objected that 'twas too big for a bird, far too big, and stared and fidgeted all the way to the foot of the hill. I thought she'd settle when we passed into the meadows, but she only grew more and more tetchy, until by the time we made the Forêt des Enfans, she was like a duck who sees the cook's boy approaching. The first ranks of firs opened to us, and we passed slowly among them. There was no sound in the forest save the scraping hiss of the runners, the muffled clop of the hooves, and then, suddenly, my mistress' voice shrieking at Carmontelle to turn around at once.

"Children, Berthe," she panted when at last he'd managed the feat of turning four horses and a sleigh on a narrow forest road. "On the road. Didn't you see them?"

I'd seen long aisles of trees, shaggy and dark, with the prospect of Paris shimmering like heaven beyond them. Now I saw nothing at all. "No, madame," I said coldly.

"A dozen or more. Beggars, like the ones . . . you know. I expected to see them, but not so close to Beauxprés. They're everywhere, aren't they, so many of them, so hungry. . . . Surely they can't expect me to feed them all. And if I feed them today, they'll only be hungry again tomorrow."

"The poor are always with us, madame."

Well, she said nothing to that: indeed, what could she say? She did not mention the children again. Nor did she attend her mother's funeral, or visit Paris, or Versailles, or Lausanne. She did send gold to Baume-les-Messieurs to buy Masses for the baronne's soul, wept like a fountain for a month and wore black for a year. Me, I mourned for Olympe, who had doubtless received Mme la baronne's dying breath, closed her eyes, bound her jaw, bathed and arrayed her outworn body for its journey to the grave. Olympe, who called herself a cautious woman but could never resist a bit of lace or a fashionable hat. I feared she'd saved little enough of her wages, and she was now too old to find another position and too proud to enter an almshouse. I prayed she'd not starve or freeze in some Saint-Antoine doorway. I much fear she must have.

That winter, the winter of 1784, was terrible—not as bad as the winter of '88, mind you, but bad enough. The cold seemed endless, and the suffering also. In the village, the peasants burned dung or froze, for monsieur had exercised his right of triage and claimed all the dead wood for his own use. The aviary furnaces roared night and day, and still, without Noël Songis to nurse them, parrots and macaws, toucans and honey-birds fell sick and died by the dozen.

Because of the warmth, I went there whenever I had an hour to spare—provided I knew monsieur to be occupied elsewhere—and often I would discover a feathered corpse among the drooping greenery, or two, or three. Once, a small, bright bird dropped right into my lap, jerked its claws, spread one wing, and stiffened. Dead, it looked too lapidary to have ever been alive: its tail was peridot, its wings lapis lazuli and turquoise, its body burnished gold, its head carnelian. Folding the wing, I gathered it up, half thinking to find it as cold and heavy

in my hands as the mechanical nightingale the chevalier du Faraud
had given Linotte. But its body was still warm, and its feathers softer
than swansdown. I remember thinking one day I'd find my mistress
like that, still and soft and broken, or Linotte, or even the magpie
Justin, freed at last from Beauxprés and the vigilance of the tutors his
father had procured for him.

Tutors. Bah! Jailers, rather: thick-necked, iron-handed, gimlet-
eyed jailers. If they were masters of mathematics and philosophy, why
then I was Voltaire's mistress. They stuck as close to the boy as his
shirt. Closer. I doubt he could turn over in his sleep or fill his chamber
pot without one or both of them taking note of it. And the tutors were
not the worst of the torments his father forced upon him.

One day, passing the library, I heard a scream. I jumped. Well,
anyone would have: a screech like a crow's alarm, and me not expecting
it.

"Damned! Damned! Damned!" the crow mourned. 'Twas more
than flesh and blood could bear not to hear who was being damned
and how, so when my heart had calmed somewhat, I stood close by
the door and listened.

"Superstition!" monsieur was shouting. "Hell is only a nursery
tale, and damnation a goblin to frighten infants into good behavior.
Your precious monks had you for five years, and look at you—no
strength, no will of your own, no accomplishments, good for nothing
but praying day and night. And what good's *that*, I ask you?"

The answer came very firm. "To praise Him who is our Creator
and our Savior. And to purify our souls."

I heard the smack of flesh against flesh, then monsieur's voice:
"I'll tell you what comes of purifying your soul. Nothing save a puling
weakness. You shame me, Justin. You shame the name of Maindur."

"Hearing Mass is not nothing," said Justin, and I vow there was
no weakness in his voice.

" 'Tis less than nothing—less than the twittering of birds."

"I beseech you, monsieur, to beware how you place your soul in
jeopardy."

"My soul, if indeed I have such a thing, is no concern of yours.
You will obey me. Does not the rule of Saint Benedict enjoin you to
obedience? Does not your God Himself command you to honor your
father?"

"The Devil quotes scripture."

"Call me Devil, will you?" Smack.

A pause, and then Justin's voice again, growing as he spoke ever stronger and more passionate. "Saint Paul has written that if a man would serve God with his whole heart, he must leave behind his father and mother, his home, his wife and children. As I'd leave you, monsieur. Yet I swear upon the bones of Christ that I'll not seek to return to Baume-les-Messieurs, that I'll obey you cheerfully and dutifully in all you ask of me, if only you'll let me be confessed and hear Mass. If you do not trust my vow, at least allow the curé to come to me here. Once a week is all I ask. Monsieur—Father—I beg you."

This last was said so earnestly, so reasonably that the Devil himself must have been moved. Monsieur was not. His answer came through the door as the whistle and thwack of a crop or a stick. I did not hear Justin cry out, but then I did not listen long. My store of pity, as of patience and loving-kindness, was more barren than Mme Pyanet's larder.

And what's pity, after all? A poor, threadbare emotion, of no more use to its object than a cloak of sighs to a freezing man. Yet a cloak of sighs may warm a soul. And I was so angry in those days, so troubled in my heart and unquiet in my mind, that I begrudged madame even that thin comfort.

One winter's night at the turn of the year, I was roused from a sound sleep by the frantic tinkling of my mistress' bell. Grumbling, I crept out of my bed, lit a candle, wrapped myself in a shawl, and made my yawning way to the China apartment. She was sitting up in her bed, shivering like a flame in a draught, her eyes liquid and her voice quavering as she bade me light the candles and build the fire high. Had I inquired, she might have told me why she'd been weeping, but I'd have sooner comforted mère Boudin. I did as I'd been told, then inquired coldly if that would be all. Indignant, she said it would not, and kept me busy with meaningless tasks until dawn.

Next evening, she ordered me to make up my bed in her dressing-room.

She'd taken to drinking sweetened wine before she retired, and that night emptied nigh on a full bottle of the vile stuff before crawling drink-sodden into bed. I fell asleep to a snoring like a rusty winch, and awoke some hours later to a terrified moaning. I don't know why—old habit, perhaps—but without thinking I leapt up and took her to my breast.

She pushed me away, her eyes wide with horrors only she could see.

"Beggars," she whispered. "Famine. Pestilence. War. Death."

I felt a prickling down my spine, as of tiny claws—it could equally have been fury or fear I felt, and in truth, with me the two are closely allied. None too gently, I took her wrists and shook her.

"Madame has had a nightmare," I said when sense returned to her eyes. "Little wonder, after the great quantity of wine madame drank before she retired."

She lifted cold hands to her ashy cheeks. "Very like," she said in a child's voice, then, "I have soiled myself, I think."

I scolded while I changed the linen on her bed, scolded while I built up the fire and heated water, scolded while I cleaned her and clothed her afresh, scolded while I emptied the slops out the window. She drank like a salt-merchant, I told her, and ate like a honey-bird. She'd grown lazy and gluttonous and forgotten all the good advice Dr. Tissot had given her. When was the last time she'd ridden Fleurette? I inquired. When was the last time she'd done anything at all?

If she'd answered me, we might have quarreled. I might have said the unforgivable at last, she might have sacked me, and angry as I was, I might even have gone. My tale would then have been a different one, and I no longer alive to tell it.

There are times when I regret that night, when I wish with all my heart that I had gone forth from Beauxprés to live, and to die, like ordinary folk. Eternity has made a philosophe of me, who am all unsuited to the role. Once, looking at the White Cat's dog Toutou asleep in her glass and rosewood case, it came to me that Beauxprés itself was such a case, and we the curiosities protected and imprisoned by its transparent walls. What collection are we part of? I wondered. In which Heavenly mansion are we stored? And then I laughed, for I had a fancy, like a vision 'twas so clear, of an angel's eye upon me and an angel's face lost in wonder at the art that had preserved me here so long.

Well. Think me mad if you will. Jean has called me mad, yes, and ungrateful, too. Had I gone out into the world, he says, my body would be cold clay by now, and my soul annealing in the flames of Purgatory. Confess, he says, his gesture encompassing silver fountain, unfading flowers, Sèvres sky, Colette playing at ball with a pair of bodiless hands, a yellow-haired demoness loitering at the garden gate—confess that this is better than dying.

Than dying? Of a certainty.

Than death? I cannot say.

In Which Brother Justin
Goes Questing

By the spring of 1784, nearly three years had passed since the vicomte had set out on his quest, and a full year since his—or rather Reynaud's—last request for money. Monsieur had given up hope of him. Oh, he *said* nothing—adversity had not changed him so much as that—but when Just Vissot and Claude Mareschal began to plant corn-seed in their fields, monsieur began to plant hero-seed in M. Justin. He'd have had more success planting peas in a rose garden and having them grow into rose bushes. I suppose the boy had seen men grasp the hilts of a sword and wave the sharp end in the air, just as he'd seen men grasp the stilts of a plow and dig the sharp end in the soil. But he'd no more aptitude to one thing than to the other, which is to say none at all. As for skills useful for questing, he could ride—providing the horse walked slowly. And he could tell north from south—providing he had a compass. He could endure a prodigious lot of discomfort in the way of hunger and cold, and he was astonishingly persistent.

In a fairy tale, of course, his faults wouldn't have mattered. Either he counted as the youngest son, in which case he'd inevitably achieve the quest. Or else he was only the middle child, in which case he'd inevitably fail. In neither case would his ability to stick to a horse or wield a sword weigh in the balance. But monsieur (when he wasn't chasing after chimerical doves) was a man of reason, and reason told him that an adventurer is likely to survive longer and go further in the world than a monk. Justin must therefore learn to be an adventurer. Q.E.D.

Once the original impossible premise had been accepted, monsieur's regimen seemed sensible enough: wrestling, swordplay, geography, tactics, ornithology (to help Justin keep the Dove alive once he'd found it), dancing (to make him light of foot), riding, hunting, and rock climbing. The stone-eyed tutors kept the boy at it from dawn to dusk. Whenever I chanced to look into the stable-yard, there he'd be, stripped to his shirt and gutting a rabbit or hacking his sword at a stick, his face white and set as cold porridge, while his tutors watched him with the indifferent patience of cats at a mouse hole.

Such scenes, though painful to behold, were easily enough avoided by avoiding the stable-yard. Far worse were the dancing lessons administered by M. le duc in the Miniature salon; those, I had no choice save to witness. The progress of those lessons seemed to unfold in tableaux, like a series of etchings in the style of M. Hogarth of England, for example. I imagine them bound in red calf and untouched for a century or more, the edges stained from being much handled when new. There are four plates in the series. We may call it "The Minuet."

The prints' common setting is a noble salon furnished in the highest style of the last century. A sofa and a rolled-up carpet weight the left-hand side of the composition. A satinwood clavichord, painted with dogs coursing a deer, balances it on the right. The curtains of the salon are drawn, and the walls are hung to the ceiling with miniature portraits whose variously gay and grave smiles give them an air of bystanders at a public spectacle.

The first plate is titled "Révérence à la presence." A pretty woman sits at the clavichord, frowning short-sightedly at the music before her. A slightly older woman stands beside her and behind—her maid almost certainly, from her plain cap and look of bland disapproval. Her hand hovers by the music, ready to turn the page. In the middle foreground, a young man and a girl address themselves to the dance. The young man bows, leg thrust forward, hand on heart, face a mask of politesse. The girl is sunk in a graceful curtsy, her thin face a feminine mirror of her partner's, her eyes, like his, upon the central figure of the dancing-master, who commands both his pupils' attention and the composition: a tall, upright, hawk-faced man in an outdated peruke, holding a long, beribboned cane in one hand and a copy of Rameau's *Le maître à danser* in the other.

In the second plate, "Pas balancée," there has been a collision.

The girl reels against the sofa; the young man steadies himself on the clavichord. The pretty woman stretches her hands beseechingly towards master and pupil, who eye one another like the archer and St. Sebastian. The maid has covered her mouth with her hand; 'tis impossible to tell whether her fingers conceal a gasp of horror or a smile.

The third plate shows the young man fallen to his hands and knees. The dancing-master stands above him with the beribboned cane held high like a flail and his face contorted with rage. The girl, one hand upon the salon door, casts an unreadable look behind her. The pretty woman has buried her face in her hands. The maid bends to the sheets of music, which have fallen to the floor. This plate is titled "Temps de courant et demi-jeté."

In the fourth and final plate, called "Contretemps de minuet," the centerpiece is the book lying open at the dancing-master's feet under the broken pieces of the beribboned cane. To the left, two large men bear the unconscious young man from the salon, his arms drawn over their necks and his feet dragging. Their attitude is solicitous, almost tender, but their faces are the faces of devils attendant upon the damned. To the right, the pretty woman has fainted in the arms of her maid, who stares past her at the dancing-master. He, in turn, stares after his pupil. From his face, you'd swear that he was afraid.

An unpleasant subject, to be sure, though no more unpleasant than a Rake's Progress, and the work is very fine. See how the engraver's needle has caught each expression—the young man's martyred look of endurance; the girl's narrow face locked tight as a dungeon door upon her emotions. He conveys the tall man's rage in the curl of his nostril and lip, reveals his fear in a slight widening of the eye. And the pretty woman, when you examine her closely, is not so pretty after all, the delicate skin around her eyes ruched up by tears, the full mouth deeply tucked at the corners.

Ah, bah! What good is it, dragging such scenes of Hell into Paradise? I'll shut the portfolio now, and put it away. I don't expect I'll look at it again.

The spring of 1785 came at last: wet, cold, and grudging. The driest thing about the place was my mistress' cough, and the greenest was the mold on the scullery floor. In the village, everything was scarce: wine, clean water, straw, clothing, hope. The only thing there was plenty of was mud, which couldn't be eaten and couldn't be burned, but could be flung over the powdered heads of the duc de Malvoeux's few remaining lackeys, and was, whenever one chanced to show his face in the village. In the château, we neither starved nor froze, yet we suffered from hunger and cold and moody starts. M. Malesherbes fretted over losing flesh; I fretted over Pompey.

I was sure he was alive, less sure that he was safe and warm and fed. I imagined him holed up in the Forêt des Enfans like a wild animal, sharing a den with a bear, perhaps, or lairing with wolves. Anything seemed possible to me, except that he was dead. Yet there was no rumor of him in the village or among the servants, and after much agony of imagining and wondering, I concluded that I must consult with Mlle Linotte. Why I thought she'd have news of him, I'm sure I don't know, unless it was that I'd grown so accustomed over the years to thinking of her and him in the same breath. In any case, I went to seek her out.

"Seek out" I say, though finding her was always more a matter of luck than diligence. Whatever the time, whatever the weather, Mlle Linotte was as likely to be out as in, and never where you'd expect a duc's only daughter to be. I looked in her apartment. No Linotte. I looked in the cabinet des Fées. No Linotte. I looked in the library, the stables, the formal garden, the aviary, the kitchen. No Linotte. At last I remember thinking, distractedly, Pompey'll know where she is, then sitting down upon the Unicorn stairs and weeping as I hadn't wept since I was a child.

I don't know how long I'd been there when a small, cold hand touched my shoulder. 'Twas a measure of my misery that I wasn't even startled.

"Dear Berthe," said Linotte cheerfully. "You miss him terribly, don't you?"

Hastily, I blew my nose and mopped my eyes upon my apron. Linotte sat down beside me. I remember there was a glow upon her cheeks and a small, secret smile upon her lips: if she'd been only a little older, I'd have said she had a lover. About her lingered a smell of clean woods and rain, electric and ticklish. I sneezed. "You do not," I said.

The smile grew a hair more wide and a world more sly. "No."

Fury blossomed within me. "Vixen," I cried. "You're the daughter of your devilish father. You care for nothing."

Harsh words. And not only harsh, but unjust, as you will see. I'm sorry for them now. To do myself justice, I was sorry almost at once; but the harm was done. I saw the glow upon her sharpen and harden into a glittering wall between us.

"You are young," I said by way of apology. "I am not. When my heart is wounded, it does not quickly recover."

"No," she said. "No more does mine."

And she was gone.

Linotte never forgave me, I think: the Maindurs are not a forgiving race. Oh, she was always courteous, and kind in the manner of a great lady being kind to a beggar-woman, but she no longer trusted me. Ah, the tortures of hindsight! Had I held my tongue, had I waited a heartbeat to hear what she was preparing to tell me: how different would my tale be then!

How different, indeed? Whether I knew her secret or not, Linotte would undoubtedly still have learned sorcery, found the Dove, removed Beauxprés from the circle of the world. Had she trusted me, might she have asked my advice? Had she asked, would I have known what to say? Ah, well. Two hundred years of pondering these questions has yielded no answer, nor (says Jean) is it like to.

But at least I might have had two more years of Pompey. And I needed him sorely, for the village women had taken to looking at me squint-eyed. Even Nicola Pyanet did not greet me so freely as she had, taking my offering of scraps and crusts with a new air of sullenness. I did not blame her, you understand: servants lie warmer on winter nights than peasants; servants eat in times of famine; servants are clothed and shod when common folk go ragged and barefoot. When times are good and the seigneur not exigent in matters of triage and lod et vent, servants may strut their thick waists and their stout buckled shoes before their former neighbors without attracting anything worse than a few jeers. But after a winter harsh enough to claim at least one life in every family, 'tis not in the least astonishing if the peasantry take offense at the very sight of a gold-braided coat.

Jean reminds me that he was as welcome in the village that year as he'd ever been. And that, though true enough, means nothing: Jean was Jean, who could go anywhere and say anything, and folk would only laugh and slap his shoulder as if he were the village fool. Now, Jean's no more a fool than the miller's godson, who was clever enough to lead the Devil to vespers. What Jean is, is a storyteller, and a storyteller, unlike a lackey or even a groom, is welcome wherever he goes, particularly if he's been to Cathay first.

I imagine him sitting at the inn of an evening, laborers and farmers sitting around him open-mouthed as suckling babes, forgetting their rumbling bellies and their weeping children in tales of golden dragons and palaces of jade. He told those tales up at the château, too, in the back kitchen over furtive, watered-down tumblers of brandy-and-sugar. Tales of mist-shrouded mountains and temples filled with saffron-robed monks who could die and come to life again. Tales of flower-faced women with feet small as a child's, and whispers of amorous practices that would make a she-wolf blush. On the whole, we preferred Jean's tales of Cathay to the more familiar hearth-tales of ogres and wolves and brave peasant boys with which we'd once comfortably beguiled the long, dull evenings. There's little joy in the story of Chaperon Rouge when you're abroad in a forest with wolves all about you and no safe harbor, not even your grandmother's house where the wolf has been before you. Expect the worst. Trust no one. In 1785, we needed no hearth-tale to teach us these truths.

Certainly I did not, snubbed by my friends and neighbors, at odds with my mistress, forced to pick up rags and tags of gossip by hiding in the church-porch after Mass. That's how I heard Marie had swelled again, listening to the midwife mère Charreton talk it over with her cronies. 'Twas the feast of St. Michael, as I remember it, and Marie had not been to church in months, though her husband came as faithfully as ever with the eldest of his great brood of children.

"Seven children, all alive!" I remember Mme Pyanet saying. "And an eighth even now knocking at the gate of her womb. Best stitch her up when you deliver her, gossip Charreton, or there'll be a plague of Malatestes."

Mère Charreton shook her head and sighed. She was Jacques Charreton's wife, a woman of middle age, round and soft as a new cheese. A wise-wife, not a witch. The grannies tended to grumble at her—too young, they said, too full of ideas—but they took their aching joints to her all the same. She'd gentle hands and a tongue that wagged at both ends.

" 'Tis big for a famine-got child," she said, "and she carries it low. God send it be the last."

"Twins," said mère Boudin darkly. "I hear the cows are all dropping 'em, and the sows, too. 'Tis all part of the wizard's curse, mark my words."

Now, twins didn't sound like a curse to me, more like a blessing—for the owners of the cows and pigs, at least, if not for

Marie. I didn't say so, of course. The women suffered my presence only so long as they'd no need to acknowledge it.

Mme Pyanet told Boudin to watch her tongue. "If the curé hears you," she said, "you'll hardly be off your knees before Candlemas. Haven't you heard him? Le bon Dieu tries us only to strengthen us. There are no fairies and no wizards, and therefore there are no curses and no spells."

Mère Boudin squinted up her little pig's eyes and snorted. "No curses, ye say? Hasn't him up to the château had little enough luck since a certain ragged man ill-wished him? Hasn't your grain been turning black and your cheeses sour? That bull of your husband's, Mme Mareschal, did he get any calves last spring? And just last month, didn't mère Charreton here deliver your young cousin's wife of a hedgehog? What's that, eh? A blessing?"

The women turned as one to look at the midwife, who crossed herself and shuddered. " 'Tis ill-luck to speak of it," she said, just as though she hadn't told and retold it, wondered at it and exclaimed over it a thousand times. "I vow I rejoiced when he died, for surely he was no human creature, all wizened as he was, and his backbone starting—"

She broke off as the curé descended from the bell tower. He acknowledged the women's curtsies with a vaguely-sketched blessing and, turning to enter the church, brushed against me where I had tucked myself discreetly into an alcove. He started, squinted into the shadow, and said: "Ah, Mlle Duvet! You may carry a message to M. Maindur for me. Abbot Boniface wrote last week from Baume-les-Messieurs—I think 'twas last week—and bid me tell him, what was it? Words of comfort and wisdom, anyway—I remember I was much moved when I read them. He counseled patience, patience certainly, and faith—I remember that much."

"That is sure to comfort him," I said. "Thank you, mon père."

His brow knotted to a careful frown. "Those were not his *ipsissima verba*, you understand. The letter itself . . . But wait!" The frown unhitched. "I'll give you the letter to take to him. Now I think on it, 'twas addressed to him—or rather, 'twas inside a greater letter to me, on parish matters. Because M. le duc has forbidden me to speak with M. Maindur, I could not see my way, but if *you* might, Mlle Duvet?" He bestowed upon me a look of hopeful entreaty.

"Of course, mon père."

He smiled joyfully. "I'll just go bring it, shall I? 'Tis on my desk, waiting to be answered. At least the greater letter is, and I suppose the note to be with it. If you'll be so kind as to wait just a little moment, Mlle Duvet?"

He meant well, the curé of Beauxprés. He brought a sweet voice to the Mass and a gentle heart to the confessional. His sermons were soothing as lullabies. On the other side of the balance, the rats in the choir had more silver than he, and more courage besides, so that when a great storm destroyed the standing corn just before harvest, he did nothing for his parishioners save pray and starve with them.

The storm now, that was certainly the work of the beggar's curse, however the curé might deny it. Bien sûr, there'd been storms at harvesttime before, but not on the heels of the death of every cow in the ducal herd. One day they were grazing on the farther terrace, chewing their cuds and tail-swatting flies as usual. The next day, they were belly-bloated and dead as earth. Monsieur's cowman was at a loss to account for their deaths, unless they were fairy-struck or spirit-bit; and though Sangsue raged, he couldn't for his life find a way of blaming him. The day after *that*, the heavens opened and poured rain down upon the cornfields of Beauxprés, along with hailstones the size of pigeon's eggs, and wind and thunder grinding and groaning like the hunt of Hell.

Loud were the lamentations in the village of Beauxprés over the battered corn. It couldn't have been a natural storm, they said, not so violent, not so disastrously timed. Around the well, the women whispered of a dark figure seen riding the clouds, rain streaming from his hands and hair, spitting hail down upon the fields. In the kitchen, the lackeys muttered of a man in a cloak seen stirring the frog-fountain with a wand.

I don't know how monsieur got wind of these rumors, or indeed whether he heard them at all. Perhaps the tutors simply advised him, or he'd reasoned out on his own, that M. Justin was as ready to begin his quest as he'd ever be. In any case, a day or so later, monsieur called his remaining servants into the hall and announced that the chevalier de Malvoeux would be setting out next morning in search of the Porcelain Dove.

If he'd told us the cows had risen from the dead, we couldn't have been more incredulous. The chevalier de Malvoeux, indeed! You can't change a lamb's nature simply by throwing a gray pelt over its woolly shoulders and calling it a wolf.

Behind me, someone spat. Monsieur stiffened and glared over my shoulder. "You spoke, Dentelle? To wish my son well, perhaps?"

"No, monsieur." Dentelle's sneer—directed at his master, at least—was almost as astonishing as Brother Justin's sudden knighthood. I turned to stare at him. He was mouthing like a landed fish with rage.

"No and No, and a thousand times No, monsieur!" he gasped. "I spit upon your son. Your son is a puling worm, monsieur, a blot upon the proud name of Malvoeux. I am ashamed, monsieur, ashamed of serving a house so fallen into desuetude, so dwindled in power and honor, so . . ."

"Blot?" Monsieur shrieked. "Worm?" He wrenched his épée from its scabbard and stooped upon the little valet like a falcon on a mouse. Dentelle squealed and fled, the rest of us scattered to the four winds, and that's the last I saw of Dentelle.

If he hadn't taken a horse, I'd have watched the ornamental water for his body. As it was, I imagined him riding ventra-à-terre through the Forêt des Enfans until the wolves or the sorcerers got him. I also imagined him losing both horse and life to more ordinary brigands. What I couldn't imagine was Dentelle serving anyone other than a Malvoeux. I didn't miss him, you understand, nor was I sorry to see him go. But I give the little bantam his due: he put his honor before his comfort, and if his honor killed him, then he died an honest man.

It rained when the chevalier Justin de Malvoeux finally set out upon his quest, just enough to dampen what little ceremony the occasion might have warranted. Fleurette, unhappy under traveling harness, a rolled blanket, and saddlebags, stood with her nose to the ground between two stolid geldings similarly accoutred. The household once gathered in the forecourt, monsieur led the reluctant chevalier out onto the front steps, embraced him formally, and released him. Justin, with a donkey's air of being too dispirited to move, stood with his hands thrust into the deep pockets of his practical buckram coat. Monsieur gestured impatiently, and the tutors bore Justin down the steps to the waiting horses, boosted him like a sack of washing onto Fleurette's back, then swung up on their own mounts, where they sat with their hats pulled down over their eyes and their pistols at their saddlebows, as villainous a pair of brigands as you'd ever wish to see.

As for Justin, he sat on Fleurette like a condemned man on a cart, his lips silently moving and his fingers caressing a rosary of black beads. Le bon Dieu knows where he'd found it, or how he'd managed to keep it concealed, but there it was, and there he was, *pater nostering* upon it in his father's teeth.

Monsieur clenched his fists. Justin clung to his rosary. Madame wept. Linotte looked out over the fields to the forest and smiled to herself. I can't remember which of them I wanted to shake hardest.

A very dreary send-off, to be sure: almost enough to make me regret the vicomte de Montplaisir. He may have been a devil escaped from Hell, but for a moment, at least, he'd been a dashing devil. I suspect Reynaud coached him, for M. Léon would never have thought of the business of kneeling on the steps to take his sword from monsieur, or of kissing the hilt and swearing a mighty oath to find the Porcelain Dove or die in the attempt. Rising, he'd embraced his father, his mother, and his sister, then pelted down the steps and onto Branche d'Or's back, wheeling him on his haunches and galloping off down the drive with Reynaud in scrambling pursuit. The sun shone and a crowd stood by of peasants and grooms and gardeners and lackeys, all waving and cheering his departure with a good will. It didn't mean much except they were glad to see the back of him, but it looked well.

Had Mme d'Aulnoy written the scene, she'd not have changed a thing. Well, perhaps Linotte might not have turned her face from her brother's lips and run away without giving him the blessing he asked. The rest was perfect, down to the proud tears in monsieur's eyes.

There were no tears in monsieur's eyes when Justin left, only rain. "Find the Dove, my son," he said sternly. "The future of our house depends upon it."

"Yes, monsieur."

There was a pause. "Where will you ride?" asked monsieur.

"To the Forêt des Enfans, monsieur."

"Do you have any reason for your choice?"

Justin sighed. " 'Tis as good a direction as any, and better than my brother's."

Monsieur's face, which had been stone before, turned adamant. Any fool could have seen that he was feeling much, but 'twould take a greater fool than I to presume to guess what he felt. I dare say 'twas not regret, however, or pity for the son he almost certainly sent to his death.

Beside me, Linotte murmured, "Good. It took, then." Catching my eye upon her, she stiffened, then most reluctantly whispered, "He'll come to no harm, Berthe. Pompey will take care of him."

Well. You may imagine how I gaped at her, and how the speculations roiling in my head kept my attention from what was going forward. I remember vaguely that monsieur made a speech and madame clung to Justin's stirrup and wept over his boot until monsieur came down and pried her away. And I remember thinking how like an ancient martyr Justin looked, trotting away between two stolid guards to be stoned or crucified or buried alive.

The pathetic cortège disappeared among the chestnuts, came into sight again at the foot of the hill, and rode west to where the Forêt des Enfans thrust its shaggy green paw down into the ravaged meadows. Watching, I thought I saw a flash like a beacon upon the peak of the wooded hill and the horses surging forward to follow it. 'Twas far away, I know, yet I thought the tutors vanished before they were quite in the forest. Oh, and I'm sure I saw a black bird balancing on the wind below the clouds.

'Tis only fair to say that Jean swears he saw nothing like this, that there was nothing to see, that—given the rain and the distance—I couldn't have seen it even if there were, that my memory is pure, or rather impure, invention fed by hindsight and special knowledge. Well, that may be true or it may not. 'Tis equally true that I gave no further thought to Justin's fate nor pressed Linotte to explain her remark about Pompey. And if that isn't magic, I'd like to know what is.

Unlike his brother, the chevalier Justin de Malvoeux never wrote to ask his father for money. In fact, he never wrote at all. After Justin rode under the trees of the Forêt des Enfans in the rain, he disappeared as utterly as if he'd stepped into another world. We waited a month, six months, a year, and then we—or at least, I—gave up all thought of seeing him again. I don't pretend to know what hopes or fears my master and mistress may have harbored in their breasts, for they did not confide in me. I suspect they assumed him dead.

My mistress took to her bed, having—I'd almost written "enjoyed"—a rising degree of ill-health since her mother's death. She slept uneasily, demon-lulled, and suffered from constant migraines, cramps, and violent palpitations that could be relieved only by a tincture of laudanum in plain water, taken twice or thrice a day. Month by month, year by year, the tincture strengthened: six drops, twelve drops, twenty drops, forty, a hundred. She grew languorous and heavy-eyed, and her naps ran together like driblets of thick honey. Often she tossed and moaned in her dreams. When she woke, she wept; and if I asked her why she wept, she'd only say that she was weary and her head hurt and I fretted her unbearably.

Thus my mistress. And monsieur? Well, monsieur vanished, though not as utterly as his sons. We knew where he was, after all: in the aviary. 'Twas not altogether madness, for the bird-handlers—those that were left—had quit in a body at the first sprinkling of snow. Quit, I say, though they gave no notice of their leaving and took with them a pair of showy birds-of-paradise and four souimangas. Monsieur berated Sangsue, threw things, threatened to pursue the bird-keepers and hang them, and so on in his usual manner. Then he flew off to the aviary and there spent the winter caring for the remaining birds alone.

This hermitage of my master's made nonsense of my mistress' sudden notion that her apartment must be locked at night and a chest pulled across the door.

"He shall not touch me," she declared wildly. "I shall die if the duc de Malvoeux touches me!"

"Madame's husband has not set foot in the château for days. He cannot touch madame unless madame seeks him out in the aviary."

"No, Berthe. You don't understand. His hands and his lips, they run with blood. The children, the children whisper—ah!—such things as 'tis madness to know. No, Berthe. I will have the door locked at night, and you shall sleep beside me."

What could I do but agree? Mad she might be; maddening she most certainly was. Still she was my mistress, and I either must obey her or quit her service.

Two hundred years' reflection has shown me that I might have refused her, that I had a power over her that I never felt even while I exercised it, blindly, day by day. If she was my torment, then I was hers—courteous, obedient, emptying her chamber pot, washing her feet, measuring out her laudanum, powdering her breast, brushing her hair, all with the same care I might give to sorting her gloves and no greater tenderness. And all the time I was hating the power she held over me, she who was as weak as water, who wet everything she touched, just as water does. Look at me, said I to myself, soaked through to the heart with weakness and unable to stir a step without she gives me leave.

The first night I was to sleep with her, I saw her into bed, then retired to the dressing-room to strip off my gown, my petticoats, my stays, and to pull a clean white bedgown over my head. I remember

I was shaking so from the cold I could hardly tie the string at my throat. I have sworn to be honest. Though the room was in truth cold, my shaking was eagerness and disgust and fury. We two were no more, it seemed to me, than leech and patient, dog and flea. And for my life I could not say who fed upon whom.

"Berthe?" my mistress called me, petulant as a spoiled child. She was not a child; she was a woman grown and she would have left me upon the forest road for the brigands to rape and tear. Except that she did not. Except that the brigands had been children.

Sighing, I came around the screen. The chamber was dark save for my candle and the glow of the dying fire. A shadow flickered, sourceless. I heard a whistle from near the hearth, a mournful twitter. Starting, I dropped the candle, which went out. My teeth clacking, I groped to the bed and slipped under the coverlet, where I lay all cold and quivering like a struck bell. A warm foot touched my ankle.

"How cold thy feet are, Berthe. Come close and let me warm thee."

I melted, of course. Not at once, but over time, my bitterness, like bloody snow, thawed, puddled and dried up, to leave only a faint stain of betrayal behind. In our bed, madame would murmur and weep and cling to me, not to be awakened short of a slap. I rested badly at night and little during the day. For one thing, madame was seized with a fever of letter-writing—to Mme de Hautebriande, to one or two of her Parisian admirers, to Mme Réverdil, to her sister de Poix in England and her sister de Bonsecours in Versailles. While we waited for answers, she found a thousand little tasks to keep me by her side. And when Mme de Bonsecours wrote chiding her for her long silence and telling her of the changes in the mode, there was her wardrobe to be turned out, and sleeve-ruffles to be remade into ruched cuffs, and skirts to be shortened to the ankle, and her hair to be curled and tousled into a fashionable disorder, if she felt up to sitting before the dressing-mirror so long.

No one else answered at all, not even Eveline Réverdil. But the marquise wrote again, and again, regularly, two or three times in a month over the next four years. Madame answered these letters herself when she felt able, begged me to write in her name when she could not rouse herself to hold a pen. And in this correspondence at second hand, with my mistress a transparent fiction between us, I thought for a time that the marquise and I would achieve that equality she had offered in the vestry of the Church of Sainte-Catherine. Sitting at a gilded écritoire, dipping my pen in a gilt-bronze inkpot, folding the heavy, costly paper and sealing it with the ducal crest, I could almost imagine that we were in truth Hortense and Berthe, two women of an age exchanging our thoughts on friends, modes, politics, books, plays. 'Twas her account of M. Beaumarchais' play *Le Mariage de Figaro* revealed the everlasting chasm between us.

We went to see *Figaro* at the Théâtre Française. I'd read it, of course—is there a person of fashion left in France who has not?— and thought it the cleverest thing that has ever been written: excepting, perhaps, the works of M. Voltaire. But to see it! O ma soeur! I was dazzled! Astonished! Not a single unity left unbroken, and not a single moment of boredom in four hours' performance. How we laughed when Figaro plotted against his wicked master; how we clapped and cheered when he railed against him! At every damning line, I saw great nobles slap their own cheeks, laughing at themselves and—what is even more curious—making others laugh, too. A strange humor, that laughs at a poisoned dart, though it has pierced to the very heart.

She sent the play as well. I did not laugh when I read it, my life falling so far wide of its art as to infuriate rather than delight me. If monsieur was not so lecherous as the comte d'Almaviva, madame was not so lively as his comtesse, nor any lackey in the household so nimble of wit and tongue as his dashing manservant Figaro. Only in plays is the conversation of lackeys so like an épée: so light, so polished, so sharp that its victim is pricked to the heart before he knows he's been touched. In life, the grumbling of malcontent lackeys is more like a bludgeon: heavy, coarse, and without finesse. And Suzanne was not like me any more than Figaro was like Artide. They were nothing more than nobles in livery, and I thought the marquise a fool not to recognize it.

By the summer of 1787, monsieur's household was reduced to a mere embattled handful of survivors: myself, of course; two kitchen-boys, Jean and Artide, Philiberte Malateste (who hardly counted); three, or perhaps four, lackeys whose names and faces I have forgotten. Oh, and M. Malesherbes.

Yes, M. Malesherbes was still with us. Though he threatened daily to leave, his melancholic disposition made change a terror to him and uncertainty a very hell. Furthermore, he was now upwards of fifty years old and no longer au courant with the mode in sauces. Yet even the most timid hare may lose his fear when the dogs are at his throat.

One day, coming down the back stairs, I passed Sangsue holding a bloody cloth to his head and showing his long, pitted teeth in what might equally have been a grimace of pain or a smile. I ran down the steps with a foreboding of tragedy that was amply fulfilled by the scene in the kitchen. 'Twas like the last act of *Mithridate*, with broken crockery and bent iron-mongery strewn broadcast, and in the midst of the carnage, M. Malesherbes on an overturned cauldron, upheld by Artide and a chorus of scullions.

"Ah, Berthe," Malesherbes greeted me. "I am an artist, me! The prince de Conti has been wooing me ever since he tasted my riseau de veau at madame's Turkish supper in '76. The king himself has begged me to come to Versailles and raise the royal table to new heights. I am famous. I may bite my thumb at letters of character. I may sneeze upon references. I am an artist, a great artist, and I go where I will!"

Artide snorted. "You'll go to the galleys or the almshouse with every other vagabond, Malesherbes. Even artists are not exempt from branding when the gardeloups catch them wandering the roads like common mendicants."

"Hold thy peace," I said. "Canst not see the man's distracted?" To Malesherbes, I said gently: "M. le chef de cuisine, you shall have your letter of character if I must write it myself. Would you not rather stay? Without your light custards, Mme la duchesse will surely starve. And I shall miss your omelettes sorely."

The little chef deflated like a fallen soufflé. "A letter would be a great kindness," he said. "In truth, I must go even if I have none. After such words and pots as I have hurled at Sangsue, I dare not stay." He drew himself up with a forlorn dignity. "In any case, begging upon the roads is not so demeaning as a life of cooking porridge at Beauxprés."

Artide began, "You say that only because you've never begged, never known—" I snatched up a stray saucepan to shut his mouth for him, and he raised his hands in surrender. "Peace, vixen; I'll hold my tongue. But if M. le chef goes to Paris, I wager he's more likely to end up cooking mutton stew in a common inn than ris de veau in a prince's kitchen, letter of character or no."

———

As it happened, I did write a letter for M. Malesherbes. I was not called upon to provide one for Philiberte Malateste when he, too, left Beauxprés.

'Twas the last week of September, I remember, a real Saint-Michel's summer, and I was taking advantage of the warm sun to bleach madame's chemises in the drying-yard below the old donjon tower. The air was very still, the yard quiet as a grave now that Clauda had moved her tubs and her gossip down to the village washhouse. No doubt that is why, when I heard the crying of a child, my belly leapt for my throat, my toes put down roots, and my eyes froze wide.

What horror did I expect to see standing by the hedge? In truth, I know not, but certainly I did not expect to see Marie Malateste in a red Sunday apron, balancing on her hip a furious baby not long out of swaddling clothes. I gaped at her—it had been, after all, a good nine years since we'd exchanged a word.

"Good day, Duvet," she said briskly. "Malateste has finally saved up enough silver for the livery stable he's had his eye on these five years and more. You remember the inn at Pouligny?"

I shut my mouth, opened it again, failed to think of anything to say, nodded instead.

Marie set the child on the ground, took a chemise out of the basket and spread it on a hedge. Shrugging, I took another, and we worked silently together until the basket was empty. Then she eased herself onto the bench, laid back her head against the tower's weathered gray stone, closed her eyes against the sun, and sighed from her toes.

I sat gingerly beside her. "So, Mme Malateste. That's a fine child you've got there."

Marie snorted. "My youngest daughter," she said. "The latest filly of the Malateste stable."

The child glared up at me; I glared back. "A fine, healthy child," I repeated. In fact, she was indecently stout for a babe born in a lean winter, and I noted without surprise her lordly Roman nose like a goose and her unchildish, knowing air. I thought she favored her grand-dame and wondered what Pompey would have said she smelled of, apart from piss and stale milk.

Marie turned a less than doting gaze upon the infant, who was now industriously eating dirt. "My children will be the death of me."

Her voice didn't ring with iron bells, yet I recognized the true voice of prophecy. Peasants spit to avert omens. I said, "Ah, bah! Even the grandchildren of mère Malateste can't be so bad as all that."

"What do you know of it, hein? I labored with the twins for two whole days. And when this one entered the world, she nigh brought my womb with her. 'Tis held in my belly with bandages and prayer. Why, whenever I squat, I expect all my guts to come out with the shit and leave me the shell of a woman, skin and bone and hair and rags like that baby of the beggar-woman's, do you remember, when Jean and I were courting?" She shook her head and sighed. "Jean's a good man, knows how to pleasure a woman without exacting a nine-months' penance. I should have married him and taken my chances on the road or else remained unwed and contented myself with laundry. Remember how you once said there was not a blanchisseuse in Paris could touch my way with thread-lace?" She opened her eyes and smiled at me. "That was kindly said, Berthe."

Sudden tears pricked my eyes, for all the world as though I were sitting by Marie's deathbed and not in the sun with her baby playing in the dirt at our feet. After all, she had the womanly treasures she'd so longed for: a man to warm her bed, children, a house in which she was mistress. Yet, as I looked at her, it seemed to me that she'd paid dearly for them. At forty, she was thick at the waist, thin and wrinkled at the neck and breast. There were dark circles beneath her eyes and a shadow upon her face. Madame's mirror told me that my eyes were still clear, my cheeks unlined, and my breasts still full and fair. I was two years Marie's senior.

"Ah, bah," I repeated, then: "Mère Charreton is very well, but another midwife may know more than she. And when all's said and done, I doubt Jean could've kept to a single mare. You're better off as you are."

Marie shrugged and rose painfully to her feet. "When I welcomed thee to Beauxprés, I embraced thee as a friend, and although thou hast stood both friend and enemy to me since, we have loved one another, I think." Dry-eyed she embraced me and kissed me upon the mouth. "Adieu, Berthe."

I wept then. But only a little, for I was less impressionable than I'd been at eighteen.

"There's no need to say more than à bientôt," I said when I'd wiped my eyes. "Our next journey to Paris, Carmontelle will change horses in Pouligny, and I'll tell you all the gossip." My voice rang bright and false. "So. I'll carry the bébé Malateste, and we shall walk to the top of the path together."

Marie put her hand on my shoulder. "Do not trouble yourself, Berthe. I'd say farewell to Jean ere I go." She looked about her, sighed impatiently. "Now, where'd the little she-devil get to?"

Indeed, the drying-yard was empty, save for a wet spot in the dust and a heap of pebbles. "She can't have gone far," I said soothingly. "Look there in the dirt, Marie; she's crawled towards the laundry. Jean is in the stables, I think. I'll fetch her out and bring her to you there."

So Marie made for the stables and I followed the serpent's path the infant had draggled in the dirt.

She wasn't in the laundry. An angry howling led me to the room beyond where the laundresses had once stored the tubs of soap and lye. The empty tubs were still there, standing waist-high, supported on wooden planks. Marie's daughter was beating on one with her small hands and fairly screaming with rage.

Reluctantly (for her shift was soaked with piss) I picked her up, whereupon she turned upon me a look of venom that was her granddam to the life, then returned to her roaring and kicking. 'Twas many and many a year since I'd handled M. Léon in a fit of temper; I was not so vigilant as once I'd been. Before I knew what she was about, she had grabbed my amber chain with both hands, torn it from my neck, and flung it violently at the wall. It hit the stones with a rattle and disappeared behind the soap-tub.

Well. That chain was a treasure of mine, given me by madame and worth a year's wages besides. I dropped the child—gently, bien sûr—put my shoulder to the tub, and pushed. It moved reluctantly, wood against damp wood, and finally tipped off the edge of its plank, revealing a deep hole in the wall behind—no casual gap, but a dressed arch as high and wide as the tub itself. Bébé Malateste, babbling eagerly, crawled up onto the plank and leaned precariously out over the darkness beyond. I was furious enough to let her break her neck if she was so minded, but because she was Marie's daughter, I dragged her to safety by her unsavory shift before pushing the plank aside. A gap, slightly narrower than the plank, appeared in the flagstone floor. I knelt down by it and peered into the gloom, curiosity calling me as loud as my lost necklace, if not louder.

The hole was a four-stepped staircase descending into the arch and ending at a stout wooden door. The chain had fallen on the second step. I could see it well enough, but I couldn't reach it without over-balancing. Gathering my skirts about me, I stepped carefully down and retrieved it, pressing the wooden door with my rump as I bent. Had I felt the door move? Turning, I pushed at it. Yes, it moved a little, screeched, caught, opened further. Beyond it was blackness, thick as felt, and a sense of endless depths that breathed, as I listened, a cold, stale sigh.

I might have descended, if only a step or two, had not bébé Malateste scrambled down the steps and grasped at the darkness with her small fat hands.

"Chut, little one," I said, scooping her up and shaking her briskly. "Thou'rt over-young for an adventurer, thou. What would thy mother say if I loosed thee to creep through the bowels of Beauxprés? There might be rats down there, or le bon Dieu knows what ancient foulness. Hush now, and I'll give thee something nice to eat."

Far from being mollified, the little goose only screeched the louder. I tucked her squirming under my arm and went in search of her mother, thinking that by now Marie would have had time to bid farewell to Jean a thousand times over.

I found them in the stable-yard, arranged in a tableau that looked for all the world like the last act of a melodrama. For Marie had found not only Jean, as she had purposed, she'd found Artide as well.

Oh, yes—Artide. When Jean went to Cathay, Marie had been frantic for consolation. She'd despaired of a husband, was past her first flush of youth, any man was better than none, Artide was an old friend—enfin, there'd been a liaison, though it didn't last long. I'd stake my best cap she'd never looked at him when Jean was at Beauxprés. Yet to see her holding his hand, her eye resting on him as tenderly as it rested on Jean, you'd think the two men ancient rivals. As for the two men, they were as hang-dog as choir boys caught drinking the communion wine. Artide was the more ill at ease, for he perforce must give Marie his full attention, while Jean's was divided between her and the gelding tugging impatiently at the rein. I approached them with my noisy, reechy burden, and the animal rolled its eyes and danced away.

Marie loosed her old lovers and received the child into her arms. "Thank you, Duvet. No, don't come with me—what I had to say to you, I've already said." Then to her daughter, who was tearing at her bosom: "But a small moment, greedyguts, and thou shalt have thy fill of me."

The last I saw Marie, she was marching downhill to a fanfare of her daughter's piercing cries. We watched her out of sight, Jean, Artide, and I, and when she was gone, Jean shook his head and led the gelding into the stable without a word.

"She was a plump little cony once," said Artide regretfully. "And lecherous as a she-wolf. That hypocrite Malateste's bred all the life out of her. I'll wager the curé told him she'd make him a better wife so. Priests! Leeches and secret lechers, every mother's son. Their parishioners may go to Hell in a basket for all of them, so long as they've a bottle to empty and a woman to fill."

"Bah!" I said. "If our curé knows his member has another use than pissing, I for one would be vastly astonished. Secret lecher indeed! The curé's pure as new milk."

I'd have done better to hold my peace, for opposition only heated Artide's tongue. These days, when he fairly got going, he could ring more changes on "foutre" and "bougre" than the vicomte de Montplaisir. "A pure slug," he sneered. "Even if we have souls to save, which I take leave to doubt, our curé's far too lazy to save them. Confess to fornication or witchcraft or consorting with heretics, and all he'll ask in the way of penance is an *Ave* and a copper coin for the poor.

"You'll say he gives that coin to the poor, and I'll grant he does, so, yes, the curé's a good man in his way: I've no real quarrel with *our* curé. 'Tis these fat prelates, these vampire bishops and incubus monks I object to, who suck the life's blood from common men, eat their children, rip the skin from the poor to make them gloves, and all the while mouthing pieties, the stinking, crapulous—"

"Enough, Artide!" I cried, clapping my hands over my ears. "No bishop is more corrupt than your mind and no monk fouler than your mouth. Go to Rome and swear at the Pope. I can't bear to hear it again."

In Which Artide
Comes into His Own

I did hear it again, of course.

The long years of bitterness had told heavily upon Artide, cork-screwed his hopes into rage and his eloquence into invective. Thought by thought, word by word, he wove a chrysalis of hatred from which he emerged a rebel full-grown. All during the winter of 1789 we listened to him declare the queen a whore, the king a cuckold, the nobles of his court fornicators and leeches. According to him, priests were nothing more than vampires, monks sodomites, and bankers and court officials maggots growing fat on corruption. These opinions brought Artide a seat by Yves Pyanet's fire and an open invitation to the mutinous gatherings Just Vissot entertained in his grange on moonless nights. Of these last I know only that they existed. The assemblies in the inn—well, by purest happenstance, I myself assisted at one of those.

I was on my way to Clauda Boudin's to collect the week's laundry. 'Twas February, I remember, and colder than charity. The path through the wood was glazed with ice; the rocks and tree roots were disguised under snow. Before I'd even reached the great beech, I'd fallen thrice. My tail was bruised, my breath frozen in the shawl I'd tied over my mouth, and my legs numb and stiff as clappers in my iron-hard petticoats. I'd no difficulty crediting Mme de Bonsecours' recent report that France had not seen such a winter since 1709, when the red Bordeaux froze solid in Louis XIV's golden goblet.

In any case, there I was, all but dead of cold, passing the inn on my way to Clauda's. Smoke was coiling out of the tumbledown chimney, warm light escaped cracks in the winter shutters, and the long and the short of it was that I thought Yves Pyanet might not begrudge my sitting by his fire just long enough to warm my feet. Surely he'd have little other custom on a day like this.

As I approached the door, I could hear a single male voice holding forth above a chorus of murmurs and coughs. Having no special wish to witness the drunken moanings of a clutch of dirt-arsed farmers, I'd have pressed on to Clauda's had an icy gust of wind not changed my mind for me. Sick with cold, I pulled open the door and entered, and there they were, the Jobs of Beauxprés, lamenting their boils in a desert of empty cups.

The voice I'd heard belonged to Just Vissot, who stood with his back to the fire before an audience comprising Artide, Estienne Pyanet, Claude Mareschal, and Jean, who looked very much at home with his feet cocked up on a table and a tankard balanced on his belly. Quietly, I asked Yves Pyanet for a cup of mulled wine and picked my way through the clutter of stools and tables to a nook behind the chimney-corner where I could be both warm and unobserved.

Farmer Vissot was nearing the end of his oration. ". . . oil seed, of all the inedible, useless crops. My corn was beat flat as a hearth-cake by that hailstorm in July. And what few grains I saved are bound to disappear down the gullets of the seigneur's birds, one way or t'other. Firewood's dear as diamonds, flour dearer yet, and I haven't a sou for my taxes, seeing as how the cheese won't ripen in this cold and I can't get to Champagnole to sell it anyway. My only comfort is that when we've all frozen or starved, the thrice-damned birds must peck at our bones, for 'tis sure as death there'll be naught else for them to eat." He nodded heavily, put his pipe in his mouth, realized it was dead, and bent to the fire for a coal to light it.

"Like enough," said Mareschal. "Me, I have hopes of this assembly they say we're voting on come spring. Us peasants'll have commoners to speak for us, and the curé says they'll get rid of the Farmers and the taxes, and stop the likes of Sangsue"—they spat ceremonially—"from selling all our seed-grain in Paris."

Artide snorted. "Nothing'll stop Sangsue and his like from sucking the last drop of seed from each one of you and hanging the dry husk from those trees he's planted to cut up your fields. Monsieur don't care how hard the bugger screws you so long as he screws out the coin to pay his debts. The deputy don't care—he's likely some rich merchant from Besançon who keeps a carriage like a lord and dreams of buying a title. And the king cares for nothing save hunting and keeping his courtiers out of his wife's bed."

"That's not what the curé says," objected Mareschal. "The curé says that our complaints he's been taking down and sending to Besançon are going straight to the king, and that when he's read them, he'll see something done for us poor folk."

"Foutre!" said Artide. "If you believe that, Claude Mareschal, you'll believe our duc means well by us."

Mareschal objected loudly, I sighed in my corner at the high price of warmth, and Estienne Pyanet suddenly remembered that he was a patriot. "Foutre, yourself," he snapped. "King and noble, they're not the same thing at all. All the world knows that nobles are only out for themselves. But our little king, now, he's a simple man. That harpy queen of his may fill his ears with foreign lies, as Artide here's always telling us. But the king loves us, never doubt it. He'll read every word of those complaints, and then there'll be no more goat dung from the Austrian whore about how we can eat grass if we can't afford bread, just like we wasn't men at all, but only so many oxen."

Jean laughed. "I've heard much the same tale, Mareschal, but 'twas stone soup the queen said the peasants should eat, or stone-dust gruel, or even cake. You shouldn't believe everything tinkers and peddlers tell you."

"Stone-dust gruel. Well, it may come to that." Just Vissot sucked glumly on his pipe. "For if Sangsue don't take everything I own, the brigands will."

"Aye," said Claude Mareschal. "Colporteur the peddler's been telling my wife's aunt all about the salt smugglers who burned the cow-house of a farmer who wouldn't hide them, right down to the ground, mind. And then all his furniture was smashed by the garde-loups who came looking for the smugglers. The law's as bad as the thieves nowadays, that's what Colporteur says."

"Gardeloups, my ass," said Artide. "A dog's but a wolf with a master, when all's said and done."

There was a murmur of assent, a silence, and then Just Vissot said, "Baste me for a roasted rabbit if I don't hate the seigneur worse than the Devil himself. I hate his tithes and his corvée and his forest rights and his dovecotes and his aviary and his damned aristocratic pointed nose. If only M. le bird-brained duc would follow his sons into Hell, life would become ten thousand times more supportable for us all."

I felt inclined to agree with him. Jean's voice floated lazily from the opposite corner. "Come, come, goodman Vissot. Be reasonable. A good tale's a good tale, but you really don't believe all that about stone soup and the gardeloups, do you? Hate le duc de Malvoeux, very well—la sainte Vierge knows he's earned it. And his present steward's the pinch-arsed bastard of a diseased Englishman. Consider to yourself that both duc and steward are facts of life, like thunder and rain. If you get rid of these, there'll only be others behind them, maybe worse. And even if there aren't . . . Well. Can you imagine growing crops without rain and thunder?"

"Rain? Thunder?" Artide's face blotched scarlet. "What have tithes in common with rain, O fucker of horses? Hast spent all thy brains with thy seed?"

"Oh, shut up, Desmoulins," said Vissot amiably, then turned to Jean and said, "and you, mon vieux, don't be an ass. You know how things stand, you've just never thought about 'em, being the duc's groom and all. Look. I want some land. Before I can tie up the deal with the fellow who's selling it, I'm forced to pay certain dues. And these dues go not to my king, but to a neighbor landowner who has nothing to do with me in the general way of things, and gives me nothing for my money but the right to spend it. Still, I pay the dues and I buy the land, and 'tis my land, a tiny part of the wide world that is my very own. Upon it I sow, let's say corn, and, if le bon Dieu smiles upon me, I see that corn grow tall and green.

"Now my neighbor puts in another appearance. He drags me away from my land and my corn to mend his roads for nothing. Every time I cross a river, he exacts a toll from me. And when I go to market, there the bugger is again with his hand in my purse, taking a goodly portion of every livre I earn from the grain I've grown on the land I paid him for the right to buy. Even at my own fireside I'm not free of him: my grain must be ground at his mill for a fee, and my bread baked in his oven for another. And what does he do with all this money he's squeezed out of me? Does he give alms to the poor or hire honest soldiers to guard me from brigands? No. He collects birds."

"Buggering, verminous, crapulous . . ."

At this point I reached the bottom of both my tankard and my patience. "Yves Pyanet," I called out. "Friend Desmoulins has clearly drowned his wits in your excellent wine. Doubtless he'd thank you to toss him in the horse-trough to clear his head for him."

Claude Mareschal squinted through the wrack of smoke. "Peste! If it ain't la poule Duvet playing off her mistress' airs like she was a lady born."

"And the blessing of God on you, too, père Mareschal," I said. "Jean, your arm to Mlle Boudin's, if you please, and with luck, you'll make it back to Beauxprés before some . . . ah, lover of horses brings it to Sangsue's notice that monsieur's stables are unattended."

Jean rose, stretched, grabbed Artide's coat collar and hauled him to his feet. "You're right, Duvet, and 'tis kind in you to give us warning. Come, Desmoulins, back to work, or we'll soon be bleeding like asses." Then he smiled cheerfully at the company, draped Artide's arm across his shoulder, and lurched out with him into the cold, pursued by much mirthful comment on sore heads, sore stewards, and horse lovers. Estienne Pyanet then twitted me on my thoughtfulness for my fellow servants, and I returned his compliments with interest. A few moments later I left, warmed, but not at all comforted.

I'd known the peasants of Beauxprés were discontented—how could they be otherwise, given the poor harvest and the perishing cold and the countless taxes that wrung them like so many sheets? Their fathers had suffered the same in the old king's time, and their grand-fathers, and so on back to the days of Noah and beyond: generation upon generation of peasants suffering, grumbling, and enduring like cattle. 'Tis a peasant's nature to be discontented, as 'tis the nature of a noble to be arrogant or a peddler to be sly. Let the philosophes (who I wager have never spoken to a peasant in their lives) talk of reform and progress and uniform taxes, I thought. Talk is cheap. As for what good their reforms would do—well, there's a proverb in Beauxprés: "Sing to an ass and he'll fart in your face."

Oh, Beauxprés was a great place for proverbs: "One must howl with the wolves"; "Poverty is not a vice—it's a mortal sin"; "A goat must eat where she is tied." Artide had clearly taken the first to heart. I labored to come to terms with the last. Many things made this difficult—the weather, Sangsue, the cooking of the kitchen-boys, my friendless, loveless state, and above all, the letters of Mme de Bon-secours. I'd read them aloud to madame as she lay on her chaise longue, her eyes heavy with ennui and laudanum. When the marquise wrote of the war, the Assembly of Notables, and the Estates-General to which

M. de Bonsecours had been elected, she'd complain that Hortense was growing prodigious dull in her old age, and could I not skip to the gossip?

There was plenty of gossip, to be sure. Mme de la Tour du Pin was sufficiently recovered of her last miscarriage to sing contralto at one of M. de Rochechouart's musical mornings. The Irish were so droll! Imagine wearing a blue crêpe gown and feathers to the English ambassador's ball when the invitations specifically instructed all ladies to wear white! They call her the Blue Bird now. Better not mention it to monsieur your husband—he's likely to post straight up to Paris and fling her into a cage.

The queen retreated more and more to the Petite Trianon. One couldn't blame her, poor soul, with her son so ill, and so monstrous unpopular as she'd become. Did madame know Her Majesty had been hissed both at the Opéra and at the Théâtre Française? The people had never forgiven her for that affaire of the diamond necklace in '85. Surely madame remembered it—a squalid business for all it involved 10,000 livres, with both the abbé and the girl lovesick for the queen, and père Duchesne smacking his lips over it all like a glutton at a feast. His pamphlets were growing ever more scurrilous, until Mme de Bonsecours hardly knew whether to be outraged or diverted. The things he said about the queen! Messalina herself would have balked at such a variety and number of lovers. And Her Majesty was such a prude! Her only sin, in the opinion of Mme de Bonsecours, was her insistence upon playing politics when she'd no more aptitude for intrigue than the king for dancing.

These letters were a torment to me, the world they chronicled like a handful of sweet grass piled just beyond my tether's reach. I could see it, fresh and green, spangled with dew. I could imagine the smell and the intoxicating taste of it. And when I turned to my own small pasturage, what did I find? Mme Vissot's complaints that her husband was slipping the fish to Mareschal's youngest daughter. Mère Amey dead of starvation. Prodigies like the child born white as milk —skin, hair, and all, save for his eyes, which were pale blue and red like an Angora rabbit's. Unsettling, to be sure. But witty? Engaging? Interesting? Bah!

That spring, the marquise wrote that Englishness was all the rage in Versailles: English clothes, English walks, English accents. The duc d'Orléans ordered a silver service, light and undecorated in the English manner, and gave a brilliant supper to christen it. Her chef de cuisine

having taken employment with the comtesse de Fleuru, Mme de Bonsecours sought a replacement in Paris, which was all in a ferment over
the price of bread. Hardly a day passed without a riot, suddenly begun
and suddenly over, like a shower of rain. From time to time, the shower
blew up into a storm.

April 29, 1789

Only yesterday, the worthy M. Réveillon's wallpaper factory
was ravaged. He employs four hundred workers, and pays them
well, I hear—upwards of thirty-five sous a day. Ungrateful
wretches! I vow I'm so angry I can barely hold my pen. They
destroyed everything. Not only the wallpaper, gum, and paint
from his factory, but the furniture, linens, and paintings from his
hôtel as well were smashed, torn, burnt to a cinder. M. Réveillon
is a good man, too—they say he once sold everything he
possessed to keep a stranger's family out of La Bicêtre. I've heard
the mob was hired, in which case they richly deserved to be
trampled by the French guards and shot down like the ravening
swine they were. Yet there were so many killed.

Death lurks in every street, and the promise of violence in the
most innocent word or action. Paris is like a loaded cannon, and I
fear 'tis only a matter of time before it fires. We must pray, sister,
that the charge doesn't level all of France.

If Paris was like a cannon, Beauxprés was like an experiment in
phlogiston, the air quivering with anger, resentment, and hunger to
the point of eruption. Tempers flared like summer lightning; sudden
fights broke out over nothing. In May, Artide broke Sangsue's nose
and disappeared as thoroughly as Pompey. I couldn't even find comfort
in hearing Mass, so acid were the stares and mutters that greeted me
at the church. Nicola Pyanet turned her shawled back when she saw
me approach, and Clauda took and returned the linen at her door
without meeting my eyes.

In June, the dauphin died at last. Mme de Bonsecours wrote that
she'd not been able to bring herself to attend the funeral.

Here is France some twelve million livres in debt, people starving,
bread at four sous the pound, the Estates unable to agree on
anything at all, and our king proposing to spend 600,000 livres on

burying a child. Even M. de Bonsecours thinks it a pity that economy is of no account in the birth and death of princes.

Then, on the twenty-fourth day of July, 1789, Jacques Charreton delivered a thick and much-smudged packet to the kitchen door.

I didn't read it at once. Knowing now what it contained, 'tis hard to credit that I would put it in my pocket until madame awakened from her nap, then tidy her hair and check, as she asked, on her supply of laudanum in case 'twere time to order more from Besançon before I even thought of it again. Only when my mistress was settled to her embroidery did I draw the letter from my pocket, break the seal, and begin to read:

Versailles, 16 July, 1789

My beloved sister:

First, I am safe, and Bonsecours also, although more agitated than I have ever seen him since our wedding night. We may yet fly to Brussels as d'Artois, Lambesc, Breteuil, and the Polignacs have done. But M. Necker has been recalled, and as my husband has always agreed with his policies (although, I fear, not always in public), we remain in Versailles while awaiting events. This chaos in the Estates could be the making or the breaking of Bonsecours: as yet I cannot guess which. The one thing of which I am certain is that France is not altogether the same country she was before Tuesday last.

Do you recall my saying that Paris was like a cannon loaded and primed? Alas that I should have proved so great a Sybil, although, to be sure, I did not prophesy 'twould be the king himself who lit the torch. But there. Everyone knew he never liked Necker, and the saintlier our little bourgeois gentilhomme acted, the less Louis liked him. Monsieur my husband may talk of the queen's influence and Breteuil's ambitions all he pleases, but my reading of the matter is that Louis dismissed Necker in a sudden fit of Divine Right.

They say Necker tried to damp the powder by slipping out a back door on Saturday morning in the hope he'd not be missed before the Estates met on Monday. Had his intention been to condemn the king beyond doubt, he couldn't have acted more slyly. Before he was seated in his carriage, every petty secretary, clerk, and footman in Versailles knew all about it, and the news made Paris before he'd reached Montmorency.

Like the rest of the Second Estate, I knew nothing. Blithe and ignorant as a milkmaid, I drove to Paris for the theater on Saturday. Sunday, I rose, went to Mass, returned to my apartment, looked for Louison to dress me for dinner, did not find her, had to dine at Mme Valence's in a plain Circassian gown, and returned ready to dismiss the minx on the spot. She met me at the door, full of tears and lamentations and a tale of a riot at the Palais-Royal, tumbling St. Bartholomew, Necker, chestnut leaves, the duc d'Orléans, and the Champs de Mars so freely together that I could make nothing of her account. 'Twas only yesterday, when I returned to Versailles, that I heard the full tale of the tabletop Demosthenes and how his auditors denuded the chestnuts of their leaves to make them green cockades. The color of hope, he said; also, he later discovered, the color of the comte d'Artois, whom the hoi-polloi hate worse than hunger itself.

In any case, Louison had not dried her eyes before my maître d'hôtel was telling me that the Bourse and the theaters were closed and self-proclaimed patriots running riot through the streets. I dared not set foot out-of-doors that night for fear of green-ribboned brigands in search of arms and powder. M. de Bonsecours, who had proposed to sup with me in Paris, prudently remained at Versailles. I vow I was quite vexed with him. Yet when Monday dawned, and I saw from my window the cobblestones torn up from the street and piled into barriers, I was glad he'd stayed away. My husband is a gentle man; the sight of smoke rising from all quarters of Paris must have caused him unutterable pain.

At ten, my maître d'hôtel brought the news that the merchants feared to open their stores.

Prudence had counseled lying low; now prudence dictated flight. I ordered my carriage and gathered some few letters and books I wished to save, only to be told that my carriage had been impounded by the French guard. Fresh from the fray, my coachman babbled of a ragtag army of citizens pillaging armorers and bakers' shops. The mob broke into Saint-Lazare, he said, and robbed the good brothers not only of every sack of grain in their stores, but of their wine, their cheeses, even of their vinegar and oil and, most curiously, of a dried ram's head.

All that heaving about of cobbles and flour sacks must have

exhausted them, for Monday night was quieter. Half in fear, half in fascination, I sat at my window and watched men in ill-fitting blue and red uniforms build small street-fires and harry the small clusters of dirty vagabonds drifting like restless ghosts among the rubble. From time to time I heard them calling out, their terrible voices flat in the heavy silence: "Armes et pain!" they cried. "Arms and bread!"

The events of the next day are unclear, though some few facts are certain. The Bastille fell. Its commandant and guards are most horribly dead, and their heads paraded through the streets on pikes. The Swiss Guard gave up rifles to the mob without a shot fired or the least resistance. Paris is an ant's nest overturned. Versailles is little better.

Rumors abound, and no one is able to distinguish truth from the merest invention. I've heard that M. de Launay's own guards turned upon him and forced him to open the Bastille to the mob, who first promised him safe conduct, and then hacked off his head with a pocketknife. Some say that the Swiss Guard massacred a thousand citizens in the Tuileries, cut old men's throats and trampled pregnant women. Others will have it that the Swiss Guard joined the mob in burning the wall of the Farmers Général and pillaging Saint-Lazare. Jacques de Fleiselles was a traitor to the king. Jacques de Fleiselles was a traitor to the people. It doesn't matter which anymore: the poor old fool is dead and his head stuck on a pike next to de Launay's. I've heard there were eighty pensioners in the Bastille and fifty Swiss Guards. I've heard that there were twenty pensioners, or a handful; ten Swiss Guards, or a battalion. De Launay had promised the king not to fire on his subjects; he was too stupid to fire; he didn't want to risk damage to his new house across the square. Or perhaps that was M. de Besenval, who, fearing that the mob would sack his house—newly painted and provided with the most charming baths in Paris—tamely surrendered the Invalides' entire store of rifles.

Now that I've had time to reflect, I can only wonder at my own foolish astonishment. Have we not lived for a dozen years now in the midst of famine, foreign wars, scurrilous pamphlets, and taxes that rose like hawks? Twelve years ago, did not all Paris embrace Benjamin Franklin and applaud his American War? The Americans had their Concord Massacre; we French have our Fall of the Bastille. Paris and Versailles quiver as from an electric shock, and a number of the resulting sparks, alas, seem likely to catch fire.

From all quarters I hear news of peasants burning châteaux, tearing down dovecotes, shooting rabbits. Dear Adèle, have a care to thyself, and beseech thy husband to hear his peasants patiently lest they leave him without a roof to cover his head. Whatever may come to pass, I rely on the good sense of thine excellent Berthe to keep thee safe.

Thy loving sister,
Hortense de Fourchet de Bonsecours

Well. I remember I read this absorbing missive through from beginning to end, never lifting my eyes from the page to see whether madame listened or not. When I finished, she shrieked and groaned "La sainte Vierge preserve us!" then fainted untidily back upon her chaise longue. I myself was sufficiently horrified that I'd barely the wit to search for her smelling-salts, and indeed took a sniff at them myself before applying them to her nose. She came to with a start, and straightaway began to call for monsieur.

Mlle Linotte peeked in. "What's to do, Berthe?" she asked. "Is madame my mother ill again?"

"She is as you see her, mademoiselle," I snapped. "She desires speech with monsieur your father."

"He's in the aviary: I'll go fetch him if you tell me what has made you look so grim." I hesitated, and she frowned. "You forget I am a woman grown."

"Yes, mademoiselle. I forget." A woman grown, said I to myself. And a Maindur to boot. I put the letter into her hand.

She flicked through the scrawled pages, read the closing lines, reread them. A flame rose in her cheeks and eyes. "Revolution!" she exclaimed. "How monsieur my father will be furious."

Monsieur her father was furious: furious at being dragged away from his precious birds to listen to his wife's hysterical entreaties that he convey her and her daughter to Switzerland now, immediately.

"See where Hortense warns us to have a care, and talks of heads on pikes and I know not what other atrocities," she wailed. "What will become of us should the peasants burn Beauxprés around our ears?"

"Eh bien, foutre!" shouted the duc. "Let them but try! They'll learn fast enough how a Maindur deals with rebels. I'll hear no more of Switzerland, madame, nor of thy vaporish fears. Beauxprés is the seat of the ducs de Malvoeux, and in times of danger and uncertainty, the place of the duchesse de Malvoeux is at Beauxprés. Hortense is making a piece of work out of nothing. Those heads on pikes belong to common rioters, rely on it."

Then he stormed back to his birds, and there, we thought, was an end to it.

That night as I carried a posset up to madame, I heard a great pother from the courtyard of shouting voices and stamping feet. Alarmed, I turned and listened. The noise resolved into a chanted repetition of monsieur's name.

"Duc François," they cried. "François l'oiseleur!"

For an eerie moment I stood benumbed, waiting for the intolerable clamor of magic to shake the air as it had twelve years gone, when the beggar had summoned monsieur to the courtyard. A chilly draught scurried down the stairs and I looked up to see monsieur standing in the open door of his chamber. He was wearing a nightcap and a dark brocaded gown; his eyes glittered madly in the candlelight.

"You shall not have her," he shouted, and rushed past me down the steps and across the vestibule to the library.

At the head of the stairs my mistress appeared, leaning on Linotte's arm and complaining faintly of the prodigious deal of noise without. Hearing the chant, she faltered and clung to the railing.

Some heavy object began to thrust rhythmically against the doors, which gave and shuddered and groaned as with pain. Monsieur emerged from the library with his épée in his hand and started across the vestibule. The lock broke suddenly, ripped from its frame, and the doors gaped around a tree trunk, its branches roughly trimmed. Madame stumbled down the steps and clung to me. Water-kneed, I clung to her again and thought at least that we would die as we had lived.

When the doors burst asunder, there was a small hush. The tree trunk withdrew, and through the gap I saw the courtyard roiling with shadow and flame. One shadow stepped forward alone, proud as any prince over the threshold of Beauxprés. A filthy prince, clad in gray rags, his guard of honor armed with hoes and pitchforks and scythes.

"François Marie Baptiste Armand Maindur."

I started to hear the voice of Artide, rusty as the well-house pump but nonetheless familiar—Artide come into his own.

"François Maindur. Hear the will of the king of France."

Monsieur lowered the point of his épée and lifted his long nose. "I hear only a mutinous lackey backed by a herd of oxen."

An angry mutter greeted these words, more menacing, somehow, than a shout. Madame flinched, but did not retreat. Artide pulled his lips back from his teeth, reached into the bosom of his much-abused livery, and drew out a paper. Slowly he unfurled it, beckoned a flambeau closer, and began to declaim into a reverent silence.

"In the king's name. All people in the country are allowed to enter all the châteaux of the region to demand their title deeds. If they are refused, they can loot, burn and plunder; they will not be punished."

Monsieur raised his épée. "I'll see you in Hell first. Eater of shit! Peasants!"

At that the mob pressed forward into the hall. Their mouths gaped redly; their eyes rolled and stared; their faces were obscured by soot and fury. Yet I knew them: Yves and Estienne Pyanet, Claude Mareschal, Dieudonné Malateste, Pierre Desmoulins, Just Vissot, all the men in the village.

"The deeds!" Mareschal bayed. "Give us the deeds!"

Beside him, Just Vissot bellowed: "The land we farm is ours!"

"Death to the rich!" a woman's voice cried. "Death to the aristocrats!" And mère Boudin thrust herself through the press and advanced on monsieur like some malevolent fairy, one fist raised and threatening. "Give us what is ours, monster. Have a mind to the curse of the Maindurs, and for your soul's sake, give us what is ours."

Monsieur laughed. He looked upon his children's old nurse, her greasy skein of hair wound up under a red cap and white cockade, and laughed like Roland's horn. The peasants, uncertain, halted.

A hand gripped my elbow; a breath warmed my ear. "Hide the rent rolls," murmured Linotte.

I gasped and started. "What did you say?"

"The rent rolls. Hide them. Artide knows where they're kept, and they'll be ashes in a trice if they're not hidden. Hurry. I'll take care of madame my mother."

"The rent rolls."

"Yes. In the Armament room, where Sangsue keeps the accounts."

"The Armament room."

"Up the stairs and through the gallery of Depositions. Oh, Berthe, you know the Armament room."

Of a certainty I knew the Armament room, but this was no time to dispute with Sangsue my right to remove even a mote of dust from his personal domain. "Devil take the rent rolls," I said. "Let the peasants burn them."

"Go," she said. Just that: "Go."

And I went. With my skirts gathered up in both hands, I ran headlong through the dark and echoing chambers of Beauxprés, tripping over chairs and display cases, cursing the name of Maindur with every panting breath but running nevertheless as though I'd no will in the matter.

By some miracle—or spell—the Armament room was open and Sangsue absent.

Our miser was not a tidy man. Books, scrolls, quills, pen-wipers were scattered pell-mell over the trestle, and unmarked boxes shouldered undated ledgers on the shelves. Though I despaired of finding anything to the purpose, I rummaged, and luck—or some spell of Linotte's—was with me, for soon I came upon a leather box like a stocking-case crammed with dozens of tightly-rolled parchments—the rent rolls without a doubt. Slamming it shut, I snatched it up. A tin lantern stood on the window-ledge. I took that as well, and the tinderbox beside it.

Once outside the door, I stood rooted in a panic of uncertainty. Should I light the lantern? Where should I go? The document case was unwieldy, battered, all too obviously practical. Among all the ordered glory of the Beauxprés collections, 'twould stand out like a rag-seller among the queen's ladies-in-waiting.

Under my pallet? In the nursery? The devil fly away with it! In the distance, I heard shouting and the clatter of sabots on marble, sounds that awoke in my feet a will of their own. Pell-mell they carried me down the gallery of Depositions to the Violin room, down three steps into the cabinet des Fées, right at the Fan room and through the little arch that led to the donjon tower. Almost before I knew where I was going, I was down the winding stairs, across the laundry, and in the room where the soap tubs were kept, the room where I'd found bébé Malateste.

The arched door was uncovered and ajar as I had left it. Without daring to take time to light the lantern, I groped down the steps and into the darkness beyond.

In Which Berthe Uncovers the Crow's Nest and Linotte Takes Flight

I picked my gingerly way down a steep and narrow stair with the document case clutched like a swaddled infant to my breast. My skirts dragged over a thick, soft silting; under the dust, each step was sway-backed as a goat.

At the bottom I stopped to strike the tinder and light the tin lantern. 'Twas a tedious, fumbling business in the dark, but I managed it at last. The light revealed a low, stone chamber furnished with a trestle table and stools. I saw torches in the rusty cressets and great rusty keys dangling like hanged men from rusty hooks above eight doors, iron-banded and grated, four to each side of the chamber. A wide arch facing the stair framed a more inward darkness. I had found the ancient dungeons of Beauxprés.

I drew a shaking breath of stale air and held it to listen. Nothing. No rumor of sabots or peasant imprecations. No squeaking or scrabble of verminous feet.

Bon, said I to myself. Peasants have at least as much sense as rats: I'll leave the case down here. I waded through the dust to the trestle and laid my burden upon it. How large it hulked in the lantern-light! How out of place it looked, how exposed! And my trail through the dust was as clear as a way-post: Hidden documents this way.

"Bugger," I muttered. "Bugger the documents. Bugger the duc. Yes, and bugger the peasants, and Artide, and the birds, and the whole fornicating lot of them."

Something in the silence that followed my fit of spleen inspired me to an *Ave*, a *Pater Noster*, and a *mea culpa*, after which I felt somewhat calmer. Here were eight cells, and heaven only knew what deeps beyond the arch. Surely the dungeons of Beauxprés must once have concealed secrets more unwieldy than a document case.

I tried the door of the nearest cell, then another beside it, and another still. All were locked, by time and rust no less than by the heavy, useless keys: I couldn't budge them. There was one left a little ajar, and by dint of putting my back to the oak and pushing with all my strength, I managed to shift it enough to squeeze through. The cell was no wider than two coffins and barely as high as a man, with a narrow stone ledge across the far end. A perfect hiding-place, had it not been for the black water trickling down the walls. No use saving the rent rolls from fire only to lose them to rot.

That left the darkness beyond the arch gaping hungrily as a tooth-less mouth. I thought of ghosts and traps and nameless horrors. I thought of leaving the case on the trestle and pushing back the tub to hide the door again. I thought, to my eternal shame, of giving it up to the rebels. While I was thinking, I must have been moving toward the arch, for all at once I found myself beneath it, looking out into the chamber beyond.

Where the guard room had been bare, this chamber looked to be cluttered and crowded with odd bits of furniture. No, not furniture. A rack. An Iron Maiden. Divers other engines of repellent aspect. The floor was lost under a dark, mucky carpet; the air was fetid. I prodded at the mire with my toe, coughed at the ensuing acrid stink of a thousand ripe chamber pots. Bat dung. But where were the bats? I held my breath and my lantern high. No rustling; no flicker of wings, no gleam of tiny eyes. Where were the bats?

"Ah, fool, 'tis night!" I answered myself aloud. "Messires les chauve-souris take their suppers in the free air. Saint Francis be thanked they don't sleep at night like God-fearing folk!"

This time, the silence seemed indifferent to my words. I hefted the case in my arm and, after some hesitation, picked my way around the wall where the dung lay thinnest. Not thin enough, however, for every nook and crevice in the walls was foul with it. After a filthy and disheartening while, I came to another door half-hidden behind the Iron Maiden opening into a small, bare tunnel.

The floor slanted down beneath my feet, the passage twisted right and left, and suddenly my way was barred by a wall of fine-dressed stone carved with a quincunx of five-pointed stars.

Well. Afraid to curse, I kicked at the lowermost star in pure frustration. It gave, or rather the wall gave, and a low door gaped wide as Hell-gate upon an inky darkness.

Almost I turned and ran—la sainte Vierge knows I wanted to. Torture chambers and secret doors were no part of the world I knew. In a conte des fées, this door might lead to an enchanted land of emerald grasses and trees hung with rubies. In Beauxprés, 'twas more likely to lead to a dank oubliette. Still, I hadn't yet found a hiding-place for monsieur's documents. Having come so far, I couldn't go back. And if I couldn't go back, then I must go forward.

I held up my lantern, flame dancing with my nervous shuddering, raised my foot, and stepped through the secret door.

Half-expecting to be blinded by eerie light or to feel sharp blades of emerald beneath my slipper, I'd closed my eyes. I opened them quick enough when my foot came down on a hard, chill, flat surface that could only be common flagstone.

A low stone chamber, something like the guard room, save for a row of pillars down its length and a hearth fully broad and deep enough to roast an oxen whole. A perfectly ordinary room, even to the sparse and cobwebby furnishings: a joint-stool, an armchair of ancient design, a row of wooden clothes-presses against the wall, and, handy to the hearth, an iron cauldron and a tall table like a dressing-board. Oubliette? Subterranean kingdom? Bah! 'Twas nothing but a storage room.

A spell must have been on me—perhaps the beggar's or even Colette's. Why else would I have done what I did next? Why else would I have forgotten the peasants and Artide and my mistress' danger? Why else would I have laid the document case on the dressing-board—only to get rid of it, you understand—gone to the first press, bent, and tried the lid? Naturally, it would not open. I set down my lantern and tugged with both hands; the lid flew open upon a fugitive, shadowy glistening. I took up the light and held it close. The glisten was a layer of ancient cloth of gold hummocked over something hard and lumpy.

Gently I drew aside the costly, rotting stuff. Did it cover coins? Ancient plate? A hoard of barbaric jewels?

Bones. White and clean as if newly boiled, laid neatly in rows. Long bones and thin bones and curved bones and round bones, disarticulate and sorted in order of size upon a bed of yellowed linen.

Seeing a bony circlet like an irregular crown, I tried to lift it, whereupon it fell into three blade-shaped parts. I turned back the linen and discovered another tri-lobed circlet somewhat larger than the first; then another, smaller, and so on down for several layers. I carefully replaced them, tucked the cloth of gold around them, lowered the lid, sat back on my heels, and pondered. What manner of collection was this, so lovingly preserved? The care and arrangement showed a Maindur's hand, though 'twas not like a Maindur thus to hide his pride and joy under a bushel. Bien sûr, the bones were gruesome, but no more gruesome than the withered paws and foxes' masks in the Hunt closet. The collections of Beauxprés must include a thousand bones of bird and beast, clearly labeled and open to view. Why were not these among them?

In pursuit of an answer, I opened the next clothes-press, and the one next to that, and so on until I'd examined the contents of each. There were twenty-four in all: plain wood, iron-bound. Twenty of them (as I soon ascertained) were filled to the top with neat layers of bones. The twenty-and-first was packed with round objects wrapped each in fine linen.

Before I unwrapped the first, I knew it must be a skull. Nevertheless, when I peeled back the last shrouding fold to lay the grisly thing bare, I gasped and dropped it to the flags, where it shattered into dust. Perhaps I'd hoped 'twould prove the skull of some beast—a fox, perhaps, or at worst, a monkey. But when it sat grinning in my hand I could not deny that the skull was human, and the bones also; by the size of them, the bones and skulls of children.

Well, I confess I sat shaking for a space before gathering the courage to open the three remaining presses. Two of them were filled with skulls. The last contained grimmer stuff: a case of thin knives, iron hooks, coils of rotted rope which shed, when I touched them, a faint brown powder that clung to my fingers. There were also a crusted mace, four sooty irons with their handles wrapped in leather, and a brace of heavy, long knives such as a butcher might use to disjoint a pig. Separate from all this, in a compartment of its own, I came upon a tarnished silver casket like an ancient jewel chest, cunningly wrought in high relief with la sainte Vierge in glory, surrounded by angels. A reliquary? Among so many bones, what use was a single reliquary?

Within were—bones, of course—shrouded in brittle silk. This skeleton differed from the others in being entombed complete, skull and all, each separate bone polished to a dark ivory gleam with wax or much handling. Tears started to my eyes as I unwrapped them: the leg bones no longer than my forearm; the tiny, nameless bones of finger and toe; the bald skull that was like a wig-maker's form but for its grin and empty sockets.

Dark eyes glowed up at me, a soft mouth drooped, wryed, writhed over the perfect teeth. I dropped the skull in my apron and clamped my own teeth over a startled scream. The shadows fluttered; I bit my lip to blood. The lantern flame dipped and swirled.

The oil, the oil burns low, I soothed myself, and fumbled the bones back into their casket as quickly, and as reverently, as my shaking hands would allow. As I tucked the silk around them, my fingers found a wad of something dry and slick.

Parchment, said my mind even as my hand recoiled. I pried out the thick, crackling wad, unfolded it, and held it up to the lantern. A faint, crabbed writing covered it from edge to edge, indecipherable as Russian in the flickering light. The word "Maindur" caught my eye, and further down, "Beauxprés," and there, "enfant." French then, could I only unriddle the hand and the antique orthography.

The back of my hand came to rest against the hot lantern-hood. I jerked it away, silently cursing the pain and the lantern whose sullen smoking threatened to leave me benighted in this dreadful place. Hastily I crammed the parchment into my apron pocket and in a rising panic stumbled back the way I'd come.

Not until I'd reached the foot of the stairs did I recall the peasants and their pitchforks. Stay or go? I asked myself. Artide and his troops, or bones and bats?

Neither choice having much to recommend it, I stood and dithered until the lantern went out and the black air rushed in upon me, weighing on my lungs and ears and eyes, stopping up my senses as though with grave dust. Nothing stirred in the guard room, nothing leapt out or gibbered at me, and yet that darkness was more frightful to behold than a child dead of the plague, that silence more grating on the ear than the screams of a man drawn and quartered.

In the laundry, all was chaos—light, heat, the growl and snap of fire. I saw that the hedge around the laundry-yard was in flames, red-gold tongues licking the donjon as high as the windows of the vicomte's chamber of Eros. A wild desolation seized me and hurled me into the kitchen and up the back stairs into the vestibule, which, astonishingly, was dark and still as the dungeon. No smoke. No flames. No signs of life. Only furniture overturned, glass cases opened and rifled, curtains torn from windows, paintings torn from walls and an echo of shouts from the château's far reaches. No bodies. No blood. No answer to my frantic calling, though I screeched as I ran like a demented parrot: "Madame! Madame! Madame!"

A demon—black and red and horrible as death—sprang up before me, seized me by the shoulders, and shook me until my cap fell off.

"Stupide!" growled the demon. "Are you tired of life?"

"Madame!"

"She's safe enough, your precious madame, and her precious daughter, too. If you'll stop screeching, I'll tell you where to find them."

By now I'd regained enough wit to recognize Artide, to jerk myself from his grip and beat at him with my fists. "Judas," I cried. "Traitor. Have you turned your coat again?"

He bared his yellow teeth at me, raised his hands to my neck, and dug his thumbs, strong with much polishing of silver, into my throat. My breath began to fail. I remember thinking of madame, and my mother, and of the marquise de Bonsecours. How she'd scold me for my ill care of her sister, I thought, and through the roaring of my blood, I beseeched her, and le bon Dieu's, forgiveness.

"Foutre," said Artide violently, then, "I've no quarrel with you, Duvet. But you must not call me names." He released me, and I slid heavily down the wall. "Ho, you in there! Here's another little pigeon escaped from the cote. Come put her in with the others."

There'd been a prodigious smashing of glass and wood going on all this time, though I didn't really hear it until it stopped at Artide's shout. A second demon—this one thin and angular as the hoe he carried—popped up beside Artide.

"Put her in thaself, Desmoulins, if tha wants her put," said the demon irritably. "D'ye think she knows where them damned papers are?"

Artide looked down at me, blank-faced as Pompey at his most statuesque. "No," he said at length. "A femme de chambre wouldn't know a thing like that, would you, Duvet? Keep out of the way, now, and you won't be hurt. The girl and her mother are in the Cameo apartment. We're not like the nobles—we don't make war on women, unless they be whores like the Austrian, God rot her long nose. As far as I know, you're all of you chaste as nuns." His tongue wormed wetly over his lips. "Chaster."

The demon spat impatiently. "Never mind the nuns, nor the queen neither. Just ye find them papers tha promised, or we'll send thee after Sangsue to ask where he put 'em." He disappeared from my sight and began smashing things again. Artide cast me an unreadable glance and decamped.

Painfully I pulled myself to my feet. By the light of the fire outside, I saw I was in the gallery of Depositions, not far, I told myself, from the cabinet des Fées and the Cameo apartment, from madame and Linotte and safety. Three rooms separated me from them, only three rooms, and none of them long or wide to cross. Artide hadn't hurt me, at least not mortally. I could walk, and I did walk, somewhat unsteadily to be sure, the length of the gallery and into the Fan room.

Here was more desolation: cases thrown hither and thither, fans torn and scattered on the floor. Their wood and ivory sticks cracked like bones beneath my feet, and I couldn't see to avoid them, stepped I never so delicately. In the Snuff-box antechamber, a candle left burning on the mantel illuminated a sad litter of dismembered legs and twisted frames, shards of porcelain, glass splinters, gilded clips. I bent to a glitter—a small sapphire from one of the jeweled boxes— and next to it, the top of a fairy-tale box, reduced to a pair of blue eyes, a broad white brow, clustering golden curls, a crown. Good fairy or beautiful princess? Who could tell?

The door to the cabinet des Fées was ajar, and within I heard a cacophony of bangs and angry shouts. I should have been afraid, I suppose, but what with the dungeon and the bones and Artide nearly strangling me, I was sated with terrors. In any case, I walked into the cabinet as if 'twere the parish church. And there I found some four or five filthy men smashing glass cases and mère Boudin poking through the debris with a pitchfork.

"Don't touch anything, neighbors!" she was crying. "These're magic things. Ye don't know how they're bespelled, and no more do I. Unless ye've a taste for pond water and flies, don't touch 'em with bare flesh. Cold iron should keep 'em quiet."

One man—Just Vissot, by his paunch—yelped and glared at the steel coach of the Princesse Printanière. A purple rat had bitten him to the bone, and stood now on its hind legs, chittering furiously. He sucked the finger, then got a good hold on his iron spade and brought it down on the rat, which squeaked once and was silent.

A voice I knew—Yves Pyanet's—said, "Here's something looks about right," and held up his pike with a great leathern satchel dangling from it. The satchel bulged around an ungainly oblong just the size and shape of the document case I'd hidden in the dungeon.

Without wanting to, I gasped. They all turned to me.

"Ah, Duvet. Ye know this satchel, do ye?" Mère Boudin's piggy eyes glittered balefully. "No, don't deny it now—your face betrays ye. Noble's whore!" She hawked and spat. The men murmured, fingered their forks and hoes, and looked murder at me. After a moment, mère Boudin shrugged and pulled a little flask from her apron pocket, and they crowded around her like cows around a manger, leaving me free to creep towards the Cameo apartment.

"Holy Water, a Host, a nail—what're ye afeard on?"

"I don't know, and if ye do, Yves Pyanet, now's the time to say. Men!" said Boudin with fine scorn. "Babies!"

The man holding the torch waved it, sending the shadows darting. "Shut up and get on with it, ye old hag. I came for my deed, and my deed is what I want, and no dawdling."

"Patience," said Boudin. *"Ave Maria, gratia plena. . . ."*

I tapped at the door of the Cameo apartment, put my lips to the crack and whispered. " 'Tis Berthe, madame, thine own Berthe come to protect thee. For the love of God, let me in."

A pause, and a long, painful scraping as a chest was pushed from before the door. The lock-wards fell with a click and the handle dipped just as mayhem broke out behind me with a roaring and crack of blows. I rattled the handle, but the door had been relocked. I can't blame them—had I been safe within, I'd not have opened that door —no, not if Nôtre Sauveur Himself had stood without.

For mère Boudin had opened the satchel. She'd much better have let it alone—a magic bag in a magic room, and not so much as a wise-wife to advise her. Years ago I'd seen Pompey pull gold from this same satchel, and strange, hairy fruit and spicy black sausages. Linotte only got porridge from it, and monstrous gluey porridge at that. What mère Boudin and the mutins got from it was a stick, a stout wooden cudgel with a knob at the end and a life and will of its own. And life, will, and knob all three seemed set on beating the shit from the sackers of Beauxprés.

How the stick flew! Here a thwack on Pyanet's arse, there a poke in Boudin's belly, yonder a pounding across Vissot's shoulders, and everywhere such a rattling around everyone's ears as to set the whole rout of them dancing and howling like scalded cats. I laughed until I wept, laughed until my face ached and my belly quivered, and still the cudgel belabored the peasants, and still the peasants swatted at it with their shovels and pitchforks and yowled with pain.

At last Just Vissot found the door and stumbled out; one by one, the rest followed, groaning and blaspheming, mère Boudin louder than the rest. Then they were gone.

The stick took a last circuit of the room. I was still chuckling and hiccuping, but I sobered quickly enough when it came and hovered before me. Though a piece of wood has neither eyes to see with nor brow to wrinkle, I swear this same stick looked me frowning up and down before dismissing me as harmless and scudding back to the satchel, which opened to receive it and closed again with a soft, leathern slap.

Well. If I could not believe my eyes, neither could I disbelieve them. The sight of mère Boudin, leaping and squealing, her chins a-dance and her cockade bouncing, had been too grotesque for mere fantasy. Once more, laughter rose in me, wild and irrepressible. I closed my eyes and teeth upon it, quaked and quivered with the effort of keeping it down. Then the door opened behind me, and for the first time in my life, I fainted.

Swooning proved not so easy or pleasant an escape as I'd imagined. I woke up sick and dizzy and most prodigiously ashamed of myself, with my head in madame's lap and Doucette licking my cheek.

Doucette? Doucette is dead, I thought.

I must have spoken aloud, for Linotte answered me. "These thirteen years and more," she said. "This is the White Cat's dog, Toutou."

Slowly I sat upright, my mistress supporting me with a hand to my back. A tiny, multi-colored scrap of fur yipped musically by her knee.

A thousand times I'd seen the miniature dog curled in its case, silky ears spread like a coquette's curls across its silken pillow. I'd thought it an artful image, no more. Now here it was, dancing gracefully on its hind legs, a butterfly dog the size of a mouse. I was just stretching out my finger to it when madame flung herself at my neck.

"O Berthe, the terrors I've suffered, you can't begin to imagine. I've been in fear of my life. Those horrid peasants! How could they treat me so, me who has never wished them ill, nor meddled with them in any way! And when you fainted like that—why, I thought you dead. You're quite well now, aren't you, and we may be quite comfortable?"

Her voice in my ear was hoarse with fear; her body against mine was electric with it. Poor madame, I thought tenderly. Poor silly, helpless, dear madame. I took her into my arms, stroked her tumbled hair, and assured her, as much for my sake as for hers, that yes, I was quite recovered. She clutched me and sobbed. "Hush, hush, ma princesse," I murmured, rocking her. "Doucement, ma belle."

Over my mistress' head, I could see Linotte moving through the wreck of the cabinet des Fées, stooping now and again to salvage some bit of magical flotsam. The torch bobbed a little behind and above her head.

At first I thought the torch entirely unsupported; then I saw that there were fingers wrapped prosaically around it. Yet 'twas unsupported after all, for the owner of the fingers was invisible; or else the hand attached to the fingers was their sole owner. In any case, the torch was held by a disembodied hand. A dozen other hands, equally detached, hovered nearby.

I felt my cap tweaked backwards. I slapped it back into place, whereupon a plump, white hand whisked into view, shook a reproving finger in my face, patted my cheek, and darted off to receive Prince Lutin's scarlet cap from Linotte. The air around me sparkled and rang with bells—silver bells, this time, very thin and pure. Linotte was a girl of seventeen, after all.

After she'd wept herself out, madame swallowed a few drops of laudanum from the bottle in her pocket and slept. I was not so fortunate, the pain of my bruised throat and burned hand conspiring with my fear to keep me awake. Besides, how could I sleep when there was so much to be done? Linotte, intent upon her salvage, was no help at all. She paid no more heed to all my suggestions about calming the peasants, shooting Artide, flying to Besançon than if I'd been as mouthless as her dexterous attendants.

Goaded, I cried, "Heartless chit! Madame your mother's prostrate, mad peasants are pulling your home down about your ears, and your father's head may decorate a pike even as we speak! And all you do is go about your business, cool as milk."

At that, she finally turned to me. A comical sorceress she made, draggled and smutty as to her face and hair, surrounded by a nimbus of unbodied hands clutching apples, hats, boots, pots, gaudy wands and gilded nuts of all shapes and sizes. Yet I was not inclined to laughter, for under the smuts her face was stern, and her dark eyes glittered with rage and magic.

"My father has brought this upon himself," she said in a voice of snow. "And not only upon himself, but upon you and madame my mother, upon the peasants, upon the soil, upon the very air of Beauxprés. He does not deserve to live. Yet I tell you that my father is not dead, nor will he die." She sighed then, and in a voice somewhat more human, said, "So content you, Berthe. And sit down somewhere. You're fidgeting me."

In my numbed state, that speech took some puzzling out, I can tell you. And even when I'd made sense of her words, I still didn't know what she meant by them. Oh, the first part was clear enough, and true enough to swear by. The second part, however—was it reassurance or prophecy or threat? And there was the matter of the hands and the little dog Toutou and the purple rats even now mourning their crumpled comrade. Who had awakened them? Who had taught Linotte to command them?

When I opened my mouth, I had intended to demand answers to these questions, now, before I lost my mind. Yet all that came out was, "Bah!"

Linotte shrugged. "Then look for yourself." Upon her gesture, one of the empty hands darted into the bedchamber, fetched out a candle in a flat candlestick, kindled it at the torch, and presented it to me, ring politely foremost. I had the peculiar sensation that it—the hand, that is—found my bewilderment vastly amusing.

I goggled, and after a moment or two, Linotte gave an impatient snort. " 'Tis only a candle, Berthe: quite unmagical, I assure you. Take it."

Thus ordered, what could I do, save curtsy, hook my finger through the ring and take the candle and my leave with what dignity I could muster?

Quick or dead, I thought monsieur was most likely still in the château. Yet he wasn't in the hall, where I'd last seen him. He wasn't in the library. Nor was he in the Miniature salon, nor in the Egg antechamber, nor in his apartment.

They'd wrecked that too, the dirt-arses, ripped the bed as though it were M. le duc's belly and smashed the chairs and tables as though they were his bones. Crimson light shifted and flowed like fresh blood over the ruin, crimson light it took me far longer than it ought to recognize as fire glow. It took me even longer to persuade my overwrought heart that the fire itself was outside and to force my reluctant legs out to the balcony above the forecourt.

A great bonfire tossed between the château and the fountain of Latona where the beggar-wizard had stood. The peasants had built it; a heap of paintings and broken furniture showed what they'd fed it on. Sated, it roared like Gargantua, belching sparks to the sky while behind it the fountain writhed with illusory life. The man-frogs mouthed and grabbed at Latona, who, aware of her danger at last, seemed to hug herself and cower. After Toutou and the hands, I half-expected to see them up and devour her. They didn't, of course. Nor did the beggar-wizard appear to gloat over his fallen enemy, nor any peasant run out with so much as a piece of lace to coax the flames higher.

In short, the forecourt was deserted.

Then it came to me. Monsieur was at the aviary, of course. Where else would he have gone? 'Twas inevitable as a tragedy. And the aviary would draw the peasants like a magnet, too: all that glass and all those birds, beautiful as painted miniatures, useless as mounted fox paws, harmless as lace collars except for needing to be warmed and fed. To warm them, monsieur had taken the wood from the peasants' hearths; to feed them, he'd taken the grain from their stores. They'd destroy it to the last stone in its foundation. And doubtless monsieur would die in its defense.

A vermilion-winged parrot flew past me, screaming raucously. It circled the fire, then headed out over the fields towards the Forêt des Enfans.

"That'll startle the owls," said I to myself.

That is my last certain memory of that night. There are other scenes—disconnected vignettes—that return to me when I try to remember: my memories or Jean's, I can't tell which. Jean was at the aviary with monsieur and I was not, or at least I've no memory of leaving the balcony or crossing the garden or traversing the copse or hiding from the peasants. Yet I can picture the aviary's fall as clearly as if I'd witnessed it. Perhaps my soul flew there, leaving my body behind. Or perhaps 'tis only Jean's having described the scene so often.

In any case, I've only to close my eyes to see monsieur, disheveled, bald as an egg, wild-eyed, backed up to the aviary's outer door with his épée en garde. A rock arcs through the night—even had I been there, I couldn't have seen that, could I?—and a glass pane breaks high up in the building. A honey-bird darts out, yellow and gleaming blue, hovers uncertainly, flutters down to monsieur, lands on his sword arm. Monsieur stills, purses his lips and whistles to it.

I see mère Boudin beside monsieur, taking the bird in her hands. With a housewifely air she twists the tiny head front to back, tucks the corpse into her apron and turns away. Monsieur drops his épée and frowns at her with such intensity that I wonder she does not kindle with it and burn like paper under a lens.

The last scene is lit by the flare of torches. Rocks fly into the aviary and birds fly out, erupting from the shattered windows, blundering up and back and around in circles, all at sea in the unwalled darkness. One by one, they fall under the peasants' stones like rainbow fruit, and like fruit are gathered up. Monsieur watches the harvest unmoving; I would say unmoved, except for the unwavering intensity of his black gaze.

The sack of Beauxprés began an hour or so after sunset and ended about dawn. The château itself was undamaged, though the peasants had overturned almost every room within it. They'd missed some—there are, after all, upwards of three hundred rooms in Beauxprés. When Jean and I went through the place, we found the Alchemical attic untouched. The Hunt closet had also been overlooked, and the Cameo apartment spared; but the pantries had been rifled, and the apartments of M. Justin and the vicomte de Montplaisir were a wilderness of glass and wood.

Even now, I cannot bear to recount all we did that day, Jean and I, what we saw and what we felt. Nor is there any reason for it. How we found Sangsue smothered in the midden is no fit tale for a young girl, ghost or no, nor the indignities the peasants had practiced upon him before they buried him. Only I think they must have been mad to serve him so—mad or accursed. Yet if their violence were curse-brought, then what of those mobs Mme de Bonsecours wrote of, with their pikes and their cockades and their bloody trophies? Did the beggar-wizard's curse infect all of France? Or was the rot of Beauxprés, like clouded urine, only a symptom of some subtle disease eating away at our national vitals?

That night, for the first time since she had left the convent, madame retired supperless. She wept a bit, like a hungry child, then kissed my hand, murmured, "You'll take care of me, Berthe," and fell asleep.

Well, I certainly intended to take care of her, although at the moment I didn't quite know how I was going to go about it. The château was a shambles, there was hardly a bite of edible food to be found, Sangsue was horribly dead, the lackeys and kitchen-boys fled le bon Dieu knew where, and as for monsieur! Well, a walking statue would have been as much use to us, and that's the truth. Jean, who'd stuck to the duc like a louse through the alarms of the night, finally left him sitting on a rock by the ornamental pond and staring at the rubble of wood and glass and iron that once had been the finest aviary in all France. I think he was waiting for his parrots and his jacamars, his emerald cuckoos and his showy birds-of-paradise to fly home to him. He'd have a long wait, then; for their feathers were stuffing his tenants' pillows and their corpses enriching his tenants' pots-au-feu with the first meat they'd tasted in months.

Me, I was too hungry to sleep, and like a ghost I wandered the ruins of Beauxprés in search of sustenance. Had I dared, I'd have gone down to the village and begged a ladle of aviary soup from Mme Pyanet.

My wanderings took me at last to the cabinet des Fées, where Mlle Linotte was curled up on a sofa.

"Ah, there you are, Berthe. I leave Beauxprés tonight, and I wish to wear these." She sat up and thrust a suit of boy's clothes into my hands. I recognized them at once—indeed, I'd made them myself. They were M. Justin's.

"The sleeves are too short," she said, "and the culottes too narrow in the hip. You must alter them to fit me."

This autocratic speech galled me more than a little. "What about your new servants?" I asked acidly. "Aren't they sufficiently handy to alter a suit of clothes?"

"They're quite stupid," she said. "And very stiff in the joints as yet. Besides, I can't make them do anything I don't know how to do myself."

"Very well, mademoiselle. There's nothing worse than starting out on a quest in tight breeches."

My workbox, of course, was nowhere to be found, but among Linotte's gleanings were a silver needle and some lengths of gossamer; with these and a small dagger for cutting, I contrived the necessary alterations. It took some time, however, and longer for the blurriness of my eyes and the clumsiness of my fingers and the difficulty of threading a needle with gossamer, even when the needle can sew of itself.

After a search for a candle and some unspoiled cloth to piece out the breeches, I sat down to work. In my state, it all seemed perfectly ordinary: the magic needle, Linotte's intended departure, her sudden need for haste, her desire to travel as a boy. Skirts and petticoats are awkward attire for rough walking and scrambling over ditches, and (though the stories don't mention it) I'd guess that questing has its share of both.

I said that to her, and then I said, "I should've known all along you'd go off after the Porcelain Dove. You are, after all, the third child. I suppose your being an untried girl does not signify."

"Of course not, Berthe—what about Finette Cindron and the rest? They were all untried girls, and heroes as well. When the quest is yours, 'tis yours, and only you can achieve it. According to the pattern, this quest is mine."

"A good pattern, in its way, though I've always thought it hard on the older brothers." Mlle Linotte snorted laughter, and I hurried to add, "Bien sûr, the vicomte's no loss to anyone, but poor M. Justin's another story entirely."

"That's right—another story entirely. Don't worry about brother Justin, Berthe. He's quite comfortable, and much happier than he was here."

Another prophecy? I felt I'd had enough of the cursed things— yes, and of quests and magic, too. The needle would have done the seam in a trice if I'd let it alone, but I ignored its impatient wriggling, clung to it savagely, and set a tiny stitch in M. Justin's old coat. "We live in the Age of Reason," I said perversely, "not the Age of Heroes. What makes you think that questing's the action required? Walking off into the night alone, dressed in your brother's old suit—'tis not at all comme il faut. Perhaps the prophecy is a test of—I don't know— your steadfastness in the face of hardship. Perhaps you are the Por- celain Dove."

Linotte shook her head. "You're as stubborn as a stone, Berthe. Perhaps I am the Porcelain Dove. Nonetheless, I must leave Beauxprés, now, tonight, before midnight sounds."

"How do you know?"

"Oh, I know." She looked at me, teasing. "Shall I tell you a story?"

I shrugged. "Can you rip seams while you're telling?"

In answer, Linotte took up the breeches and the dagger and set to work.

"Once upon a time," she said, "there was a small girl. She had two brothers, both much older than she, and a nursemaid who was an ogress. One day when they were all out walking, they chanced to meet an old beggar-man. He was very ragged and very ugly, with eyes as yellow as the feathers of a canary bird and long gray hair growing from his chin like a billy-goat's beard. Despite his ragged cloak, the small girl could see that this beggar was in reality a mighty wizard, so that when her elder brother blustered and threatened him, it frightened her very much."

I snorted. "Threatened to feed him to the hawks, did he? I know this story, mademoiselle."

"Patience, Berthe, and listen."

Well, I'd nothing better to do, so, "Very well," I said. "Not a word shall pass my lips until you've finished: by the Virgin's blue mantle, I swear it."

She nodded and went on.

"Now, besides two brothers, the small girl had a father, and like the old beggar, he was a mighty wizard. His magic was dominion over all the birds of the air, and he was so powerful that he had only one weakness: he had no heart. He'd given it to his birds, you see, in order to strengthen his power over them, and therefore he was no longer able to feel any tender emotion. Because he lacked a heart, he often forgot his children. When he remembered them, he took them to his court of birds. There he would call each bird by its name, and the birds would fly to him and bow to him and do his bidding in all things.

"One day, he remembered the small girl. Now it happened that the small girl liked birds and alone of all his children understood their tuneful language; so she was glad to go with her father, and even more so because her brothers were not by. So they set out walking, and they hadn't gone far when who should appear before them but an old beggar-man? The small girl saw his eyes yellow as canary feathers and his chin bearded like a goat's, and recognized him at once as the ragged wizard her eldest brother had wanted to feed to the hawks. At first she was frightened lest he blame her for her brother's rudeness. But the beggar-wizard did not seem to notice her at all. Fixing his yellow eye on the bird-wizard, he said:

" 'L'oiseleur. I have come to beg a thing from thee, and thou darest not deny me.' "

At this point Mlle Linotte frowned and fell silent. I realized that I was holding the struggling needle poised in the air and that my mouth was stupidly ajar. Snapping it shut, I stabbed the needle into the heavy stuff of Justin's old coat. Eagerly it wormed through the folds, pulled the stitches taut, and darted back in again. "Bah," I said, and let it get on with the seam. Smiling, Linotte took up the breeches and the tale once more.

"At the beggar-wizard's salutation, the bird-wizard grew pale and still with rage. 'Beg, then,' he said.

"The beggar-wizard drew himself up in his old ragged cloak, and much to the small girl's dismay, pointed his taloned finger at her. 'I beg of thee thy daughter,' he said. 'Thy daughter in the room of mine. Give her me.'

"Well, I need hardly tell you that the small girl didn't like that idea at all. For now the beggar-wizard was looking right at her with the expression of a starving man who spies a sausage or a sweet cake, so that she feared he intended her for his stewpot or worse.

"Now, she knew that her father the bird-wizard did not believe in ogres—if he did, he'd never have hired the nursemaid. Despairing, she clung to her father's leg and begged him not to give her away. The beggar-wizard shot out his sharp, gray hand, seized the small girl by the wrist, and pulled her into his arms, along with the bird-wizard her father. For a moment the two wizards stood nose to nose and eye to eye, with the small girl caught between them like a hare in a trap. Then she felt a jerk and a heave, and she was in the bird-wizard's arms, and the beggar-wizard was grovelling in the dust with his sharp gray fingers rubbing his billy-goat's chin.

"'I will give thee nothing,' the bird-wizard sneered at him. 'Begone, vermin, lest I have thee flayed and thy hide nailed to the stable door as a warning to any man who would dare to lay hands on what is mine.'

"While the small girl was very glad she need not go with the ogre, she thought it might have been better if her wizard father had held his tongue, for the ogre was looking fire out of his canary-yellow eyes. Being, after all, only a small girl, she began to weep and tremble. The bird-wizard impatiently bade her be still, or he'd take her back to her nursemaid, which made her weep the more, whereupon he turned away from the court of birds and began to retrace his steps. And the small girl heard the beggar-wizard screech after them:

" 'That's thrice, l'oiseleur. That's thrice!' "

The needle had been busy throughout this astonishing tale, and as Mlle Linotte spoke the final word, it set the final stitch in the coat, knotted the thread and went still. Absently, I bit through the gossamer—it tasted most curiously of crême caramel—and took the unseamed breeches from her hands. Her normally pale cheeks were flushed and her lips pleated with the effort of holding back tears.

"The candle burns low, child," I said gently. "Can you conjure me up another?"

Mlle Linotte drew a quivering breath, expelled it, nodded, and clapped her hands sharply, rousing two of her stiff-jointed servants from the untidy pile where they lay heaped like gloves. Over the centuries I've grown used to the hands, can even tell one from another by a broken nail, a callus, a gesture. I can't say I'm fond of them, however, and when mademoiselle first animated them, I could scarcely bear them about me. But I've never denied their usefulness. Soon a branch of candles illuminated both my work and Mlle Linotte's carefully composed face.

"So," I said after a space. "You intend to find this beggar-wizard and give yourself up to him?"

"Yes."

That was clear enough, to be sure, if hardly enlightening. "Why?" I asked.

"Because I am the youngest. Really, Berthe, you are very dull tonight."

"And no wonder if I am, Mlle Taratata, seeing as I've neither slept nor eaten for two days and nights. I don't understand what this fairy tale of yours has to do with the Porcelain Dove. 'Tis the same beggar, bien sûr: his enigmatic speech marks him no less than his yellow eyes. If you ask me, even a hero would be well-advised to keep away from him—yes, and pick a less ill-omened time to go a-questing as well."

"Ill-omened? No, Berthe. Don't you see that the omens point to this being the perfect, the only time for me to begin the quest? There's nothing to keep me here—"

"Except madame your mother, who's helpless as a babe newborn, and needs her daughter. As well you know."

"And well *you* know she hardly knows she has a daughter. You love her enough for both of us, Berthe; she has no need of me." Linotte took an anxious look at a man's watch the hands had rescued, miraculously unbroken, from the Horological closet. " 'Tis gone eleven. Are you nearly done?"

The needle had come to the end of one leg and I of my patience. "You haven't answered me a single question yet," I said. "Hints and stories and evasions of all sorts—oh, yes, plenty of those. But a plain answer in plain French? Not a one! I'm a good mind to call the needle off and let you quest bare-arsed."

Mlle Linotte shrugged. "I cannot answer you, Berthe," she said. "Your questions have no plain answers. All I know is that the beggar is a wizard who lost a daughter, I know not how, and asked for me in return. When my father refused, he cursed our family to ruin unless we should find a certain Porcelain Dove. Beggar and Dove are linked. To find one will be to find the other. That, Berthe, is the logic of magic."

Although I felt little wiser than before, I could clearly see that Mlle Linotte had indeed told me all she knew. If any of it meant anything, well, she was the sorceress, not I. I sighed and told her to remove her gown and promised that by midnight I'd have her turned out like a gentleman, or know the reason why.

And I did, though 'twas a near thing, what with having to cut her hair and finding a ribbon to tie it back and rags to stuff in Justin's shoes to keep them from rubbing sores on her feet. She wanted to take along a plaguey lot of magical impedimenta, too: seven-league boots and the leather satchel, Prince Lutin's scarlet hat, a magical walking-stick, an enchanted cheese, assorted acorns and walnuts, two or three fairy jewels, the steel coach—to bribe queens with, she said —and the wand of the Fairy Friandise, purple spangles, marzipan pigs and all.

But 'twas done at last, and just on midnight, she and I stood in the stable-yard with a hodge-podge pile at our feet and a brace of torches floating over our heads. As the church bell tolled the first stroke of twelve, I fully expected a magic chariot drawn by frogs or dragons to descend from the stars and whisk my translated young mistress away.

What appeared instead was the long, low shape of a great black wolf padding paw by giant paw out of the shadows over the cobbles. My throat clamped shut with terror, or I'd have screamed fit to wake the dead. Armless hands are fairy-tale devices, and not to be taken seriously. Wolves, on the other hand, are real, with real teeth and real claws and real bellies to fill.

I must have made some sound after all, for Mlle Linotte took my arm and shook it. "Don't be frightened, Berthe," she said impatiently. "He means us no harm. He's our friend, Berthe, really he is."

Unconvinced, I gazed terror-struck into the wolf's eyes: deep, unnatural eyes, black as the midnight sky.

"Oh, dear," said Mlle Linotte. " 'Tis too much for her, Pompey. She'll faint in a moment, I know it. There's no time for this!"

Thus addressed, the wolf reared up on its hinder legs and turned into a man.

As I look back upon it, it seems to me that there were two Berthes who watched that transformation. The first was a Berthe who quaked and quivered and crossed herself and called upon la sainte Vierge to protect her. The second was a Berthe who observed how the wolf's muzzle and ears appeared to melt back into its skull, which swelled like a bladder to receive them, and how its paws split and its hips realigned under the spine and its fur matted into a velvet coat and breeches more elegant by far than anything Pompey had worn in his life.

For it was Pompey who stepped forward and very sensibly shook the two Berthes into one before catching me to his breast, where I sobbed that I'd always known he wasn't dead while he stroked my back and said he'd missed me, too. Even when I was calmer, I stood in his embrace, my cheek pressed into his jacket. 'Twas scratchier than it looked and smelled faintly doggy.

"Come on, Pompey," wailed Mlle Linotte behind us.

"There's time," he said. "Be patient." Mlle Linotte looked sulky, but held her peace while he led me to the mounting block, sat me down upon it, and squatted by my knee.

As you may imagine, I had a thousand questions; so many, in fact, that I could not ask one of them. Instead, I looked into Pompey's face and stroked his cheeks that had grown lean and lined, and his woolly hair that had threads of white twined among the black. He was thirty years old, after all. Why should I have been so astonished that he looked his age?

"Thou art grown most princely, my son," I said to him at last.

He kissed my hand. "A prince of wolves, mother."

"Tell me."

"I've ever been a poor hand at a story," he said, "but you deserve some account of where I've been and what I've been doing these six years. First, I have to go back even further than that, to when madame our mistress was so sick, do you remember? Well, I met a sorcerer in the Forêt des Enfans, a wolf-master and a good man in his way, although his way is not ours. 'Twas he gave me the receipt that cured madame, and thereafter I met him from time to time at the forest's edge. He taught me other magics, of shape-change and spell-casting and invisibility. When monsieur beat me with the riding-whip, I made myself invisible and went into the forest to dwell with him."

Mlle Linotte, who'd been dancing with impatience through this speech, broke in. "Let me tell, Pompey, and it'll go faster. Maître Grisloup taught him a lot of magic, and me, too, when I could get away, and we did what we could to soften the beggar-wizard's curse on Beauxprés. It wasn't much. We begged the wolves not to eat the cattle and gave wood to any peasant brave enough to push on past the bounds of the curse to the heart of the Forêt des Enfans. Pompey wanted to fly over the fields in the form of a crow and sow the fields with healthy seed, but Grisloup wouldn't let him. Just think, Berthe! 'Tis contrary to the law of magic for one wizard to work directly against another, just as Mme d'Aulnoy said."

By now, I was feeling more myself. "That's very interesting, child," I said. "Be tranquil now and let Pompey speak for himself. You're going no faster than he, and I've already had one long tale from you tonight."

"In truth, Berthe, there's little left to tell," said Pompey. "I was maître Grisloup's apprentice, and Mlle Linotte was mine. Now we are raised to journeymen, and our first journey is to the Fortunate Isles."

"Do you know where they lie?"

"Bien sûr," said Pompey, surprised. "Would I set out on a quest without knowing where I was going?"

Well, I came as close as my next breath to slapping his face, sorcerer or no. What stayed my hand was the fear that after this night, I'd never see him again. Thinking that a blow's a poor farewell, I swallowed my spleen and kissed his brow instead.

"No, thou would'st not, clever monkey that thou art."

"Enough!" cried Mlle Linotte. "Midnight, maître Grisloup said, not a moment after, and here we've been talking for hours. If 'tis not spoiled already, it soon will be, and the blame is not mine, Pompey, be sure of that."

Pompey turned his night-black eyes on her, holding her gaze until she looked away and sighed. "I know," she said. "Patience. I'm only a maiden sorcerer. I don't understand everything yet. When I'm ready, I will understand. Patience is part of being ready."

"When you believe that in your heart, mademoiselle, then you'll be so much closer to mastery," said Pompey severely. Turning his attention to the pile of magical objects, he shook his head. "You can't take all that, Mlle Linotte—you know you can't. Three only—and not the satchel. There are those more in need of its properties than you."

Mlle Linotte squatted beside the pile, handed the satchel to him with an ill grace, and began to pick through the rest, muttering to herself.

Pompey put the satchel into my hands. I dropped it. He picked it up. I objected. He insisted. In the end, he had his way, and taught me how to make it yield up endless food or gold or any other thing I might happen to have need of. The thing didn't take easily to me, nor I to it. By the time I'd got the trick of it, Mlle Linotte had drawn on the seven-league boots, tucked a silver walnut into her pocket, and thrust the wand of the Fairy Friandise through her belt. She was doing her best to be patient, but her hands and teeth—the former opening and closing into fists, the latter worrying at her lower lip—betrayed her failure. Clearly the time had come for farewells, and I'd no desire to drag them out.

Formally I embraced Mlle Linotte. Pompey knelt and asked my blessing before pressing me in his arms once more. Then he released me, stepped back, plucked a black feather from behind his left ear, and blew upon it. In less time than it takes me to write the words, his jacket had sprouted feathers, his legs dwindled to sticks and his body to the size of a large cat, while his nose grew more pointed and his eyes more beady until he had become, to all appearances, a very handsome crow.

He sprang into the air and circled me three times, wide wings beating strongly, black legs pumping, then took off into the night, cawing raucously. Mlle Linotte gave a joyous whoop, lifted her right foot, and strode off after him. At least I suppose she followed him; the seven-league boots took her out of sight in a single step. Me, I couldn't have seen her anyway, what with my eyes being full of tears and the night moonless and the stable-yard as black as Pompey's wings, except for the torches. I strained my ears for his cawing, but heard nothing. Except for the church bell, tolling midnight.

In Which a Curious Document Is Unveiled

The sun rose as usual the next morning, trundled peacefully across the sky, set, and rose again. Monsieur, to all appearances recovered of his shock, was for calling down the law upon his tenants. He'd been wronged, insulted, his honor trampled upon and his property stolen by mere peasants, by damned, porridge-eating, dung-footed *farmers*, and he'd see justice done or die in the attempt. Then he demanded that Jacques Ministre and Menée be sent to him and wanted to know how Noël Songis was getting on with breeding the emerald cuckoos.

Jean bowed deeply, said he'd fetch them forthwith, and locked M. le duc de Malvoeux in the library where the interview had taken place. He found me in the kitchen, where I'd retreated out of habit. Madame had been driving me distracted with "Where is my husband, Berthe?" and "Where is my daughter?" and "How my belly gripes me!" and "Whatever are we to do?" so that I'd dosed her with the last of the laudanum simply to quiet her.

"Well, Duvet," said Jean when he saw me.

"Well, Jean," said I.

And then we sat, silenced by the thought of three hundred rooms filled with the detritus of thousands of costly objets d'art, and one man and one woman who hadn't enough sense between them, were they fish, to keep them from drowning. Yet we were pledged to serve that man and that woman—had served them all our lives. We had two choices, Jean and I: serve ourselves for once and leave our charges to die, or stay and die with them. Faced with such choices as these, what use is conversation?

With a visible effort, Jean roused himself. "The first question's bread. I've no answer to it without we go begging in the streets of Besançon. For 'tis a louis d'or to stable-dirt that no one in Beauxprés will give us so much as a moldy crust."

I'd put off this moment as long as I could, having thus far kept body and soul together on orts scraped from the pantry floor—disgusting stuff to be sure, but real. Now it had come down to magic or starvation, my clenching belly chose for me. "Bread, at least, I can supply."

Rising, I fetched the satchel from the chimney corner where I'd hung it two nights before. "This is a magic satchel," I said. "And if you don't mend your look, you'll get nothing from it but rotten eggs and stale water." For Jean was scratching his stubbly cheek and eying me with the look of a sane man penned up with lunatics.

"Very well," he said at length. " 'Tis a magic satchel. In the last twelve years, I've swallowed a wizard's curse and men who lie down to sleep upon beds of fire and a dragon with whiskers six ells long. I suppose I can swallow a magic satchel, so long as my belief yields me a mouthful of wine to sweeten the draught."

"Le bon Dieu willing, it shall." Then I closed my eyes tight and muttered the charm Pompey had taught me, full of doubts as St. Thomas.

I'd asked for a meat pie. I got a sausage, raw and gristly, as punishment, I suppose, for my lack of faith. Astonished that I'd gotten anything at all, I thanked the satchel as Pompey had instructed me, whereupon it relented and produced not only the pie I'd asked for, but a baguette as well and a stone bottle full of good Normandy cider. Jean fell upon the pie like a starving man, which indeed he was, and between the two of us, we made short work of it.

When we were done, Jean belched happily, leaned back against the wall and laced his fingers across his belly. "Yon bag's as fine a cook as M. Malesherbes, in its way," he said. "I'm almost resigned to living again. Still, we're in a fine mess, Duvet, and no mistake."

I had to agree with him. "The only reasonable thing to do is to put them in the berline and take them to their friends."

"The duc de Malvoeux has no friends," said Jean. "Nor yet no family, at least that I've ever heard of."

"And the marquise de Bonsecours has enough to worry her without an hysterical sister and her mad husband."

"Yes. And besides, the horses have disappeared."

We looked at one another and sighed.

"How far do you think we'd get on foot?" I asked.

"Who's we? Monsieur and madame and you and I? The bottom of the hill, or perhaps the end of Just Vissot's far meadow. If his cowman should chance to be nodding, we might even make the Forêt des Enfans, but I doubt we'd make it through."

"Because of the curse," I said.

"Because of the curse, because of the brigands, because monsieur would fall down a gully, because madame would fall in a stream. Alone, you and I might possibly make Besançon, if you wore a coarse gown and kept your Parisian jaw shut."

Pain squirmed in my breast when Jean spoke of Besançon—pain like the breeding of maggots.

"I will stay by my mistress," I said. "You may do as you please."

Jean shrugged. " 'Twill make a good tale someday, how I locked the mad duc de Malvoeux in his own library and fed him meat pies from a magic satchel. I'll stay."

From pure relief I wanted to embrace him, to kiss his hands and rain tears upon them like the heroine of one of madame's novels. We'd never been on that kind of terms, however, nor did I wish to be. So I said only, "That tale'd be sure to get *you* locked up—as a maniac or a mutin, the one or the other. Still, making this place habitable again's too great a task for one. I'm content to have you stay, if only you promise not to make a tale of it."

"Surely you can't mean to put the entire château to rights!" he exclaimed.

"Not at once, no. Just the kitchen for us and the library for monsieur, perhaps his apartment as well. Those will do for the winter. Come spring, we'll see what more."

Jean gaped at me. "Come spring? What are you saying, Duvet? We'll stay, bien sûr, maybe a month or two, until things in Paris have settled and we can get word to madame's sister."

The maggots swarmed up again, worse than ever. "I've already said I won't go," I snapped. "Leave Beauxprés? Sacré Dieu, Jean! Where will Pompey find me if I leave Beauxprés?" And I leapt from my seat and commenced to pace the length of the hearth, wringing my hands in my apron and declaring I'd wait for the Porcelain Dove, yes, if it took Mlle Linotte twenty years to find it.

Jean watched me gawp-mouthed for a space, then, "Duvet," he said firmly; a little louder, "Berthe Duvet!"; finally at full voice, "BERTHE!" which startled me so much I froze in mid-stride with my apron all wadded up in my hands. Then he came to me and pried open my fists and smoothed down my apron, talking gently all the while.

"There, there, ma belle," he murmured. "That's better, now, n'est ce pas? All sweet and calm, now, there's nothing here to fright thee, just old Jean who loves thee. Gently, gently, now, sit and rest thyself. Thou hast done nobly, nobly. Chère Berthe, ma belle, ma bien aimée."

Sensitive as a snail out of its shell, I didn't want him touching me and would have struck his hands away had I not been too weary to move. Still murmuring, he led me to the settle and fetched me a cup of water. I began to weep. He clucked soothingly and took up my apron corner to wipe my face. A great wad of yellowed parchment fell from the pocket, thud, at his knees. "What's this?" he asked.

"I don't know. I found it." Remembering where I'd found it, I shuddered. "Leave it be, Jean; 'tis a filthy thing." I dipped the corner of my apron into the water he'd brought me and held it to my burning eyes.

" 'Tis not so dirty," he objected, examining it. "Though it looks to be older than the Devil himself." He turned it crackling in his hands. "Can you read it?"

"No. Yes. I don't know whether I can or not. When, pray, have I had the leisure to try? I found it only yesterday—no, the night before, when . . . you know. Give it here, and the satchel, too. Madame'll be waking soon, and you don't want monsieur starving to death, do you?"

"Hunger may bring him to his senses. Come on, Duvet, just the first line. It may be about the quest."

I'm sure I don't know what made Jean so insistent. He swears it must have been some spell upon the parchment. But to hide a document so carefully and then to bespell it so that whoever discovers it, will he nill he must read it: that doesn't sound like wizard's logic to me. Unless the spell were Colette's, to bring the truth to light and expose it, grim and festering, to the healing air. In any case, 'twas easier to read it than to argue with Jean, so I carried it out to the stable-yard where the light was better, sat on the mounting block, spread the parchment on my knees, and squinted at it. 'Twas not an easy task to decipher it, the hand being crabbed, the ink faded and blurred in spots, the language antique, and the spelling more erratic even than madame's.

" 'By order of my father, Jorre Maindur de Malvoeux,' " I read, " 'duc de Malvoeux, Seigneur of Beauxprés and Montplaisir, I something something words—dying words, I think—as he speaks. His, his confessor—' " I looked up. "This is a dying confession, Jean. We've no right to read it."

Jean glared at me. "Where's your famous curiosity, Mlle la chatte? Jorre Maindur was the first duc de Malvoeux. This is important, I tell you: I feel it in my bones. What if it says where to find the Dove?"

I turned over the first sheet and glanced over the second. " 'Little children, use them for . . .' O Jean, I cannot read this!" Yet my eye had seen and my brain understood the rest of the sentence, and the one following, so that even as I protested, I read.

"One hundred and twenty!" I exclaimed. "Mère de Dieu! That such wickedness could exist in the world!"

"Name of a name! One hundred and twenty what? What wickedness? Read it out to me, Berthe Duvet, or I swear by my mother's grave that I'll take it away to someone who will, and leave you to manage monsieur and madame and the peasants all by yourself."

He looked like he'd do it, too. Turning back to the beginning, I began to read aloud.

Now I come to it, the confession of Jorre Maindur de Malvoeux. Days ago I fetched it from the Armament room where I put it after that day, and ever since I've been like the ass of Buridan, who starved beside two stacks of hay because he could not decide between them. Except that the stacks, in this case, are both poisoned and filthy, or at least one is, and the other may be, and Oh, how I wish I'd never begun this history or found the confession or promised Colette to be truthful and to tell all!

Today she's been as shy with me as a wild bird eying a crumb of bread, in and out of the library, picking up first this book and then that, perhaps reading a page or two, sighing, putting it down, sliding glances at me and my desk and my wad of ancient parchment. I've told her I don't know if I can bear to read the repellent thing again, far less copy it word for painful word.

"Please, Berthe," was all she said.

And that's what her eyes say now, looking at me from the table between the long windows, the table at which monsieur would write his breeding records, his observations, his letters of inquiry to Brisson and Réamur and Mme la présidente de Baudeville.

" 'Tis not comme il faut," I say.

"Nevertheless," she says.

"You will upset yourself," I say.

"Nevertheless," she says.

"Here is the original, then—read that."

"No," she says, and shudders. And indeed I am shocked that I have suggested it, when I think of the pains it cost me to puzzle it all out and how she'd have to read and reread it through a dozen tortures, a dozen slow deaths. I will spare her that, at least.

By order of my father, Jorre Maindur de Malvoeux, duc de Malvoeux, Seigneur of Beauxprés and Montplaisir, I copy these his dying words as he speaketh them. His confessor, granting him absolution for his sins, hath requir'd of him that he cause this document to be made so that his son and his son's sons may know the truth of their inheritance.

Jorre Maindur de Malvoeux would have it known that in his youth he was a stout man of his hands, born to the sword and bred to battle. The year he saw light was mark'd by English Edward's provoking that quarrel the which staineth our good soil of France with French and English blood unto this very day. Child and man, his life was toucht by death; for his mother perish'd in the Great Mortality and his sister also, his three brothers falling or at Crècy or at Poitiers. In that last rout was his father slain and he himself wounded even unto death. Yet he recovered of that wound, being young and quick to heal, and fought again, gathering around him a company of doughty men, whose swords drank deep of English blood as well in pitched battle as in siege, in mark of which the King was pleased to name Jorre Maindur Baron de Montplaisir. Then pride did swell in Jorre's breast and Satan did whisper in Jorre's ear that great fortune awaiteth that wight who feareth not to grasp it in his hand, though it burn him to the bone. And so it came to pass upon a day that Baron Jorre and his company rode the Jura mountains in that debatable land to the east of Bourguignon that oweth sure allegiance to no lord, neither French nor Swiss nor German. And from the Western height of the Forêt des Sapins,

Jorre Maindur saw the fair hill of Beauxprés set among the broad meads that named the place, and the sight of it struck his heart and his soul as it were a fair woman.

And now my father falleth a-cursing of the day he ever saw Beauxprés and a-praying for God's mercy upon his sin of covetousness, babbling wildly so that I scarce may tell his words one from the other. But soon he leaveth praying and calmeth and biddeth me write again, thus.

The fate of Jorre Maindur was set that day, and the fate of all the sons sprung from his loins. For seeing Beauxprés, he desired to have it for his own, and who would dare say him nay with an hundred armed men at his back, and they prepared to die upon his word? Like the Devil's own hunt fell they upon Beauxprés, slaying the lord's garrison and his household, saving only the lord himself and his young daughter, whom Jorre purposed to take to wife. In that battle, a sword thrust under his shield did sever the strings of his arm so that his left hand would no longer serve his will save at great pain and striving. Nonetheless did Jorre Maindur take the château of Beauxprés for his own, and the seigneury and title thereto, fairly giving its former lord a thousand florins for the right to them and to his daughter's hand. The which, much loathe, he rendered up to him, and went his ways mourning. Then did Jorre Maindur, lord of Beauxprés, commence to harry the country round about, piling up in his coffers a great store of gold so that he might one day take his ease as lord of a rich domain. And when that day was come to pass that Jorre Maindur de Beauxprés at last set aside his sword and shield, he dwelt within his château with his fair wife in peace and amity for a year or more, until a strange restlessness came upon him that could in no wise be appeased. And thereafter, from the Year of Our Lord 1375 when Coucy marcht upon the Swiss, even as lately as this year just past, Jorre Maindur de Beauxprés slaked this restlessness as thou shalt hear hereafter. Ah, my son, my son, it is pain like unto the pangs of Hell for me to rehearse my crimes before thee, who hast ever been to me a good and loving son. For the price thereof shall weigh upon thee heavier and more costly than a century of Masses, and thy heirs shall have the paying of it from generation to generation. Of that price will I speak anon, but my confessor hath laid it upon me to tell over the full tale of my iniquities that thou, Guillaume Maindur, mayest know why and wherefore thy inheritance cometh to thee thus encumber'd.

And here doth my father look straitly upon me and enjoin me to keep silence and falter not in my writing, however heinous or distasteful his tale may grow. Though he knoweth well of my hunger for knowledge, of things forbidden no less than things seemly to know, and oft hath visit'd the high chamber in which I have begun to gather the appurtenances and paraphernalia proper to that most worshipful Science of Alchemy. So I reassure him as I may, and he doth continue, thus:

Of his own will, Jorre Maindur, who is now duc de Malvoeux, doth now say and confess that four times each year as the fit came upon him, he did take little children and use them for his pleasure, committing upon them most unnatural vices as sodomy and divers sins of luxury, and afterwards slaying them. In the course of thirty years, he us'd one hundred and twenty children thus, with no soul ever the wiser. In all precautions his nurse Barbe Grosos instructed him, and until her death served him as chief procuress and sole witness of his pleasures. For one deep midnight chancing to hear the cries of a child, she discover'd her nursling in the act of murder, whereat she utter'd no word of disgust or surprise, but watcht all in silence. After, she helpt dismember the corse to boil it, and all the while question'd me close until I confest this to be the second child I had thus kill'd; the second child in as many months. Then did she rate me for my rashness that took two so hard upon one another, though I protested that both were beggar children who would never be miss'd. Wherefore did my nurse Barbe Grosos put forth a plan: *viz.* that she would gather together such children as might be to my liking as it were in a hospice or a shelter for the poor, and three or four times in a year would I choose among them which would be my plaything. Penance thus preceded sin, for thou knowest, Guillaume my son, how tenderly we clothe and feed these pauper children, and what a name of sanctity attendeth the memory of Barbe Grosos, who would not suffer a child to go hungry or bare, but cleans'd the filth of poverty from them with her own hands. So kindly did she meddle with them that children came willingly to Beauxprés to be swallow'd thereby. Fathers of large families gave us their daughters and sickly sons, and many a harlot abandon'd the fruit of her shame at the postern gate by night. Some of these babes we sav'd alive; some Barbe Grosos herself strangl'd in pity of their weakness or deformities. Among so many children, some must by nature fall sick and die, and so no wind of gossip arise to sweep away all.

Here doth my father fall silent and chew on his nether lip until the blood floweth and I ask him whether this be all his confession or no? He answereth me that it is not, but he knoweth not well how to proceed. So I question him straitly, having a great curiosity thereto, how that he did use the children and what he did with the mortal remains thereof. And with much moaning and calling upon the name of God, he beginneth thus:

I confess that since the days of my youth have I committed numberless enormities against God and His Commandments, mightily offending our Savior Jesu Christ thereby. Being without curb or rein, as a child I did all I desir'd to do, and found pleasure in all manner of wickedness. Prompted by my luxurious nature, voluntarily and for my pleasure have I spilt my seed upon the bellies of little children, either before they died or while they were *in extremis*. While they yet lived did I inflict upon them divers sorts and manners of torments, as cutting them with knives, or striking them violently upon the head with a mace, or hanging them up on a hook so that they half-strangl'd, before I let them down again with soft words and caresses. While they languished, being thus cut or hang'd, I committed upon them the vice of Sodom. I have kiss'd them when they were dead, and sever'd their heads and limbs, and perform'd luxurious acts upon the trunk as long as some warmth remain'd therein. The most beautiful of them would I lay open their bellies to gaze upon their internal organs and weigh their hearts in my hand. And sometimes as they died did I sit upon their bellies to watch the moment of their souls' flight. In these pastimes did Barbe Grosos my nurse aid me in tasks beyond the skill of a one-handed man, as binding a child or hoisting it upon the hook, filling the cauldron with water and gathering the bones therefrom when the flesh was boiled away. But Barbe Grosos had no hand in conceiving this evil. I am the only begetter of these crimes. In their commission, I follow'd my imagination and my will, without the advice of any one, only for my pleasure and fleshly delight and not for any other intention or any other end.

Here is my father seiz'd with such a fit of coughing and retching as is like to heave up his guts, after the which he lieth like the dead until I am bold to hold my dagger to his lips. At which he starteth up and saith:

Such were my sins, my son. Concerning them, I can say only that I was born under such a constellation as made me hot of blood and liver and a great hoarder of secrets. Heavy though my sins may be, they weigh in the balance not a feather's weight against the crime I have committed against thee and thy heirs, my crime of heedlessness and pride. For I lookt upon a child with lust, and she no fatherless beggar nor hedge-got starveling, but a free man's daughter dwelling deep in the Forêt des Sapins, who most hospitably did give me wine when, hunting the boar, I lost my companions. Never have I seen a child more beautiful, neither man nor maid. She was a very infant still, no greater than thine own small Raoul, but very plump and fair, her hair like a raven's wing on her shoulder and her eyes like great dark stars. Ah my son, meseems I see her still, smiling at me with her mouth like a rose half-blown. The red blood ran so close under her white skin that I long'd beyond all telling to let it spill and run over her flesh and mine. So thinking, a rage did fall upon me in such wise that I reckt nothing of secrecy, but only of mine own lusts and desires, so that I pluckt her up to my saddlebow in the sight of her father and all his household. Blind with passion, I rode with her to Beauxprés, and her cries in my ears were the sweet singing of birds or choirs uplifted in ecstasies of praise. Such sport I had of her that day as sated my carnal desires for nigh on a year. And by my hope of Heaven I swear that, prickt I never so ingeniously, no child after suffer'd so sweetly as that little maid, so black and red and white.

Here I see the salt tears well in my father's eyes. Wherefore a foreboding now cloudeth my heart that what is yet unsaid surpasseth in evil that which is already said as Alchemy surpasseth all other magical arts. Presently my father speaketh, but very weak and low, so that I perforce must beg him to begin anew.

'Twas dawn, I said, before all was done and the child's plump limbs stript to clean, white bones. I wrapt them in silk to be plac'd apart from the others in a casket, the which I desir'd Barbe Grosos to procure presently from a certain goldsmith in Besançon. Being clean and vested, I was sat down to break my fast when my men-at-arms gave me to know that a madman clamor'd without the gates and would not be silenc'd, but call'd for his daughter and the sieur de Beauxprés without ceasing. And they said he had stood clamoring thus since the day before when I was out a-hunting, to the much distress of my lady wife, who sent to find me and they could not. Bold in my sins, I laugh'd and mounted and bade the gate-ward to raise the portcullis so that I might ride forth to meet the child's father. For what could one man do against Jorre Maindur de Beauxprés de Malvoeux? And thus it is that great pride goeth before a fall: for in very sooth, one man hath humbl'd me and brought me low, both me and my heirs forever. Heed well my words, Guillaume my son, and write each one as I say it, leaving none aside nor adding none to the account, for this mournful tale is my legacy to thee, no less than my money and my lands.

I cry out to my father to have done with his warnings and abjurations, and disclose without further ado the price of his iniquities, a price that I, not he, (if I understand him aright) must pay, whether I will or no. Then doth my father bare his teeth in rage and miscall me bastard and blockhead and I know not what else until, calming, he proceedeth thus:

When I rode out to him, the child's father threw his arms to Heaven and cried out in a terrible voice.

Then my father heaveth him upright in his bed with the sweat springing from his brow, and from his mouth issueth forth a stranger's voice, terrible and harsh and clangorous.

Hélas, my daughter, my Colette! Hélas, my dove, my slaughter'd lamb! Thou, devil, hast slain her, hast rent and tormented her with no more pity than Herod shew'd unto the Holy Innocents. Her sinless blood cryeth to me from thy butcher's hands and thy lips that have kiss'd her mortal wounds. Her screams linger in the air about thee, and the stink of hot iron laid upon her tender flesh. Butcher of Beauxprés, thou shalt suffer as she hath suffered. As thou hast flay'd her body, so shall I flay thy soul, and bind thee to fear as his slave forever. I, Gabriel Favre, Gabriel called the Sorcerer of the Forêt des Sapins, do curse thee, Jorre Maindur, Ogre of Beauxprés, with a prophecy. Watch thou thy every word, thy every thought of greed or pride. For there will come a day when thou or one of thy blood will for pride's sake deny a poor beggar a thing that he requireth of thee. It may be a thing as common as thread or as precious as thy only son: as the debt is mine, so shall I choose its payment. But whatsoever it be, fils or fils, thy denial shall cut short the line of Maindur and cast it into darkness for ever and aye.

Now the clangorous voice stilleth, and my father falleth back upon his bed with the breath rattling in his throat. He muttereth low, so that I can catch but one word of five or six, as *children*, and *blood*, and *Yesu*, and *children*, and *charity*, and *sweet nurse, sweet Barbe*, and then *blood* and *blood* and *blood* again. After a space he falleth silent, and then clear and weak he speaketh thus:

Whatever a beggar may ask of thee, my son, that thing see thou give him, though the giving rend the very roots of thy heart. For the sins of the father will be visited upon the sons, yea, unto the seventh generation and beyond.

I do not know whether these were Jorre's dying words or no, for there follow some smeared and blotted phrases of which I can make neither head nor tail, and then a small blank space, and then a paragraph in the same hand as the rest, but more crabbed, with each word shouldering into the next. It has cost me some pains to make it out, and many arguments with Jean over whether Guillaume would have writ "fille" in place of "fils" when neither word fits the sense.

. . . interr'd yestereve, in the choir of the village church, as he would have it. Signs and portents there were none, though I kept most narrow watch. Excepting only that when a certain black-cloak'd mourner pass'd the bier, I smelt a charnel stink. And a shadow fell over mine eyes as of a multitude of wings, and a piping in my ears as of a thousand birds. The peasants now call the fir forest the Forêt des Enfants, and whisper of an ogre dwelling therein, who doth eat small children and suck their bones. My father repented his sin; his confessor absolv'd him. He had all hope of salvation and eternal bliss. Yet when I inquire of my homunculus concerning him, the manikin answereth not but laugheth immoderately. To what fate hath Jorre condemn'd us, with his knives and his ropes and his great cauldron? Sleepless have I ponder'd the wizard's prophecy, and constru'd the meaning thus: that a Maindur once denying the wizard his due will damn all Maindurs to Hell forever. For my father I care not, but for myself I am loath to risk Hell-fire for a sin not of my committing. What is that beggar like to require? Gold? Blood? My homunculus that knoweth the secret of the philosopher's stone? Sooner would I part with my life than my fille I labor'd so sore to gain. For without my fille all my alembics and grammaryes and vials of mercury and rare earths are as naught.

In Which Both France and Madame Are Transformed

After reading the document, we didn't speak to each other for one whole day, Jean and I, though we worked companionably to feed monsieur and madame and bring order to the kitchen. Even when we'd recovered the power of speech, we made no further mention of Jorre's confession or the horrors it revealed. We had no need. Its spawn lay all about us, blasted and rotten, fouling the air we breathed with poisonous exhalations of decay.

Jean vows he put the thought of it from him. 'Twas all so long ago, after all, and he'd horrors enough to contemplate closer at hand. Now Jean is my good friend, and he had not seen the bones, so I'll not name him liar. For myself, who had not only seen the bones of the innocents Jorre had slain, but had touched them . . . Well, I was haunted, sleeping and waking, by the echoes of screams and the shadows of weeping eyes and tiny, pleading hands. I tried to exorcise them with chatter of practical matters, of wood and candles and suchlike aids to daily comfort. 'Tis all very well, I said, to have a magic satchel that gives you anything you ask of it. I prefer, me, to get my wood from trees, my eggs from hens, and my bread from a baker's oven.

Jean agreed with me and talked of buying a cow, a cock, and some hens from Claude Mareschal.

"Very practical, to be sure," I said. "Just where will we get the coin to pay for them? And the grain to feed them?"

Jean shrugged. "M. le duc de Malvoeux is a rich man, Berthe. He's coin in store we never dreamed of, I'll wager, and hidden so Artide would never find it."

"Bah!" I said. "And bah again! If 'tis so well hid, we'll never find it either. I doubt this horde exists, me. Sangsue kept monsieur's gold, as well you know, and the peasants left no more of it in his money-box than they left flesh upon his belly, poor devil, just some few bloody shreds of écus and . . ."

"Enough, Berthe—I take your meaning. Well, we'll trade for them, then."

"With disemboweled clocks and dismembered glass cases?"

Jean scowled and begged me to leave off talking of horrors.

"Then must I leave off talking altogether," I said, "for we are sunk to our chins in horrors. Forget the cow and chickens, at least while I try to persuade this magic satchel you trust so little to spit up the coin to pay for them. If it won't, I seem to remember a wand in the cabinet des Fées that conjures up gold."

Jean threw up his hands and beseeched le bon Dieu to give him patience. "Magic is for sorcerers, Berthe. We aren't sorcerers, nor have I any desire to be one, nor to consort with a witch. And that's what you'd be, Berthe, did you start playing with wands and suchlike."

I objected that 'twas the wand, not me, did the magic, to which he answered that he didn't care to listen to silly arguments, and he'd leave me to shift for myself did I not find some less tainted source of coin. Whereupon I threw M. Malesherbes' favorite omelette pan at him and told him to go, then, if he thought he'd be better off elsewhere. He said there'd be no need for him to go if I were only a little reasonable, and I said—well, I don't remember what I said, only that it made him laugh, which made me angrier. We bickered back and forth like children until in the end we agreed that I'd write the marquise de Bonsecours explaining (with diplomatic omissions) how it was with her sister and her sister's husband. Then Jean would creep down to the village after dark and give it to the curé, who, we thought, might be able to get it to the abbot at Baume-les-Messieurs, who might be able to convey it to the marquise at Versailles. Or at her hôtel in Paris. It was, in any case, worth a try.

Never since first I copied out *pater noster* on my slate have I struggled so with words. After ruining a sheet of our precious stock of paper with a blotted and incoherent account of murder, destruction, and madness, I decided simplicity would be best. Having sent the note, I do not pretend to remember it word for word—'twas something like: *Beauxprés intact. M. le duc de Malvoeux and madame your sister unharmed but much distressed. Please be assured, Mme la marquise, that I will care for her until my last breath, which will certainly be delayed by your sending 50 livres by messenger as soon as may be.*

By the time I'd finished this missive and sealed it with madame's ring, the sun had dipped into the Forêt des Enfans and Jean had decided that no power in Heaven above, Earth below, nor Hell beneath would force him down the rocky path to the village.

"They wanted to kill us, Berthe, and they would've, too, if they hadn't lost the stomach for it after butchering Sangsue. You can't call me a coward; I've faced dragons in my time and yellow-faced demons, and I'd face them again if I had to. What I don't have to face is our neighbors, not tonight. We'll find some other way to send the letter to the marquise."

"Bah, Jean. You're as stubborn as M. Justin's mule and not half so sensible. You don't trust Pompey's bag and you won't take my letter to the curé. What shall we do for bread, hein?"

Sullen-faced, Jean shrugged. "Le bon Dieu will provide."

"Poltroon! Tête de merde! I'll take it myself!"

"Take what?"

The voice was so familiar to me from many years of daily hearing, that before I remembered I'd last heard it screaming for blood, I answered, "A letter to Mme la marquise de Bonsecours."

"A letter to the marquise, eh?" Mère Boudin stepped through the door and held out her hand. "Give it me."

I stared at her. She'd clearly not washed herself since the burning of the aviary, for her cheeks bore traces of soot and long, dark smears of blood, as did her arms and her naked feet. She stank most vilely of smoke and anger-sweat and something else, something familiar, though not on her. Roses and civet. Ah! Madame's Eau de Vénus, that was it! And that gown Boudin was wearing. Could it be that old gown of madame's I'd made over for myself?

"Becomes me, don't it?" she said, complacently smoothing the corsage. The satin strained over her great breasts and uncorseted waist, the seams gaping over the unclean flesh beneath. Become her? It made her look like a burst sausage. And a sallow-faced woman should never wear goose-turd green.

"Yes, we're all better clad than we were," she went on, "and better fed, too, though there's more feathers than meat on most of them birds. I thought I'd pay a neighborly visit, as among old friends: chat, take a glass of wine, see how ye keep yerselves."

Jean, who'd been standing by with his mouth ajar, shut it with a snap. "Well, now you've seen."

"Yes," said mère Boudin, seating herself comfortably by the fire we'd lit with shards of furniture. "Keeping pretty well, ain't ye? Seigneur et dame de Beauxprés, eh? And how does the former seigneur and dame? Dead or alive?"

I thought of monsieur as I'd last seen him, perched behind the long table in the library like a hawk in molt, shoulders hunched, hands searching the ruined surface aimlessly, calling for Noël Songis. And madame, curled up in her daughter's bed, sweating, sneezing, spewing, and sobbing for a drop, a single drop of laudanum.

"Alive," I said shortly.

Boudin's eyes narrowed. "What's he planning to do to us? In Christian charity, ye owe an old friend so much, and if y' don't feel friendly to me, why, Mme Pyanet, she refused to come with us that night. Surely she deserves a warning of monsieur's plans."

Oh, fear's an unreasonable thing. There we sat, Jean and I, helpless as nestlings, and there stood Boudin, crammed to her gums with stewed crane and cross-eyed with fear of us, or rather of that crane's former owner, M. le duc de Malvoeux. His sixteen meaningless quarterings terrified her; his useless triages and lods et ventes and corvées filled her with unspeakable awe.

Boudin looked from me to Jean, who, predictably, shrugged. "You know the duc as well as I," he said.

This brought her upright and bristling. "Ye'd play with me, would ye? Pat and claw, like a pair of cats, and don't the mice squeak pretty? Well, this time I'm the cat and ye the mice, ye and your precious duc de Malvoeux. I spit on his taxes and I spit on his revenge. There's worse things than the mad duc coming to Beauxprés, and out of my good heart and for old friendship's sake, I'll do for ye what ye're too proud to do for me, and that's give ye fair warning.

"Tell the duc that the Franche-Comté is alive with brigands burning and murdering honest men in their beds. 'Tis only a matter of time before they reach us, tell him. Say also that a courier's been stopped in Grenoble with a letter from the Austrian whore to her brother.

There'll be fifty thousand Austrians marching through here before long if another courier was luckier. Or not so lucky—they say the end of the message sent the bearer to his grave, so that he was happy to be caught, and in gratitude denounced the queen's plot to poison our king, may God preserve him, and set up her lover in his place."

Jean and I listened to this tirade with mounting fear—of her words, bien sûr, and also of her dying of an apoplexy. She was scarlet-faced and sweating, her wrinkled dugs heaving over the neck of her —my—gown. While I'd hardly mourn her passing, the villagers would never believe we hadn't somehow killed her.

"There'll be order now," she was screaming, "and plenty, and peace. There'll be no more leeches like thee, Berthe Duvet. I tell thee, and tha may tell M. le duc de Malvoeux, that the world he has known is thrown down and destroyed and will never come again."

That fine piece of rhetoric was her final salvo. Having fired it, she stamped to the outer door and went away, leaving the two of us shaking as with a fever.

After a time, I conjured a sup of brandy from the satchel, which Jean wasn't too mistrustful to drink at a draught.

Needless to say, Jean didn't go down to the village that night or the next or the next. We discussed his walking to Baume-les-Messieurs to give the letter to the abbot himself, and we discussed his walking to Besançon, where he'd likely get fresher news than he could come by in a smaller town. Yet he was as nervous of leaving Beauxprés as I was nervous to be left, and day after day passed without him walking anywhere.

In the first week in August, we were surprised by the curé tapping hesitantly at the kitchen door. He'd not set foot under monsieur's roof in five years, and he stood just inside in an agony of fear, clutching his broad-brimmed hat and darting nervous glances at the stairs. Like mère Boudin, he desired to know how things stood with monsieur and madame. 'Twould have been a comfort and a release to me to confess myself to him, but one look at his knotted brow and his pale, frightened eyes told me I dared not.

"They're well enough," I said. "Grieved over their tenants' hatred. Worried about the king, may le bon Dieu bless him. Longing for news of madame's sister in Paris."

"As to Paris, I've heard nothing myself. The abbot has sent a note counseling patience and faith. My parishioners have chopped up the seigneurial pew. I don't quite see my way, Mlle Duvet, indeed I do not."

Did he imagine I'd comfort him? When the shepherd loses his faith, what then are the sheep to believe in? "Well, perhaps you might see your way to enclosing this note to the marquise de Bonsecours in your next letter to the abbot," I said tartly.

The curé, who'd been drooping like a beaten dog, picked up his ears a bit. " 'Tis little enough you ask, Mlle Duvet. I'll see to it immediately. This letter to the abbot—nothing easier, I'm sure." He turned to leave, then turned again, one finger upraised almost in his old manner. "A word of advice, Mlle Duvet, if you'd not take it amiss? You might be thinking of calling upon your old friend Mme Pyanet. Let it go for a little while yet. There's high feelings down in the village about the rent rolls, and superstitious nonsense about a magic stick and floating hands and I don't know what else. I am persuaded 'tis only the exhalations of unlearned and over-excited brains. Yet I'd not like to see you suffer any, ah . . . inconvenience over it."

One of the hands floated into sight, carrying a twiggy broom. The curé, being somewhat short-sighted, didn't immediately see it.

"To be sure," I said, chivvying him towards the door. "Thank you, Father. God be with you."

"And with you, my daughter. Now, you're quite sure your mistress is bearing up under her affliction?"

I looked him firmly in the eye and lied. "Quite sure, Father."

The hand gave me the besom and darted up into the rafters.

"What's that?" cried the curé, squinting up after it.

"What's what?" I glared at the hovering hand. It made a rude gesture. My heart heaved into my throat. "Oh, a bat, I dare say, or some kind of bird. All sorts of things got stirred up when the peasants came to call, you can't imagine the rats in the cabinet des Fées; in fact, I've got to go chase them out right now, that's why I picked up this broom. You were most kind to come, Father."

Puzzled and gentle, he frowned at me. "To be sure," he said. "A white bat. God bless you, my daughter." He sketched a cross over me and went away shaking his head.

The hand streaked down from the rafters, slammed the door to, flicked at the air the curé had signed, twitched my cap over one ear, and whisked away before I could slap it.

"Good thing the curé didn't see you," I told it. "Inconvenienced! Why, they'd burn me for a witch."

The marquise didn't send the fifty livres; neither did she send an answer to my letter. The curé made another sally up the hill to tell me he'd given it to a courier from Dijon, who'd assured him that the roads were peaceful and the threatened brigands as invisible as a noble's charity: there'd be no trouble getting the letter to Baume-les-Messieurs, not the least trouble in the world. So perhaps 'twas between Baume-les-Messieurs and Paris it miscarried. Or between Paris and Versailles. In any case, Mme la marquise neither came nor sent word.

The year moved on to harvest. Whenever I looked out over the meadows, I saw peasants moving in their fields, reaping, binding, stacking fodder for their cows. Some of them wore red caps, and those few strains of harvest rejoicing that reached my ear had a curiously martial sound to them. Truly, the times had changed.

Once in two weeks or thereabouts, the curé would ascend the path to give us the news. He told us that the Assembly had abolished feudal rights and dues; that Louis was no longer king of France but of the French; that church estates were the property of the nation. I confess that I wasn't much interested, though I should have been grateful that he came at all, with the villagers feeling as they did about monsieur and monsieur feeling as he did about the clergy.

He was such an innocent, that curé. How shocked he was at the reports of riot and mayhem, as though revolutions did not spawn riots as middens spawn maggots. Once he brought me a horn-cornered journal from Paris describing a riot of fishwives in Versailles and pointed with a trembling finger to an engraving of three cockaded "citizenesses" astride a rampant cannon. I'm sure I disappointed him terribly when I only nodded absently—very distressing, to be sure, mon père—less worried over the dissolution of the world as we'd known it than over the curé's possible reaction to the sudden appearance in the kitchen of a hand or monsieur.

Well, we couldn't keep him confined *all* the time, could we? 'Twas his château, after all, and it wasn't as if he could do much damage, even if he became violent. Mostly in those early days he sat by the ornamental pond or climbed among the aviary ruins, more bewildered than enraged. Oh, sometimes he'd rant and threaten and thunder, just like the old days. But there was no one to carry out his threats, no Sangsue to flog us, no Malateste to flay us. There was no one save monsieur, who could do us little harm now that the peasants had broken his épée.

Madame was an altogether different case. Madame had run mad. Where once she'd seldom stirred from her chaise longue, now she couldn't sit or lie quietly for a minute before she must leap up to pace, to search for this or find a place for that. When she was not pacing, she was huddling in a corner, screaming with fear of the birds, their battering wings, their darting beaks, their talons, oh, their talons slashing at her hands and face. Why didn't I chase them away? Dear God, did I hate her so that I'd watch her be pecked to pieces? And her head hurt so. Where was her laudanum? Why had I hidden it?

Well, when I told her that the only laudanum left in the house was a sticky residue on her chamber floor, she tried to go and lick it up, and when I tried to prevent her she fought me with a wild and feverish strength. That was the first time I locked her into the Cameo apartment and fled to the kitchen. It was not the last.

You understand 'twas not disgust drove me thus to abandon her. I still loved her, pitied her, bled from my heart for her anguish. But I could do nothing to ease her pain, though I tried, even to the extent of asking the satchel for laudanum. It gave me dried valerian, handfuls of it, smelling like cat piss and making a most vile-tasting tisane that I gave to madame nonetheless, on the chance it might help her. She threw it in my face at the first sip, and that was that. Afterwards, I tried to keep her clean, emptied her chamber pot, left food and water on a tray with a little cup of the valerian tisane, just in case. Then I locked her door and went my ways.

In the winter of 1790, as if things weren't bad enough, the magics Mlle Linotte had left behind her began to fail, or at least to grow wonderfully capricious in their workings. The hands were the first to go, disappearing one morning without so much as a wave of farewell. I clapped for them until my palms stung, even ventured up to the Alchemical attic and down to the cellars in search of them: not a nail-paring could I find. Although they made my skin creep, I'd found them useful, obedient servants, and the first time I hauled water from the well myself, I was sorry enough they were gone. Jean laughed when I complained, welcomed me home from fairyland, and predicted that the satchel'd be the next to go.

He was right, bugger him. 'Twas the Eve of Saint-Denis, as I recall, when I took the satchel on my lap as usual, closed my eyes, murmured the charm, and put in my hand to find pease porridge instead of the fish I'd asked for. This was not an entirely uncommon occurrence: the satchel wanted to be wooed, that was all. "Sweet satchel," I said, "thy generosity is as the love of God, ever-flowing. We thank thee for this good pottage, and beseech thee to add unto it a boiled trout, in honor of the holy Saint-Denis whose feast-day is tomorrow."

Again I put in my hand, and again I found porridge—cold, gelatinous, with unground pease lurking in each bite like shot in a hare. And porridge is all it would give me, begged I never so prettily.

"That's it," said Jean at last. "Put it in a pot and heat it up— we've nothing else to eat. In a day or so, perhaps the cursed thing'll have recovered itself, and if it hasn't, well, we've still got that gold you conjured out of it. 'Tis enough for a cow, and pease and beans for planting."

The following Sunday, Jean pocketed a portion of the gold and set out for Besançon. Early though it was for it, we'd had one snowfall and the sky threatened more. I objected that Besançon was three days' walk in good weather.

"Perhaps Just Vissot will sell us a cow, if the curé asks him for us. This is not a good time to be proud, Jean."

A week of lumpy porridge had put Jean sadly out of temper. "Ah, but 'tis a good time to be cautious," he said sourly. "Remember this gold is magic gold, and magic's as fickle as a dockside whore. I'm going to Besançon, and there's an end to it. If I can't find a cow to buy, there'll surely be goats and hens, and if the gold disappears after I've gone, well, they won't be so ready to come after me if the roads are heavy going."

He was gone so long I thought he'd run away or been killed— two weeks and more. I was miserable. No one to talk to save a sweating lunatic, a raving madman, and the White Cat's tiny dog Toutou, who wasn't quite the wonder she had been.

When first awakened, Toutou had been able to dance a sarabande, leap through a finger-ring, and speak two languages, though her French was very poor. She would chatter to madame by the hour, and sometimes could make her laugh with her antics. By imperceptible degrees, her sarabande degenerated into a little dog staggering about on her hind legs and her clever speech into yipping and yapping. She could still step through a finger-ring, but when her thousand colors faded into white blotched with brown, I had to accept that she was only an ordinary little dog, a pretty papillon, ridiculously small and quite useless. Madame said she looked like a rat and that her yapping made her head pound. So I moved Toutou and the purple rats to the kitchen, where at least they served to keep more ordinary vermin at bay.

Madame had by now regained at least so much of her sense that I was able to coax the tisane down her, which soothed the pain in her belly. The fits continued, however, racking her so cruelly that I would have had to be as hard as Jorre to have witnessed them. I learned to watch for signs—sneezing, abstraction, shivering, a certain clamminess of the brow and shrinking of the pupils—and when I observed them, to take my leave and lock the door behind me. Sometimes I could hear her screams as far as the gallery of Depositions.

In contrast, monsieur seemed almost rational. Wherever I might go, gallery of Swords or Alchemical attic, there he might be also, striding back and forth in unutterable agitation, disputing hotly with thin air. Philosophy, politics, natural science—everything he'd read or thought in his life spilled from his lips in a passion of argument, all to persuade some invisible interlocutor that wizards cannot exist in a rational world, that the sins of a man four hundred years dust are not the responsibility of his descendants, that the complete understanding of the natural world is the sole hope of mankind. This insubstantial debate was real to him, more real than cold or hunger, certainly more real than I. If I touched his arm or addressed him, his eyes would catch on me a second, no more, before sliding back to the ghost of whatever philosophe he was currently refuting.

An annoying madness, monsieur's, most especially when I'd wake in the middle of the night to hear him expounding the finer points of Locke, say, or Voltaire on the scientific method: a lone, hoarse voice assaulting the indifferent darkness with logic. At such times I prayed for Jean to return and protect me. Not from monsieur, who didn't seem to see me, but from a growing sense that the worlds he and madame inhabited were real, and I only a phantom of my own imaginings.

By the time Jean returned, I truly believe I was more than half mad myself. I remember watching him trudge through the formal gardens, leading a brindle cow by a ring through her nose, carrying one large wicker basket strapped to his back and another dangling from his hand. The cow looked cold and unhappy, as well she might, having walked further than any cow wants to walk in a lifetime, uphill much of the way and in the snow, too. I quite felt for her, imagining her milk freezing in her udder, the snow collecting in hard frozen balls in her hooves, the grass sparse, hard to find, and prickly on her great, soft tongue.

"Ho, Duvet! I've brought us a cow! And chickens, too—three hens and a cock." Jean grinned at me through stubble like burned-over corn. "Success, Duvet! Aren't you going to thank me?"

The question woke me from my stupor. "Thank you? Well, I suppose I must, if the cow doesn't die from exposure where she stands and the hens have survived the bumping and cold. You certainly took your ease. Did you enjoy yourself in Besançon, Jean? Tumble a whore or two? Attend a play, perhaps? It's been as good as a play here, the past two weeks, I can tell you, with monsieur eating air and clouds and madame seeing devils in the pear tree, as the saying goes."

"Softly, now, Duvet," said Jean, angry in his turn. "I came as quick as I could. And the cow'll be more likely to live if you take her into the kitchen where 'tis warm while I search out some hay for her to eat."

As it happened, Jean had attended a play in Besançon, quite by accident, on his way to the house of a man he'd heard had a cow to sell. The man lived up in the citadel, where he'd retreated during the unpleasantness of July and August. Jean had to climb a hundred steep stone steps, bribe a guard with fairy gold, then climb another thousand steps or so, and what should he find when he reached the top but the way blockaded and the central courtyard cordoned off and packed as full as it would hold with dignitaries and carters and beggars and shopkeepers. At the far end of the court by the wellhouse stood a great scaffold and a crowd of men upon it, declaiming and waving their arms in a theatrical frenzy.

"I couldn't very well get a cow through all that brouhaha even if I could've pushed through it myself. So I stepped on a few toes and elbowed a few ribs to get closer, then craned with the rest.

"I'll tell you, Duvet, 'twas a sight worth climbing any number of stairs to see: the fortress of the Bastille, only a little bigger than ma-dame's dressing-case, complete in every part from the portcullis to the cannon and carved out of a stone of the Bastille itself. Behind it stood a type in a red cap and a cockade reading poetry while two other types crawled around the model moving little soldiers here and there and winching down the little portcullis. More poetry, some shouting about liberty, equality and fraternity, and then they raised a tiny white flag from the tower, winched the portcullis back up again, and talked of the Age of the Common Man. Then red-cap opened a big chest and brought out such a collection of horrors as you can't imagine—a metal corset they said was an engine of torture, and heavy manacles and lengths of black chain and pictures of the prisoners, thinner than skeletons, with white beards down to their waists. There were real skeletons, too, that they found in the lowermost cells when they were taking the place apart—or at least engravings of them—and a genuine fragment of the crust formed on the cell walls by the breath, sweat, and blood of the men unjustly imprisoned there. The nobles—the aristos—have much to answer for, Duvet. They do indeed."

I couldn't disagree with him, but felt bound to remind him that he'd thrown in his lot with those aristos nonetheless. Even as Jean spoke, our own personal aristo could be heard in the distance, declaring that a seigneur stood as a father to his tenants, and like a father, must often seem cruel to be kind.

Jean grimaced and sipped at his fresh milk.

"Why'd you come back?" I asked him curiously. "You had gold, a cow, the world before you. The Age of the Common Man, is it? You're more common than most, Jean. Why didn't you go out and claim your place?"

Startled, Jean looked at me. "This is my place. Besides, after I left, I heard a rumor of gold turning to dung. I'm a wanted man, Duvet. I dare not leave Beauxprés."

After that, the days and nights passed, each finding us colder, hungrier, more frightened than the last. Forgetting Pompey, the wolves howled close in the snowy wood. Forgetting monsieur, the peasants stole wood from the ruins of the aviary. Jean stabled our precious cow in the back kitchen, stole fodder from the Mareschal's grange, and chased Just Vissot's second son down the hill with a pitchfork. Me, I'd never worked so hard in my life. If a pot wanted scrubbing or a loaf of bread kneading, who was there to scrub or knead it save I? Jean was too busy milking, mucking out, hoeing, besides feeling himself above such merely domestic labor. You'd have thought I'd asked him to keel the pots with his manhood, so loudly did he prate of my insulting it when I suggested he lend a hand in the kitchen.

As for madame, she was both better and worse. Better, in that her food stayed with her when she ate it and the fits came not so often as they had. Worse, in that her spirits were so excited that nothing I could do could calm her, not even brushing her hair. And she was sad with it, grief-stricken even to rage, weeping like Niobe over the children, the ghostly children who had no one to love them and so could not rest. Fearing she might cast herself from a window in her despair, I nailed her shutters. And when she said she felt stifled, imprisoned, caged, I opened another room to her: the cabinet des Fées.

How often in the dark years to come did I worry at the bone of my guilt like a starving dog? I blamed—I still blame—myself entirely. She was my mistress, my charge, my bien aimée, and mad as a hare in spring. I should have kept her by me, or tied her to the bedpost, or at the very least removed the various magical hats and nuts and flowers of forgotten uses scattered about the cabinet des Fées to some more distant chamber. I should have; I did not. Instead, I left her locked up, alone, despairing, without even a purple rat for company. And one evening in the spring of 1791, I unbarred the door of the cabinet des Fées to see a large dun bird perched on the arm of the sofa.

My first thought was how terrified my mistress would be and how long 'twould take to calm her, if indeed I could calm her at all. For a moment, I wished there were laudanum in the house as profoundly as she. Then, ashamed, I called out to her:

"Have no fear, madame. 'Tis a real bird—I see it, too. A peahen, nasty thing. I'll just chase it away, and then 'tis time for your warm milk. Nothing to be frightened of, madame, I assure you. Just a peahen. Perfectly ordinary."

That she made no answer to my babbling did not alarm me, for I pictured her cowering under the bed, too terrified to squeak. I did think it strange that the bird didn't take flight at my shouting, but hopped down from its perch and paced curiously towards me, snaking its neck to keep me in view. 'Twas indeed a common peahen, save for being uncommonly large and sleek and plump in the breast. I couldn't imagine how it had gotten in, nor how, in the midst of famine, it had contrived to survive so long uneaten.

I edged around behind it and stamped my foot. "Vas-y!" I said. "Filthy bird." It fluttered into a heap of pale material that happened to be lying on the floor and tangled its claws in the gauzy stuff. Tucking its head into its breast feathers, it peered at its feet, then raised its black beak and uttered a hollow and mournful scream.

Whether 'twas the gesture of looking to see what had caught it or its unbirdlike calm, I was suddenly sure that the peahen was madame.

Well, I dropped my tray, of course, and 'twas a question whether I'd follow it to the floor, so dim did my eyes grow and so weak my knees. At the crash of crockery, the peahen—my mistress—battered her wings and pranced amid the ennetting folds. In fear that she'd break a wing or a leg, I stepped over the mess, knelt, and clucked my tongue soothingly.

What held her, I saw, was the robe-chemise of white muslin I'd dressed her in that morning. Tears started to my eyes, and I reached out blindly and much too fast. With a hiss, she pecked at my hand and tore the fleshy part of my thumb.

I swore and sucked the blood from my hand while she eyed me with a bright, black, suspicious gaze. Her feathers were all huffed out with temper. When I moved, she rattled them at me and caterwauled again.

The vanity of peacocks is proverbial. "Softly, ma belle," I said to her. "Thy beauty deserves a nest far richer than this poor muslin, fit for common fowl as ducks and geese, but not for a queen of birds such as thou. Only be still and let thy handmaid free thy feet, and she will give thee a nest of gold such as will make all other birds stare and wonder. Softly, now, now . . . Ah, bah!"

She'd pecked me again, drawing blood, and now she set up such a screeching and fluttering that I could hardly hear myself shouting that she was ungrateful and unkind and deserved to be stuffed with watercress and roasted. Shocked, I clamped my hands over my traitorous mouth.

Presently I remembered that Noël Songis used to subdue fractious birds by mantling their wings in a heavy drapery and went into the bedchamber to search for a shawl. This took far longer than it should have, for sometime during the day my mistress had turned out the chests and drawers, so that petticoats, ribbons, stockings, fichus, bodices, ruffles, corsets, and gowns were drifted and strewn across the floor. Cursing her again, I dug through the mess, and all the while she screamed as only a peahen can scream.

At last I found a shawl and was preparing to fling it over her from behind when monsieur appeared at the outer door.

He looked very much as he'd looked in the days after the beggar first cursed him—glitter-eyed, crack-lipped, beak-nosed. He appeared to be half-naked under his brocade dressing-gown, and a rough beard shaded his craggy cheeks. He pursed his dry lips and whistled, low and piercing.

The screams stopped; madame bobbed her head searchingly. Monsieur whistled again, a tuneless air that grated on my ears. It had quite another effect on madame, who settled down upon her feet and cocked her head at him. Slowly he approached her, knelt and lifted her, cradled her breast in the crook of his arm, and with his free hand unwound the muslin from her claws, whistling softly as he worked. When she was free, he stroked her wings. She folded her neck sleepily, then stretched it again, nestling her head under his chin to mingle the black feathers of her crest with his black beard.

At the time, I thought the beggar's curse accomplished, the duc and his duchesse stripped of goods, reason, of their bare humanity. Now, I'm not sure but that they foiled the beggar at last. For, in this their extremity, monsieur and madame at last found some measure of peace. Monsieur had a bird to care for. And madame had the love of her husband restored to her, with all the tender devotion he'd never shown her, not even in the first flush of his passion.

In Which the Crows Feast

Two years passed, or perhaps three. I'd never understood, before, how Mme Pyanet could forget how old she was and whether 'twas last year or the year before that Jacques Charreton broke his arm and Hugenin Mareschal wed Elizabel Vissot. In a village as small as Beauxprés, there's not so much to remember, I thought. And that, I learned in the years after madame's transformation, is why forgetting is so easy. When life consists of keeping oneself alive, daily events are much of a kind. The satchel does or does not produce porridge. Monsieur does or does not set snares that may equally catch rats or rabbits, or once, madame, out for a dust-bath in the stable-yard. Now *that* was a set-to, attended by cursing and screeching and some little blood—monsieur's, from madame pecking his hands as he tried to release her. Made sliced meat of them, she did: he'd have borne the scars until the day he died, if Mlle Linotte hadn't made him immortal. The scene I recall as if 'twere yesterday. But the year? 1791? 1793? I cannot remember. They were all so much the same that not even an enchanted quill can choose among them.

The seasons, too, were much the same. As the beggar's curse seeped into the soil of Beauxprés, the earth grew barren; as it sublimed into the air, the atmosphere grew cold and unfriendly to life. Winters, to keep from freezing, we spent the days and nights huddled in the kitchen with the cow and the chickens and Toutou and the purple rats—even madame and monsieur. That was bad enough; but the springs were worse, when we could see the pale gauze of young grass and leaves clothing the meadows all around while dirty snow lingered in the stable-yard. The exotic shrubs and trees planted by monsieur's father all died, so that even in July and August the gardens were as brown and gray as December. A few weeds still grew—knot grass and angelica and scarlet pimpernel—enough to choke out the vegetables in Jean's little garden.

Except when Jean crept down by night to steal a cabbage or a handful of beans, we held ourselves aloof from our neighbors. Strange to descend the path only as far as the fallen beech, to hear mère Mareschal scolding her grandchildren or père Mareschal cursing a laborer and not go down to speak with them; stranger still to hear the church bell calling me to Mass and not answer. At first 'twas fear of mère Boudin and Artide and their rabble that kept me from the village, then fear of what I saw when I stood by the beech and peered down between the trees to the well. The washhouse roof hid the well itself, but not the stripped sapling the peasants erected beside the well and decked with tri-colored ribbons, nor the papers and posters they tacked to the church door, nor the earnest, angry gesturing of the men who read and argued over them. After a time, I ceased going even so far, and was on the whole content to see no more of our neighbors than the pale curls of smoke from their chimneys and the morning and evening processions of their cows to the milking.

For their part, the villagers seemed equally content to see nothing of us, and shunned the hill as religiously as Jean and I shunned the valley. Even the curé had not ventured up the path for a year or more, so that I started as though I'd seen a ghost when I came upon him one day lingering by the horse trough.

He was a little fatter than he had been, and had given up his cassock and priest's bands for a brown coat and a patriotically-striped waistcoat. His height and his uncertainty were unmistakable, however, as was his answer to my greeting.

"Yes, yes, citizeness, I am enchanted to see you well. Ah, is Mme la du . . . That is"—he looked about him anxiously—"is the citizeness, ah, Maindur, is she by any chance receiving visitors today?"

It took me a moment to recognize madame in this novel form of address, though not so long as 'twould have taken the curé to recognize madame herself, hunting insects in the dirt not a stone's throw from his feet. Sternly I stifled the urge to introduce him, asking instead what had brought him to the château.

His eyes flitted uncomfortably from the château to the ruined gardens to the brassy sky to me. "Ah," he said. "Oh, dear. What the mayor will say if he comes to know I've been here, I daren't imagine. Aristos, you know. Anti-revolutionaries. If they're still alive. And the letter. I shouldn't have accepted it in the first place, but I just can't see my way clear to giving it to citizen Desmoulins. A *personal* letter, after all, quite harmless, I'm sure."

To endure so long without news, and then to be approached by this white rabbit of a curé twitching his nose at me and talking nonsense—why, 'twould try the patience of a saint. I cocked my fists upon my hips. "Then you're more sure than I, *citizen*," I snapped. "What mayor? What aristos? What letter?"

Humbly, he pulled a small packet from his pocket. "Of course, citizeness Duvet. I beg your pardon, I'm sure. A peddler gave it me. He said he'd had it of a vagabond, le bon Dieu only knows how *he* came by it. It could only be from the marquise, you see—from citizeness Bonsecours."

My heart rose in my throat. "To be sure," I said. "Just a letter from, ah, citizeness Bonsecours to her sister. What could be more natural?"

"If I thought 'twas political, or seditious, or anything of the like, I'd feel compelled to give it over to citizen Desmoulins. He's mayor now, did you know? A great patriot, too great a patriot for an out of the way place like Beauxprés, I fear. God willing, he'll soon be off to Besançon where he can do some real good."

I looked at him narrowly. "Yes," I said. "Of course he will. I always knew Artide Desmoulins would go far. Well. Thank you for bringing us the letter."

The curé looked down at the packet he still held in his hand. "I don't quite see my way," he began unhappily.

"Bah!" I snatched it from him. "So. You did not give it me. Now, mon père, go away."

The curé opened his mouth as if to protest, closed it again, shrugged, blessed me, and left me with the precious packet, directed in Mme de Bonsecours' familiar, sprawling hand to citizeness Maindur, Beauxprés near Champagnole, department of Jura.

Judging from the state of it—tied up with a bit of grimy string and stained with grease and candle-drippings—it had had a hard journey. Miraculously, the wax seal was unbroken. I broke it, unfolded the thick, coarse sheets, and read.

20 Floréal, year II of the Republic

Beloved sister:

I write you from Port Royal.

No, I've not taken the veil, though I'm a widow now and apt for the cloister, were there any left to retreat to. As you may know, there are not, not even Port Royal, which is no longer either convent or Port Royal. Still, 'tis a house of detention, and I once more among its detainees.

I am here upon suspicion. Suspicion of what they do not say, save of being the daughter of a Farmer Général, the wife of a treasury official, and the mother of an émigré. With such familial ties, I must surely harbor anti-revolutionary sympathies. Most especially as the revolution, in the persons of a handful of zealous sans-culottes, murdered my poor husband last September while he was visiting a friend in the Conciergerie. The butchers, the Septembrists, broke into the cell with axes and pikes and slaughtered them both out of hand. Hundreds died that day—forgers, prostitutes, malcontents, priests, nobles, patriots of all persuasions. I cannot weep for them. Some of them were surely guilty, if not of anti-revolutionary plots, then of other crimes. I save my tears for my husband, innocent as an hour-old babe, and for myself, who am become the citizeness widow Bonsecours, whose husband died in the Conciergerie.

I confess to missing Bonsecours. I miss him so sorely that I've been forced to conclude that I must have loved him—if such a decorous, domesticated, half-irritable comfortableness as we shared can be called love. Certainly 'twas not the passionate and single-minded devotion described by my fellow widows in their communal lamentations. Daily they water the earth with tears and shake the air with such a storm of sighings and moanings as render the cloister walk inhospitable to all save themselves. Me, I prefer to solace my grief in the acacia court, among the young men playing whist and talking politics. Between bouts of tears, the widows whisper to one another that I am all mind and no heart, as utterly without human feeling as citizen Robespierre. So you see that little has changed at Port Royal.

Or rather everything is changed. First there is the name—Port Libre. What a name for a prison! I can still laugh at the irony of it, and at the inscriptions they've written up on the walls of the refectory:

"Liberty includes all the rights of man—reason, equality, justice."

"The Republic brings society happiness: she unites all men under the banner of common interest."

"The free man cherishes his freedom even while he is deprived of it."

Nothing of women, of course. Women are accustomed to cloisters.

I remember when I was a pensionnaire, beating my head against the convent wall and the convent will that barred me from the world. The wall remains, and the will to suppress individual difference. But now the world and I are on the same side of the wall. Men and women, financiers and flirts, rakes and politicians, pious and profane, young and old: all have been stripped of titles and former lives—just as the nuns had been, now I come to think of it—and set to work for the glory of a Higher Authority.

You'd not credit, ma soeur, how whimsical that Higher Authority can be. It snatched the comb and iron from a coiffeur, replaced them with a knife and ladle, and made him our chef de cuisine. Yet he's a coiffeur still, frizzing the vegetables and scorching the soup until they're barely edible. We pray daily for his early visit to that famed coiffeuse Mme la Guillotine, for a man who thus murders food must surely be guilty of a myriad lesser crimes.

By some administrative oversight, our maître d'hôtel is well-suited to his post, having been in his former life a Farmer Général like monsieur our father. Coaxing gold from reluctant pockets and giving it to an overlord is second nature to him, and I must say that he executes his duties with as much reverence for citizen Haly our warden as ever he felt for Louis our king. As for our musicians, our sempstresses, our femmes de chambre and our teachers of the young, they perform their duties as well as can be expected of former barons, duchesses, and marquises. At least they bring some grace and wit to their tasks, which is more than can be said for our masters, those mustached and bearded lords of creation who only two years since were carters, butchers, and wine-merchants. Their notion of equality and fraternity is to address princes as "thou," and their notion of freedom to threaten us with La Bicêtre or the Conciergerie if we seem lacking in revolutionary zeal.

Ah, sister, here am I complaining, and I've not the smallest

cause of complaint; for Port Libre is the gentlest, the pleasantest
of prisons. The food is not good, bien sûr, but 'tis wholesome. We
have clean air to breathe and clean water to drink. Our windows
are unbarred and our cells have no locks upon them. Those of us
with gold or jewels to sell live in cells above the rue d'Enfer no
more than four to a room, with views of the observatory, fires in
the grates, and plenty of fresh straw in the mattresses. For us
pensionnaires de luxe, 'tis hardly like a prison at all. In the
evenings, we take our candles to the old refectory and sit there
reading, sewing, writing, knitting. The Salon Port Libre. Very à la
mode, my dear. One amuses oneself excessively. There's music
every night. Sometimes we dance and sing. Last autumn, citizen
Coittant wrote a song in three parts to the vaudeville air
"Visitandines." A small chorus presented it in concert. I'll give
you a verse of it, just for the flavor.

> *On one side you see the sage*
> *With his reading occupied;*
> *On the other, youth and age*
> *Laugh and talk and versify. (Bis)*
> *In your presence, sweet mistress,*
> *In your council's inmost part,*
> *Love doth hold a court of hearts*
> *And a school of tenderness.*

Such trifles comfort us, evoking happier days. When I listen
to the baron de Wirbach draw sweet music from his viole d'amour
or Vigeé declaim an ode, when I play charades and bouts-rimés,
watch the young people flirt together under their parents'
indulgent eyes—why, I might almost be at Bonsecours again, or
Malmaison, or indeed any château with a house party in residence.

There are a number of young girls here—not so many as
there were, to be sure, but many of them well-born and some of
them pretty enough to turn the young men's minds from thoughts
of death. Our gaiety is tenuous, however, and grows ever more
strained as time, money, and hope all run thin. When I came here
last spring, we imagined that we at Port Libre were among the
privileged, whose guilt, if it existed, would never be proved.
Those whom the Tribunal summoned to trial were often
acquitted, and those whom they sent to spit through the
guillotine's window were more often common thieves and forgers

than ex-nobles. Now, no one is privileged. No one is safe. M. Fougeret is dead, and Victor de Broglie, and the gay and gallant vicomte de Ségur, who passed the time before his trial singing airs to the ladies. New prisoners arrive daily in great numbers: informers and former revolutionaries; Mme de Simiane who was Lafayette's mistress; nuns, who are kept in such isolation that all we know of them is their voices, shrieking their innocence. And today, the newest, most innocent prisoner of all, a baby daughter born to the citizeness Malessi.

The curfew bell sounds. I have bought an indulgence from Haly to keep my candle lit another hour, but I do not think 'twill last so long. I shall end this letter, this long and disjointed letter, direct it to Beauxprés, and send it tomorrow wrapped in my dirty linen and one of our revolutionary paper bills.

All my life I've written letters—to our mother, our relatives, a wide circle of friends and acquaintance, to my husband, to you. Correspondence has always been as necessary to my happiness as a well-cooked dinner, and I've found it the more sustaining for its generosity: an act of charity that returned to me a hundredfold. Now my charity is sown upon the wind, for many of my friends are dead and many more are fled or in hiding, I know not where. And you, my sister. Did Beauxprés survive the uprisings and burnings? Did monsieur your husband? Did you?

I cannot bear to think otherwise. I will imagine you in the China antechamber with your Berthe at hand to pick up a shawl or a train of thought with equal grace. She's still at Beauxprés, I make no doubt. She reads aloud as you embroider and tenderly dries the tears you shed for your unhappy sister,

Hortense Bonsecours

I shed more tears over this letter than I'd thought were left in me. I wept for Mme de Bonsecours, for Paris, for the beautifully dressed, beautifully mannered citizens and citizenesses who were dying with the world that had bred them. And I wept a little for myself.

In Which We Hear Word
of the Sorcerer Maid

I had decided to make myself a new chemise. The thought came to me like a lightning-bolt one day while I was winching up a bucket of water from the well. Beyond the meadows, the Forêt des Enfans told me 'twas high spring in France, and here I was winter-bound in Beauxprés, wood-smoked, frostbitten, and verminous. My skin was rough as an ass's hide, and my filthy clothes chafed me unbearably. I imagined how a new chemise would lie upon my back, as white and soft as an angel's wing. I'd alter one of Mlle Linotte's, I thought, remove the point d'esprit lace, cut some off the bottom and use that to let out the sides. I might have grown thin as a needle on porridge and cabbage soup, but I still had more bosom than Mlle Linotte.

I left the bucket on the coping and hastened up to the Cameo chamber to turn my vision into reality. Chemise, needle, and gossamer all found, I settled myself in a window seat and began to snip and sew, setting each tiny stitch carefully and neatly, as maman had taught me.

I was threading the needle, I remember, squinting at its eye that seemed to be squinting back, when a flash of scarlet snagged at the edge of my vision. If 'twere not that I'd seen no colors save gray and black and brown and white for so many weary months, I doubt I'd have noticed it, so far away and so fleeting, like a smuggler's signal lamp, there and gone. Indeed, I was hardly aware why I put down my needle and looked down the long slope to the chestnut drive. Yes, there it was again—scarlet, flashing in the barren branches of the chestnuts, again and yet again, higher than a man's head would be, too slow for a bird. If I close my eyes, I can see it even now, that scrap of scarlet moving among the naked chestnuts. And I can still see the wonder that presently emerged from the end of the drive and lurched up the slope: a great cart piled high with chests, trunks, and bundles of canvas, drawn by four oxen. A man astride a dun horse plodded on beside it; a second man walked at his stirrup. The scrap of scarlet was the gown of a woman lounging among the bundles and trunks like Cléopâtre.

As I gaped at this spectacle, this wheeled enigma, it drew purposefully nearer. It passed below my window on its way to the fountain court, and I dropped my half-sewn chemise upon the window seat and hurried through the ruined chambers down to the hall. The hinges of the front doors were seized up with rust, and by the time I'd forced one side open and come out on the steps, the cart had halted and the man who'd been riding the dun horse was halfway to the door. Immediately he saw me, he swept off his high-crowned hat and touched his nose to his knee in a profound reverence.

"Le Destin, your most humble servant, madame. May a simple player dare express blessings of the most heartfelt upon this most joyous of occasions? The birth of an heir! By my faith, madame, words fail me."

Clearly they hadn't; they had, however, failed me. Utterly. When I did not reply, he lifted his nose just enough to allow his eyes to squint doubtfully up at me. "This is the château Beauxprés, is't not? Whose duchesse is just made lighter of a son and heir? My faith, beauté, tell me whether 'tis or no, that I may not stand here wagging my arse for thy sole amusement."

He was a big man, I saw as he came upright: blunt-faced, with a mouth that curled most charmingly at the corners and an astonishing waterfall of dark ringlets. He wore a yellow velvet coat cut very long in the skirts and breeches so full they were like short petticoats tied at the knee with knots of green ribbon. A curious costume, and his shoes the most curious part of it, being a kind of patten laced up over his stockings with red ribbons. Oh, and the stockings were blue, though not the same blue as his cape.

Observing how I goggled, he clapped his hat on his head and his hand to his heart. "My faith," he said with a lift of his chin. "I'm not such an eye-mote as that, surely? Art simple, to gape at me thus? Go to thy major-dome, girl, or the steward, or better yet, thy master the duc, and tell him Le Destin has penned a play in honor of his son's birth. A *play*. You understand 'play'?"

I suppose he'd ample reason to think me simple, yes, and deaf and mute as well, for his every word threw me further into speechless confusion.

"Le con!" he cried at last and swung around upon the steps to address his company. "Thou, La Grotte. 'Twas thou the old peddler told of a duc with a new heir, and we've journeyed two days out of our route on the strength of it. Where is this duc, madame? Produce him at once!"

The scarlet-clad Cléopâtre stretched upon her canvas barge and yawned in a perfect excess of ennui. " 'Twas Rosemont's peddler," she said wearily. "Let Rosemont produce the duc."

The man who'd been on foot bounded up the steps and bowed in the same manner as Le Destin, only not so low. He was younger than the master player, and even more outlandishly clad in a grass-green tunic and yellow leggings under a cloak of cramoisi. A handsome man, with a firm jaw patchily shaven, and long, yellow hair tied up in rags to preserve the curl.

"I'll warrant she wants a taste of our wares as *bona fides*," he said cheerfully. "Comedy? No, she looks a high-minded piece. Ah, I know." He looped the tail of his cloak over one arm, flung the other wide, and in a sonorous voice began to declaim:

> " *'Heavens high,' he said, 'have taken my life from me.*
> *When I die, care thou for the sad Aricie.*
> *Dear friend, if my father one day disabused*
> *Mourns the fate of a son he has falsely accused,*
> *Say my blood and my plaintive shade may be stilled*
> *If he kindly succor his captive good-willed*
> *And give her . . .' On this word, the hero's soul fled.*
> *In my arms lay his corpse, disfiguréd*
> *By the wrathful gods' triumph; an object the eyes*
> *Of the tenderest father could not recognize.*"

"Why, that's from *Phèdre*," I exclaimed. And when he broke off to goggle in his turn: "Théramène's speech on the death of Hippolyte. The last time I saw it was at the Comédie Française, oh, more than ten years since. It always makes me weep."

Le Destin lifted his hands and eyebrows in vast surprise. "She does talk after all," he exclaimed. "And she knows the *Phèdre*. Now. Does she know whether this be the château Beauxprés where the duc de Malvoeux is on the point of christening an heir?"

By this time, I'd somewhat recovered my wits, though I was still mightily puzzled what to make of this mountebank and how I might answer his questions. "Yes, this is the château Beauxprés," I said slowly. Whatever else I might have said was lost in Le Destin's whoop of joy as he dashed down the steps and whipped up the oxen to pull the cart into the stable-yard, calling to me over his shoulder that his troupe would take their dinner in the stable, and he'd wait upon my master thereafter, at his earliest convenience.

The players were with us for a week in all, and I vow upon my mother's soul that was the strangest week of my life. The players seemed to see nothing amiss at Beauxprés. That afternoon, I led Le Destin into the empty library, where with utmost gravity he bowed before a wild man and a peahen and complimented monseigneur le duc de Malvoeux and his duchesse on their beautiful château and even more beautiful newborn child.

Monsieur regally inclined his shaggy head and ruffled his wife's feathers; madame screamed and briefly preened her breast. Le Destin smiled broadly, thanked her effusively, and vowed she'd find his play worthy her generosity.

" 'Tis quite outside the usual style, madame," he assured her as he backed towards the door. "I wrote it myself—a most fantastical pastoral romantical comedy, madame, just the thing for a christening fête, nothing coarse, nothing bawdy: I assure madame she may invite the curé, the bishop himself without fear of a blush. On Sunday, then, after the christening." And he bowed himself out.

The players spent the next day erecting a stage in the stable-yard and the succeeding days rehearsing scenes before an audience composed of a brindle cow, a miniature dog, five purple rats, and a handful of chickens. There were five players in all—two women, two men, and a boy who claimed sixteen years. I suspect he'd stolen at least four of those years, perhaps from the actress Belle Étoile, who confided to me that she was three-and-twenty. I'd have put her closer to three-and-thirty, me. But there, who knows better than I that an actress' life is of the hardest, and that nothing ages a young skin so fast as white-lead and rouge? Why, even La Grotte, who'd the form and step of a young maid, showed without her paint the lined eyes and faded lips of a matron. She was Rosemont's mistress, I think, and Belle Étoile called herself Le Destin's wife. The boy was a cousin. They had given him some outrageous name, what was it now? Rosidore? No, L'Espérance, that was it.

For four days, they dashed back and forth between cart and stage, tearing their hair, darting behind curtains, tumbling, dancing, shouting out cues and declaiming speeches. I watched them for a while, but could make neither head nor tail of their play. There seemed to be at least one magician in it—perhaps two—and a shipwreck. At one point La Grotte, dressed as a boy, made sad eyes at Rosemont in a purple turban and a long black cloak. Come sunset, they laid aside their trumpery robes, built a fire just outside the stable and spent the evening beside it, mending costumes and singing.

Naturally enough, they expected to be fed. I wondered what they'd make of the lumpy porridge that had perforce become the staple of our diet. However, the satchel liked them, or perhaps was simply stimulated by whatever magic had lured them to Beauxprés. In either case, when I reached inside, I found ragôuts and roasts and haricots aux amandes sufficient to feed us and players as well. Le Destin proclaimed himself ravished by such bounty, and begged that the beauteous fount of it—by which he seemed to mean me—deign to hear them sing. Before I'd even sat down, he tucked a violin under his chin and bowed a lively melody, once, twice, and on the third repetition, La Grotte opened her faded lips and sang in a sweet, unfaded voice:

> " *The old King comes from far away (E-y-a)*
> *To still the dancers' sport and play (E-y-a)*
> *For he fears both night and day*
> *That bold young men may steal away*
> *His queen of April morning.* "

She sang other airs, too, alone and in chorus with Rosemont or Belle Étoile, of love and liking and long days wandering, complaints of faithless lovers and greedy fathers who'd marry a maid to a man thrice her age. Breton songs of witches and ghosts; Provençal songs of happy and unhappy love. More often the latter than the former, however: happy lovers have better things to do than sing.

Actors change little down the years. Whatever the century, whatever the circumstances, they are always and ever passionate, self-absorbed, and oddly innocent. Reality is of less interest to them than philosophy to a beggar's child. Rags are royal robes, if the property list says so; raddled crones are beautiful princesses. They'd been told that Beauxprés was the glory of the Juras. That 'twas also a rat-haunted ruin did not seem to signify. And as for *when* they thought it was! My curiosity being piqued by their outlandish clothes, I asked Le Destin who was king in France. He wrinkled up his nose and scratched his head and finally answered me, with the air of a man who's capping another's joke, that the king was a queen, par Dieu, at least until he was out of skirts. By which I understood, after some pondering, that his Louis was the fourteenth of that name, still unbreeched and under the regency of Marie de Médicis.

My next question was, had the players been dragged forward to our time or had we slipped back to theirs? That I could not ask them, nor could they have answered, nor, I suspect, would they have cared, as long as they'd an audience to play before, even such an ill-assorted audience as we.

As for the play—well, the play proved to be as curious as the circumstances. Le Destin swore he'd writ it himself. Stole it himself would be closer to the truth, from second-rate writers of pastoral romance and third-rate copies of ancient Greek comedy, with patches of old folktales where his other borrowings were threadbare. The verse, I fear, was all his own. However much the actors urged it on with kicks and sawing at its reins, it limped along like an old horse on a hard road: clip, clip, clop; clip, clip, clop.

Had I attended *The Sorcerer Maid* in Paris, the first speech would have sent me out of the theater in search of more spiritual amusement. In Beauxprés, I laughed over its spavined jests and wept over its clapped-out sorrows with as much fervor as I'd have accorded Racine and Molière rolled into one.

The performance took place on a Sunday afternoon. I'd heard the players clattering about the stable-yard and the court all morning, and when Le Destin called us out at last, I saw they'd been preparing for a large audience. The cart was pulled up before Latona and her frogs, and all the space between stage and front steps was filled with benches, stools, upturned mangers extracted from the stable, and slats balanced on buckets. Two chairs, for the seigneur and his lady, were set on the highest step. Monsieur—who'd understood the occasion just well enough to cram a wig over his wild hair—arranged himself in the largest chair. Madame fluttered up and perched on its arm. I pulled the second chair a little aside and sat in that while Jean reclined on the steps at my feet.

As soon as we were settled, a flute began to tweetle behind the moth-eaten curtain, which fell aside to reveal a stiff cloth scene inexpertly daubed with some five or six trees. Plank-built frames stood at either side of the stage, their upper parts forked like branches and stuck with a few rags of green cloth. A rope was strung between them, and a mound of green canvas lay beneath. A forest, beyond doubt.

The flute soared to ecstatic heights, cracked, and fell silent. Three knocks off-stage heralded Rosemont, resplendent in an azure turban and a salmon-pink sash. You could tell he was troubled in his mind, for his brow was deeply wrinkled, and he sighed and shook his head from side to side like a horse refusing the bridle. When he'd reached the midpoint of the stage, he clutched his breast, flung wide his arms, and confided his woe at the top of his voice.

"Alas and alas! Is't not grief enough that my master Alcendre should be the most wicked mage in five kingdoms, without he be the most demanding as well? Nothing but spells, enchantments, charms, and cantrips from dusk until dawn. And then, from dawn until dusk, I am set to gather simples, philtres, decoctions, and essences. With my own hands I must gather them, I, Charmant, a king's son. Behold how I am tried!"

Rosemont—Charmant, I suppose I should call him—then drew a scroll from his bosom, and with a flick of his wrist unfurled it across the stage and into the wings. "Dog's eye, bat's wool, monkey's paw, pig's—I cry you pardon, madame—pizzle, black cat's blood: tedious to gather, unpleasant to carry. And the list grows more curious still. Worm's nail, mandrill's tail, hen's tooth, liar's sooth." He looked up. "Liar's sooth! I ask you. And there's yet more."

He'd been rerolling the list as he spoke, and now only a foot or so of threadbare fabric dangled from his upraised fist.

"The Horse of the North Wind, the Cloak of the Wizard of Norroway, and, finally, the Sorcerer Maid." He shook his head. "The Sorcerer Maid. The use of the rest is clear enough to the merest dabbler in the Arts Magical. But what can he want with a Sorcerer Maid? We are not, after all, a school of women! And where does one seek a Sorcerer Maid? To the East? To the South? To the North? To the West? Perhaps my master's new slave can advise me. Oh, Dove," he called off-stage. "Oh, Porcelain Dove!"

Beside me, monsieur stirred uneasily, and I feared Le Destin's play was about to reach a sudden and unforeshadowed denouement. But he quieted when the boy L'Espérance fluttered onto the stage, all tricked out in white, with a cap of white feathers and a feathered cape. Twice he wheeled around Charmant heels-over-head, then leapt up into one of the framework trees and somewhat breathlessly, spoke:

> "Far over the sea dwells a maiden most bright
> Redder far than the rose, than the lily more white.
> Her voice is enchantment, her eye is a flame,
> The Sorcerer Maid is that sweet lady's name.
> My mistress was she, and my playmate most tender;
> I was parted from her by your master, Alcendre.
> My tale is most woeful; most desperate her fate,
> Oh, hear me, oh help me before 'tis too late."

Then, in a clear, piping voice, L'Espérance—Bah!—the Porcelain Dove—revealed to Charmant—and to us—the argument of the play.

As I've said, Le Destin's plot was nothing more than begged-and-borrowed claptrap. A lovely virgin, an aging wooer, his young apprentice—the *dramatis personae* tell all. Disguises, lovers' misunderstandings, idiot brothers, a ballet—the only new things in it were the aging wooer's being a wizard and the lovely virgin's showing more spirit than the species commonly exhibits. La Grotte played the Maid as a termagant, all tossing ringlets, flashing eyes, and heaving bosom. Le Destin undertook the role of the wizard Alcendre in scarlet velvet, black lace, a black wand, and an expression of doting malice so hideous to behold that 'twas no wonder La Grotte laughed his suit to scorn. Affronted, Le Destin stamped his feet, tore his peaked wig, and flourished his wand in a circle until he'd wound up a terrible curse:

> "Refuse my love? Unhappy maiden,
> Unhappier still prepare to be!
> Want and woe shall be thy guerdon,
> Grief and madness thy true love's fee.

> All shall prove
> As I foretell
> 'Till Porcelain Dove
> Doth break the spell."

Then he seized the Porcelain Dove—not L'Espérance, you understand, but a stuffed white bird tied with thread to La Grotte's wrist—and exited, cackling.

"The Dove!" cried monsieur, which made me start. "The Porcelain Dove!"

Madame reached up with her beak to preen his wig and croon soothingly in his ear until he calmed and sighed and listened with an air of puzzled attention to the Maid lamenting the loss of her pet with much wringing of her hands and beating of her fine bosom. This display not unnaturally attracted the attention of her two brothers, Pridamont and Clindor, who, learning the cause of their sister's distress, swore to retrieve her Dove though they should die in the attempt. Pridamont was rude and ruddy, Clindor clerkly and pale. Their sister thanked them at length and sent them on their way with kisses and blessings.

The next scene was an inn, with Pridamont and Clindor before it, quarreling over the choice of their way. Presently the innkeeper came out, her hands over her ears, demanding to know what the noise was about. The innkeeper, played by Belle Étoile, was a widow of bountiful charms whose chilly aspect warmed immediately she caught sight of the ruddy Pridamont. Pouting prettily, she offered the gentlemen wine and roast fowl and feather beds so soft they'd swallow a man up to his ears and make him think he'd died and gone to Heaven on a cloud. Would the gentlemen be pleased to step within and try them? Before she'd finished her speech, Pridamont had her by the waist and on the other side of the inn door. Clindor sat upon a mossy bank and sulked.

A flute sounded, stage right. Clindor started violently and stared into the wings. "The Dove!" he cried. "Dear brother, the Dove! Like pearl it glitters through the gloom. It beckons me! Dear brother, come!"

An acrobatic turn ensued. The Porcelain Dove pirouetted upon the rope strung above the stage, treading it so lightly I could almost swear he flew, while Clindor tumbled comically in pursuit. With ever-increasing daring, the Dove leapt and slid, and when at last he came to rest at full length upon the rope, he plucked a single feather from his cloak and touched it to Clindor's brow. Clindor's mouth stretched slowly in a rapturous smile, and falling to his knees, he lifted worshipful hands to the heavens.

A rattle of thunder, a puff of black smoke, and when it cleared, there was Alcendre, coughing a little and fishing in his pockets. After one or two false casts, he pulled from his waistcoat two golden cords, one of which he tied to the Dove, the other to the rapt Clindor. Then he explained he'd done for Pridamont by identifying him to the gardeloups as a desperate smuggler and, chuckling evilly, dragged off his prizes, stage left.

There followed great banging and swearing backstage; after a space, a breathless grenadier entered stage right with his wig awry, marched into the inn, tore a disheveled Pridamont from the innkeeper's arms, loaded him with chains, and led him briskly away, presumably to prison.

The Sorcerer Maid, who'd been watching all this through the circle of a magic ring, flung it pettishly downstage and declared she'd regain the bird herself.

> "Be gone, weak tears; beat strong, my heart!
> I now eschew the maiden's part
> To stride the world in man's array,
> Cast Evil down and win the day!"

The next scene found the Maid, fetchingly breeched and wigged, entered into service with Alcendre. Naturally, she fell in love with Charmant, who, equally naturally, was already in love—with the Dove's vision of the Sorcerer Maid. There was one particularly affecting moment, when Charmant was bemoaning his love to the soi-disant youth Cléomède. In the course of confiding to Cléomède how he intended to declare his love to the Sorcerer Maid, should he ever encounter her, Charmant by little and little leaned closer until he was within a pig's whisker of kissing Cléomède full upon the mouth. 'Twas in this compromising pose that Alcendre surprised them.

> "Is this how you serve me? Ungrateful! Unkind!
> Charmant, O thou falsest of false humankind.
> All my lore have I taught thee, my wisdom laid bare;
> Is this now thy thanks? By Hades I swear
> I'll slay thee! Yet stay! Why threat Charmant's life
> When thou, Cléomède, art sole cause of this strife?
> Begone from my sight, saucy boy; ne'er return!"

Of course the Maid pled with Alcendre to forgive her. And of course he relented so far as to set her an impossible task. If Cléomède brought him the Horse of the North Wind, perhaps he'd let him continue as his apprentice. But Cléomède was to accomplish the task alone, with help from neither man nor woman.

The next scene was the forest—somewhat better supplied with trees than it had been—and the Maid sitting on a mossy bank with her head in her hands. "Cent mille tonnerres," she mourned. "The Horse of the North Wind! As well ask for the chariot axle of the Sun or the barrow of the Man in the Moon! Sorcerers are a greedy race."

L'Espérance fluttered down from a tree and alit at her feet. This time, the feathers sewn to his cap and cloak were black.

"You can't give up so soon, mademoiselle," he cawed. "Why, you've barely begun. There have to be three tasks: you know that."

"And each more impossible than the last," said the Maid despairingly. "Go away. You heard what he said. No man can help me. I've got to find the North Wind by myself, *and* where he keeps his Horse, all before I can even think how to go about stealing it without his discovering me and blowing me to Cathay."

The Crow cocked its head at her, impatience clear in every feather. "Oh, mademoiselle, mademoiselle. A crow is not a man, not though he read and speak as fluently as any bishop's clerk in France. Take heart, therefore, and put on your boots. You've a journey before you and some danger to face at the end of it. But you're a brave girl, and you won't be facing it all unsupported."

For answer, the Maid sighed and shrugged and pulled from her pack a pair of cracked leather boots, which she tugged onto her feet. As she swung the pack onto her back, I caught sight of a wand sticking out of it. I knew that wand, me. I couldn't be mistaken—how many wands could there be beribboned like a maypole and crowned with a purple jewel? Yet how came a troupe of bad provincial players to have among their properties a duplicate of the wand of the Fairy Friandise? Wondering, I stared and stared at it, and what with staring and wondering I missed the change of scene, so that the Maid's arrival at the North Wind's palace took me by surprise, as though she'd made the journey by magic in very truth.

Le Destin, it seemed, had kept back his best effects, for the palace of the North Wind was splendid if somber, as one would expect the dwelling of the grim Boreas to be. Bidding the Crow farewell, the Maid entered the stable and offered herself as stableboy to the North

Wind's head groom. There followed a comic scene involving the head groom, the Maid, a dung-fork, and a flatulent horse which had Jean holding his ribs and weeping with merriment. I, too, found it amusing, if a little coarse, especially when the Horse of the North Wind copiously demonstrated why not all foul airs are born in marshes. The Maid was inspired to a stream of scatology that would have shocked the curé, had he been there, into a fit of the vapors.

So easily the Maid found the object of her virgin quest. The stealing of it was not so easily achieved, for the smoke-gray stallion was so wild that even his master the North Wind approached him with respect and a magic bridle. Furthermore, Boreas always cared for the Horse with his own hands, nor would he accept any help in unsaddling or rubbing down or putting away tack. A thousand times the Maid despaired of accomplishing even her first task.

"He's as bad as maître Grisloup," she complained to the Crow. "One brush out of place, one straw too few or too many in the bedding, one blanket left hanging unfolded, and 'tis the back of his hand or the tip of his lash and 'Polish those bits 'till they *shine*, lad!' I'll never catch him napping, not the North Wind."

The Crow bobbed his head thoughtfully. "Then we'll have to catch him waking. How fast is he without the Horse?"

"As fast as he is with, only he can't keep it up long. He's out of training, you know. I've seen him blown and sweating just running across the stable-yard."

"There are kingdoms smaller than the North Wind's stable-yard," said the Crow. "Yet I can run farther and faster if I must. And the Horse. How fast is he?"

"Not so fast as lightning, nor yet so fast as thought. Much faster than a bird in flight or any animal upon four legs." The Maid shrugged. "As fast as the wind, in fact."

The Crow tousled its wings in an irritated way. "I cannot run so fast as that, yet, perhaps if he is over-blown . . ."

"What are you going to do?" asked the Maid.

" 'Tis the merest spark of a thought; a breath would extinguish it. Only, should you see a chance, jump on the Horse and hold on for your life." And then it flew away, leaving the Maid puzzled and fretful as before.

The next scene was the stables, with the Maid opening the door to Boreas and the Horse returned from a storm, the pair of them so blown out they could scarcely raise a breeze between them. Boreas fairly tumbled off the Horse's back, and was leading him into his stall when a playful whickering was heard off-stage. The storm-gray steed stiffened and tasted the air with flaring nostrils.

"Quiet, lad," said Boreas, and tugged impatiently at the magic bridle.

The whickering again, and then the Horse upped so suddenly with his great head that the North Wind lost his grip on the magic bridle. Before he could grab it again, the Maid was on the Horse's back and clinging to his mane like a burr as he reared and wheeled and thundered out of the stable with Boreas cursing and puffing at his heels.

A trim black mare stood at the palace gate, her tail invitingly raised. As soon as she caught sight of the Horse of the North Wind with the Maid on his back, she tossed it flirtatiously, picked up her heels and made for the Southlands, running before the Horse faster than an eagle flies, faster than a hare or a rat or any animal on four legs, though not quite as fast as the wind. Stride by stride, the Horse of the North Wind gained on her, his lungs heaving like an air-pump, sweat and foam streaming from his sides and mouth. When they reached the border of the North Wind's country, the mare's tail was flicking in the Maid's face and her breath was laboring; she was slowing, stumbling, halting to stand, her trembling legs splayed, as the Horse, rampant, reared to mount her.

Poor Horse, to be led so far and then to have his prize snatched so rudely from under his very nose! For the mare disappeared, and suddenly a gigantic Crow was flying up between his forelegs. He came down stiff-legged, jolting the Maid half off his back, whinnied wildly, and stood trembling. If he hadn't been so tired, he'd have bolted again. As it was, after a moment he put down his head and began to pull at the short grass.

A thousand leagues away, Boreas sat cursing and rubbing at a cramp in his leg. As weary as his Horse was, he was wearier still. Yet before he went home to his bath and his bed, there was something he wanted to know. He stood up and called out in a voice of tempest: "Thou, Thief! I clothed thee, I fed thee, I paid thee good gold. Why then hast thou robbed me?"

The Maid stood in her stirrups and replied: "Fury drives me, duty calls me. I have what I need and will fret you no more."

This answer did nothing to appease the North Wind, who raged and roared until I feared for the Maid; but he was too leg-weary to follow her.

Slowly, to spare the Horse, the Maid rode over land and sea to the island where Alcendre had his dwelling. Before she reached the tower, she drew rein, dismounted, and went to the Horse's mighty head. As the Crow watched from the crupper, she breathed her own breath into the Horse's nostrils and whispered long into the Horse's ears. Then she removed the magic bridle from between the Horse's teeth and hid it in her pack.

"Clever girl," said the Crow approvingly. "I'll be away, then." He spread his wings and crouched ready for flight. "You have the black feather? You've only to blow upon it to call me."

"I know, Pompey," said the Maid. And after a small pause, awkwardly: "I am grateful for your help."

The Crow laughed raucously, hopped into the air, and flapped heavily into the trees.

I started and looked sharply at Jean, who was gazing at the stage like a man enthralled.

"Did you hear that?" I hissed. "She called the Crow 'Pompey.'"

"Chut," said Jean. "Alcendre enters."

A glade before a tall white tower. The Maid sat the Horse with Alcendre at her stirrup, caressing the Horse's flank with one bony hand. It seemed to me he'd aged a hundred years in the space of one act; perhaps 'twas only the monkish robe with which he'd replaced his scarlet suit. He'd changed wigs, too, from black to white, and gummed a wispy beard to his chin. In short, Alcendre was the image of the beggar-wizard down to his clawlike hands and his burning amber eyes.

I remember that I noted this metamorphosis with as little wonder as I'd noted the transformation of a painted scene and two ill-carpentered trees into a real forest. "How skillful," I thought. "How clever." Then I thought nothing more at all. 'Twas as though I'd shrunk to two eyes and a memory, with no room under my cap for judgment or feeling.

The beggar-wizard gave his apprentice a sour look. "Well, girl. Hast got the Horse, I see. Did any man help thee?"

"Only the North Wind himself, Master, and that entirely by chance. May I have the Dove now?"

"One task achieved achieveth naught, as thou know'st full well. Thy second task is to bring to me the Wizard of Norroway's black Cloak."

The Maid bowed, and he hobbled into his tower without further word. When he'd disappeared within, the Maid slid down from the Horse and glared at the closed door, her eyes a little narrowed and her jaws clenched in a look of fury restrained. Gently the Horse nudged her shoulder.

"I pitied him, Horse," she said, stroking his cheek. "I never blamed him for hating my father, not when I learned what cause he had to hate the name of Maindur. How foolish I was to think he'd except me from his hatred."

The next scene was a ship bound for Norroway, with the North Wind blowing vengefully and the Maid seasick, and the crew casting dark looks at her and her Crow. They muttered about witch-boys and they muttered about Jonahs, and the harder the North Wind blew, the louder they muttered. They'd just settled upon throwing both Maid and Crow overboard as a sacrifice to the elements when the North Wind, howling his rage, seized the mainmast and snapped it like a bone.

This was the shipwreck I'd seen the players rehearsing, with the stage tossing and rocking between moments of terrible stillness when it lay in the trough of a wave whose crest hung above it like a rocky gorge before tumbling down upon the deck and shattering into foam. Maid and Crow forgotten, the crew sprang to their stations. Yet Boreas did not go unappeased. The wind swept the Crow up and away; the water claimed the Maid.

Gasping and flailing, she fought the waves and seized upon the top of the mainmast, which chanced to be floating nearby. Miraculously, it bore her up through the storm. More miraculously still, it carried her safely to shore where she washed up at the feet of an ancient man in a rusty black cloak: the Wizard of Norroway.

Stiffly he knelt down beside her, his cloak billowing out behind him in the wind, and bent to raise her in his arms. With some difficulty he sat her up, thumped her on the back, and held her as she began to retch up seawater. When she was done, he wiped her mouth with a corner of his cloak.

"Easy now," said the Wizard gently. "Easy, lass. Lie you still a moment, and when you're feeling better, we'll go up to my house and

I'll get you something to eat. Though you're a strong sorcerer, you're mortal yet."

Thanks to the Maid's weakness and the Wizard's age, they were a tedious while scrambling up the cliff, and perforce stopped often to rest. During one of these halts, the Wizard said, "Fortune was with you, lass. I was expecting an omen, or else I'd not have been here."

The Maid had only strength to shiver and nod and haul herself a little higher up the cliff. But when at last they stood panting at the top, she asked, "Did you get it?"

"Get what, lass?"

"The omen."

"The omen?" The Wizard opened his arms and his rusty, black cloak and folded the Maid within them to nestle by his side. "Yes," he said. "I did."

By this time in my life, I'd met two sorcerers and heard tell of another, and the Wizard of Norroway was like none of them—although in time, I thought Pompey might grow to be as kind and wise. Observing the Wizard tend and teach the Maid, I seemed to see the shadow of the youth he'd been: lean-faced and sharp-eyed as an eagle, fearless as a lion, solitary as a bear. He was old now, a thousand years or more, he said. His magic kept him alive, but he'd not bothered to keep himself young, so that his shoulders stooped like folded wings, his hands were gnarled and spotted, and his plaited hair trailed down his back in seven bleached rope-ends.

"Magic is a strange thing, lass," he told her once. "You can learn all its rules and doctrines, read grammaryes until you're blind, question imps and fairies and kobolds and dwarfs for twice a thousand years, and still magic will surprise you. Any country witch-wife can cast a spell. And not the wisest, oldest, strongest wizard that ever lived can control precisely where 'twill land or how 'twill work itself out."

Young and headstrong, the Maid smiled, sure that her spells would cast true. Old and wise, he smiled back at her. I've often taken comfort in the knowledge that he was right and she was wrong. He was a kind teacher, the Wizard of Norroway. 'Twas no wonder that the Maid grew to love him and to feel the burden of her quest as a grim weight upon her heart.

One day she went to the Wizard's rock above the cold North Sea and blew upon the Crow's black feather. I knew she feared him lost in the storm; as she blew she wept. Yet within a pair of moments he flew to her call, incongruous over the ocean as a whale in a mountain stream.

"Well, mademoiselle," he croaked as he flopped to earth beside her. "You've waited long to summon me. What news of the cloak?"

Having called the Crow, the Maid seemed loath to speak to him, at least about the Wizard of Norroway's black cloak. First she wanted to know where the Crow had been, and why he'd sent her no word.

"Here and there," said the Crow to her first question, "and I came as soon as you called me. Now. What about the cloak?"

The Maid fidgeted her fingers, a child's trick her mother had often taken her to task for. "There's nothing to tell, Pompey. I can't take it."

"Take heart, mademoiselle. We'll think of something will turn the trick, just as we did with Boreas. And this wizard is mortal, which should make the task easier. Why, you might simply slip it from his shoulders as he sleeps."

"Well, yes; I'd thought of that. But I can't do it." She sounded young for her years, a child protesting the horse is too high, she'll fall off, she knows it.

And 'twas the child the Crow answered, his harsh voice soft as down. "He's been kind to you and you don't want to rob him. I'm glad you feel so, mademoiselle—it does your heart credit. Yet here is a quest to be achieved and you the one fated to achieve it, by blood, by nature, and by training. Do you refuse to take the Wizard's cloak, the Dove will never come to Beauxprés and the wounds of the past must fester on unhealed."

"Then the Dove will not come to Beauxprés. Is that so great a tragedy, Pompey? I am sorry for my mother's sufferings, bien sûr— she is only silly and vain, and those are not mortal sins. But my mother has never been so kind to me as this Wizard of Norroway, so heedful of my thoughts and opinions. When he looks at me, he sees me. Not his own desires and fears: me. He knows my soul more truly than any, save you. I cannot betray him. I will not."

Though that sounded like the end of the matter, it wasn't. They argued it back and forth as I'd often heard them argue before, over the application of a spell or the use of learning Latin. Linotte was impassioned, Pompey reasonable and sympathetic and unyielding as stone. Faintly I understood 'twas my fate they were arguing—my fate against the Wizard of Norroway's. If I wasn't to go on as I was, trapped in the beggar-wizard's curse upon the blood of Maindur, Linotte must betray her new master's trust and her own love for him. Or she must betray her father, her mother, her brothers, Jean, me.

"Let them suffer," she cried at last. "Let them die. They'll die in the end anyway. And what about the suffering they've caused, like Jorre, with their willful self-love? My mother cannot see past her laudanum and her tambour frame. And my father—my father sees only his birds."

" 'Tis not for you to condemn them to death," said Pompey.

" 'Tis not for you to condemn the Wizard of Norroway," said Linotte, and stood up from her rock. "Whatever I do, I'll have innocent blood on my hands: either Berthe and Jean or the Wizard must die. Yet Berthe and Jean chose to stay by my parents, knowing what they were and how they were cursed. Leaving the Wizard his cloak seems to me the lesser evil."

Something in this speech had surprised Pompey—what, I could tell no more than I could tell how I knew he was surprised. A crow has no brows to raise, after all, no lips to "O." Perhaps 'twas some lifting of his neck feathers made me think he was startled and, I thought, a little relieved.

"You must trust me, child," he said gently. "Take the Wizard's cloak. If your weird permitted you to ask him for it, I'm sure he'd give it freely."

This speech enraged Linotte past all sense. "Trust thee?" she screamed. "Trickster, shape-changer, savage, why should I trust thee?" Like a child in a rage, she plucked the black feather out of her bosom and flung it off the cliff. "I'll never call thee again, carrion-eater, bird of ill-omen. I need not thy help to be what my blood and destiny make me. I am the youngest child of the house of Jorre Maindur. Murder should come easily to me." And on that word, she spun away inland, running as though she sought to outrun fate.

The feather lifted and flirted out over the fjord before an updraft sidled it back to earth at the Crow's feet. He examined it birdlike, one eye then the other, pecked it up like a grain of corn, and tucked it under his wing. A most unbirdlike sigh, a hop, a beat of his wings, and he was gone. And we were in the Wizard of Norroway's stone hut, waiting with him for Linotte.

He knew she was coming, no doubt of that, and seemed oddly undismayed, though a little abstracted, if the way he was fiddling with his cloak-pin were anything to judge by. I hadn't really noticed the pin before—a flimsy-looking thing, brown and twiggy. After a space, he rose and walked to the hearth, where he stooped over the fire, presenting his back to the Maid as she stormed in, red-cheeked and breathless. The hut was not large. Two steps took her near enough to rip the cloak from the Wizard's shoulders and fling it across the room.

I can't say I was astonished when the Wizard turned from the fire and sat placidly at the table, no more put out by the loss of his cloak than he'd be by the loss of his sandal. Linotte gawked at him, then erupted into a spate of tears that flooded over her cheeks and chin like a mountain stream at thaw. The Wizard let her weep for a while, and then he said, "Hush, child. These tears do not become the Sorcerer Maid who overcame the Wizard of Norroway and took his magic cloak from him. You'd better take the brooch as well."

Linotte lifted her swollen eyes to him. "No," she said thickly, and blew her nose on her sleeve. "No. I won't take it. He asked for the cloak. That's all I have to give him."

"It won't do him any good without the brooch. You must give him both."

"No. He won't know the difference. And even if he does, he can't send me back to get it. Keep the brooch, Master. Live another thousand years."

The Wizard of Norroway smiled at her, then slipped up the pin of the brooch of rushes and removed it from the shoulder of his long robe of white fur. He raised the hand of the Sorcerer Maid from her lap, laid the brooch in her palm, and closed her fingers over it. When his hand left hers, he withered away into dust.

Grim-eyed, the Maid marked her cheeks and brow with the Wizard's dust, rose, gathered up the cloak, shook it out, and pinned the brooch at its neck. Without a backward glance, she stepped out the Wizard of Norroway's front door straight into the beggar-wizard's tower.

"So, apprentice," said the beggar-wizard. "Hast brought me the Cloak of the Wizard of Norroway, as I asked thee?"

"As you see, Master."

"Thou wert long enough about it. Yet 'tis no matter. Thou art here now, and twice welcome for thy absence."

This was a new tune, and no mistake. The Maid eyed the old man narrowly, as did I. He'd thrown a kind of glamour over himself so that his four hundred years sat more lightly upon him than they had, and fixed his lips into a rictus that did duty as a smile. He wore Le

Destin's scarlet velvet suit—upon which now flourished a costly fungus of gold embroidery—and a long, black, curling wig. On one beringed hand, as stiff and out of place there as the smile on his lips, perched a gleaming white bird.

"So that's the Porcelain Dove," said the Maid, and reached out her hand to it. Beside me, monsieur growled low in his throat; from the corner of my eye, I saw his fingers twitch and scrabble upon his thighs. It seemed to me that the beggar-wizard glanced out towards us and that his smile broadened. Or perhaps he only rejoiced to see Linotte so eager—who knows? His joy was a cruel joy in either case, the cat's joy in lifting a single claw from the wing of her prey.

"First give me the Cloak," said the beggar-wizard; and with a bitter tenderness, she laid it across his knees and watched hot-eyed as he fingered it.

"I hope it brings me more joy than thy first gift, ma mie. The Horse of the North Wind will suffer nor saddle nor bridle—no, not so much as a hand laid upon him. He's been the death of two good grooms."

The Maid cast down her eyes. "The cloak will not harm you," she said.

"Nevertheless. Now for the third task, that pays for all." The beggar-wizard laid the cloak aside and, taking up his staff, rose from the high carved chair he'd been sitting in. As he stood, he grew more upright, more lordly, until he seemed a king among wizards: crowned with black cloud, a scepter of thorn in his left hand, and in his right, a living, feathered orb. Blood and night robed him, and his words crashed and rattled like rocks in a landslide.

"Hear thy fate, O Child of Maindur. Life for life is my right, and life for life shall I have. Thy third task is to give me a daughter of my getting, to love and rear and teach in the place of my lost Colette. Thou wilt therefore wed with me, and be my wife at bed and at board until that thou dost conceive and bear forth a girl-child alive."

As though the words had been rocks indeed, they beat upon the Maid until she huddled to the floor with her hands to her ears. She had not wept when the Wizard of Norroway fell to dust; she did not weep now. Like her father at the sack of Beauxprés, she only gazed upon her tormentor as though the very intensity of her look might silence him.

The beggar-wizard returned her gaze, a smile upon his bearded lips. "Well, girl?"

Linotte lowered her hands to her lap and shut her eyes. "A year and a day," she said. " 'Tis my right."

"Thou wert more than two years in Norroway, and in the house of Boreas less than one. Thyself hast set aside the binding of time. Never think to take it up again, now it chances to serve thy turn."

The Maid nodded. "Three days to decide."

"No."

She opened her eyes and glared at him. "Three days to prepare, then. No bride should go to her marriage without time in which to bid her maidenhead farewell and make her a gown to be wed in."

"You consent?" Triumph and suspicion warred in the wizard's voice.

"I do." Very clipped, and the breath bated at the end of the phrase, awaiting his response.

He grinned like a skull. "Thou shalt have thy three days, ma mie, alone, as thou hast asked, providing thou keep to the island and seek not to venture abroad. In earnest of which promise, do thou kiss me."

Stiffly the Maid gained her feet and stepped towards him. On his fist, the Porcelain Dove cucuroo'd in its pearly throat. She halted and considered it, her dark eyes unfathomable.

"Yes—'tis fair, my Dove. But not so fair as my dead child. Come. Thy kiss."

Another step brought her to him. She lifted her face and, firm and unshrinking, laid her lips to his. Then she turned and went from him, down through the tower and out to the stable where the Horse of the North Wind, looking sadly neglected, greeted her with soft whickers of joy.

The three days of the beggar-wizard's grace the Maid passed in the stable, grooming the matted hair from the Horse's coat, cleaning his stall, sitting on an upturned bucket with the wand of the Fairy Friandise in her hand and, at her feet, the Horse's bridle and the silver walnut she'd brought with her from the cabinet des Fées. Once she waved the wand, whispering words over it she'd learned of the Wizard of Norroway. It gained her a sticky handful of marzipan pigs and the usual cloud of purple dust. The dust eddied about the Horse, who snuffled at it, then shook his ears and neighed gustily. The Maid stared at him and the purple sparkles so incongruously bespangling his mane, and helplessly began to laugh, her laughter as painful as weeping. She fed the marzipan pigs to the Horse, cast her arms around his neck and stood with her head tucked under his jaw while the purple glitter faded slowly into the air.

Well. I could make nothing of that, nor of the calm with which, next morning, Linotte cracked open the silver walnut and found—to no one's surprise—a gown as bright as the stars.

I confess I'd always wondered what such a gown would look like, how it would be fashioned, and above all, how she'd manage to put it on without a maid to lace it up for her and drape the skirts. So 'twas with a professional interest that I watched her strip off her boy's clothes, shake out the gown, and cast it over her head. Alas, the gown was so bright that I couldn't look directly at it, but must squint with slitted eyes at the quicksilver folds rippling down Linotte's body to clothe her in a seamless glory of light. Prosaically, she combed out her short black hair with her fingers, and before leaving the stable, waved the wand of the Fairy Friandise, ate a marzipan pig, and pulled the dust around her like a sparkling mantle.

All that came before and after the wedding, I remember well. The wedding itself I don't care to remember. 'Twas like no nuptial Mass I've ever heard sung, that I will say, the groom himself conducting the rite in accordance with rubrics as strange as they were foul. In comparison to the ceremony, the eerie witnesses seemed like old friends. There they were: Jorre's victims, the children of madame's bedchamber, the creeping infants, the staggering babes, the little maids and lads of five or six years' growth. I could hardly bear to look at them for wondering if they'd been disturbed by my pawing through their bones and which of them, living, had owned the skull I'd shattered to dust. Yet look on them I must, for they impressed themselves upon my senses even with my eyes shut: rank upon rank of childish faces, still and unreadable as servants' faces, waiting.

At last the rite drew to an end. The wizard, plunging his hand into a brazier filled with aromatic coals, drew forth a ring that glowed red. This ring he thrust onto the forefinger of the Maid's left hand. I saw her pale lips move—a spell of warding, I suppose, for she neither winced nor withdrew her hand from the burning gleed. Then the watching children sighed and faded from sight, and the beggar-wizard, smiling, took his bride by the hand and led her up to bed.

Helplessly I watched as they mounted the winding stair, their steps illuminated by the gown as bright as the stars. When they came to the top, the gown's light fell upon a small, round chamber, empty save for a wooden bed of ancient and rustic design. The wizard turned to the Maid and touched her above the heart, and the gown as bright as the stars flowed away from his hand like water to gather in a gleaming puddle at her feet. Her hands moved to cover her breasts and her sex. He laughed; they fell away again to hang passive at her sides.

A flick of his hand, and his own garments fell from him—all save the rusty black cloak he wore hung over his shoulders, fastened at his throat by the brooch of rushes. He let fall, too, the glamour he'd cast upon his person. I don't know how a man four hundred years old might be expected to look, few such having been recorded since the days of Abraham and Methuselah. This man was seamed of skin, sunken of belly and chest, shrunk of shank, gray and lax from head to horny foot, save for his manhood that rose in dark and angry salutation to his wife.

Taking her hand, he led her to the bed, laid her down upon it, knelt between her legs. He stroked her impassive face, her neck, her shoulders, her breasts, his hands moving like insects across her white skin. And all the while he stroked and caressed his wife, when he mounted and as he rode her, his eyes were fixed, not on her, but on monsieur, and he smiled at him an old man's gap-toothed smile.

Beside me, I felt monsieur stir, heard his harsh breath in his throat like a death-rattle that had no end. I thought—I prayed—that I'd go blind, go mad, die with the horror of the wizard's revenge. Linotte's hand crept up her husband's haunch. He glanced down at her, startled, and she moaned and heaved her hips and locked her shapely legs around his withered buttocks. For the first time, he bent his head to kiss her. The black cloak covered them, its rusty darkness making whiter by contrast the arm Linotte twined about her husband's neck. Finally he gave a great thrust and cried out; shuddered and gurgled deep in his throat, then collapsed upon his wife in the lassitude of passion spent.

How many nights to get a child, I thought. Will he force us to watch them all, and the birthing, too? And: how many years have we sat here?

Upon this thought, I found I could move my hands, discovered I'd clenched them so hard over my mouth that both my palms and my lips were torn. As I wiped away the blood with my apron, the black mound upon the bed gave a heave and the beggar-wizard flopped over onto his back. Linotte dragged herself upright and put back her hair from her face. Her pale skin was flooded with scarlet, as were the sheets and pillows beneath her. Her bleak eyes looked down upon her husband.

I followed her gaze to a corpse, shrunken and fast falling into decay; a corpse in the hollow of whose throat was thrust the pin of a round brooch improbably woven of rushes.

In Which the Porcelain Dove
Comes to Beauxprés

The vision of the Sorcerer Maid faded with the wizard's corpse, and in the place of his tower I saw only bare boards, a badly-painted scene, two framework trees, and a grassy knoll fashioned from a heap of green canvas. Actors there were none. The prophetically named Le Destin, Rosemont, La Grotte, Belle Étoile, L'Espérance—all were returned to their proper time and place, or translated at the wizard's death le bon Dieu alone knows where.

Though Le Destin was gone, his properties remained at Beauxprés, including the oxen and the dun horse, which increase of our stock pleased Jean greatly. He'd been snoring against my knee after the vision faded and, when I woke him, owned not the smallest memory of seeing Linotte or the beggar-wizard or Pompey. Charmant had tricked Alcendre in the end, he said, and ridden off on the Horse with the Cloak on his back, the Maid at his saddlebow, and the Dove on his fist to live happily ever after. He remembered it all perfectly, him. As for the sudden departure of Le Destin and his troupe unpaid, he'd no explanation save that actors are an unaccountable race.

Thus Jean then; thus Jean now. I do not believe he lies. What Jean wishes to see, that is the thing he sees. A comfortable magic, that has warded him against an army of horrors, not the least of them this vision of Linotte's wedding. Oh, the shame I felt, to be constrained to sit and watch the rape, powerless to look away or call out or even to throw fruit! And there is some shame, too, in having written it all for Colette to read, lest in some sense I have served her as her father's spell served me.

Or was it her father's spell? He saw monsieur, I am sure of it, watched him watching him take his daughter's maidenhead, and unastonished to find himself so observed. The ghostly children he did not see, or at least did not acknowledge, nor did he know of Linotte's adventures anything more than she herself revealed. As Pompey was fond of saying, and the Wizard of Norroway also, the patterns of magic are as capricious as they are compelling, and not the most learned wizard on earth can cast a spell to perform only his desire and no more.

I was writing about Jean.

He would not believe me, wondered that I would care to invent such filth, and left me as I was consigning all the inhabitants of Beauxprés, servant, master, and child, to the deeps of Satan's hottest sinkhole and good riddance to them. Nor did the next day encourage me to a more charitable disposition. Jean could hardly bring himself to speak to me. Monsieur and madame made a Charenton of the library, caterwauling and raving enough for a hundred maniacs. Me, I carried on as I had before, save for a revolution in my belly that cast my food back up my throat as soon as ever I swallowed it.

I was spewing porridge into the horse trough. When Linotte returned to Beauxprés, I thought I'd never be warm again, or well, or happy. I thought I'd be dead soon, the sooner the better. And when the spasm released me, I leaned my brow on the edge of the trough and wept.

Through my weeping, I heard birds.

Birds! Only imagine the shock, after perhaps four years of silence, to hear larks, doves, nightingales, finches, linnets, singing full and liquid paeans to the sun, which, for a wonder, was warming my back as it had not been warmed since I couldn't even remember when.

My over-tried heart counseled flight. The last marvel, it told me, had not been of a particularly comforting nature; why should I be eager to greet the next? I'd be wisest to run to the kitchen, bar the door, and hide me in the chimney corner until whatever horror the birdsong heralded had run its course and departed. Thus my heart. My feet, in the meantime, carried me past the kitchen door and around the north wing to the forecourt and Latona and the long, blasted lawn to the east. And there my eyes showed me the chestnut trees blooming and leafing out like chicks hatching while a tide of gold and new green rushed up the slope: grass shooting up and rippling in the warm wind, marguerites and cowslips and anemones hurriedly unfurling their leaves and petals.

I screamed for Jean.

As I think I've said before, pain and pleasure sound much alike. Jean came running from his garden at full tilt, hoe raised and ready for mayhem. "What's wrong now, Duvet?" he panted. "Have you run mad?"

Well, that struck me as funny, the way he'd said it, and I began laughing so hard I couldn't answer him, only point over his shoulder and sputter. He dropped the hoe, took me by the shoulders and shook me until my teeth chattered. "Shut it, Berthe Duvet! Do you hear me? Just shut it!"

Still laughing, I forced him around to face the chestnut drive, brilliant as emerald in the clear air. His jaw dropped. He put his fists to his eyes, rubbed, and looked again. A cloaked figure on a storm-gray horse emerged from the end of the drive and started up the hill.

"Who's that?" he asked plaintively. "Another sorcerer? And who's that with him? D'ye think they're dangerous? I tell you, Duvet, I don't think I can endure much more."

My turn to shake him—more gently than he'd shaken me, bien sûr—and to make soothing noises. "Now, now, Jean—'tis only Mlle Linotte, returned from her quest. Remember, she went dressed as a boy? Of course you remember. As for who's with her, I'd guess the vicomte de Montplaisir and M. Justin. The tale is told, Jean, and we've come to happily ever after. There'll be nothing more for you to endure. You'll see."

I was wrong.

If this history of mine were in truth a conte des fées, I could make an end here, with Linotte, like Persephone, bringing spring to Beauxprés. I could purloin my closing lines from Mme d'Aulnoy or even M. Perrault, some scene of restoration and reconciliation replete with tears and smiles and wedding bells, change the names to suit, and Jean at least would be satisfied that I'd ended my tale the way a tale ought to end.

Colette, on the other hand, would not be satisfied with such a romance, however elegantly composed. From a child she has always insisted upon knowing the truth. Oh, the questions she asked! What was beyond the mist? Why would Léon not come out of his room?

Where was monsieur? What happened to Pompey? And when we told her le bon Dieu alone knew the answer to *that*, why she'd stamp her little foot and vow she'd find out for herself. Which she set herself to do, with her readings and her scribblings and her magical experiments in farseeing.

How like Linotte she is. And how unlike. Colette's magic is all making and doing and knowing; Linotte's was all breaking and undoing and hiding away. And that, I think, was the wizard's parting malediction upon monsieur: that his daughter sacrifice her youth and her joy and her maidenhood in the quest of the Porcelain Dove.

Yet Linotte had her moment of triumph, and at first her return was glorious as even Jean could have wished. Like an April queen she trod the carpet of new grass and flowers that sprung up beneath her horse's feet. A rainbow of small birds arched above her and her two brothers rode behind as guard of honor. On her fist, borne high and forward like a standard, perched a bird whose feathers gave back the sunlight with a hard, polished gleam, a bird whose beak was coral, whose eyes glittered red as faceted glass. The Porcelain Dove.

The Horse's iron-shod hooves rang upon the cobbles of the fountain court, then halted by the front steps where Jean and I were standing. Through my blur of tears, I saw only a shadow crowned with flowers and haloed with light. The Sorcerer Maid spoke.

"Fetch monsieur my father, Berthe."

That was all Linotte's greeting, in a voice as hard and bright as the Dove's feathers. No sign of being happy to see us or grateful or relieved the château was still standing; just "Fetch my father, Berthe," as though I were a lackey. Bah!

"Bah!" I said. "Fetch him yourself, you. You're good at fetching things."

She'd no reply to this save silence. I tented my hand and glared up defiantly; she bent her head to meet my gaze. Her eyes were red and swollen-lidded and shadowed with pain; her face a dozen years older than the face of the girl who'd cracked the walnut and put on the gown as bright as the stars. Still angry, and ashamed now with it, I shrugged, turned, entered the château, crossed the hall to the library, and rattled the broken handle.

"Monsieur," I shouted. "Oh, M. le bougre duc de Malvoeux. Come out, O descendant of monsters. Thy daughter awaits thee, O fornicator of birds. She's brought thy thrice-cursed Porcelain Dove, and I pray to le bon Dieu that 'twill peck out thy eyes."

Silence. Then a scream worthy of madame, a great crashing, and the handle torn from my hand as he pulled open the library door and stumbled past me to a scene I'd no desire to witness: the coming together of duc and Dove. I'd had my fill of birds, me.

I slid to the floor and sat hugging myself, waiting for it all to be over. Madame stalked out of the library, trembled her feather aigrette at me, pecked at my shoe, and paced with heavy dignity across the hall to the door where she jerked a beady glance over her back and waited. I sighed; but my time for defiance was past. I hauled myself wearily to my feet and followed her.

When we reached the forecourt, Linotte was down from the Horse and standing on the steps with the Dove held high. Messires Léon and Justin had their eyes fixed on it, as did monsieur and Jean and madame. Flies in amber, all six of us—ten, if you counted the horses, the mule, and the Dove—held prisoner by perfect uncertainty. Who will make the first move? What will it be? Almost I ran upstairs to consult the *Contes des fées*, before I remembered 'twas burnt.

The Dove cooed softly, swelled its neck into a bristling ruff, fanned its tail, tucked its coral beak coyly into its breast feathers. Monsieur whimpered and stretched out his hand, and the Dove flew to it, tame as a cote-pigeon, and dug its coralline claws into his fist. And that, suddenly, was all the Porcelain Dove appeared to be—on my hope of salvation I swear it: an ordinary white pigeon, such as you may find cooing by the hundred in any seigneurial dovecote in France.

The absurdity of it all rose to my brain like mercury. So much worry and effort, so much betrayal and waste of freedom and life. So much suffering. All for an aristo's whim to possess a white pigeon. Artide, I am thy sister. Mère Boudin, I embrace thee. Were Sangsue alive again and his members intact, I would have killed him all over again, torn his eyes from his head and his tongue from his mouth, severed his hands and fed him his manhood. I was ready to do the same by monsieur, if only I could find a knife. Yes, and chop the Porcelain Dove fine and bake it in a pie.

Thus I stood fuming in a scarlet haze while the brothers alit. Madame, catching sight of the vicomte, squawked prodigiously and flurried up to his shoulder. The vicomte, seeing nothing but a peahen attacking him, swore and beat her away. Before I knew what I was about, I'd my fingers dug into his shirt-front and was pounding him with all my might. "Salopard! Unnatural! Violator of children! Did thy father teach thee to beat thy mother, eh?"

He was very thin and dirty, his flesh white as a dead fish, and weak, too, or else he'd have made short work of me. As it was, it took him a moment to detach me, and he said only, "Are you mad, whore? Beat my mother? My mother's not here. Just a fucking great bird. I hate birds."

I spat at him. "That bird *is* thy mother, Montplaisir. Wouldst thou love her the more were she in her proper shape?"

"Enough," shouted Linotte, sounding very like her father. "Berthe, you presume. And Léon, she's quite right: the peahen is our mother."

Léon laughed at that, hoarse and mirthless, his pale eyes like dirty ice above his curling lip. "A peahen! To be sure, sister. And my brother here's a moon-calf, my father an ogre, and you're the queen of the fairies. I'm grateful to you for breaking me out of the château d'If, Linotte, but my gratitude has limits."

Linotte, who was thoughtfully observing madame, did not seem to hear him. "This is a great pity," she said, and reached for madame, who screeched and pecked peevishly at her. "Peste! Will she let you handle her, Berthe?"

Well, I didn't know whether she would or not; nonetheless, I sat on the step beside her and slowly put out my hand. After bobbing at me a moment, she hopped onto my lap and folded her legs.

"Good. Now feel at the back of her head. Do you find a pin?"

Gingerly I searched among the sleek feathers, touched a hard, round, cold knob, nodded. "Bon," said Linotte. "Now. Draw it out slowly—it mustn't break. That's right. Now, you must kiss her to seal the change."

I looked up from the naked woman who was suddenly, magically, sprawled across my knees. "Surely monsieur her husband . . ." I glanced around for monsieur, found him billing and cooing with the Dove.

" 'Tis best done by someone who loves her," said Linotte gently. "Quickly, now. Kiss her."

A touch on my cheek, a hoarse, parroty voice in my ear. "Yes, kiss me, Berthe. If it pleases you."

It did please me. Her mouth was very soft and her arms about my neck comforted even as they clung. I'd forgotten how loving she could be, how sweet it was to have her nestle in my bosom like a child. I kissed her lips and face, stroked her graying hair, and thanked le bon Dieu for her bony weight in my arms.

I'd have been content to go on doing those things for a while longer, but almost at once Linotte slung the Wizard of Norroway's cloak from her own shoulders and draped it over madame.

"Come, ma mère," she said. "There's work yet to be done. You may rest later, as long as you wish, but now's the time for laying ghosts and breaking curses. A wound must be searched before it may be healed—that's what my master taught me."

Her voice dropped and her brow twitched as with sudden pain. Is her mourning for the Wizard of Norroway, I wondered, or for Pompey? Which thought caused such a pang in my own heart that 'twas only with the half of my attention that I helped madame to her feet, folded the cloak decently around her, and pinned it closed with the brooch of rushes. Where was the boy? Why had he not come to comfort me? Was it only that I had no feather to call him with?

I heard Jean saying, "Duvet knows more than I. Duvet knows all about it. She was the one found the document I told you of, she never said where nor how."

I turned to see Mlle Linotte considering me, her arms folded across her chest. "Well, Berthe?"

My mind being so full of Pompey and wizards and crows, I couldn't, for a moment, think what they could be speaking of, and bemusedly begged her pardon.

'Twas Justin enlightened me. "When my ancestor murdered the beggar-wizard's daughter, I doubt he buried her in consecrated ground. 'Tis our belief the curse cannot be fully lifted until her bones are found and buried and her soul released to judgment."

"Jean has told us," Linotte interrupted him, "that you once found a document: the dying confession of my cursed ancestor."

My blood ran cold in my cheeks. "I found it, mademoiselle."

"Did you find anything else?"

"Yes, mademoiselle."

"What did you find?"

"Bones, mademoiselle."

"Take us there."

Thinking that even Nôtre Sauveur had only been required to descend once into Hell, I hesitated until madame touched my arm and said, "Yes, Berthe. All the little birds: I must go to them at once."

At the word "birds," monsieur turned his eyes from the Dove to me, and now all the Maindurs were staring at me, expectant and vaguely threatening, like goats waiting to be fed. Well, you can't argue with mad folk any more than you can argue with goats. So I turned on my heel down the front steps and led the way around the north wing and through the stable-yard to the scorched and blasted laundry-yard and thence to the room of the tubs and the arch and the stairs leading down to the dungeons of Beauxprés.

" 'Tis very dark," said Jean nervously.

"Nevertheless," I said, and started the descent. Whoever came behind me made a light so that I could see to set my feet; above and around me, the murk pressed close and heavy.

Forty paces across the guard room took me to the door of the torture chamber.

"Pah!" said Léon. "How it stinks! Worse than the château d'If, by damn."

"Bat dung," I said.

"And behold the bats that made it," said Linotte, gazing ruefully upwards to the ceiling, thick with dark, untidy spikes. Whatever other living things the curse had killed or driven from Beauxprés, the bats had manifestly thrived.

A dazzling light darted through the gloom to rest, cooing mournfully, upon the Iron Maiden. The bats, their slumbers disturbed, rustled and hissed; those caught by the silver glare dropped from their roosts and skimmed noiselessly into deeper shadow.

I was inclined to let the Dove guide the family Maindur to its ancestral chamber of horrors while I awaited them above in the warmth of the new sun. Monsieur was already ankle-deep in the muck, making for the Dove like iron for a lodestone, with Justin wading close behind, followed by Linotte and madame clinging to her belt. As monsieur drew near, the Dove took wing, circled, and flew into the tunnel beyond the Iron Maiden, taking the light with it. I'd certainly have turned back then, unneeded and glad of it, had I not felt the hungry darkness pressing at my back, sucking urgently at my eyes and ears.

After all I had witnessed and suffered, it took more than a moonless dark to terrify me, nor was I subject to phantasmical terrors. Yet I never doubted that all the malice of Hell waited in that darkness to consume me should I lose sight of that silver gleam. I hitched up my skirts to my knees and floundered after it. Jean must have sensed something of the same threat, for I heard him stumbling behind me, and last of all, the vicomte de Montplaisir, cursing a steady stream of filth.

The opening to the passage was as I remembered it, and the passage itself, bare and twisted. The door at the end was open as I'd left it, and the chamber beyond filled to overflowing with liquid silver. Half-blinded, I blinked and squinted at the squat columns, the wooden table, the document case, the wide hearth, the iron cauldron, and in the midst of it all, madame, monsieur, and Linotte standing frozen in attitudes of wonder. Slowly I came a little down the room to where I might see the row of clothes-presses. The lid of the nearest was raised, and Justin, on his knees before it, spilled cloth-of-gold over its side in a brilliant, molten flow.

"Sacré Dieu," Jean murmured behind me. "What is all this?"

"Chut," I said, and stepped quietly nearer.

Linotte and my mistress stared over Justin's shoulder. Their eyes and mouths were round as rings, Linotte's with simple shock, my mistress' as if the bones she beheld were the bones of her own children. As for monsieur, his back was to the chests, and his worshipful gaze fixed upon the Porcelain Dove that roosted upon a great rusty hook near the top of a pillar. In its soft, clear light, the hook showed a sullen red, like old blood.

The tableau hardly wavered when the heir of Malvoeux thrust himself into it. "What's this?" he said, his voice so rough I couldn't tell whether he were eager, angry, or afraid. "Bones, by the devil's arse-hole! Think you the old bugger ate human flesh?"

"For pity, Léon, hold thy peace," said Linotte.

"For pity certainly," said Justin, "and also for thy soul's sake, that goes in sore danger of Hell-fire."

Léon snorted. "Hell-fire? I don't believe in Hell-fire, brother, nor in thy milk-and-honey Heaven. I don't believe in pity, and I don't believe in God. I do believe in the pleasures of the senses, and I believe in nothing else: in which philosophy I think our ancestor also rejoiced."

"Whatever else our ancestor may have been, his confession is witness that he feared God at the last," said Justin.

"Foutre," said the vicomte.

Jean spoke up behind me. "Those chests, are they all full of bones?" he asked wonderingly. "How will you know which belonged to the wizard's daughter?"

Linotte sighed. "We must bury them all, nameless as they are. I should have known no ancestor of ours would have contented himself with killing a single child."

"All my pretty birds," said madame softly. "Don't cry. Soon it will be time."

Her voice was sane, though her words and her appearance were mad enough, what with the black cloak clutched around her and her silvered hair falling in swags over it, her naked feet all clottered with dung and her white legs showing above. Her face was calm and her eyes fixed tenderly on air in which, if I squinted, I could catch a glimmer of bright wings. Or was it children's faces? Though I couldn't see them clearly, 'twas apparent that my mistress could. Here was a cue for bitterness, if not on my own behalf, then on Justin's and Léon's and Linotte's, whom she'd never known or loved half so well as these ghostly children four hundred years dead.

Looking upon her, all I felt was love.

"Ah!"

"Ah!"

A cry of triumph and a cry of pain. Justin, opening the last press, had found Jorre's knives and ropes side by side with the silver reliquary, none of them so neatly disposed as they'd been before I went rummaging through them.

Linotte's was the cry of triumph. She stooped upon the reliquary, snatched it up, bore it to the table, set it next the document case, and opened it.

"Colette Favre," she said, half-wondering, half-bitter. "Soon you will rest in peace."

"Peace," echoed Justin, tears breaking his voice like a boy's. But when I turned to look at him, I saw that the tears were not a boy's tears, nor did he look sad, precisely, despite his anguished cry. I thought his face shone; and where his tears fell upon the ancient instruments of torture, they ate into them like drops of acid. In less time than it takes to write it, the knives and the ropes, the hooks and the irons and the mace were gone, sublimated into nothing by a Maindur's tears.

I'd been conscious for some little time of a pain in my elbow, now grown sufficiently sharp to drag my attention from the unfolding scene. It proved to be Jean's fingers, digging into the flesh of my arm like eagle-claws gripping a rabbit; though he himself looked more like the rabbit than the eagle, poor man, with his face all ashen and glazed with fear.

"Dragons," he muttered. "Priests that died and rose again. I did see them, Duvet. In Cathay. Upon my mother's soul I swear it."

"Yes, Jean," I said without irony. "I believe you. Furthermore, I believe you faced them with the courage of a Frenchman."

Shame pulled a tide of blood up his cheeks and across his brow, and he eased his grip on my arm.

I touched his fingers. "They'll be needing you soon, mon brave, to help with the chests. Unless mademoiselle enchants them out of here, I can't imagine how you'll accomplish it."

"The chests." Jean's fingers pinched me convulsively, then relinquished their hold. "We'll need ropes."

"We'll need ropes," Linotte was saying briskly. "And strong arms—yes, yours too, Léon. I will not use magic here."

Getting twenty clothes-presses full of bones out of Jorre's dungeon was easier, I suppose, than getting the infidels out of Jerusalem, for in the end, we did succeed. A noisy business, and not as reverent as it might have been, involving not only ropes, but making wooden slides and improvising pulleys and lighting flambeaux in the old cressets. I daren't think what the bats must have made of it all, not to mention the rats, the crawling things, and all the less substantial vermin I felt sniffing at the skirts of my senses. Linotte and Jean planned the most part of it, and did most of the work as well; for madame was incapable of hauling and lifting and maneuvering, Léon resistant, monsieur indifferent, and M. Justin, though willing, utterly useless. I did my part, me, and all the more gladly for my impression that the darkness of the dungeon recoiled from the noise and light of our undertaking.

By the time we had all twenty clothes-presses sitting in the laundry-yard, the day was nearly gone and I was as bone-weary and sore as I'd ever been in my life. Monsieur sat upon one of the chests, I hardly need say gazing at the Dove, which had perched upon another. I'd dearly have liked to sit on one myself, the stone bench being occupied by the vicomte, but sat in the laundry door instead. Aching legs are no excuse for sacrilege.

"Where's the priest?" said M. Léon suddenly. "Where's the consecrated ground? Don't tell me, sister, that having dragged our ancestor's leavings thus far, we must now drag them down to the village!"

Linotte stared at him open-mouthed. Having thought so far, she'd clearly thought no further. And now dusk was drawing in, with night not far behind. A small breeze tickled the back of my neck. Darkness, I thought. Bats. I shivered.

" 'Tis time," wailed madame. "I promised them!"

"Yes, ma mère," Justin's voice came from behind me. "As you say. 'Tis time. I am no priest, nor is this consecrated ground. Yet I trust to God's grace to bend both to His purpose."

I turned and stared at my mistress' younger son, back from wherever he'd been for so many years. He didn't seem a day older than
when he'd left, but he did seem different—calmer, more easy of stance,
his hands folded quietly at his waist, his eyes at rest upon his mother's
face. Where once he'd put me in mind of St. Sebastian awaiting the
arrows, now he put me more in mind of a martyr awaiting his crown.

"Wherever have you been?" I asked him.

"In Paradise," he said softly.

And so he had, in a manner of speaking. He told us how he'd
crossed the fields to the Forêt des Enfans, how he'd heard a bird
singing and followed the song, which was the purest, the most melodious, the most beautiful he'd ever heard. By and by the song led
him to a small glade bright with all the flowers of the field: marguerites
and violets and lilies-of-the-wood, gillyflowers and eye-bright and wood
anemones, all blooming, regardless of season, with gentians and asters.
In the center of the glade grew a pomegranate tree—strange visitant
to a forest of firs—and in that pomegranate tree perched a white bird
that sang without ceasing of the love and glory of God. Adoring, Justin
knelt to hear it. A moment only, he assured us, barely long enough to
realize his unworthiness to behold this miracle. Two heartbeats, no
more, of perfect joy and peace. Then the bird and the tree gave way
to his sister and his brother, two horses, and a white mule.

He'd wept, of course—why, I almost wept when he told us of it,
imagining Heaven thus opened to me and snatched again from sight.
"And long before I'd done mourning," he finished, "Linotte hauled
me up off my knees and onto the mule." Unsaintlike, he glared at her.

"I made that bird," said Linotte with an air of defense. "Or at
least Pompey made it, with instruction from maître Grisloup, to keep
you from harm."

"Le bon Dieu made the bird," said Justin; and what I heard in
his voice was less faith than conviction, as a man would say, "The sun
will rise tomorrow."

Léon blew a fart with his lips.

"Have some respect, Léon," said Linotte sharply. "Nonsense,
Justin. I myself helped Pompey to cast the spell."

"The spell may have been Pompey's," said Justin. "The vision
was nonetheless true. Magic and miracles are much akin, when practiced in love and fear of le bon Dieu. And, look you . . ."

Putting his hand in his pocket, he drew it forth clenched and slowly opened his fingers to display upon his palm a single black seed about the size of a small pearl, perfectly round, with a bit of dry pulp sticking to it.

"From the tree," he said reverently. "The pomegranate tree."

Léon laughed, a harsh derisive bark in which I heard both pain and envy. "I piss upon your tree, brother," he said, "and I spit, sister, upon your bones. Fuck your little birds, madame; monsieur my father, bugger your Porcelain Dove. I reject them all, every one, absolutely and for ever."

With that, he rose from the bench and would have swaggered out of the laundry-yard had Linotte not muttered such words as to freeze him fast as a pond in February. Through the fading light, I could just see Justin's reproving frown and Linotte's answering shrug. "All the children of Jorre should be present," she said, "and whether it please you or no, brother, I am a sorcerer."

"A sorceress, a woman," he began, a shadow of his old whine falling upon his voice.

"Bah!" I interrupted him. "If you can believe that le bon Dieu has used one of mademoiselle's spells to His Own mysterious ends, why not this one also? Can you do nothing, you children of Jorre, without bickering and babbling? I'd be ashamed, me, to argue theology while night falls upon these poor infants, still unburied."

"Berthe is right, my son," said madame. "Can you not see how they suffer, hear how they plead for rest? They're weeping, Justin. Can you not hear them?"

From his face, I saw that he could. And then, as if a heavy door between us had suddenly swung open, I heard them, too. There was nothing eerie about the sound of them: no screaming or tormented cries, only the weary, dreary wailing of children who have no hope of being heard or comforted.

Justin clapped his hands over his ears. Linotte covered her face; Jean, peasantlike, hid his eyes in his sleeve. My own cheeks grew wet, and my chest heaved with sobs while the darkness grew and the wailing with it until I hardly knew whether I wept from pity or terror.

This is Hell, I thought.

I heard my mistress cry out—an unmistakable cry of joy—and a light shone through my tears.

A small light, very bright, like a firefly bobbing above one of the chests of bones.

A second light, somewhat fainter; a third, sparking gleefully into the black air. And suddenly there were too many lights to count, a myriad feux follets dancing over the chests that held their bones. Save that the chests weren't chests anymore, but a fountain: a wide marble basin white as bone, with a tree in the midst of it all of silver, and ghost-fires twinkling in its branches like stars. Casting aside the black cloak, madame knelt and lifted her hands to the tree; one by one the ghosts flew to her, clung to her, clothed her more brightly than the gown bright as stars.

Tenderness rose in me, watching her. This was my Adèle, long imprisoned in despair, laudanum, and hysterical fits, released at last to her best self. She knelt by the fountain like a figure of charity, with the ghost children like cherubs clamoring about her. One by one she took them to her overflowing breasts and suckled them; one by one she breathed on them and released them to fade gently into the night.

At last only one light was left. Hesitant, it hung upon the air a little way from her.

As she had its fellows, Adèle gathered this last soul to her breast. Like its fellows, it transformed into a child, a little black-haired maid, white-skinned and soft-limbed: the wizard's daughter beyond doubt. Unlike its fellows, this child kicked and struggled until Adèle set her down upon the earth, whereupon she retreated to the chest where the Porcelain Dove was perched and frowned upon the assembled Maindurs. The Dove-light shone upon her small face that was inscribed with hate and reined-in fury.

"Colette," said Adèle, offering her breasts to her. "Be comforted."

"My father is dead," the child answered. "Your daughter killed him. I cannot be comforted while he howls in Hell."

"The choice was his," said Justin loftily.

"The choice was your ancestor's who slew me." Her voice was as old as her face, I remember, and as bitter as alum or her father's voice when he mocked Linotte. "He wept over me even as he parted my flesh, and bade me, as you have, to be comforted. I swore I would not, and still I will not. I've not done haunting you, madame."

Adèle smiled. "Haunt me, then."

Oh, her composure shattered at that! Suddenly childlike, she stamped her foot, and her face twisted as though she'd weep. I yearned to go to her. I yearned to turn away. And just as I thought that my yearning must tear my heart in two, the Dove spread its gleaming wings. I watched as it circled thrice around the yard, landed on Léon's shoulder, its pure light pitiless upon his scabrous face, his predator's eyes, his sparse and fading hair. For a moment it sat there, and then took off again, the flurry of its glassy feathers drawing a line of blood along his cheek, releasing him from Linotte's spell to growl and stumble from the yard.

And now the Dove had settled upon Justin's fist and cocked its ruby eye at the hand clenched above his heart, the hand that held the pomegranate seed. With trembling reluctance, Justin unfolded his fingers and extended his flattened palm to the bird, who pecked up the seed and left in its place a single ruby bead of blood.

When the Dove came to her, Linotte held Colette's reliquary out before her like an offering for it to perch on. It came to rest and its silver light upon the silver casket glared brighter than the moon, brighter than the stars, flooding every corner of the drying-yard with a constant lightning. And in that radiance I saw the chests open of themselves, and the bones pour out of them like Judgment Day and swirl together in the middle of the yard in a triumphant danse macabre, wild and leaping, reaching to Heaven whither their souls had flown, coming to rest at last in the form of a bone-white tree set in a wide basin of dark marble veined and knotted like wood, the whole glowing dim and softly dimmer until all I could see through the gloom was a pale shadow of branches and the Dove perched among them, and a single bobbing feu follet like a fallen star.

A hand touched me. I startled. It grasped my shoulder firmly, then gave me a friendly shake as if to say, How goes it, my girl? Justin gasped, "Que Dieu me garde!"; Jean muttered, "Merde! Not *them* again"; Linotte laughed and called for lights.

Then a thousand lanterns appeared on the hedges and along the laundry-yard wall, and by their yellow light we saw that we stood in a garden first-cousin to Justin's forest glade. The bodiless hands were returned from wherever they'd been hiding all this time. There were hundreds of them, fluttering around us like great white moths, patting our clothes and stroking our hair and faces in happy greeting. Jean lifted his own hands to shoo them away, caught sight of his arm, gaped and stared. For he was no longer clad in the torn and filthy frieze he'd been wearing for five years, but in fine twill, plum-colored, with real lace at the wrists. Laughing, I smoothed my gauze apron and my striped silk skirt, then rose and danced for the joy of clean linen against clean skin. Adèle, in white muslin and a Roman scarf, took my hands and danced with me, light-foot over the starry grass.

———

While we danced in the garden, the château was made whole by the bodiless hands: each cup and piece of lace, each bibelot and miniature, each glass case and inlaid table intact, in place and as bright as the day it was made.

Later, I found some few things missing, mostly from the cabinet des Fées: the boots of seven leagues, the silver walnut, a swan's egg, the homunculus, a horse on wheels, the wand of the Fairy Friandise. That night, lighting madame to the China apartment, I saw only that the riches of Beauxprés had been restored in all their bewildering vanity. The horrors that had flooded my life these past five years— the rioting peasants, Artide, the barren rooms, the balky satchel, madame's metamorphosis—receded from my mind like the insubstantial tide of an evil dream. The quiet, brightly-lit chambers, each a treasury, a wonder opening onto further wonders: these alone seemed real. These, and my mistress leaning on my arm, giving up her garments to me, sighing with pleasure as I stroked the brush through her hair, kissing my mouth as I bent to tuck the coverlet around her, falling asleep with her hand under her cheek.

First, I thought I'd lie down beside her, and then I thought I'd go to the kitchen and drink a glass of wine, if I could find one.

Beauxprés appeared so much as it had in the days of Menée and Malesherbes and Jacques Ministre that I half-expected, as I entered the back kitchen, to see them gathered around the fire gossiping quietly with their coats unbuttoned and their stockinged feet propped on the fender. Instead I saw only Jean sitting in what had been Menée's armchair, silent, solitary, and uncomfortably upright. I took Malesherbes' place at the other side of the hearth, and for a space we sat thus like a pair of firedogs, saying nothing and thinking less.

By and by a hand came in bearing a flambeau, followed by Mlle Linotte, who held cradled in her arm a large and dusty bottle.

When I saw the light descending the stairs, my heart speeded painfully. It expected Pompey, I think, though my head knew very well that he would not come—could not come, without Linotte's calling him. And Linotte had cast away his feather. Remembering this, I returned her greeting coolly and did not offer to stir as she hunted through the kitchen for a cork-pull. She did know where to look, I give her that, and what to do with it when she found it.

"I learned this for maître Favre," she said as she deftly unsealed the bottle. "He liked having the daughter of a duc open his wine and empty his chamber pot. To such pettiness does a man sink, when his brain's rotted with hatred."

I thought of several things to say to this, none of them useful, settled upon a formal, "Mademoiselle is most kind," took the glass she handed me, and sniffed at it contents. Brandy, well-aged, and by the color and the satiny taste of it, worth more than Just Vissot's farm.

Linotte had not heard my tone or had chosen to ignore it, for she raised her glass to me and said, "Not at all, Berthe. Say rather that mademoiselle is most content to find you alive and well after so long and tedious a trial."

"As are we, mademoiselle," said Jean with feeling.

Linotte laughed. "I'm sure you are," she said. "Tell me about it—everything that's happened since I've been away."

Jean drew an eager breath and opened his mouth to begin. Well, I'd no patience, just then, to hear him narrating our sufferings like a messenger in a tragedy. So, "To say true," I interrupted him, "very little has happened worth the telling. We'd much rather hear the adventures of mademoiselle."

She sniffed at the brandy, sipped it, sighed, and: "Like you, I've little to tell," she said at last. "I quested, I labored, I achieved. The bibliothèque bleu contains a thousand similar tales."

"And which account would be the most like mademoiselle's?" I asked slyly. " 'La Princesse Printanière'? 'Prince Lutin'? 'Finette Cindron'? 'Barbe-bleu'?"

Seemingly, my shot struck home, for she bit her lip and glanced askance at me. I met her eye innocently enough, waiting to hear her answer. But all she said was, "The Dove is come to Beauxprés and the prophecy fulfilled. That tale's ended, Berthe. Let be."

"Amen to that," said Jean, contemplating his empty glass. "What I say is, when the tale's over, 'tis over, and time to write 'finis' and be done. All fairy tales end the same way, after all."

Linotte held out the brandy bottle to him. "And how do they end, Jean?"

"Mademoiselle is most generous." Taking the bottle, Jean poured himself a liberal tot. "Why, with people living happily ever after, of course."

"And what does that mean?"

"Well, generally it means they marry."

"Do you wish to marry, Jean?"

He choked on a mouthful of brandy and coughed. "I? Marry? Who?"

I snorted at that, whereupon he slapped his palm against one blazing cheek and spluttered, "Oh *no*, mademoiselle! I mean, I beg pardon, I'd not cause mademoiselle the least offense, but I'm getting old, mademoiselle, and I've never loved any woman but Marie, not to marry, anyway."

Linotte fixed her bright black eyes on me. "Well, Berthe, what about you? Do you wish to marry?"

"No," I said, calmly enough. "Not at all."

Linotte sipped with an aggrieved air. "Well, then, how do you think this tale should end?"

"With the good rewarded and the evil punished," said Jean. "M. Léon, he should be nailed in a barrel lined with iron spikes and rolled down a mountain. And that foxy manservant of his, that Reynaud, he should be made to fit his name with a red bushy tail and four black paws and a whiskered nose."

"And sent to England," agreed Linotte. "I've already seen to M. Reynaud's reward, never fear. As for Léon, he has locked himself into his chamber of Eros, and all the words he has for me are 'foutre' and 'bougre' and 'leave me in peace.' I see no cause why I should not grant his wishes. My father already has his reward. He is in the aviary with the Dove. When last I saw him, his hands were bloody with stroking it."

I shivered. "And how will you reward the good?"

"Justin wants to become a holy hermit. Madame my mother wants things to be just as they were, only better."

"And Colette?"

Linotte shook her head. "Colette is a ghost. I have no power over her, either to curse or to bless. My mother has bade her haunt her; 'tis for my mother to appease her."

"Well," said Jean after a pause, "it seems to me that all is as it should be, except for there being no wedding. A pity mademoiselle didn't encounter a prince in her travels."

It occurred to me that she had, if Le Destin's play had any truth to it at all. "Surely the wizard had some handsome apprentice, some charming servant to be mademoiselle's reward?"

"There was nothing and no one handsome or charming in the house of maître Favre," said Linotte shortly. "No apprentice. No servant. No prince."

"A pity," said Jean sadly. "Well. Mademoiselle's most kind to ask our advice, but we're only servants. All that's nothing to do with us."

I'd resolved to add nothing further to this prodigiously foolish discussion. This, however, was too much. "Bah!" I said. "A queer tale it'd be without us! You may be sure that monsieur would've gotten himself killed and madame starved or frozen to death. Where'd your happy ending be then, pray tell me, with no one save vermin to witness mademoiselle's triumph?"

I glared at Jean, who shrugged, and at Linotte, who said softly, "Just so, Berthe. And I owe to you and to Jean a debt of gratitude I do not well know how to pay."

"Three wishes," said Jean out of the ensuing silence. "In the tales. If they don't marry, they get three wishes."

"And each wish more foolish than the last is the way it usually goes," I said, "with the wisher no better off at the end than he was before."

Jean pounded his fist on his knee. "No, no, Duvet, it doesn't have to be that way at all. I've thought it out, and the way I figure it is if your requests are neither too humble—like a sausage, for example—nor too grand—like being God—then you'll do well enough." Hopeful and uncertain, he turned to Linotte. "You can grant wishes, can't you, mademoiselle?"

Linotte shrugged. "Bien sûr," she said. "Am I not a sorcerer?"

"Well, then," said Jean. "First, I wish for my body to be comfortable. Second, I wish for my spirit to be at rest. Third . . ."

I leaned across Linotte and shook his arm. "Have a care, Jean, lest you find your wishes leading you to early burial in a silk-lined coffin. *My* first wish is to know how mademoiselle intends to go about granting all this rag-bag of wishes."

"Dear Berthe," said Linotte. "Cautious as always. I'll make you a present of your answer and not count it one of the three. There's a spell my master taught me that will remove Beauxprés from the circle of the world and set it among the enchanted realms. Whoever dwells within its pale will live happily indeed—well-fed, in good health, supplied with whatever he likes most. An earthly paradise, in short."

Strange as it now seems to me, at that moment Linotte's enchanted realm was all my heart's desire. Of late the world hadn't been so pleasant a place that leaving it seemed unbearable. If only I might see Pompey again! But Pompey, I reflected, was a wizard, and as likely to visit me out of the circle of the world as in it. I'd nothing to lose, and an eternity of comfort to gain, so—

"Bon," I said. "That is my wish, then. To stay in Beauxprés with my mistress, sharing her Paradise as I've shared her Hell. You promise us eternal health, bodily comfort, and peace of mind. What more could one want, after all?"

"What more indeed?" said Linotte. "And you, Jean?"

"This magic realm of yours, it will have horses in it?" asked Jean cautiously.

"If you wish."

"I do. And women? Other than Duvet here and you and madame my mistress, I mean."

Linotte laughed. "That's four wishes, Jean, if I count your first two. Yet I'll grant it. After all, you've wished for bodily comfort, haven't you? And Berthe here desires peace." She tapped her cheek with one finger, a gesture that reminded me of Pompey. "They wouldn't be human, of course."

Jean bridled. "Not human, mademoiselle? What do you take me for? I am a God-fearing man, me, and will have no commerce with beasts or demons!"

Now 'twas Linotte's turn to stare in offended surprise. "What right have you, Jean Coquelet, to question my judgment? Where am I to get these human women for you, hein? From the village? From a brothel? From the side of the road? Do I ask if they'd like to warm your bed, or do I just translate them naked into your arms? A strange way you have of fearing God, I vow."

Jean protested, but after some little argument, supposed he'd learn to make do with the demons, providing mademoiselle did something about their cloven hooves. Linotte, laughing, said he'd get used to them.

While they bickered, my mind was brushed by the tail of a loose end. Linotte had spoken of madame, and of monsieur her father, and of both her brothers. "What of mademoiselle?" I asked abruptly. "Will she stay here in her enchanted realm and live happily ever after with the rest of us?"

"Without a prince?" Jean couldn't have sounded more shocked had I suggested she dance naked in the Palais-Royal. "Our tale may be told, Duvet, but mademoiselle is still young, and much too fair, if she'll permit me the liberty, to die a maid."

"Oh, I'll not die a maid," said Linotte dryly. "That, at least, I may safely swear. As for a prince . . . Well, there are fewer in the world than once there were. To answer your question, Berthe: No. I'll not stay at Beauxprés."

"Mademoiselle must do as she thinks best," I said irritably. "She's done well enough so far, except for losing Pompey somewhere along the way. Where's Pompey, mademoiselle? Where's your old tutor, who was kinder to you than your own flesh and blood? What reward for his constancy, hein? Did you cut off his head and tail and release him from the evil enchantment that made his skin black?"

Well, she looked up at that, I'll tell you. For a moment she held my gaze, then dropped her eyes as if suddenly uncertain of her ground.

"Of course," she said, "he was dear to you. Indeed, I half-thought I'd find him here, but I should have known he'd not return, not so long as monsieur my father was lord of Beauxprés. The truth is, Berthe, that I sent him away in a fit of temper. I thought he was telling me to do a horrible thing. 'Twas a misunderstanding—I realize that now. At the time, I hated myself and him and, being unable to banish myself, banished him instead. Now I would beg his pardon, ask him to take me once more as his apprentice, for I know I have a great deal yet to learn of life and magic both. I'd call him if I could, but I can't, and I don't know where or how to find him."

By the end of this speech, she sounded so forlorn that my anger was overturned by an upheaving of pity. As I've said, I was always a little awkward with Linotte, so all I could do to show it was pat her arm and say, "There, there, mademoiselle. You'll find him, I'm sure. And when you do, tell him Berthe would be glad to see him, should he choose to visit."

He never came.

Perhaps Linotte never found him to give him my message; perhaps she found him and never told him. Perhaps he tried to come and couldn't get through Linotte's spell without breaking it. Perhaps he couldn't get through it, tout simple. Sometimes I wonder whether Linotte couldn't get through it either, and if that's why *she* never returned. I've wondered, too, what tale she entered when she left, and whether she found Pompey, or true love, or adventure, or only a solitary death at the end of it. I wish I knew, just as I wish I knew what happened to Peronel, and Marie, and Mme de Bonsecours, and Olympe, and Malesherbes, and Artide, and mère Boudin, and all the rest of those whose tales, for a time, ran alongside mine.

When first I picked up this quill, the things I did not know and understand filled my soul with a regret as sour as wine hoarded long past its prime. Writing, I have poured them all out upon this paper, and find, now that I have come to the end, that their bitterness has leached away. I'm left with the paper itself, a monstrous stack of it thick as a folded blanket, covered with what I know and understand. And the sight of it makes me feel as light and clear as an empty bottle waiting to be filled with new wine.

As I write these words, I sit in the enchanted garden that was once a laundry-yard upon the stone bench where I once sat with Marie, the bench Adèle calls Berthe's throne. My lap-desk rests upon my knees, heavy with the weight of my tale. This paper is the last blank sheet. This ink is the last drop wetting the belly of my crystal nestling.

By the bone-white fountain, Adèle and Colette rehearse Colette's new play. Adèle is tearing a passion to tatters and Colette is sprawled on the grass at her feet, laughing helplessly. Jean has told me the play is a prodigious droll tragedy concerning a pair of servants waiting for their master who never appears. Not to spoil the performance, I have not yet read it, but I have helped Adèle to sew all the dresses for it —artful rags of brown and gold like the Forêt des Enfans in October. Justin, perched upon the basin's rim with the playbook in his hand, listens to his mother rant. I see that he is smiling.

On the bench beside me, Jean is whittling goose feathers to a fine, sharp point.

I've told him that my quill is magic, that I'll need no more pens, that my tale is almost at an end. He says he'd prefer to be prepared when I recall some conversation I've left out and need a sharp pen for adding it.

Adèle drops her hand from her brow and bends to pull Colette to her feet. Justin shuts the playbook and offers it to Colette, with a comic little bow and a remark that sends her off laughing again. Adèle cuffs her son's head lightly, ruffles his hair, turns and sees me watching. Now she beckons, arms outstretched, and calls to me.

"Here, Berthe, Colette has a part for you to play. Come and see."

ACKNOWLEDGMENTS

Greer Gilman for reading this as many times as I rewrote it and always keeping the threads untangled.

Ellen Kushner for helping me find Beauxprés, both in France and in Boston.

Ann Downer, Mary Hopkins, Deb Manning, Pam Summa, and Elizabeth Willey for honesty and critical acumen. What they don't collectively know about reading mss. isn't worth knowing.

Anne Hudson for invaluable help with research.

Dr. Patricia Craddock for getting me into the Bibliothèque Nationale.

Dr. Patricia Papernow for advice on matters psychological.

Faye Ringel Hazel for finding and translating La Grotte's song from the Provençal.

Patri Pugliese for explaining the ins and outs of the minuet.

Adelaide Kent, Beverly Momoi, Mimi Panitch, Caroline Stevermer, and Patricia Wrede for analysis, encouragement, and hole-spotting.

Jo Ann Citron, for asking the hard questions and living with the struggle for the answers.

HISTORICAL NOTE
AND
BIBLIOGRAPHY

Beauxprés was never in the Jura Mountains or anywhere else upon the earth. The small medieval town of Nozeroy, however, looks very much like it, and can be found 70 kilometers south of Besançon in the Franche-Comté. There was never a Jorre Maindur, but there was a Gilles de Rais, and anyone familiar with accounts of that unlovely gentleman's trial will recognize Jorre's description of his own crimes. There was no Mme de Bonsecours among the prisoners at Port Libre, but there was a M. Coittant, who kept a detailed diary of his stay there, which was reprinted in Charles A. Dauban's *Les Prisons de Paris sous la révolution* (Paris, 1870).

Anyone seeking further information on the bibliothèque bleu and French folklore may consult Robert Danton's *The Great Cat Massacre* (New York, 1985). Most of my history comes from Simon Schama's *Citizens* (New York, 1989), and most of my gossip from a variety of memoirs and letters. For the cultural history, I am indebted to the work of Braudel and his school of Annalistes. Because of their work among the city halls and armament rooms of France, finding out exactly how much a lady's maid earned in 1775 is much easier than you'd think.

Braudel, Fernand. *The Structures of Everyday Life*. New York, 1981.

Manceron, Claude. *The Age of the French Revolution*, Vols. I–V. Paris, 1979; New York, 1989.

Maza, Sarah. *Servants and Masters in Eighteenth Century France*. Princeton, 1983.